A SPARK WITHIN THE FORGE

BASED ON THE NOVEL SERIES *AN EMBER IN THE ASHES* BY

SABAA TAHIR

Published by
ARCHAIA

A SPAR
THE F

K WITHIN
ORGE ™

STORY BY

SABAA TAHIR

SCRIPT BY

NICOLE ANDELFINGER

ART BY

SONIA LIAO
INKING ASSISTANCE BY ANNETTE FANZHU

COLORS BY
KIERAN QUIGLEY
WITH MICAELA TANGORRA
(ARANCIA STUDIOS)

LETTERS BY
MIKE FIORENTINO

ARCHAIA ™
Los Angeles, California

COVER BY
SONIA LIAO

ASSOCIATE EDITOR
ALLYSON GRONOWITZ

DESIGNER
MICHELLE ANKLEY

EDITOR
AMANDA LAFRANCO

EXECUTIVE EDITOR
SIERRA HAHN

Ross Richie Chairman & Founder
Matt Gagnon Editor-in-Chief
Filip Sablik President, Publishing & Marketing
Stephen Christy President, Development
Lance Kreiter Vice President, Licensing & Merchandising
Arune Singh Vice President, Marketing
Bryce Carlson Vice President, Editorial & Creative Strategy
Kate Henning Director, Operations
Ryan Matsunaga Director, Marketing
Elyse Strandberg Manager, Finance
Michelle Ankley Manager, Production Design
Sierra Hahn Executive Editor
Dafna Pleban Senior Editor
Shannon Watters Senior Editor
Eric Harburn Senior Editor
Elizabeth Brei Editor
Kathleen Wisneski Editor
Sophie Philips-Roberts Editor
Jonathan Manning Associate Editor
Allyson Gronowitz Associate Editor
Gavin Gronenthal Assistant Editor
Gwen Waller Assistant Editor
Ramiro Portnoy Assistant Editor

Kenzie Rzonca Assistant Editor
Rey Netschke Editorial Assistant
Marie Krupina Design Lead
Grace Park Design Coordinator
Chelsea Roberts Design Coordinator
Madison Goyette Production Designer
Crystal White Production Designer
Samantha Knapp Production Design Assistant
Esther Kim Marketing Lead
Breanna Sarpy Marketing Lead, Digital
Amanda Lawson Marketing Coordinator
Grecia Martinez Marketing Assistant, Digital
José Meza Consumer Sales Lead
Ashley Troub Consumer Sales Coordinator
Morgan Perry Retail Sales Lead
Harley Salbacka Digital Sales Coordinator
Megan Christopher Operations Coordinator
Rodrigo Hernandez Operations Coordinator
Zipporah Smith Operations Coordinator
Jason Lee Senior Accountant
Sabrina Lesin Accounting Assistant
Lauren Alexander Executive Assistant

BOOM! Studios, 5670 Wilshire Boulevard, Suite 400, Los Angeles, CA 90036-5679. Printed in China. First Printing.

ISBN: 978-1-68415-762-4, eISBN: 978-1-64668-350-5

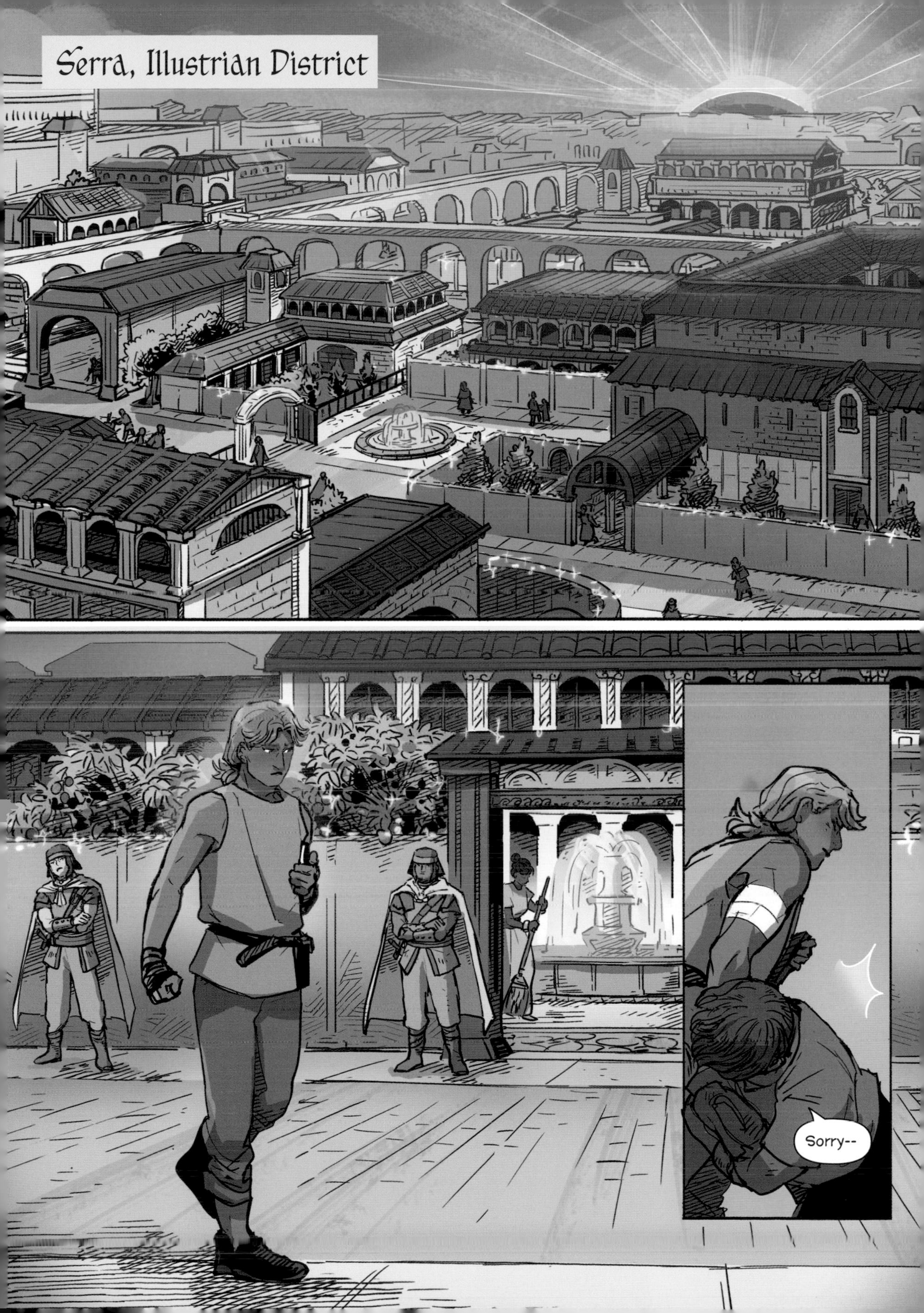
Serra, Illustrian District
Sorry--

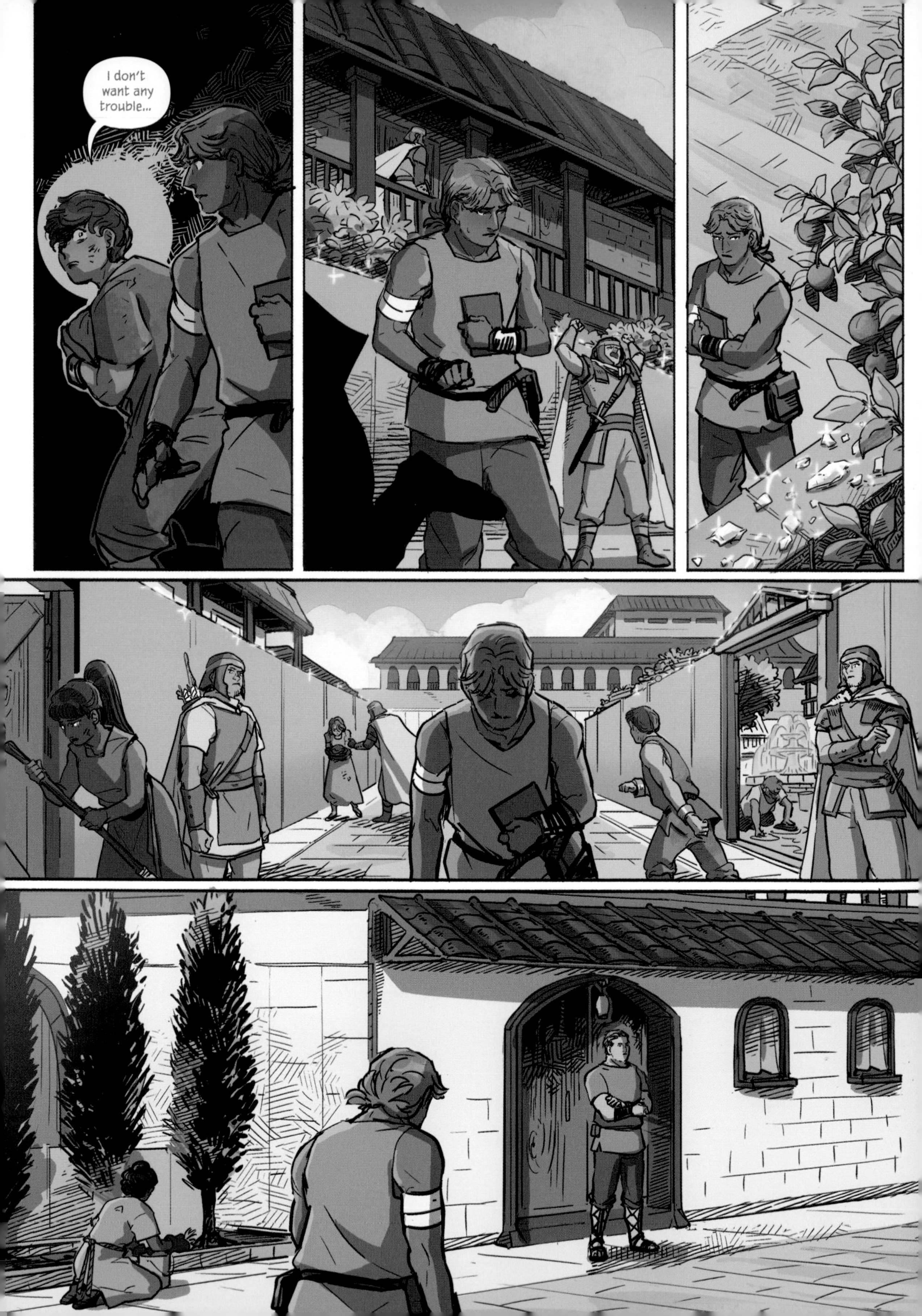
I don't want any trouble...

Morning, Zamil.

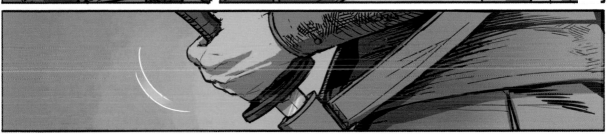

Darin.

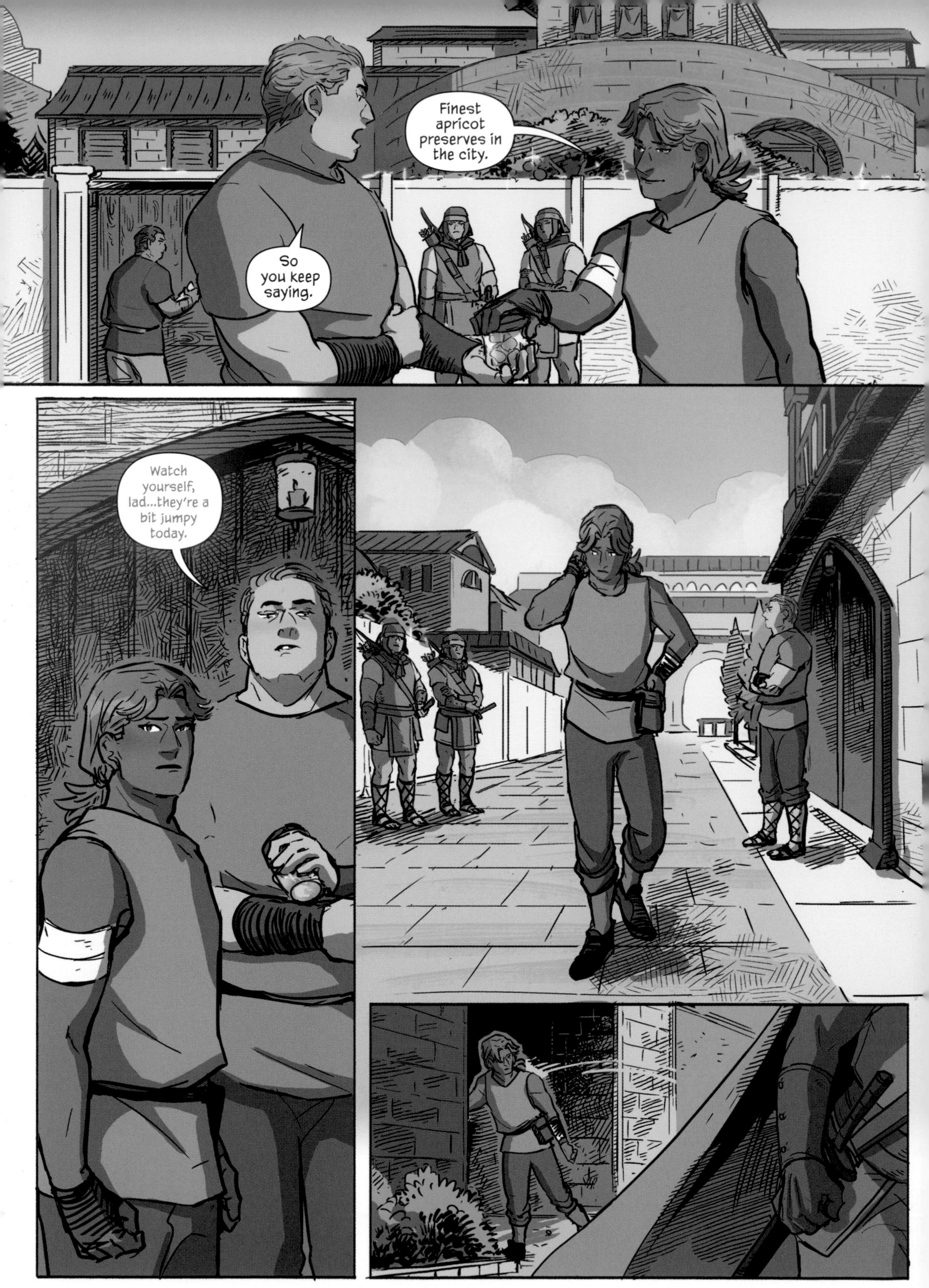
Finest apricot preserves in the city.
So you keep saying.
Watch yourself, lad...they're a bit jumpy today.

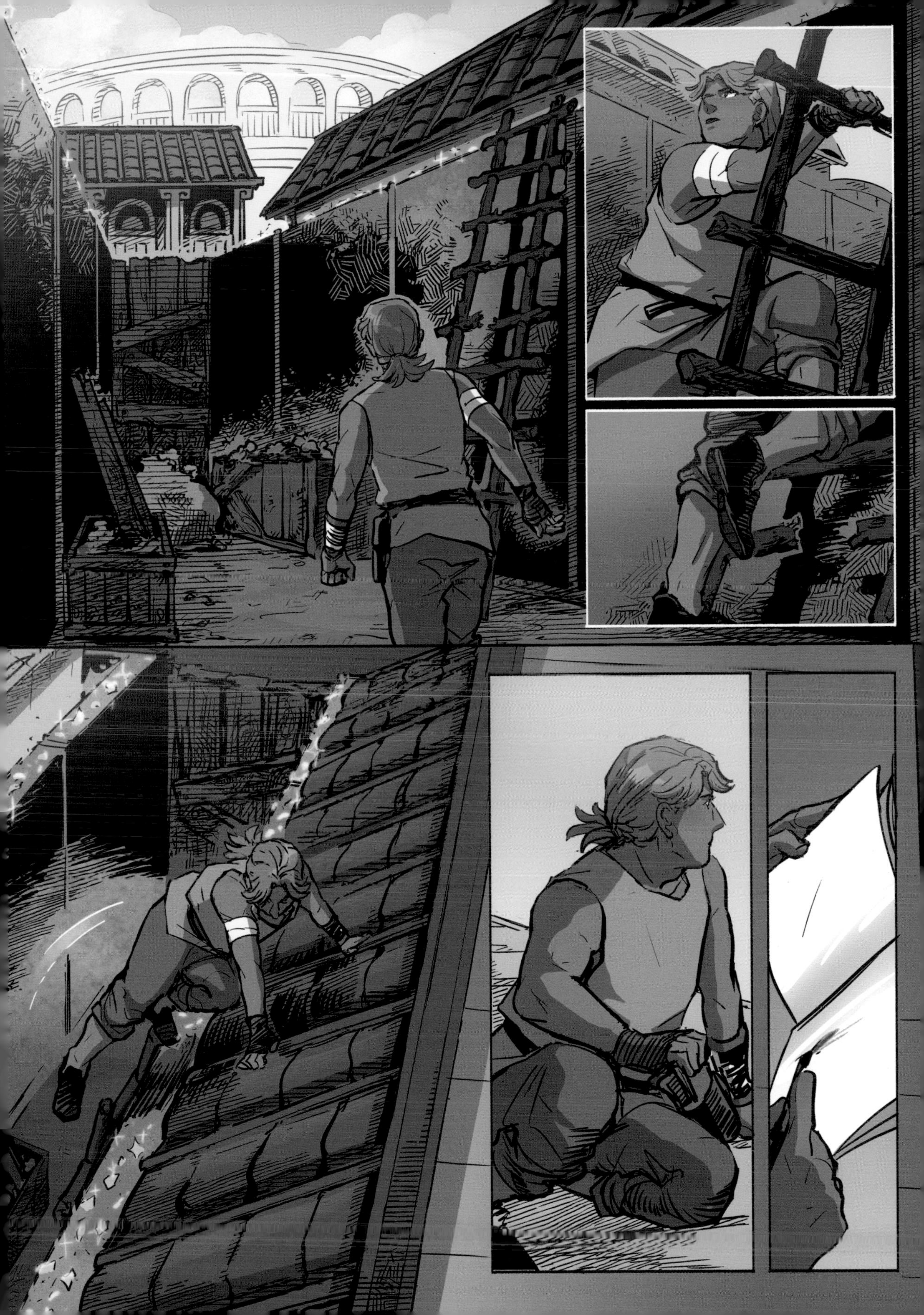

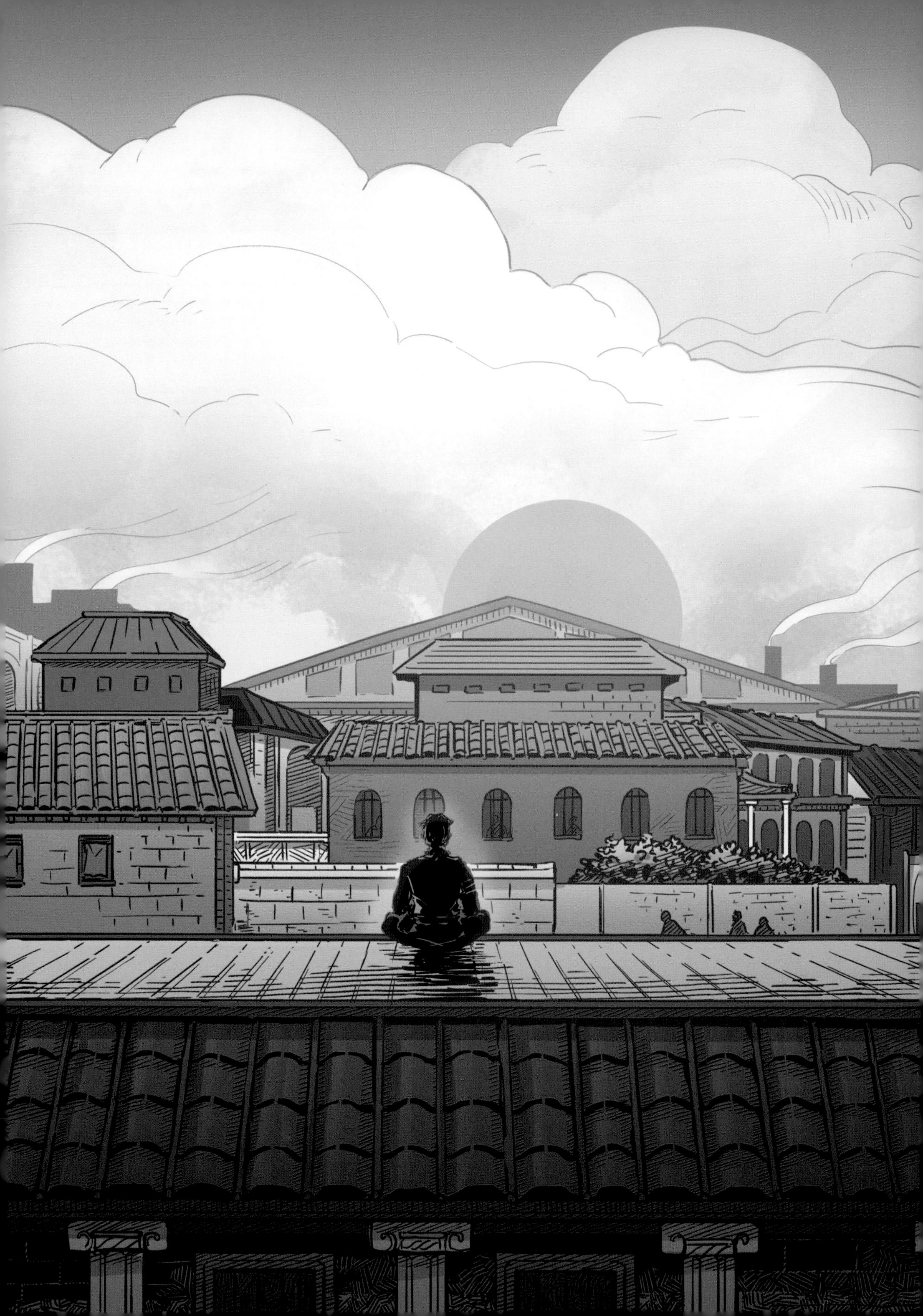

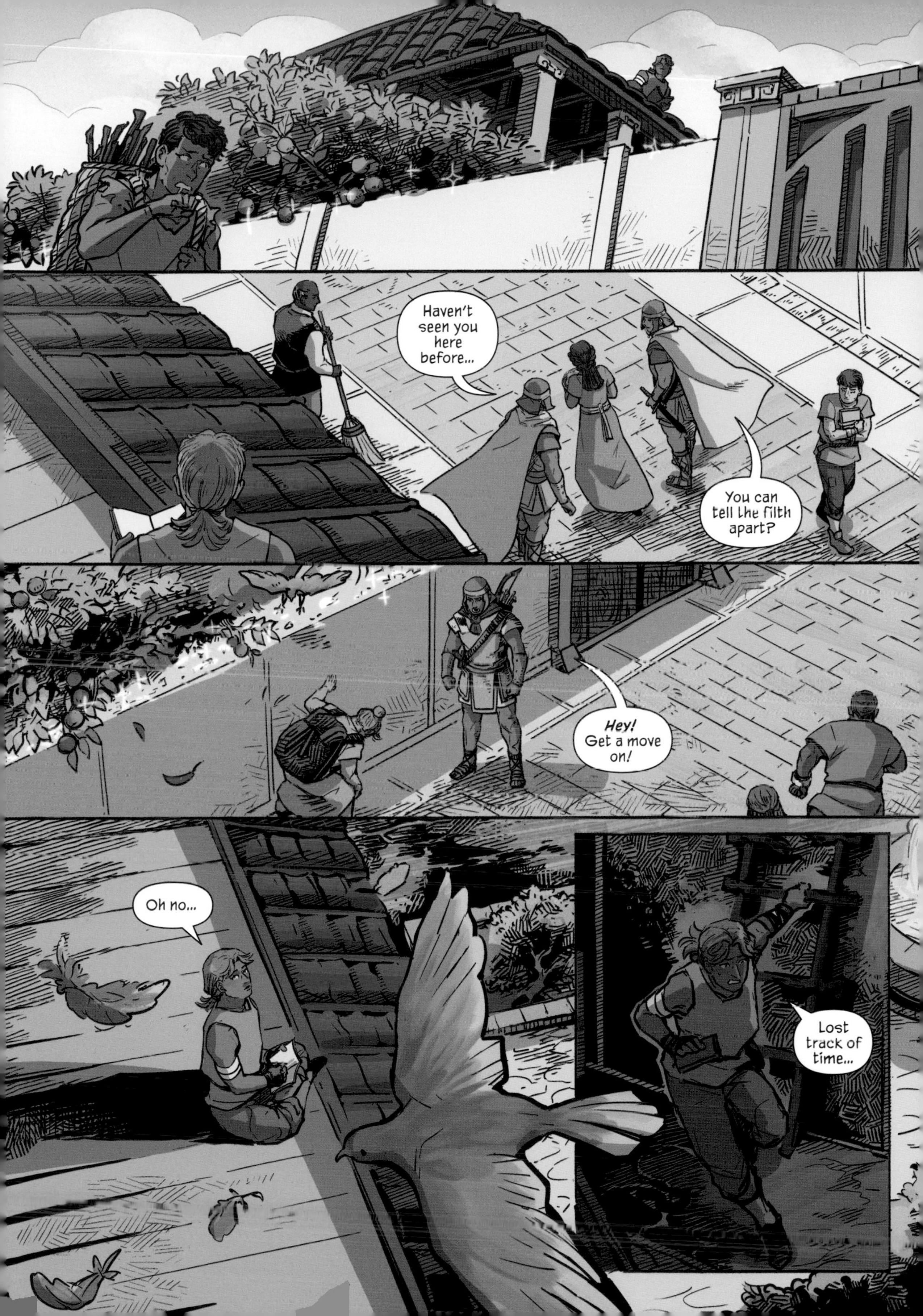
Haven't seen you here before...
You can tell the filth apart?
Hey! Get a move on!
Oh no...
Lost track of time...

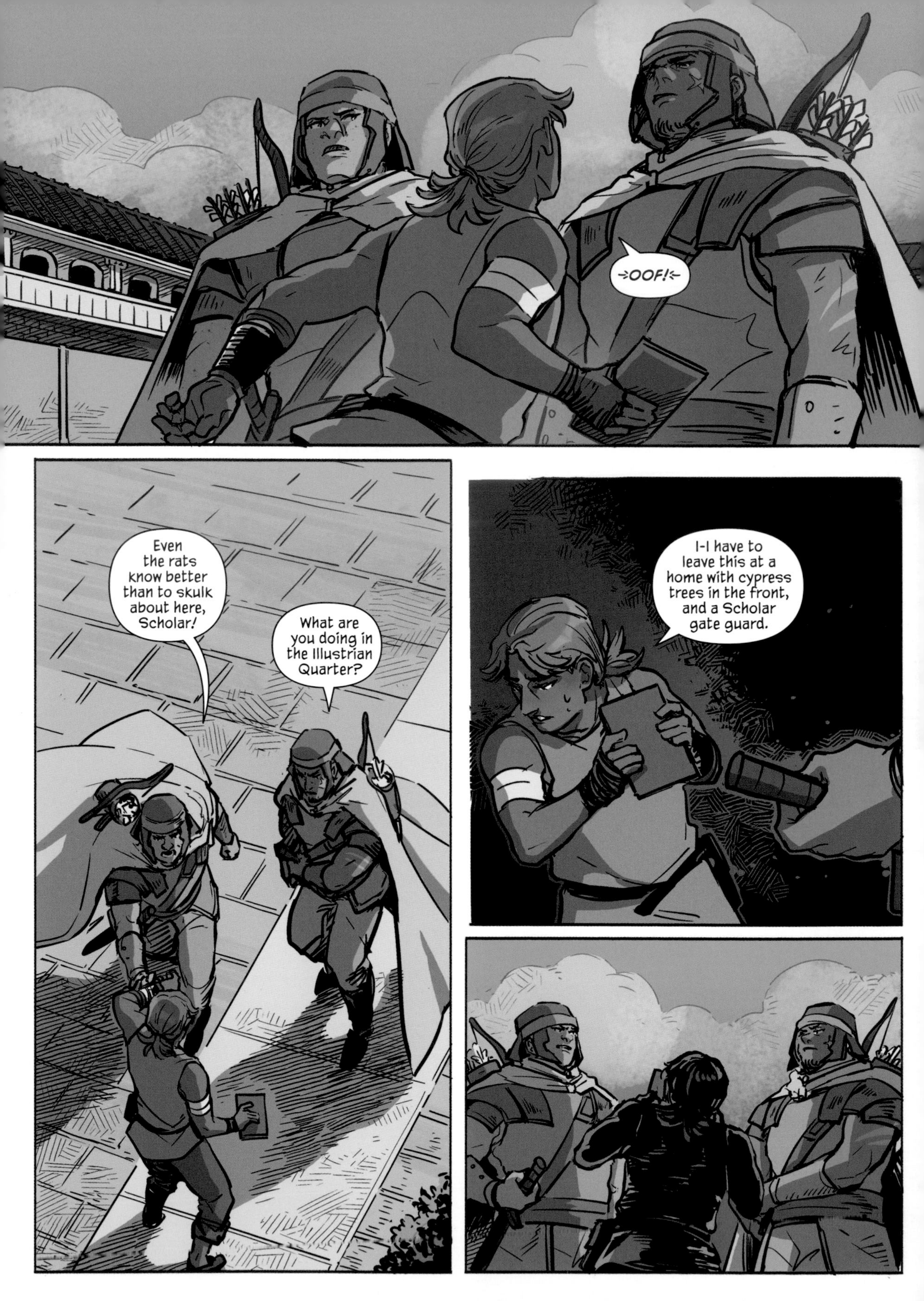
OOF!
Even the rats know better than to skulk about here, Scholar!
What are you doing in the Illustrian Quarter?
I-I have to leave this at a home with cypress trees in the front, and a Scholar gate guard.

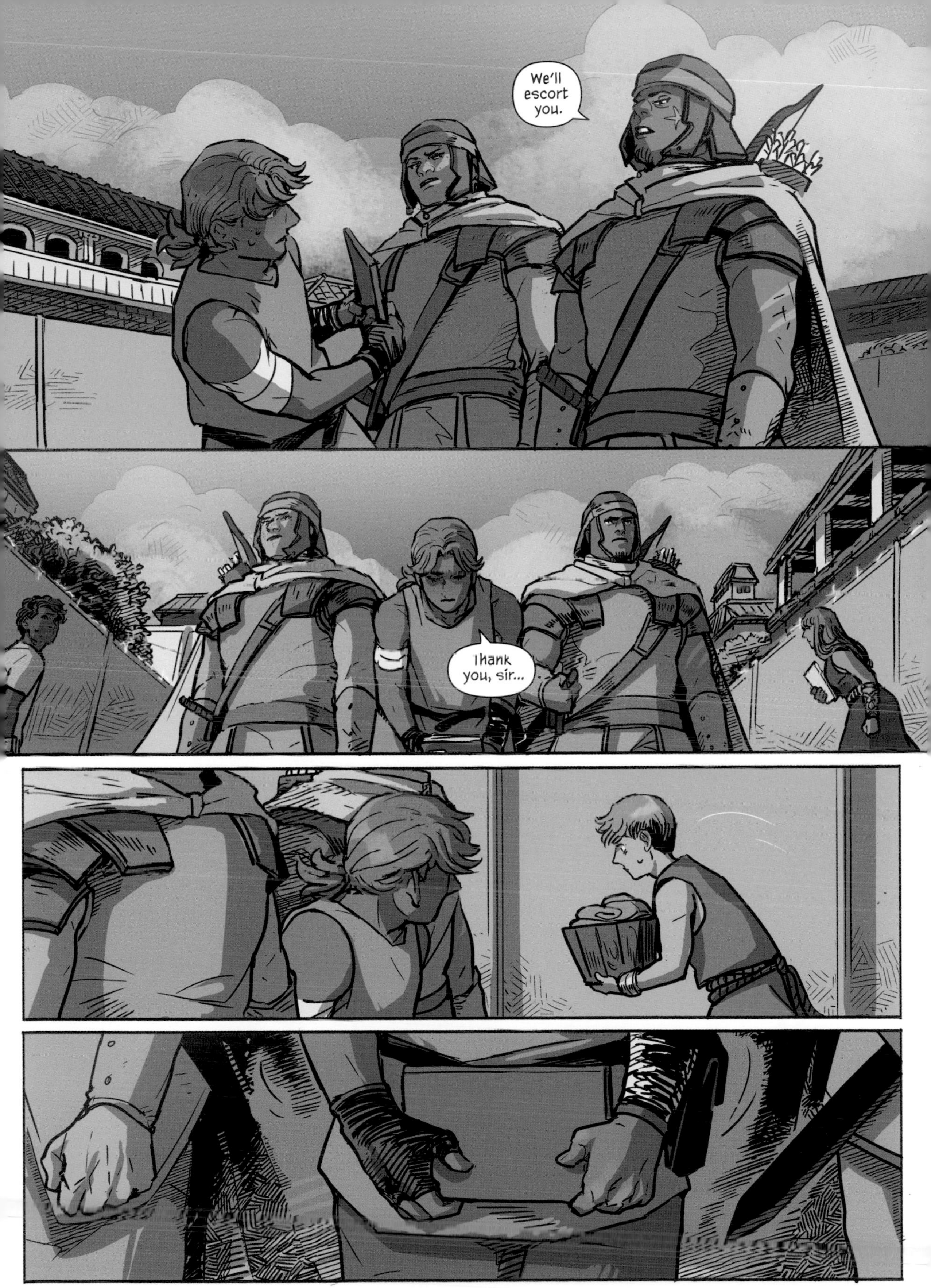
We'll escort you.
Thank you, sir...

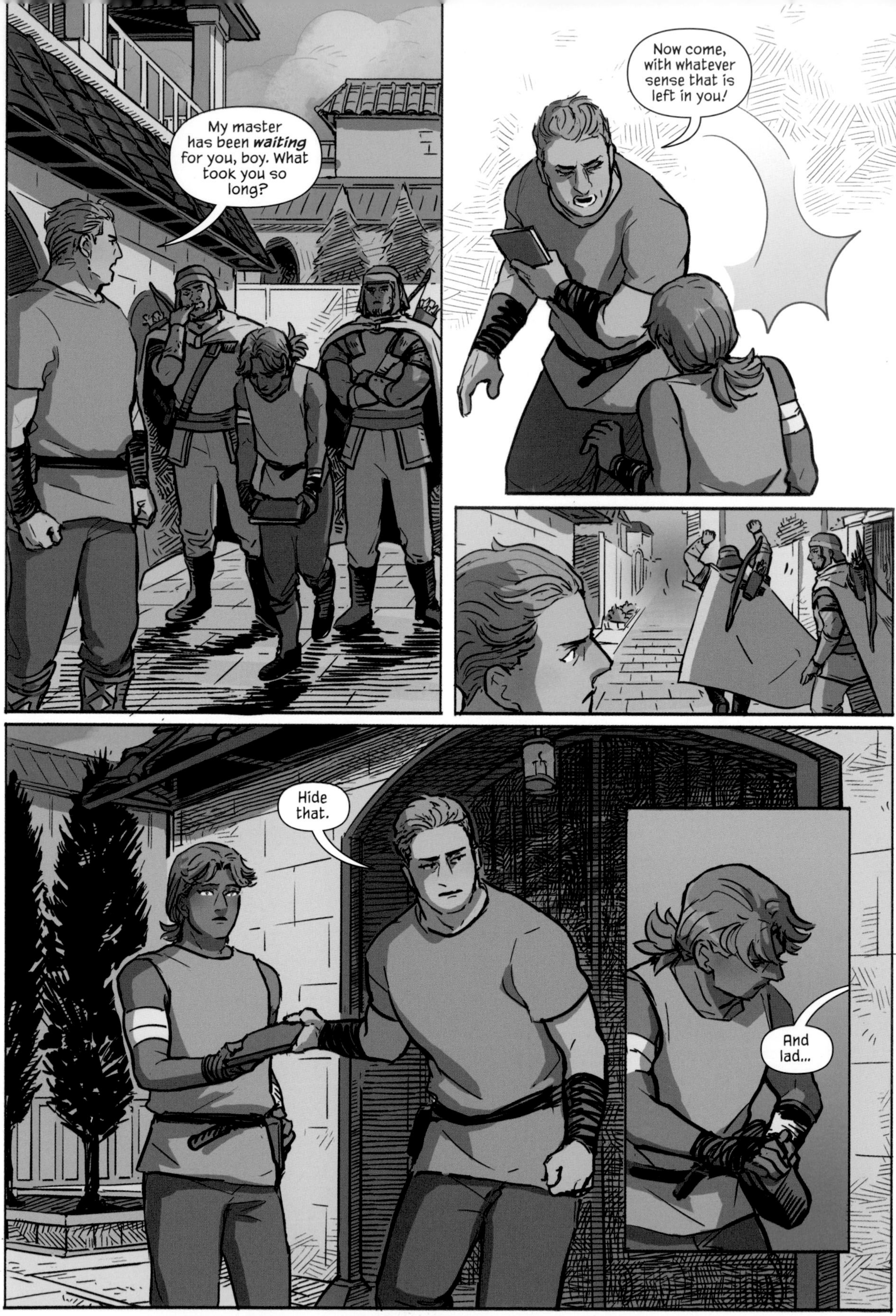
My master has been *waiting* for you, boy. What took you so long?
Now come, with whatever sense that is left in you!
Hide that.
And lad...

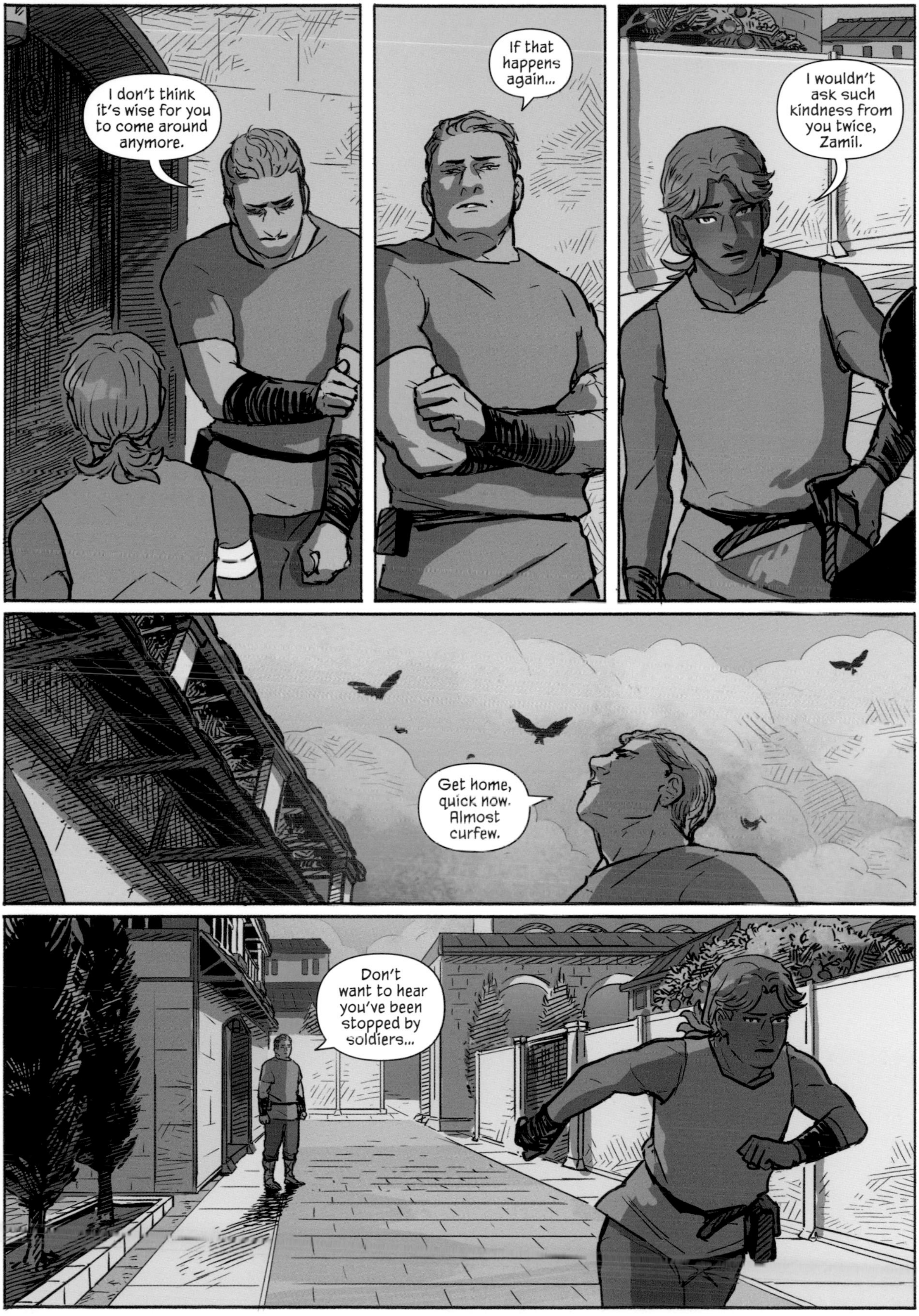
I don't think it's wise for you to come around anymore.
If that happens again...
I wouldn't ask such kindness from you twice, Zamil.
Get home, quick now. Almost curfew.
Don't want to hear you've been stopped by soldiers...

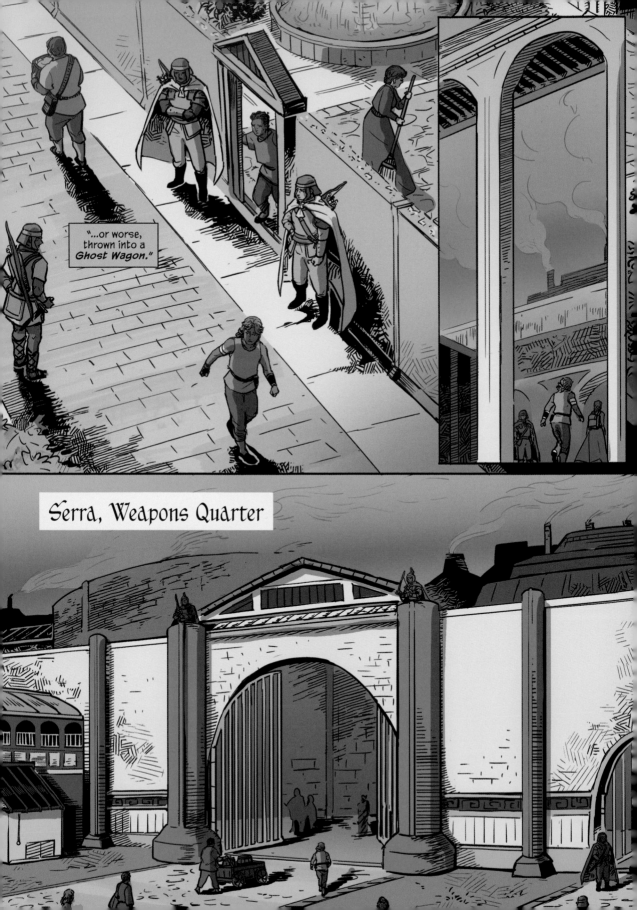

"...or worse, thrown into a *Ghost Wagon.*"

Serra, Weapons Quarter

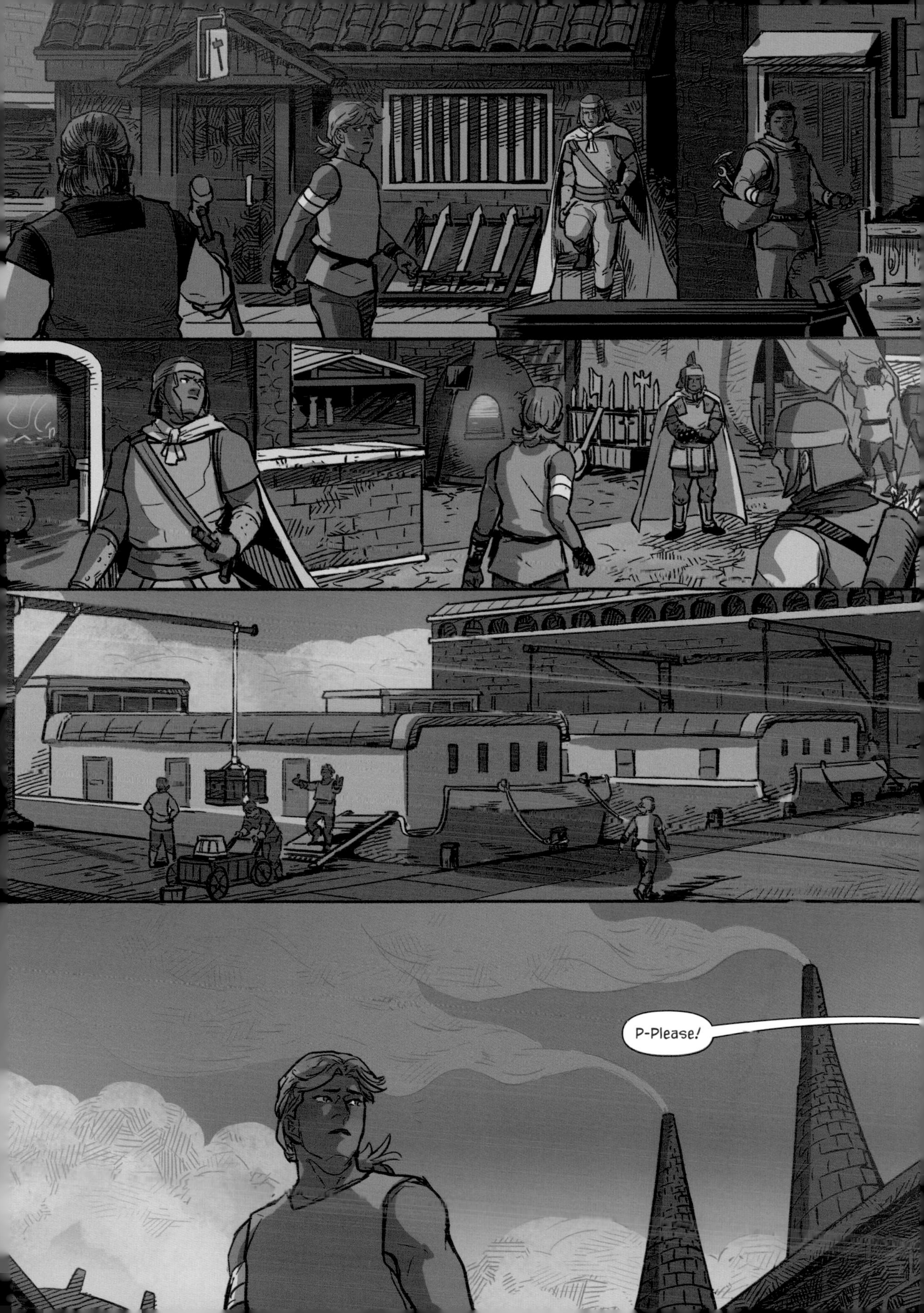
P-Please!

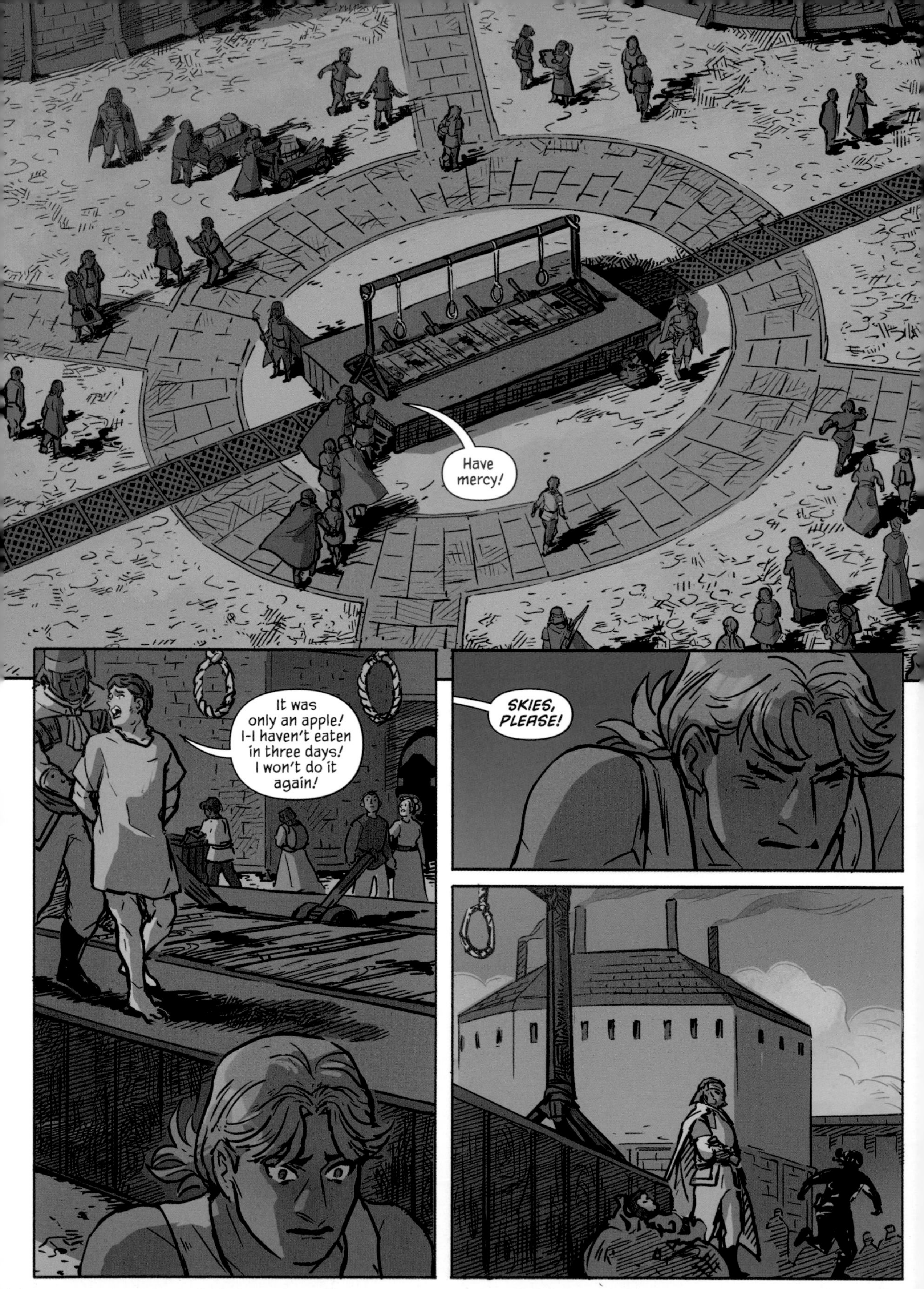
Have mercy!
It was only an apple! I-I haven't eaten in three days! I won't do it again!
SKIES, PLEASE!

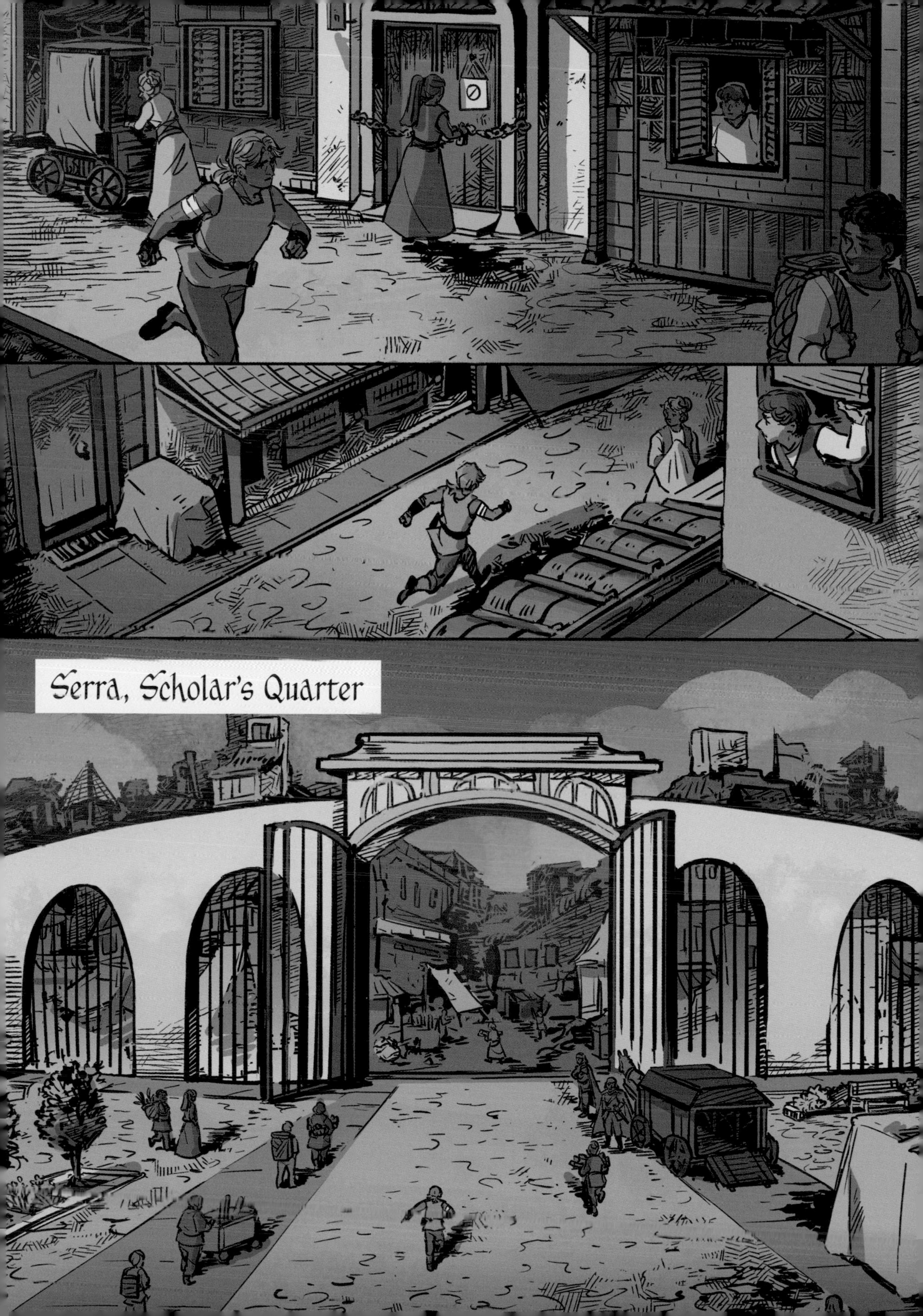
Serra, Scholar's Quarter

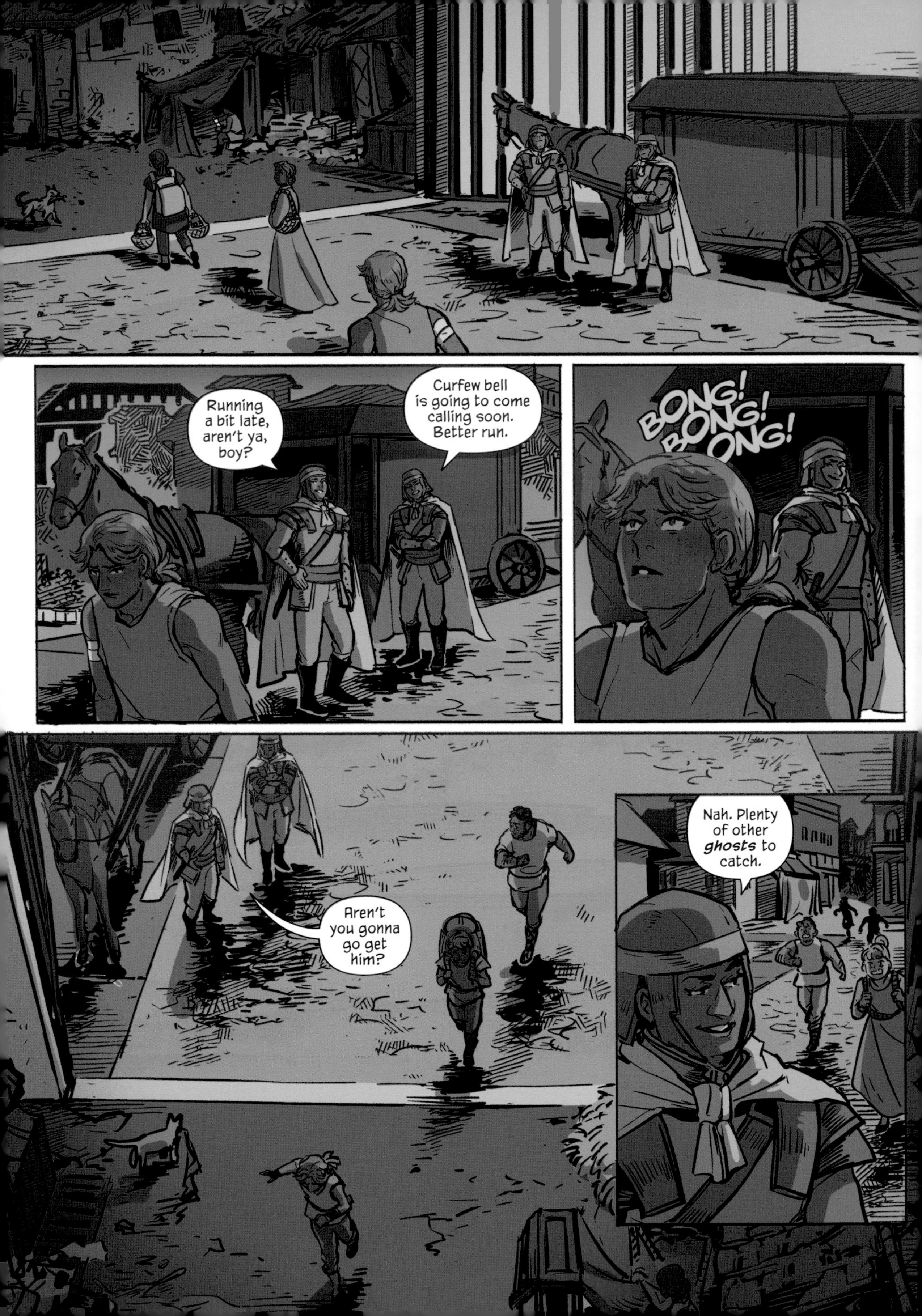
Running a bit late, aren't ya, boy?
Curfew bell is going to come calling soon. Better run.
BONG! BONG! BONG!
Aren't you gonna go get him?
Nah. Plenty of other ghosts to catch.

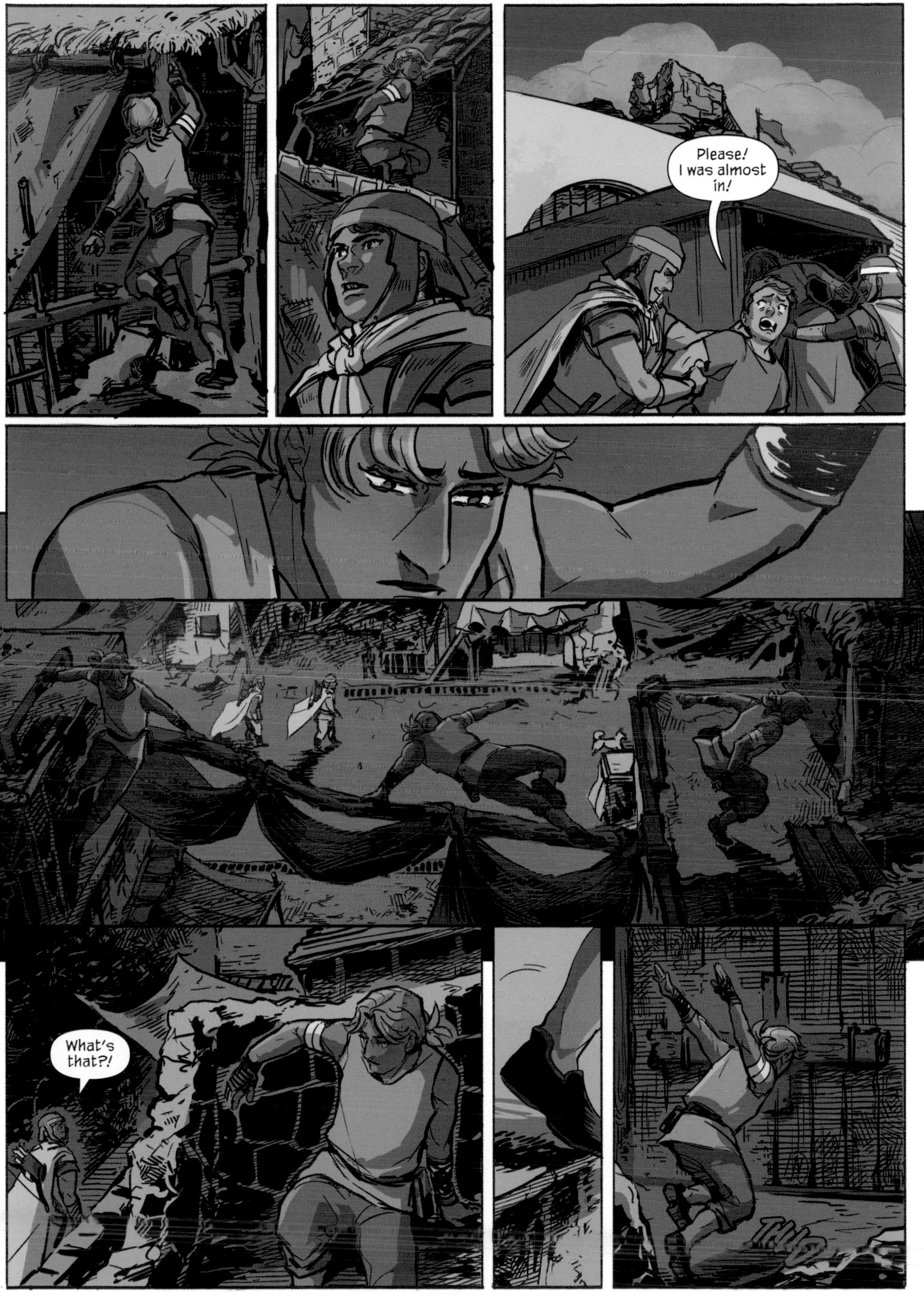
Please! I was almost in!
What's that?!

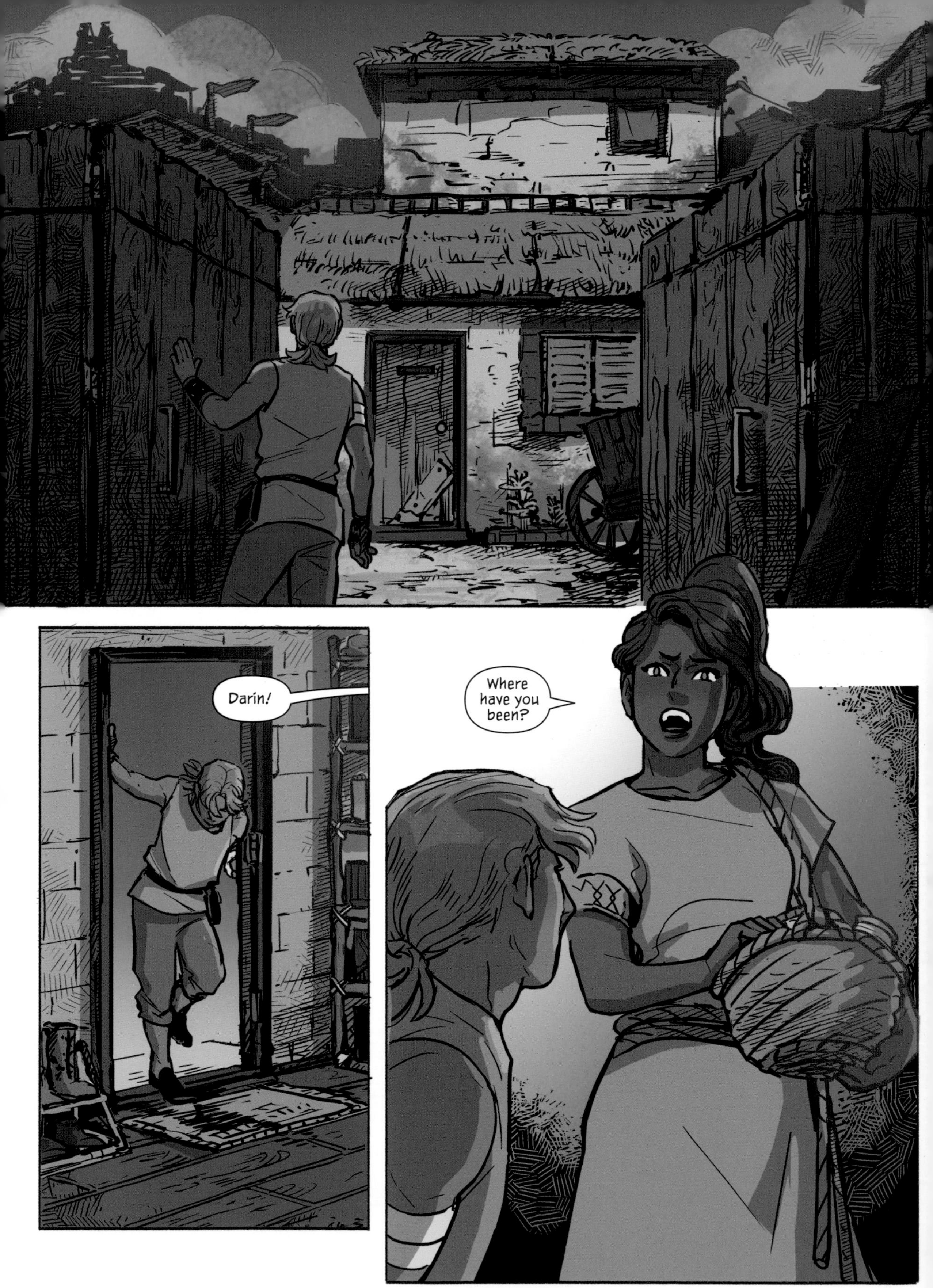
Darin!
Where have you been?

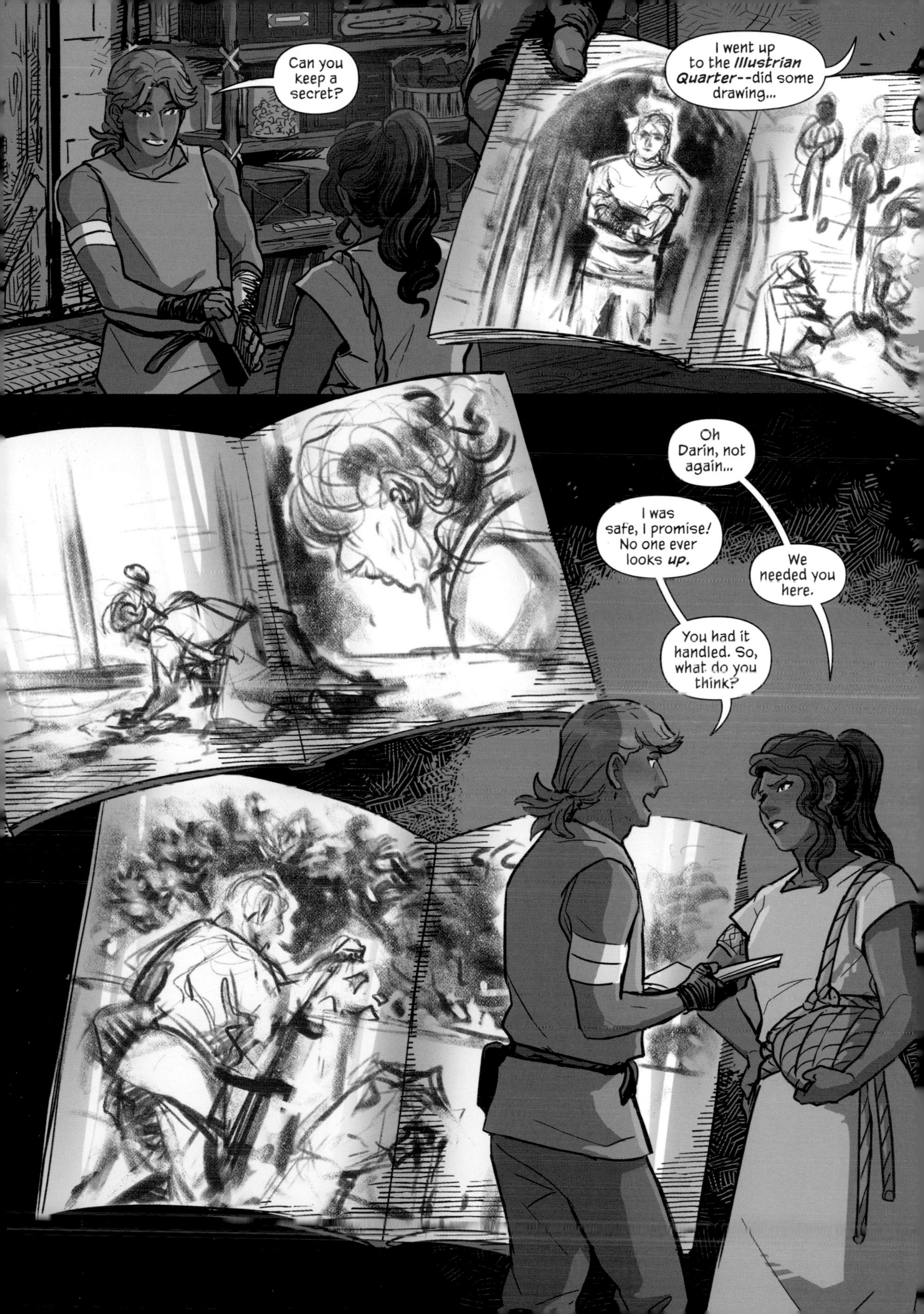

Can you keep a secret?
I went up to the Illustrian Quarter--did some drawing...
Oh Darin, not again...
I was safe, I promise! No one ever looks up.
We needed you here.
You had it handled. So, what do you think?

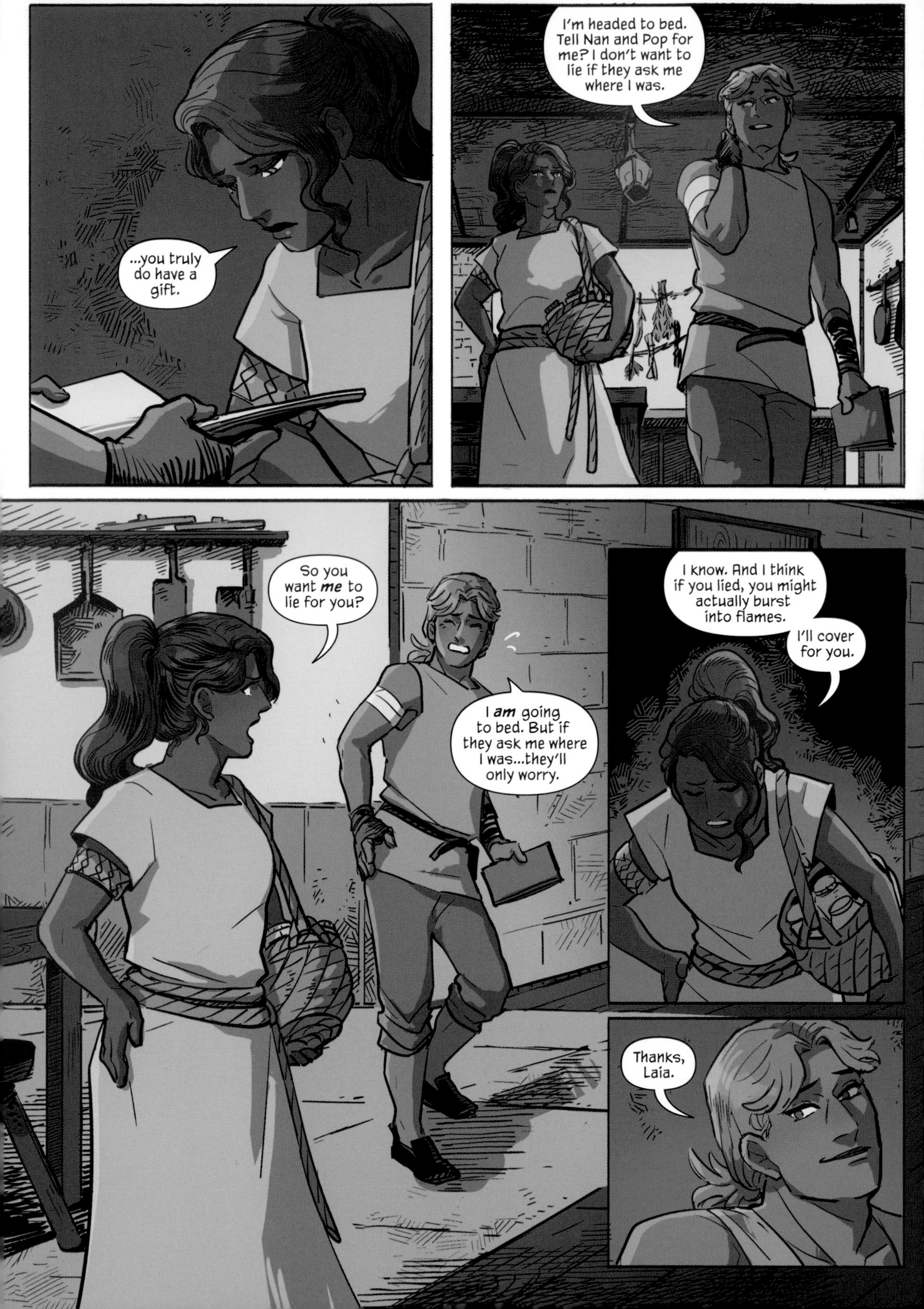
...you truly do have a gift.
I'm headed to bed. Tell Nan and Pop for me? I don't want to lie if they ask me where I was.
So you want *me* to lie for you?
I *am* going to bed. But if they ask me where I was...they'll only worry.
I know. And I think if you lied, you might actually burst into flames.
I'll cover for you.
Thanks, Laia.

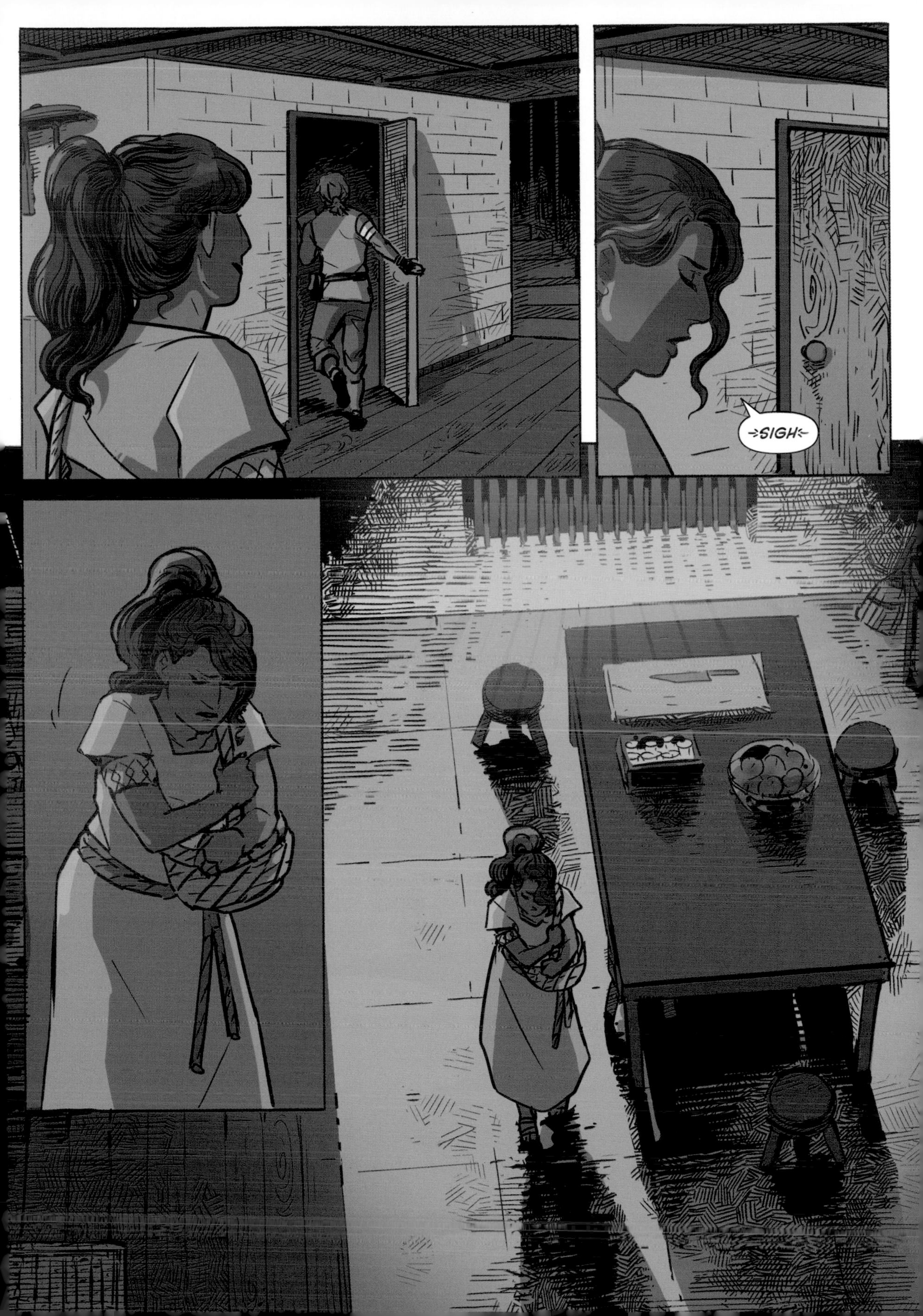
SIGH

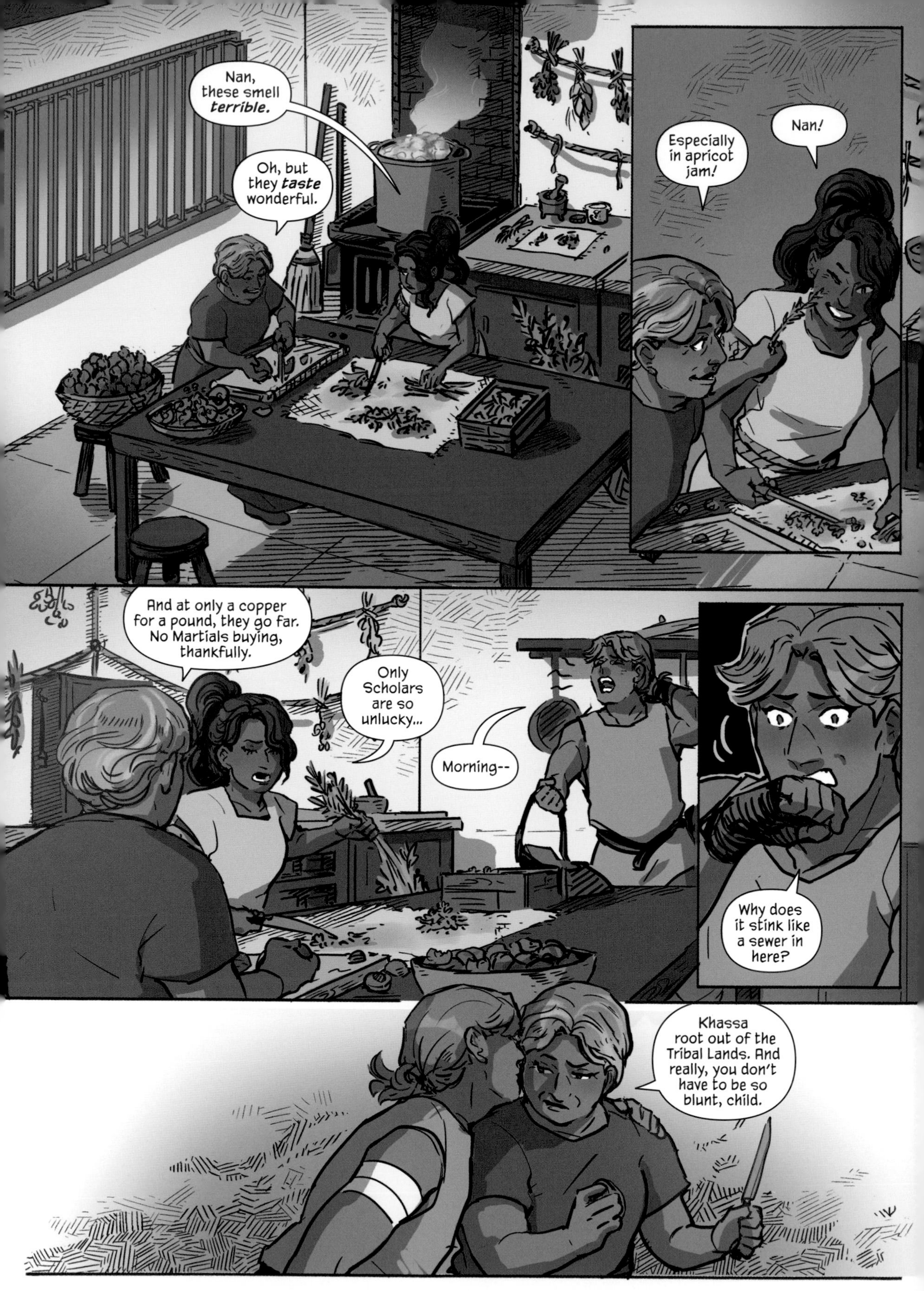
Nan, these smell *terrible.*
Oh, but they *taste* wonderful.
Especially in apricot jam!
Nan!
And at only a copper for a pound, they go far. No Martials buying, thankfully.
Only Scholars are so unlucky...
Morning--
Why does it stink like a sewer in here?
Khassa root out of the Tribal Lands. And really, you don't have to be so blunt, child.

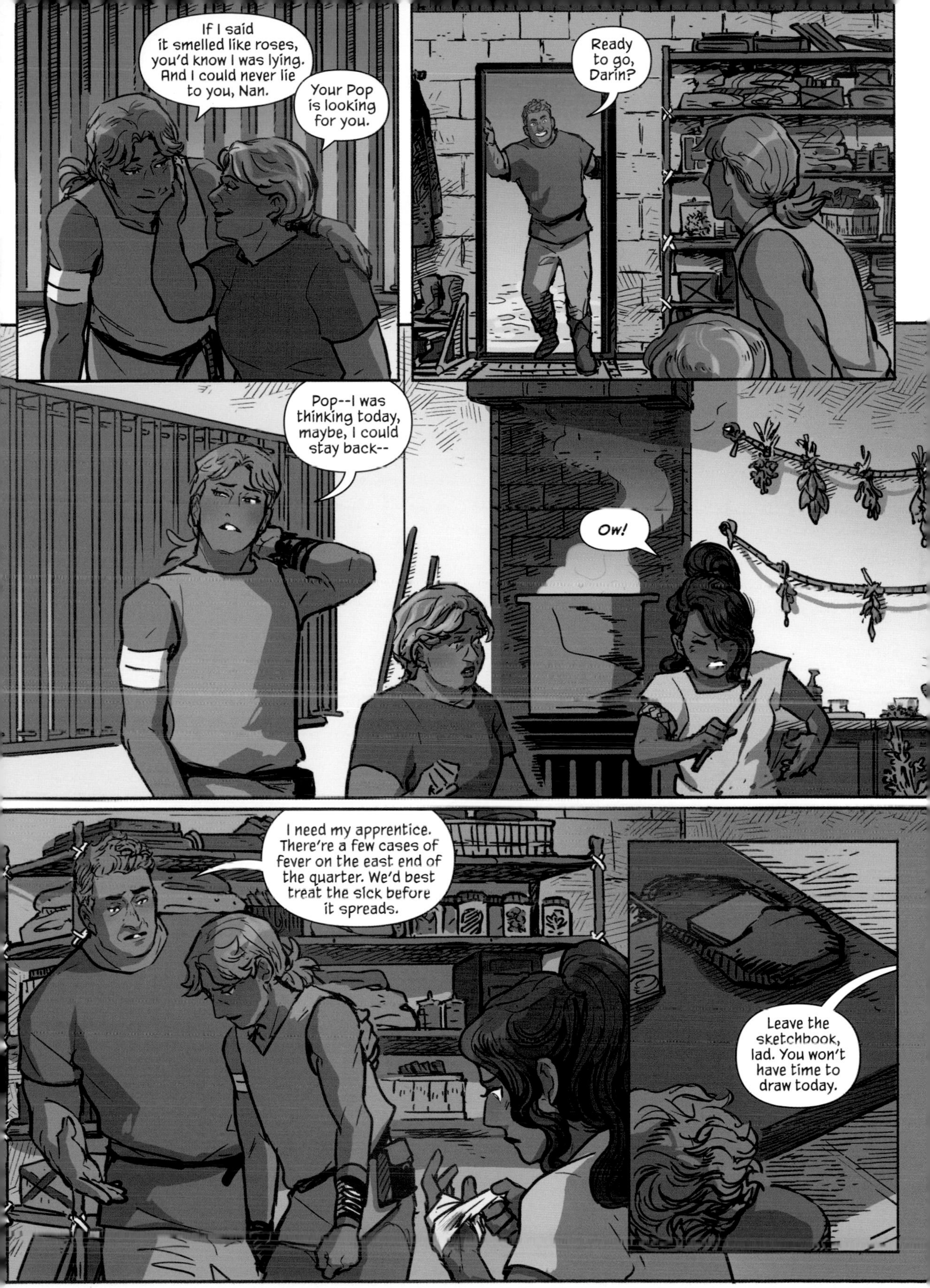
If I said it smelled like roses, you'd know I was lying. And I could never lie to you, Nan.
Your Pop is looking for you.
Ready to go, Darin?
Pop--I was thinking today, maybe, I could stay back--
Ow!
I need my apprentice. There're a few cases of fever on the east end of the quarter. We'd best treat the sick before it spreads.
Leave the sketchbook, lad. You won't have time to draw today.

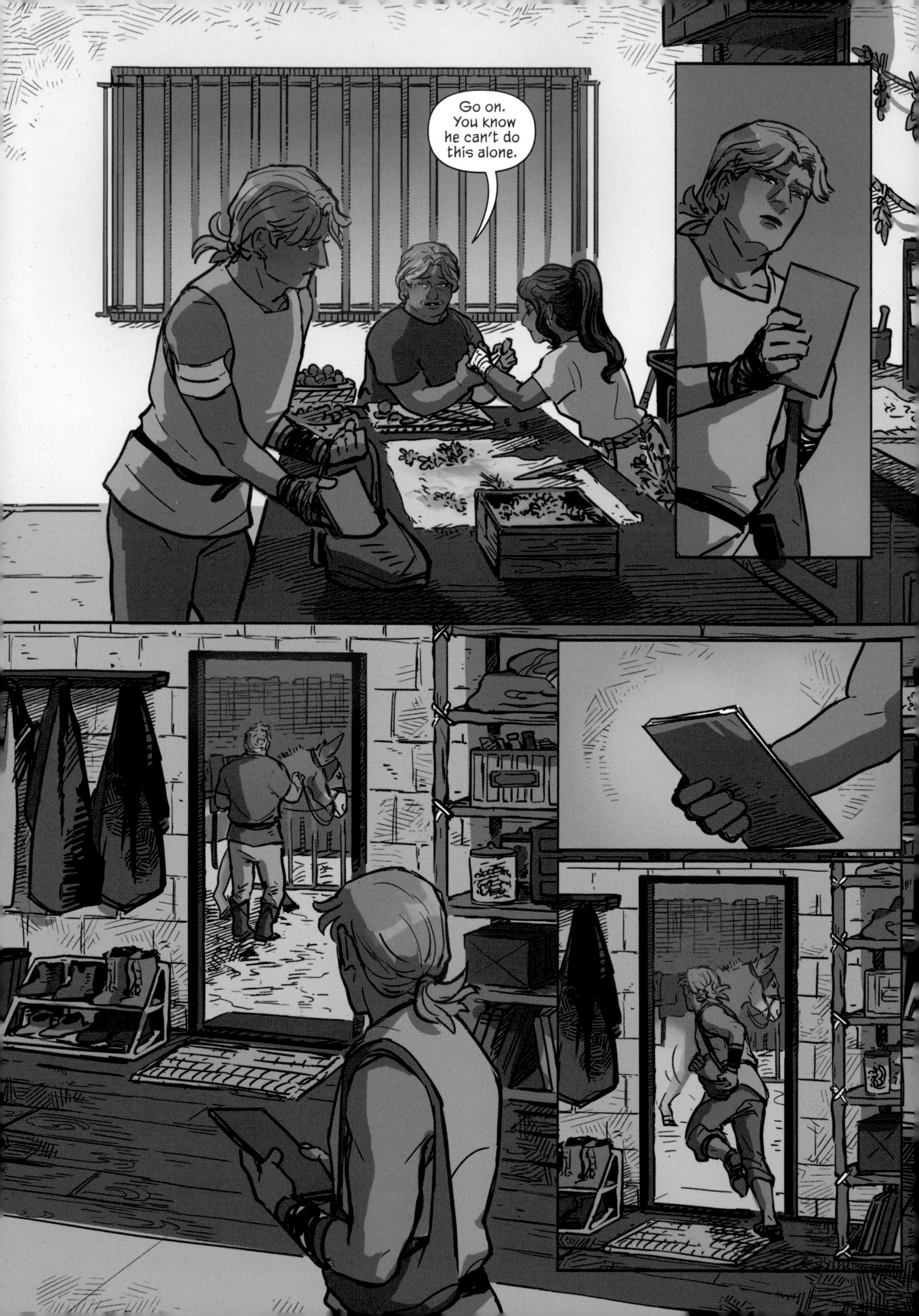
Go on. You know he can't do this alone.

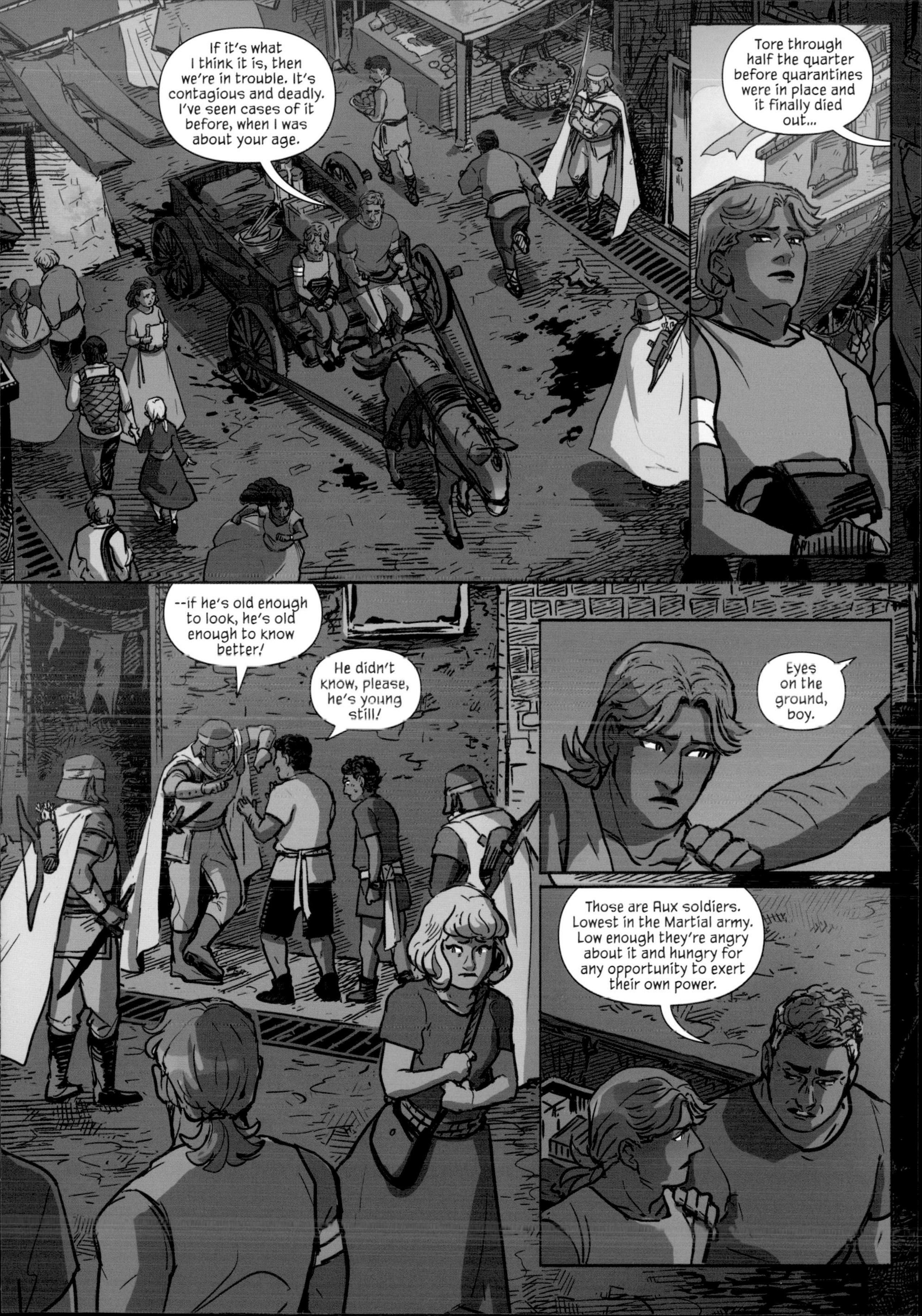
If it's what I think it is, then we're in trouble. It's contagious and deadly. I've seen cases of it before, when I was about your age.
Tore through half the quarter before quarantines were in place and it finally died out...
--if he's old enough to look, he's old enough to know better!
He didn't know, please, he's young still!
Eyes on the ground, boy.
Those are Aux soldiers. Lowest in the Martial army. Low enough they're angry about it and hungry for any opportunity to exert their own power.

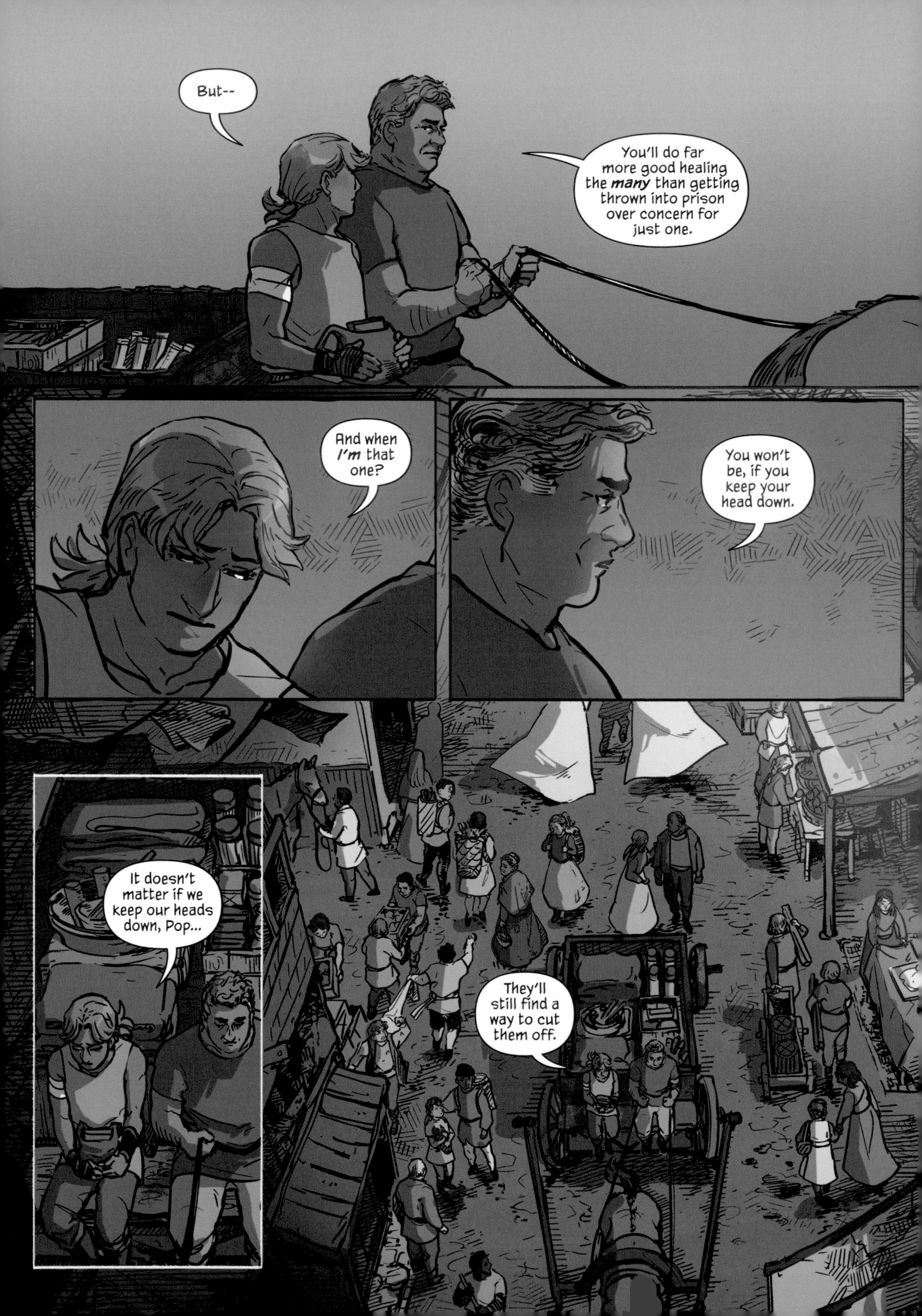
But--
You'll do far more good healing the *many* than getting thrown into prison over concern for just one.
And when *I'm* that one?
You won't be, if you keep your head down.
It doesn't matter if we keep our heads down, Pop...
They'll still find a way to cut them off.

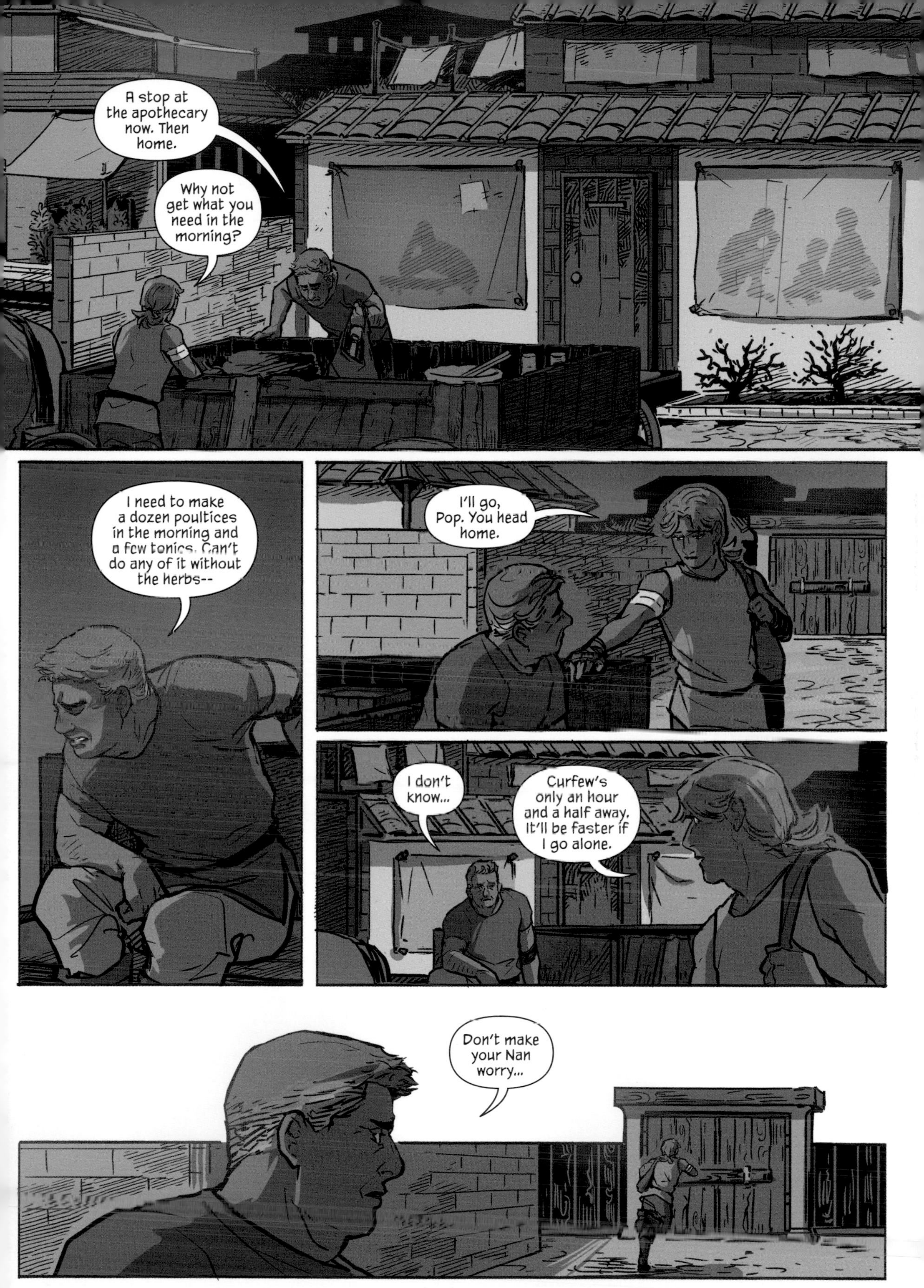
A stop at the apothecary now. Then home.
Why not get what you need in the morning?
I need to make a dozen poultices in the morning and a few tonics. Can't do any of it without the herbs--
I'll go, Pop. You head home.
I don't know...
Curfew's only an hour and a half away. It'll be faster if I go alone.
Don't make your Nan worry...

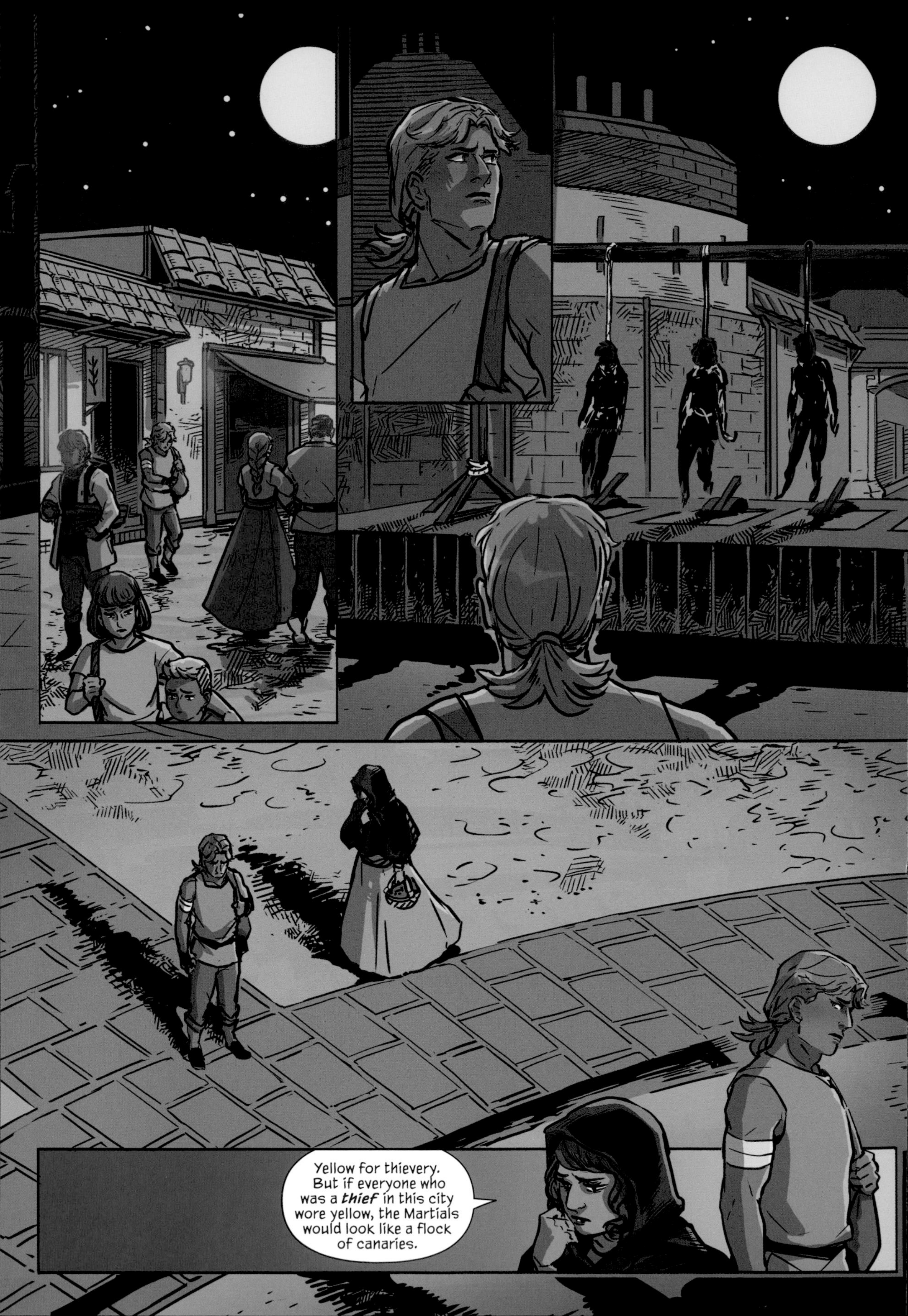
Yellow for thievery. But if everyone who was a *thief* in this city wore yellow, the Martials would look like a flock of canaries.

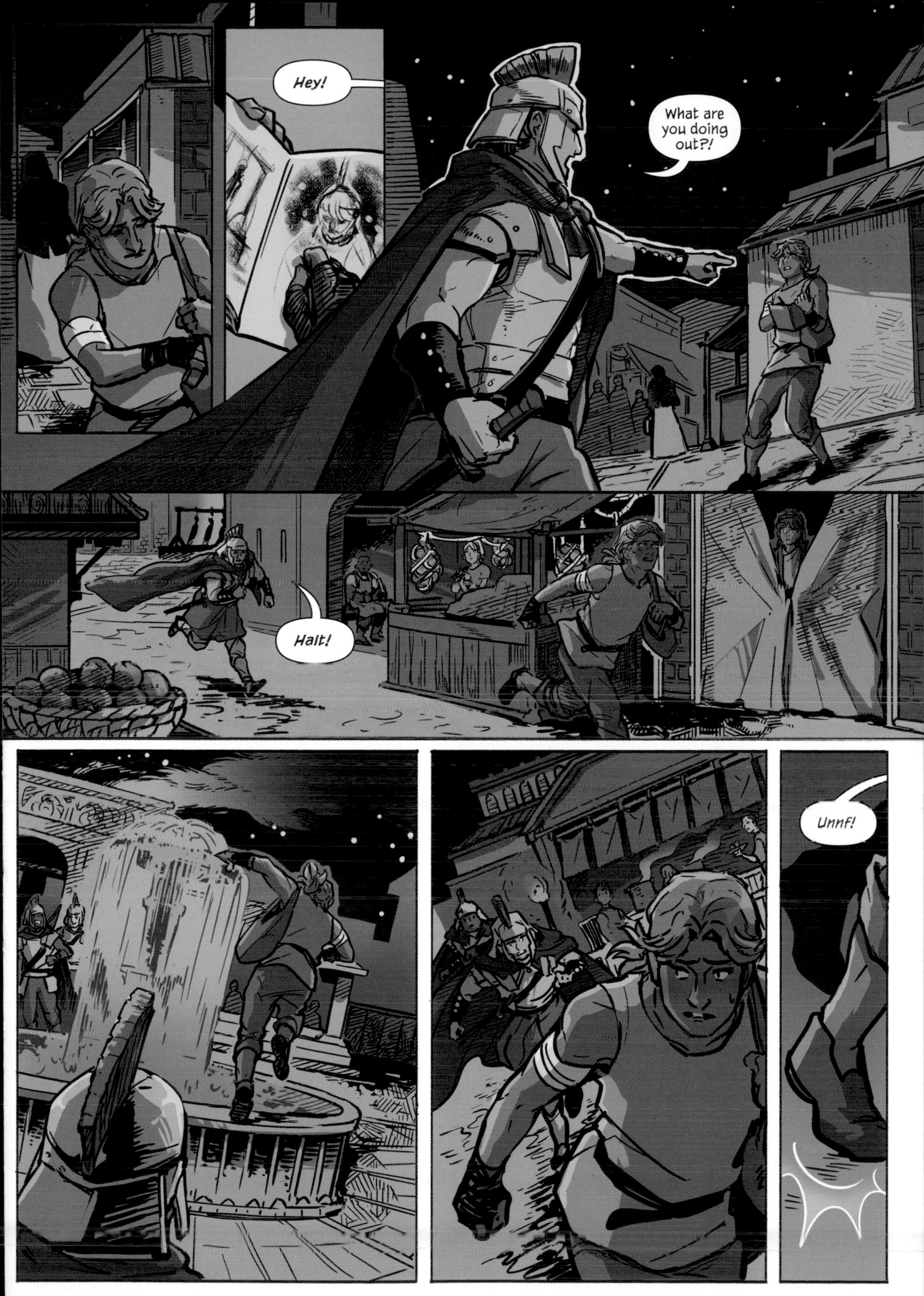
Hey!
What are you doing out?!
Halt!
Unnf!

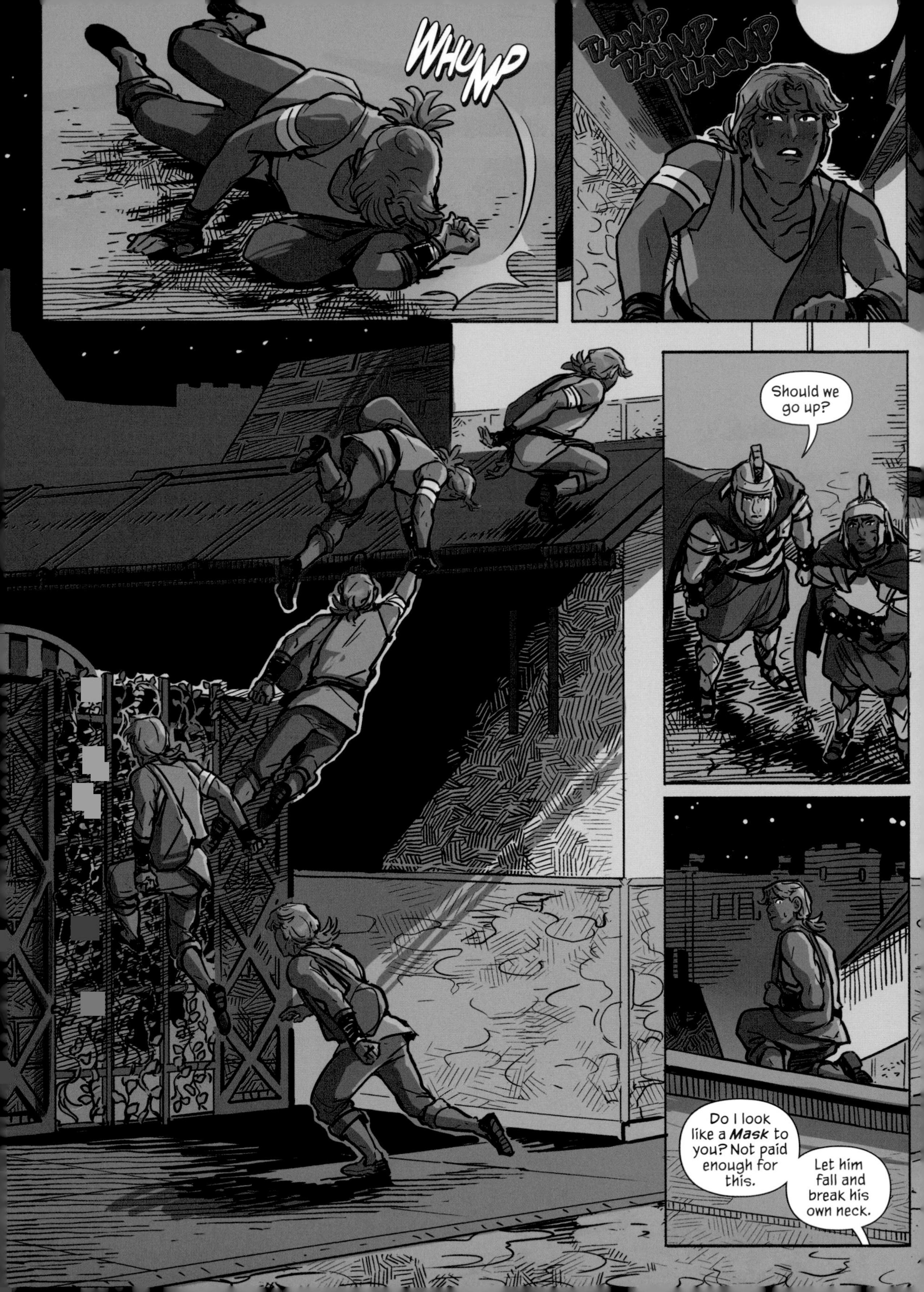
WHUMP
THUMP THUMP THUMP
Should we go up?
Do I look like a *Mask* to you? Not paid enough for this.
Let him fall and break his own neck.

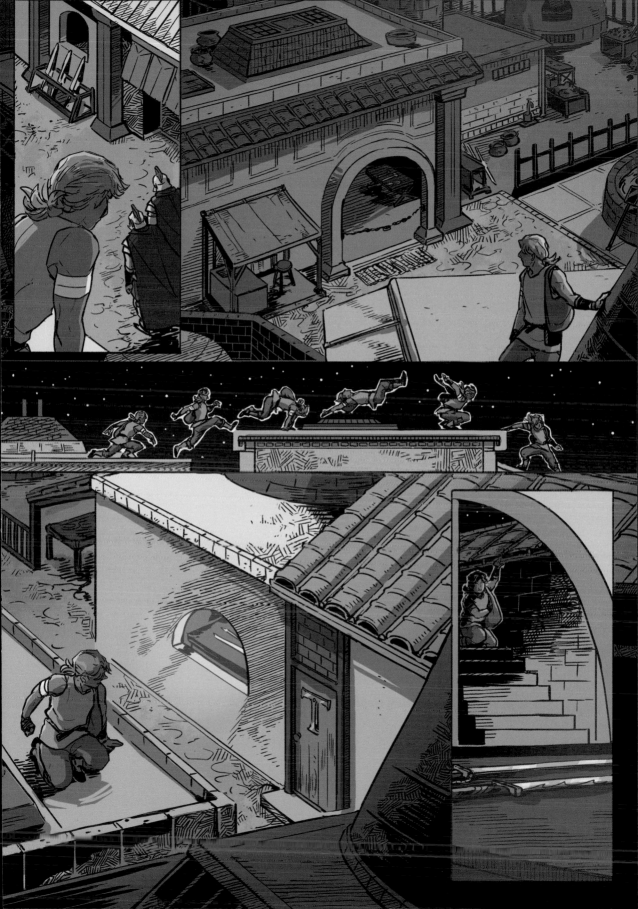

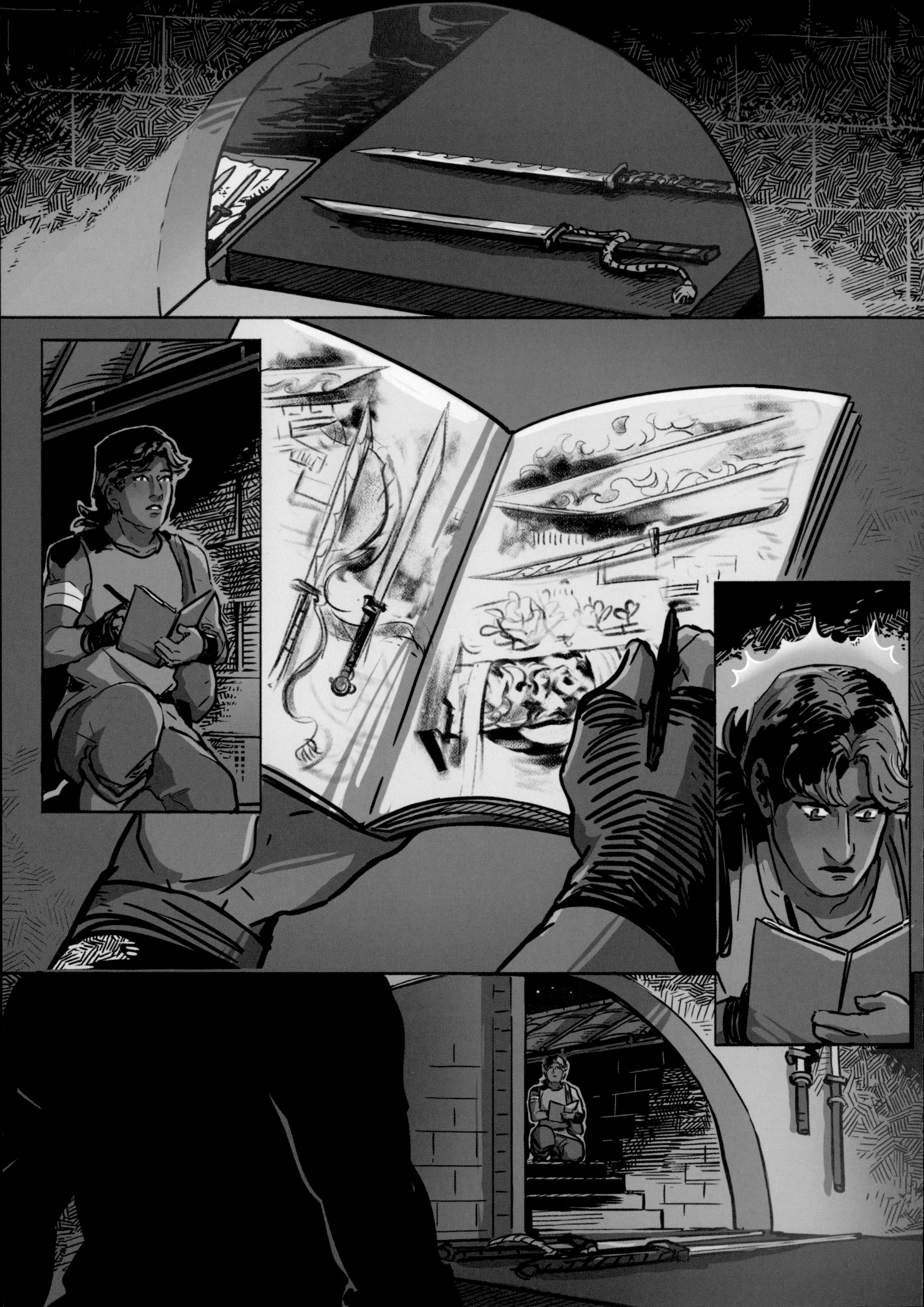

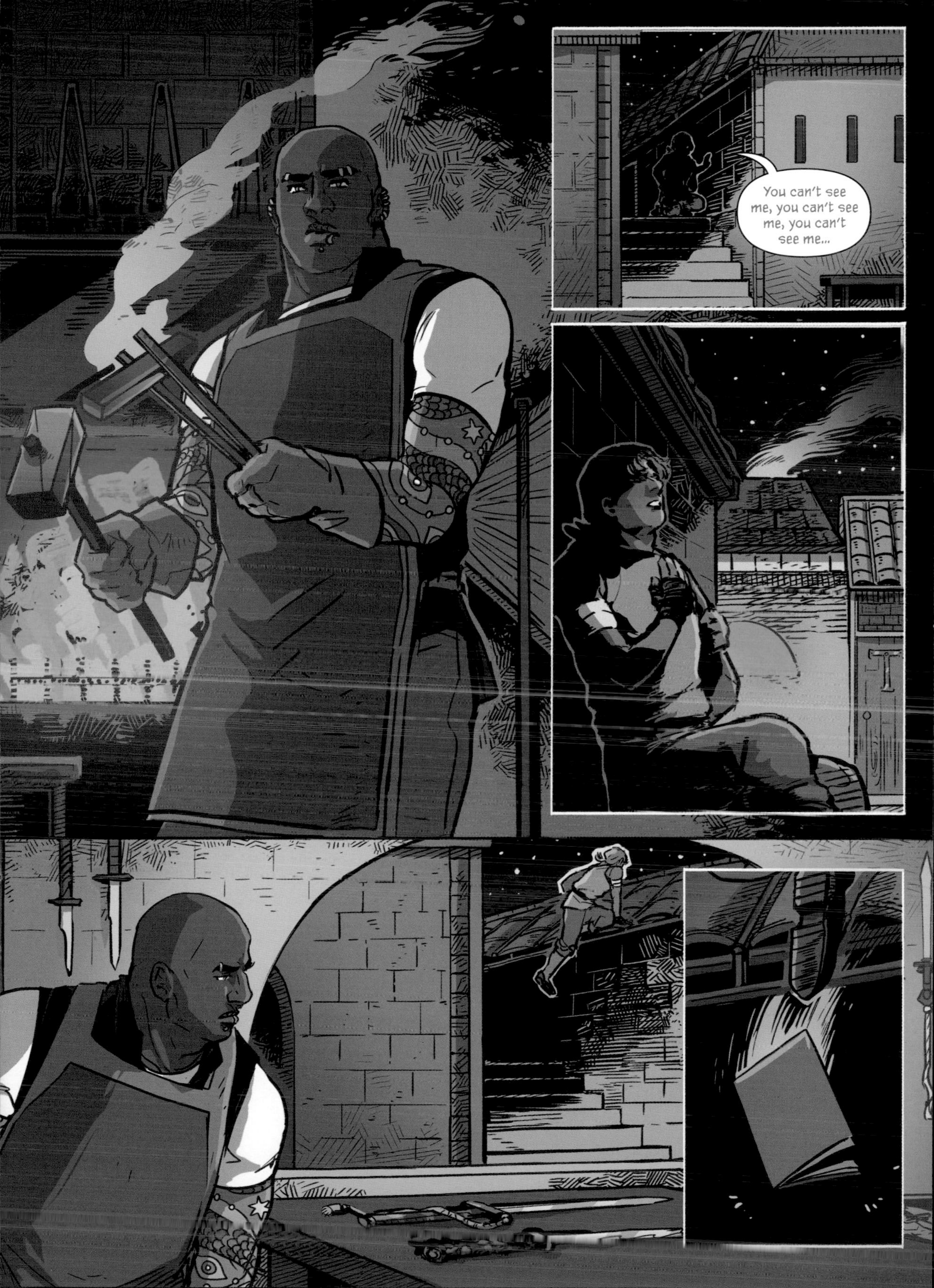
You can't see me, you can't see me, you can't see me...

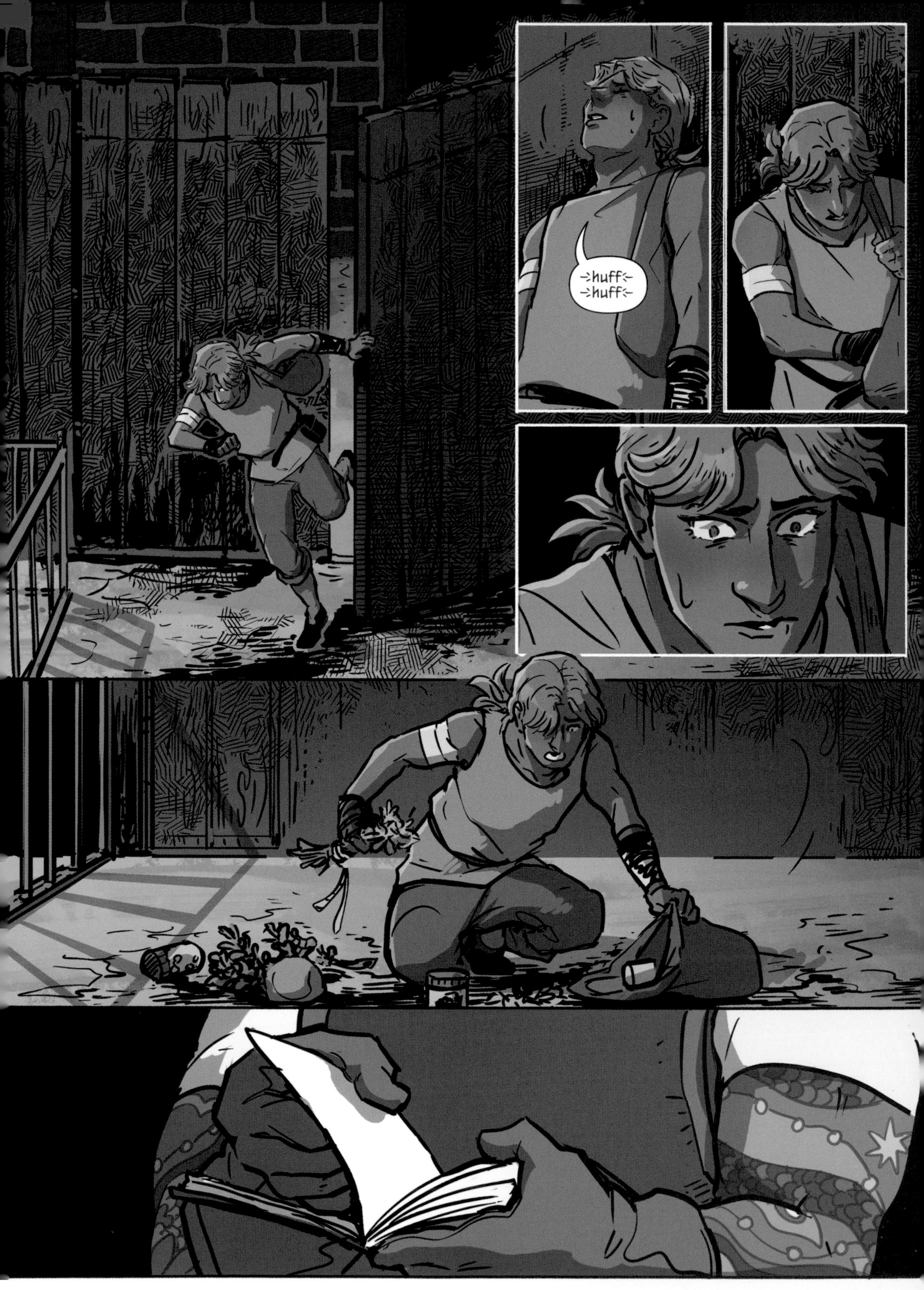
huff huff

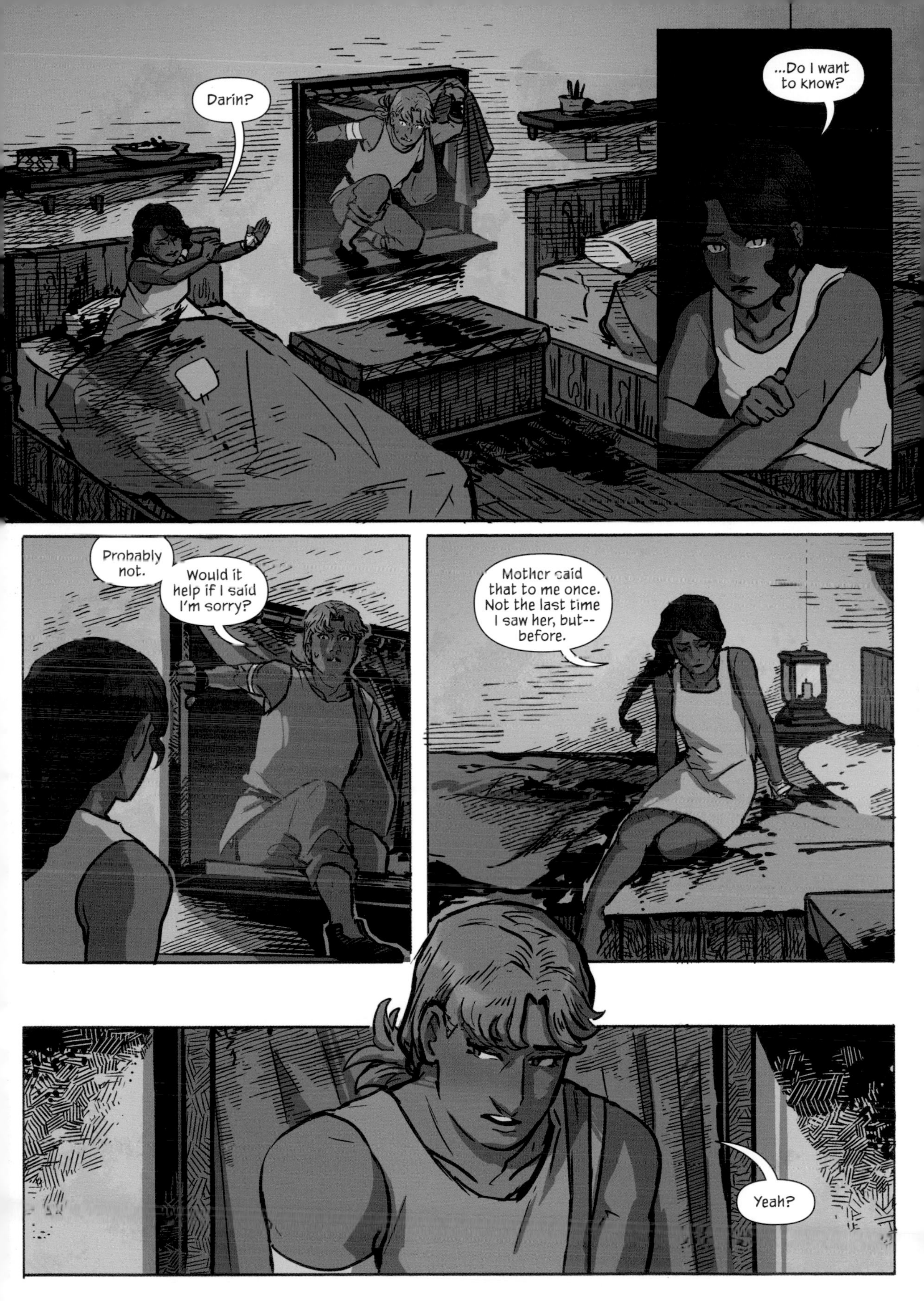
Darin?
...Do I want to know?
Probably not.
Would it help if I said I'm sorry?
Mother said that to me once. Not the last time I saw her, but-- before.
Yeah?

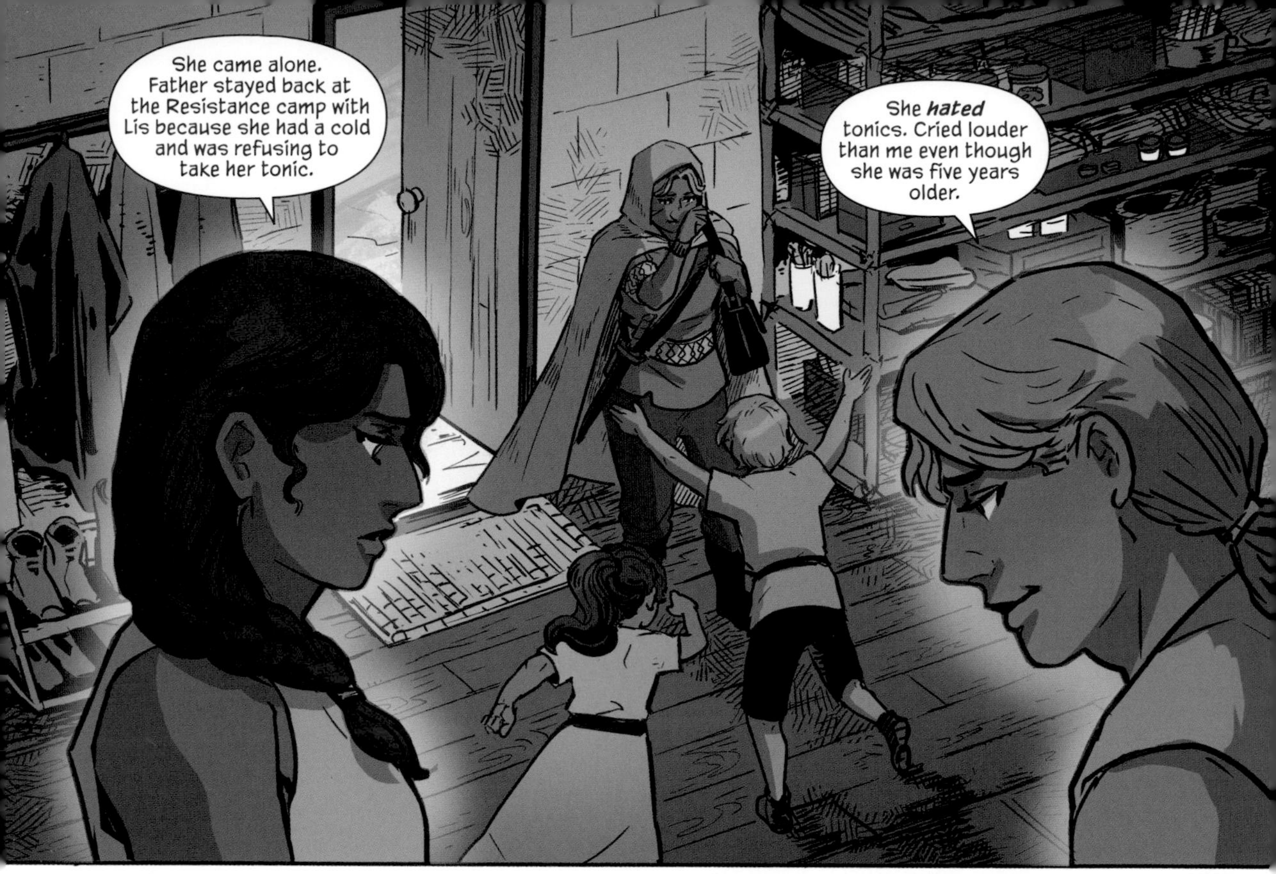
She came alone. Father stayed back at the Resistance camp with Lis because she had a cold and was refusing to take her tonic.
She **hated** tonics. Cried louder than me even though she was five years older.

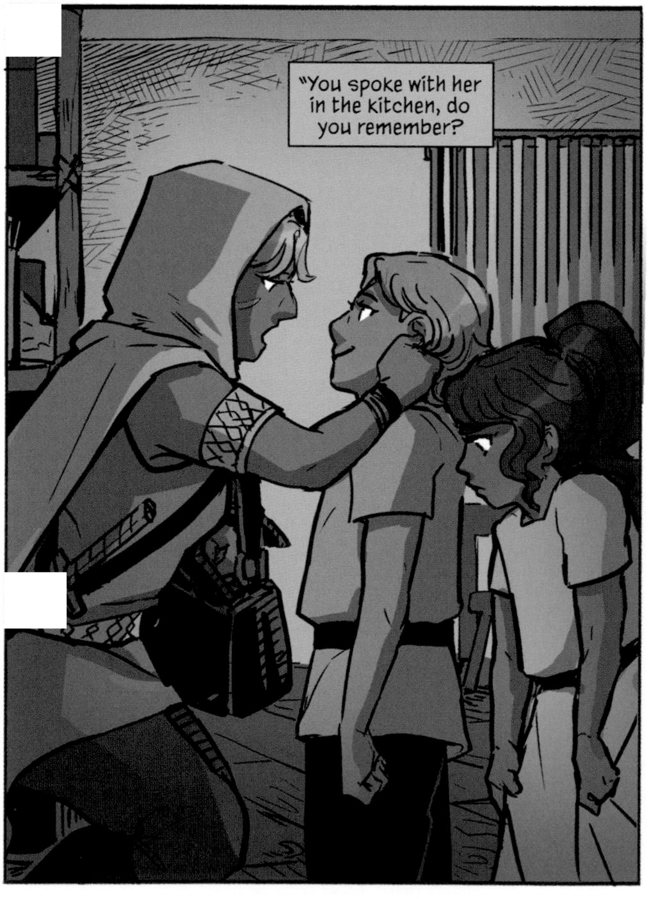
"You spoke with her in the kitchen, do you remember?

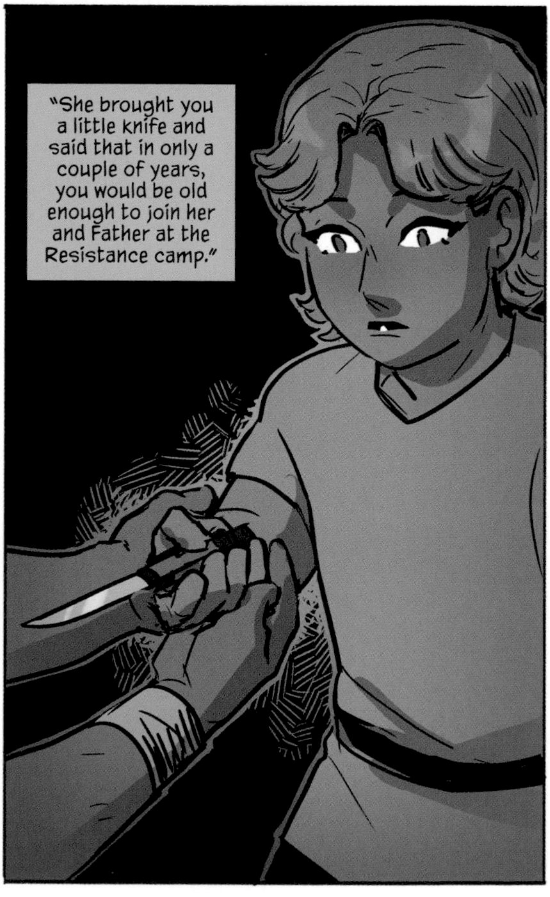
"She brought you a little knife and said that in only a couple of years, you would be old enough to join her and Father at the Resistance camp."

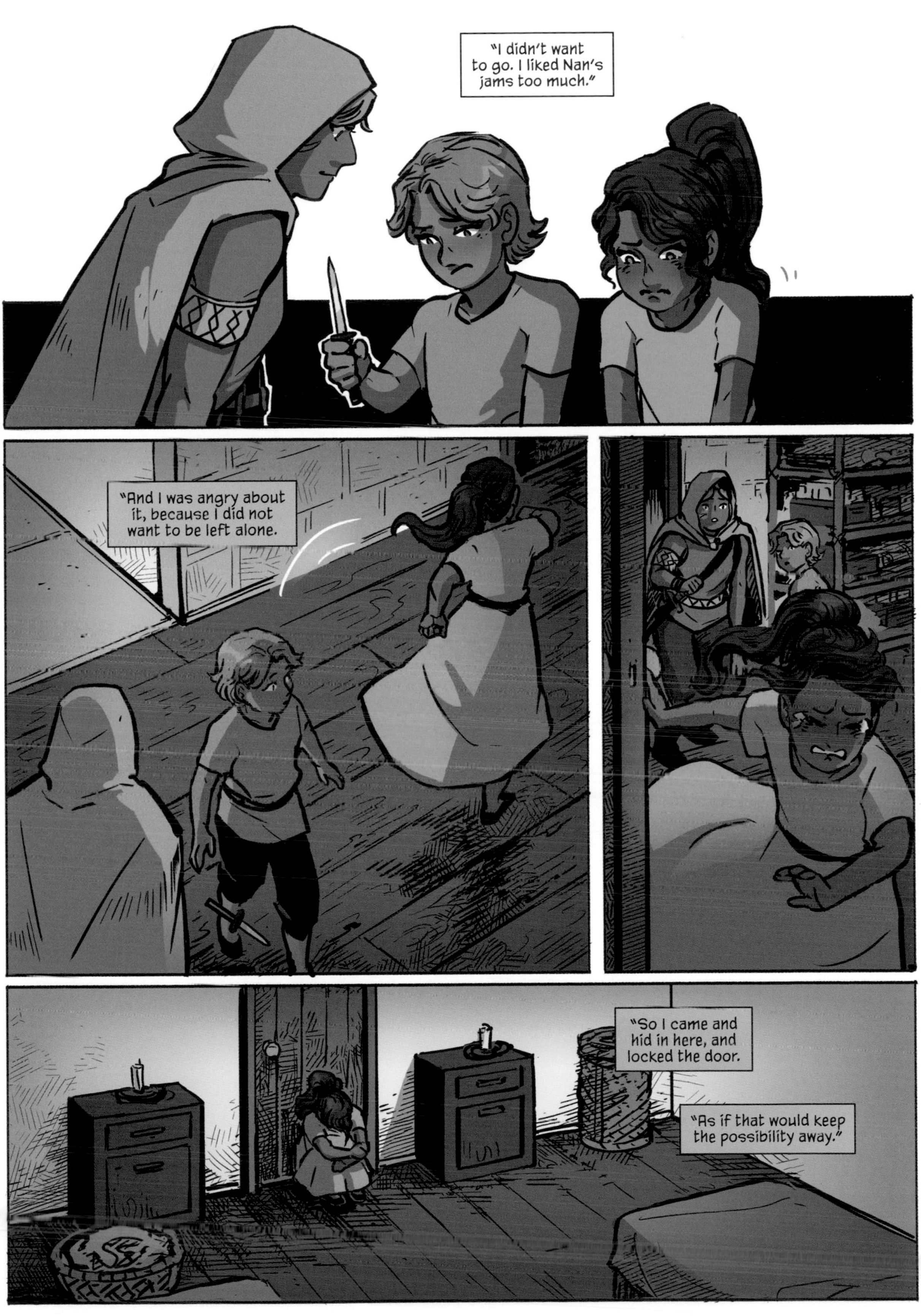
"I didn't want to go. I liked Nan's jams too much."
"And I was angry about it, because I did not want to be left alone.
"So I came and hid in here, and locked the door.
"As if that would keep the possibility away."

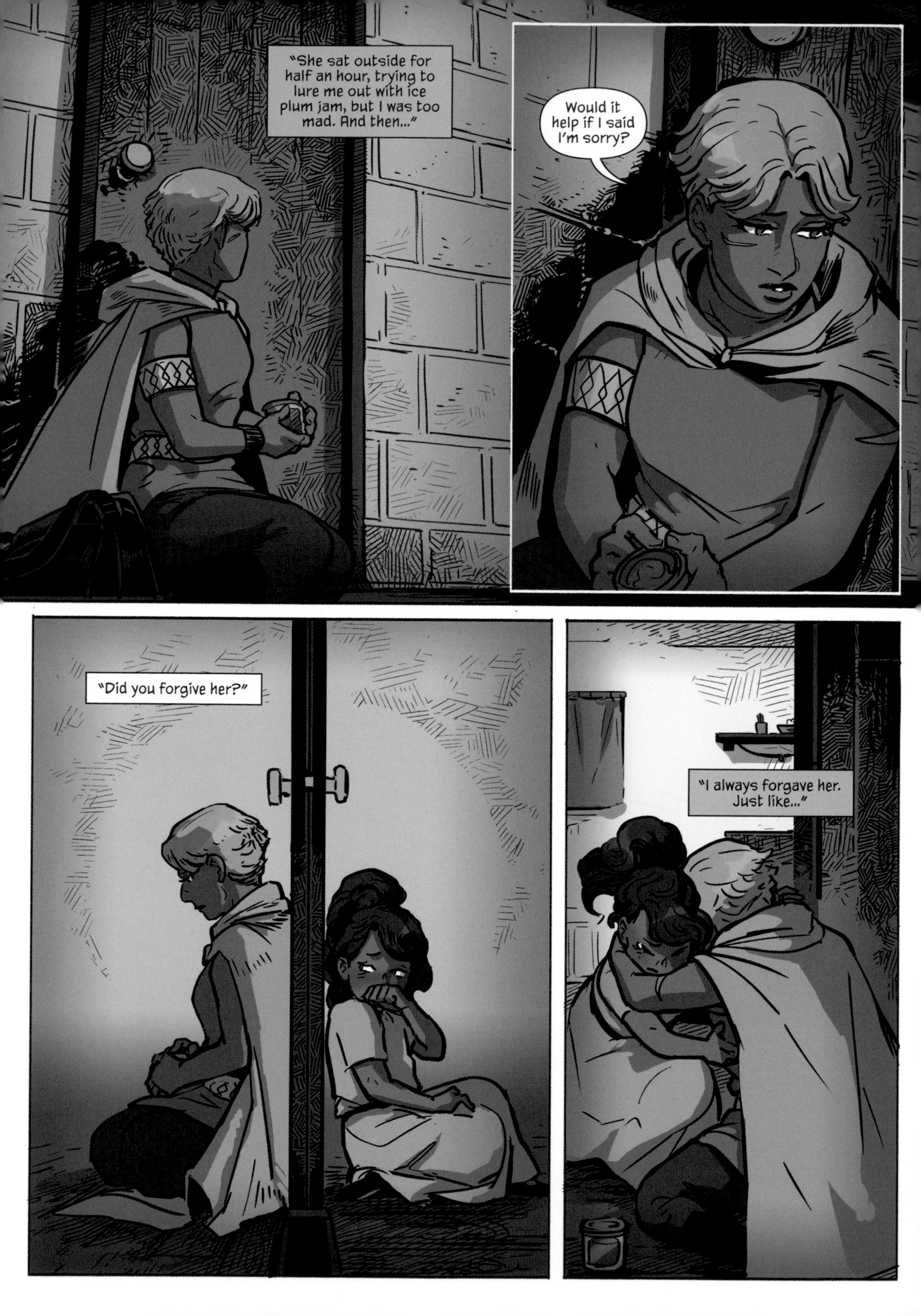
"She sat outside for half an hour, trying to lure me out with ice plum jam, but I was too mad. And then..."
Would it help if I said I'm sorry?
"Did you forgive her?"
"I always forgave her. Just like..."

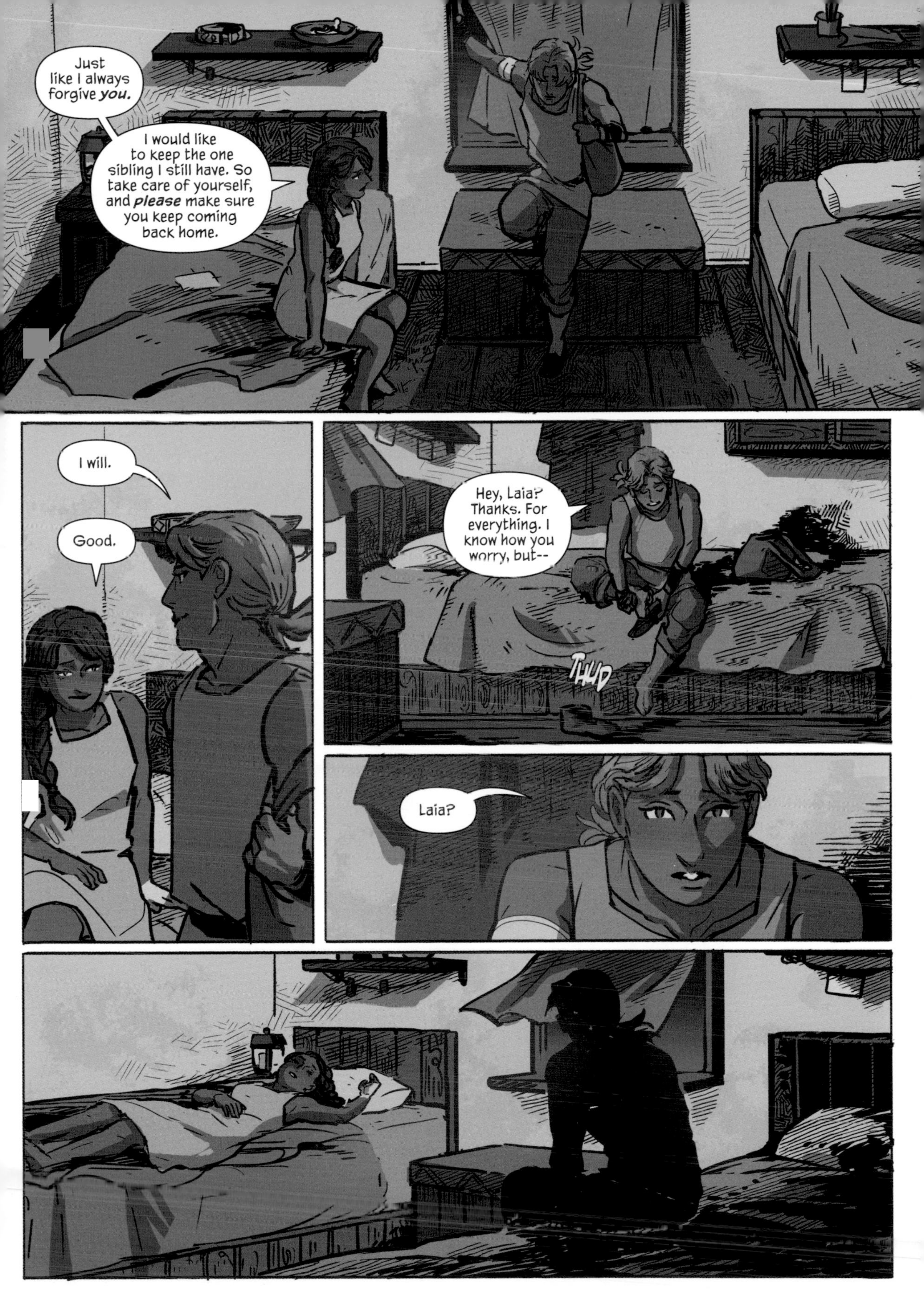
Just like I always forgive *you.*
I would like to keep the one sibling I still have. So take care of yourself, and ***please*** make sure you keep coming back home.
I will.
Good.
Hey, Laia? Thanks. For everything. I know how you worry, but--
THUD
Laia?

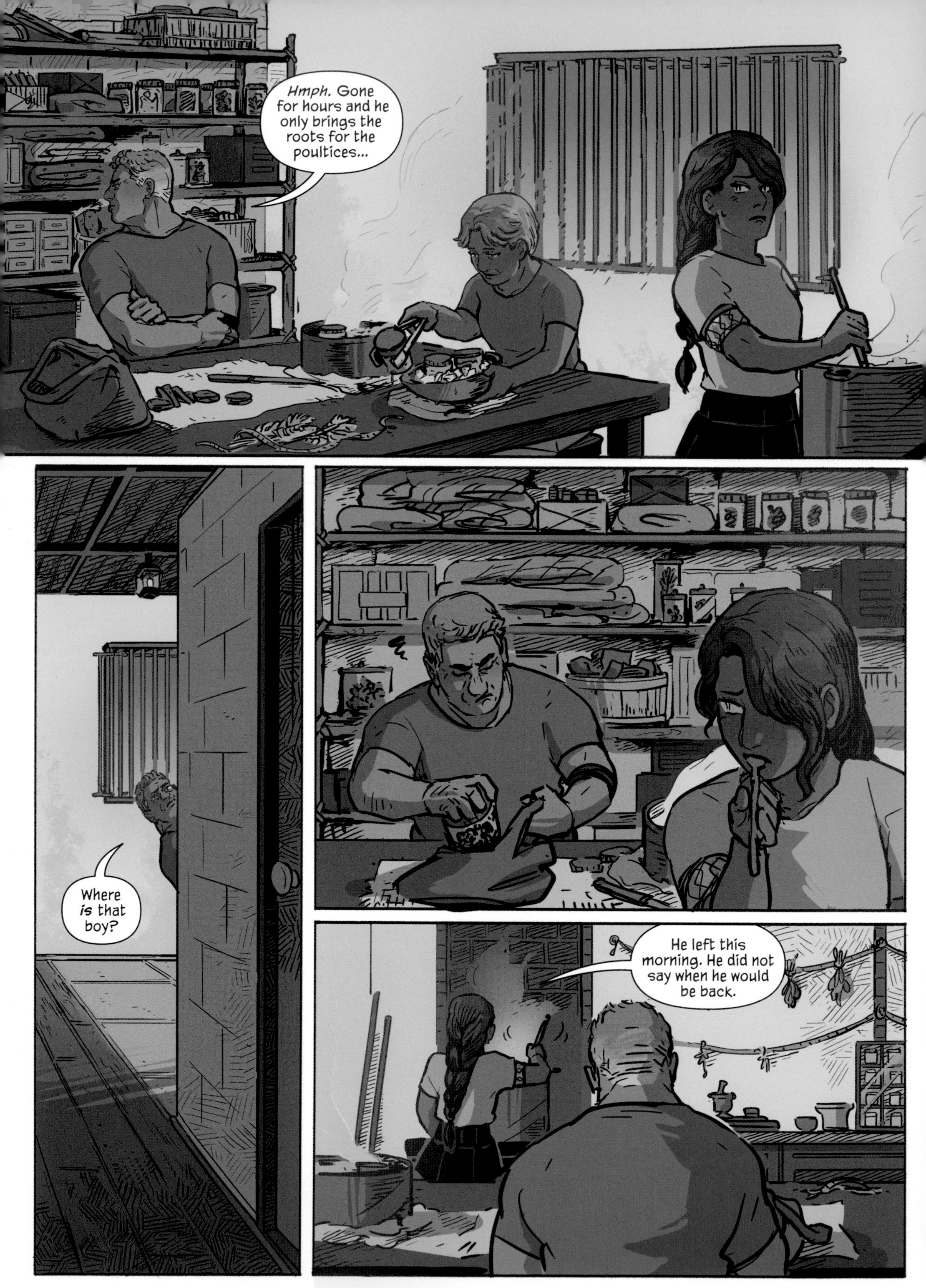
Hmph. Gone for hours and he only brings the roots for the poultices...
Where *is* that boy?
He left this morning. He did not say when he would be back.

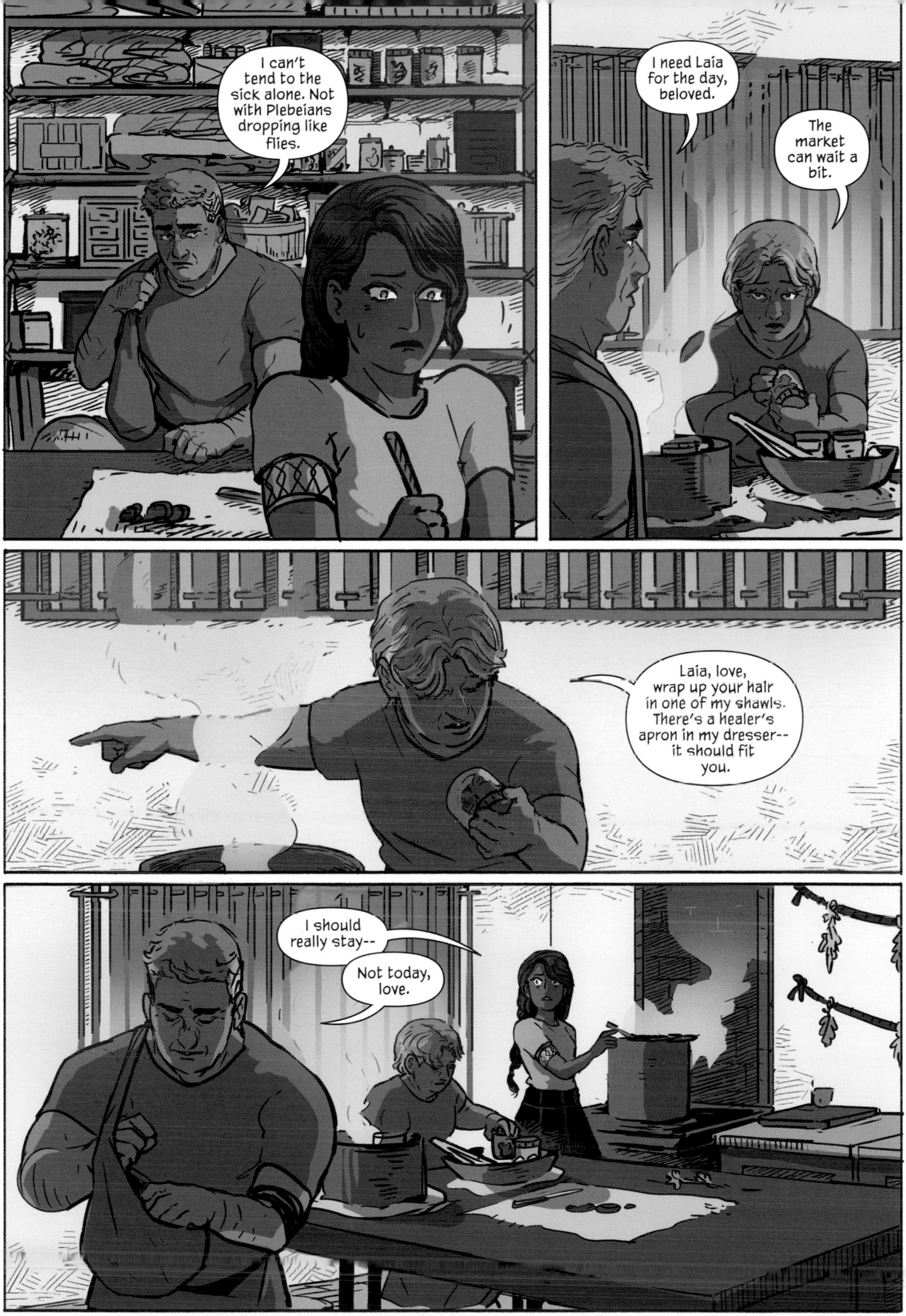
I can't tend to the sick alone. Not with Plebeians dropping like flies.
I need Laia for the day, beloved.
The market can wait a bit.
Laia, love, wrap up your hair in one of my shawls. There's a healer's apron in my dresser-- it should fit you.
I should really stay--
Not today, love.

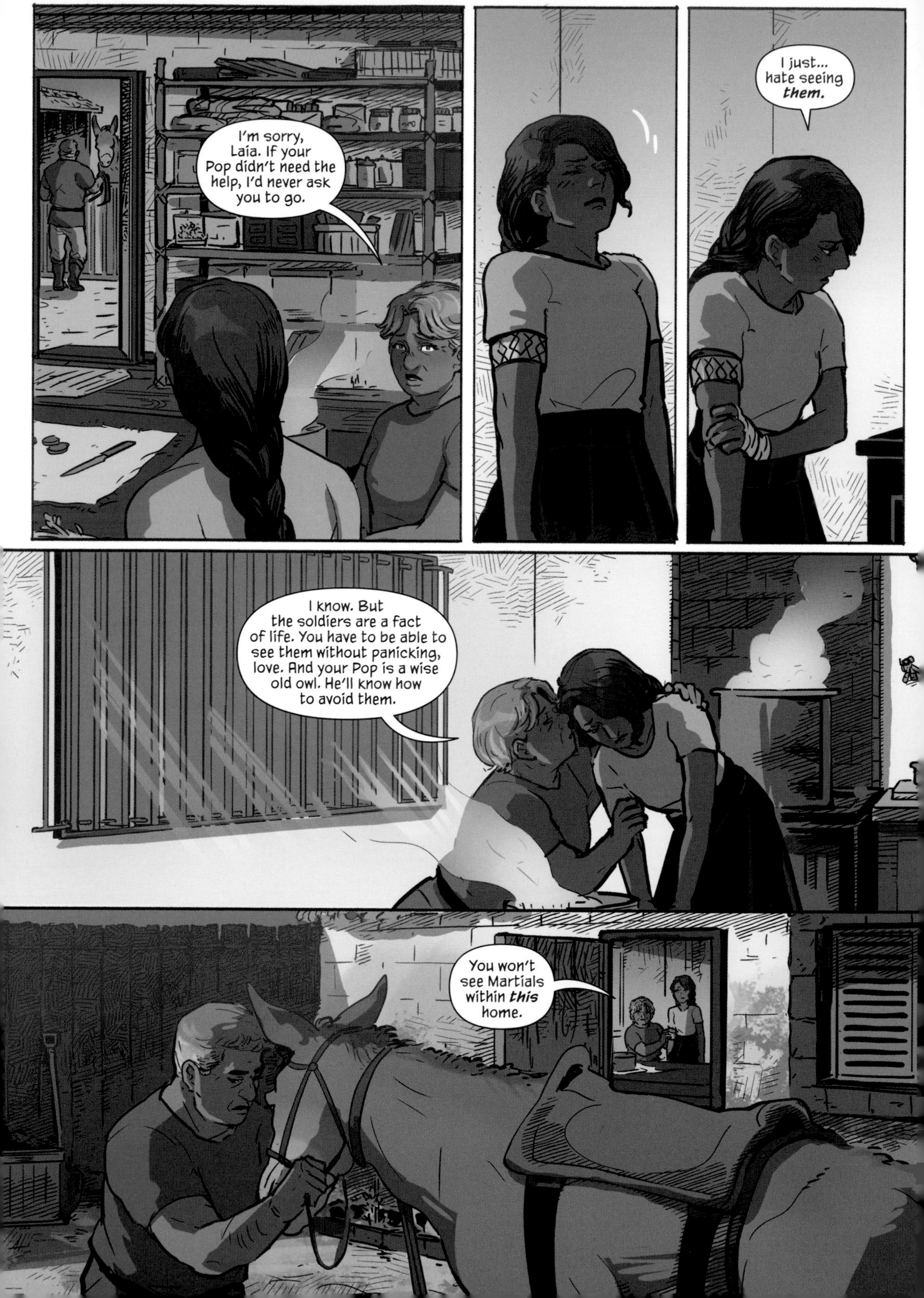
I'm sorry, Laia. If your Pop didn't need the help, I'd never ask you to go.
I just... hate seeing *them.*
I know. But the soldiers are a fact of life. You have to be able to see them without panicking, love. And your Pop is a wise old owl. He'll know how to avoid them.
You won't see Martials within *this* home.

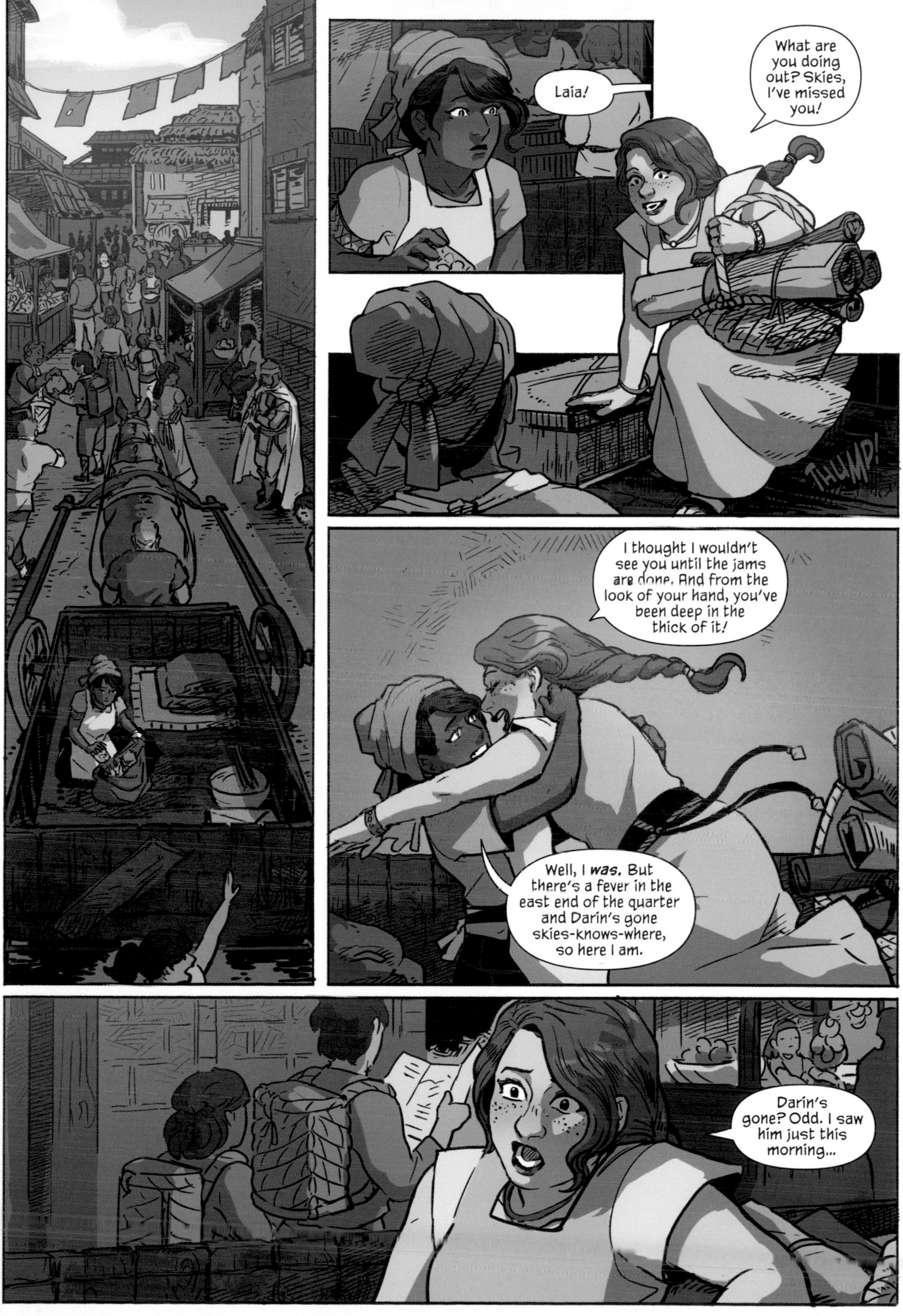
Laia!
What are you doing out? Skies, I've missed you!
THUMP!
I thought I wouldn't see you until the jams are done. And from the look of your hand, you've been deep in the thick of it!
Well, I *was.* But there's a fever in the east end of the quarter and Darin's gone skies-knows-where, so here I am.
Darin's gone? Odd. I saw him just this morning...

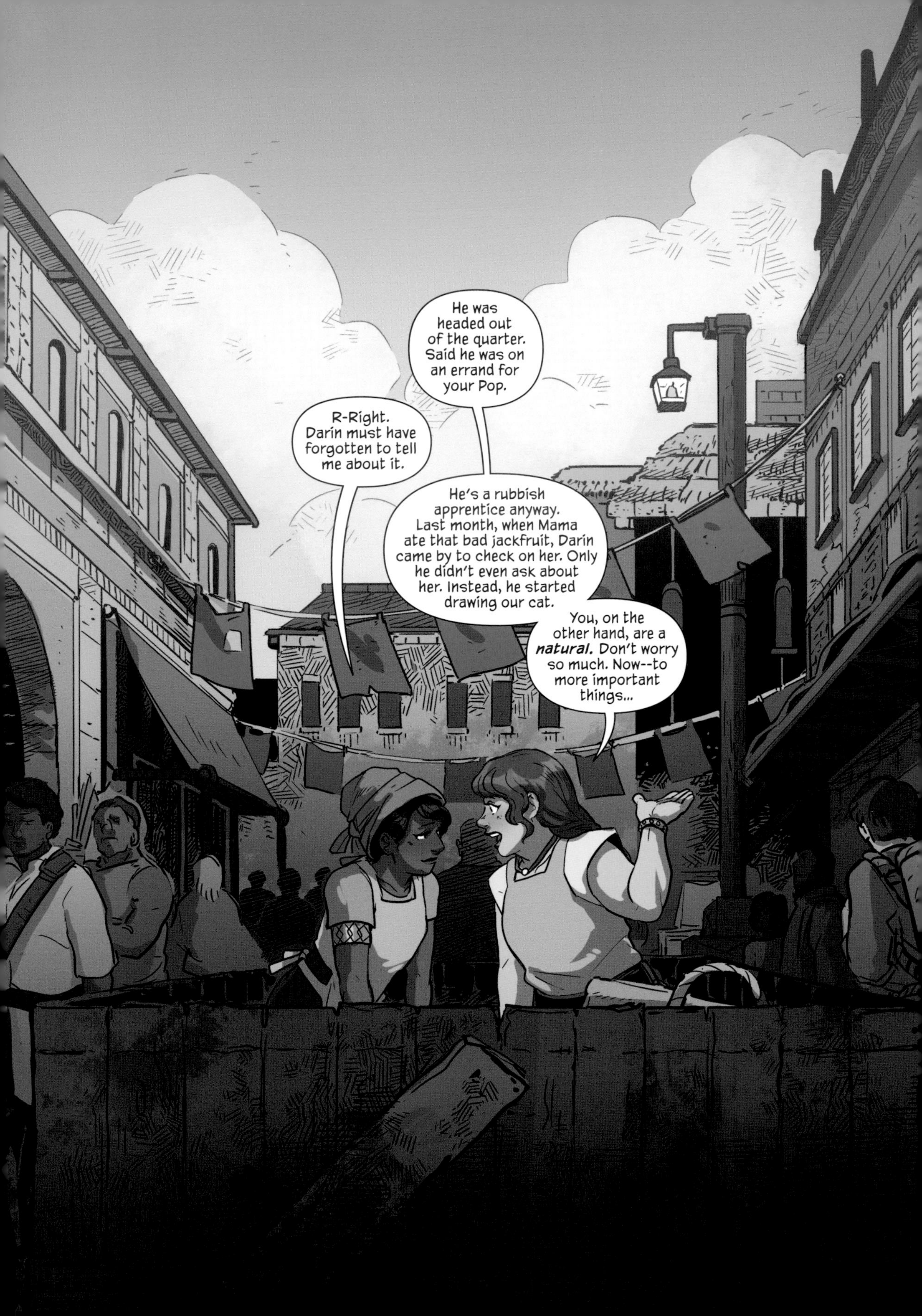
He was headed out of the quarter. Said he was on an errand for your Pop.
R-Right. Darin must have forgotten to tell me about it.
He's a rubbish apprentice anyway. Last month, when Mama ate that bad jackfruit, Darin came by to check on her. Only he didn't even ask about her. Instead, he started drawing our cat.
You, on the other hand, are a *natural.* Don't worry so much. Now--to more important things...

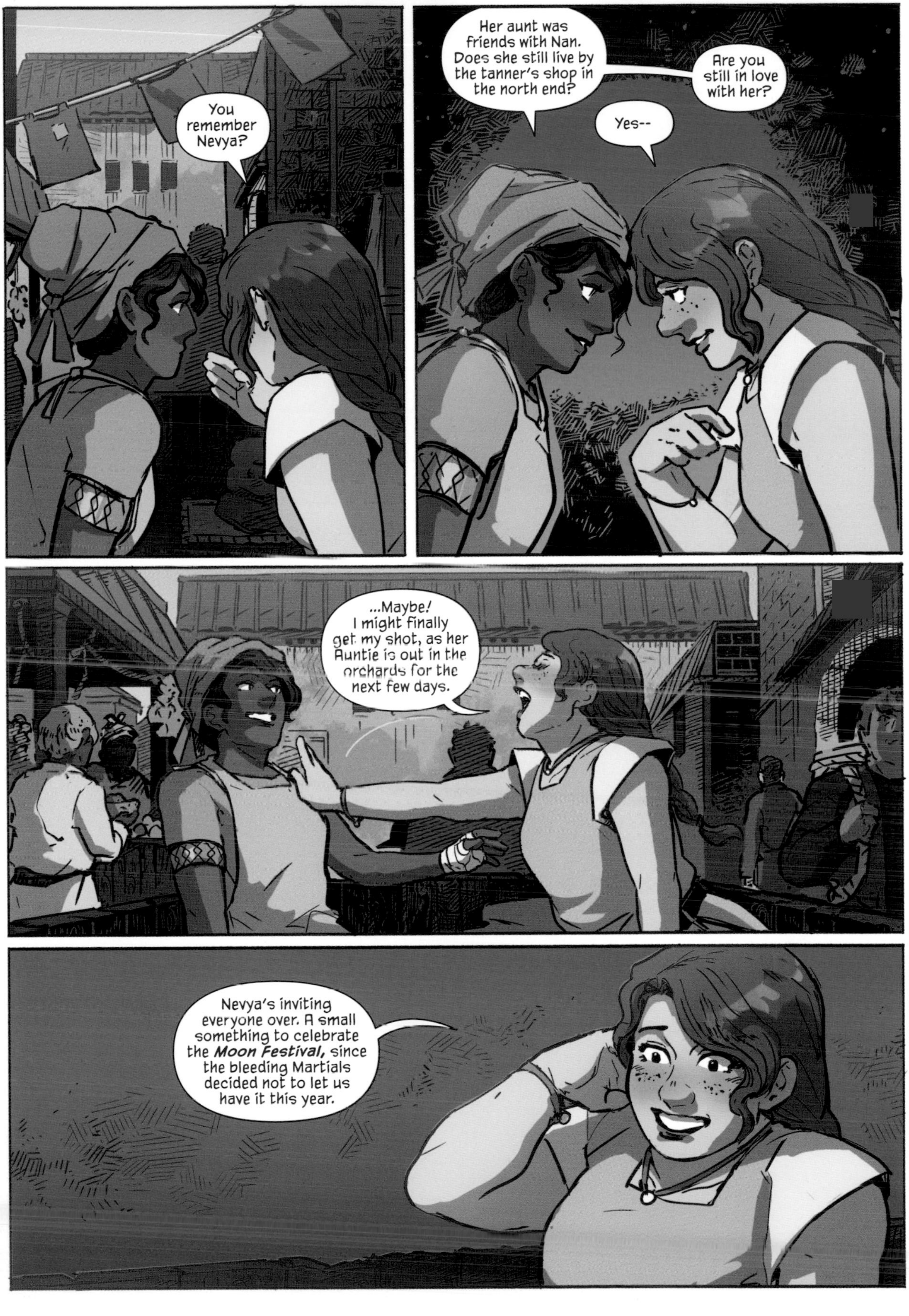

You remember Nevya?
Her aunt was friends with Nan. Does she still live by the tanner's shop in the north end?
Are you still in love with her?
Yes--
...Maybe! I might finally get my shot, as her Auntie is out in the orchards for the next few days.
Nevya's inviting everyone over. A small something to celebrate the *Moon Festival,* since the bleeding Martials decided not to let us have it this year.

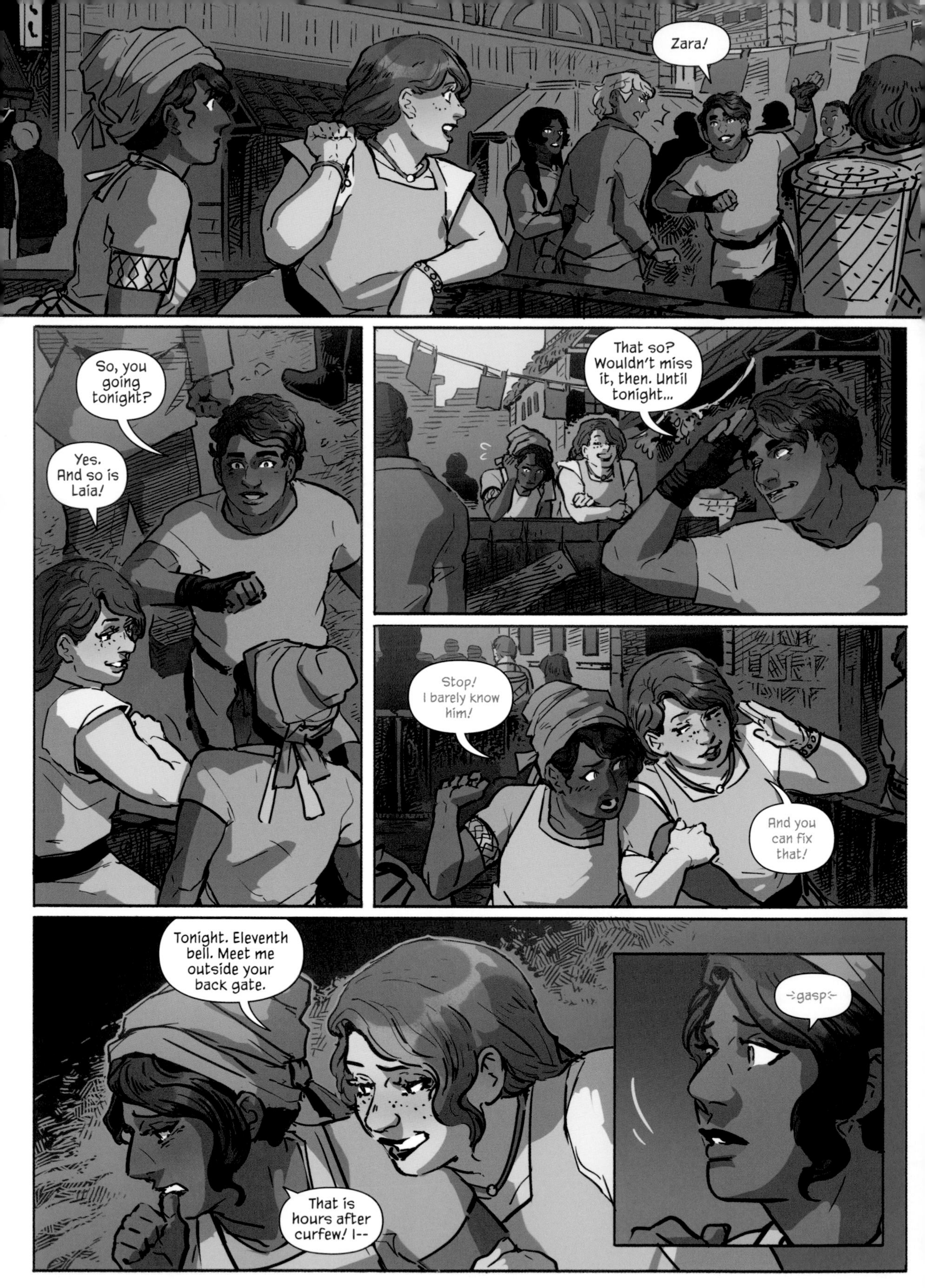
Zara!
So, you going tonight?
Yes. And so is Laia!
That so? Wouldn't miss it, then. Until tonight...
Stop! I barely know him!
And you can fix that!
Tonight. Eleventh bell. Meet me outside your back gate.
That is hours after curfew! I--
gasp

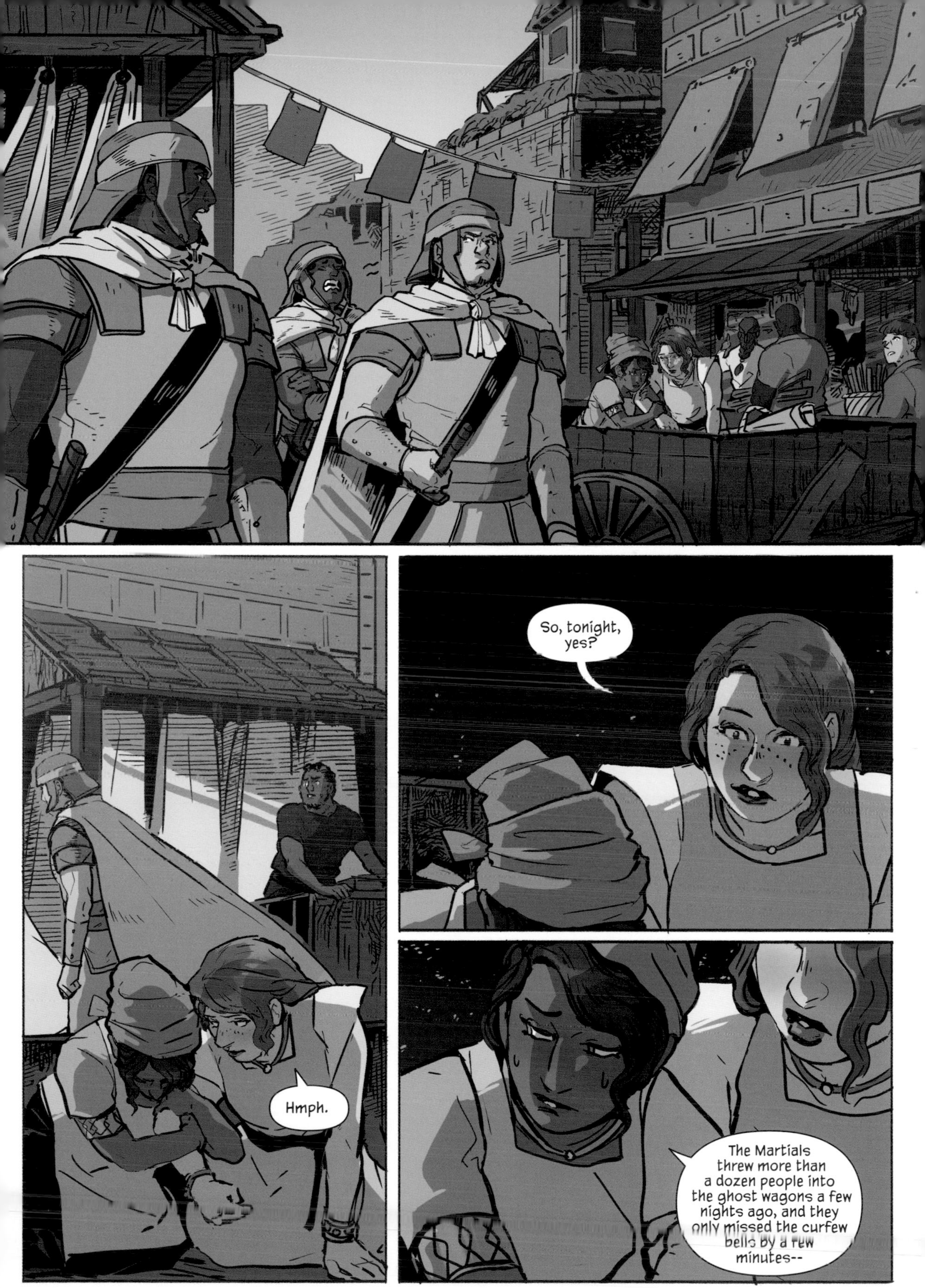
So, tonight, yes?
Hmph.
The Martials threw more than a dozen people into the ghost wagons a few nights ago, and they only missed the curfew bells by a few minutes--

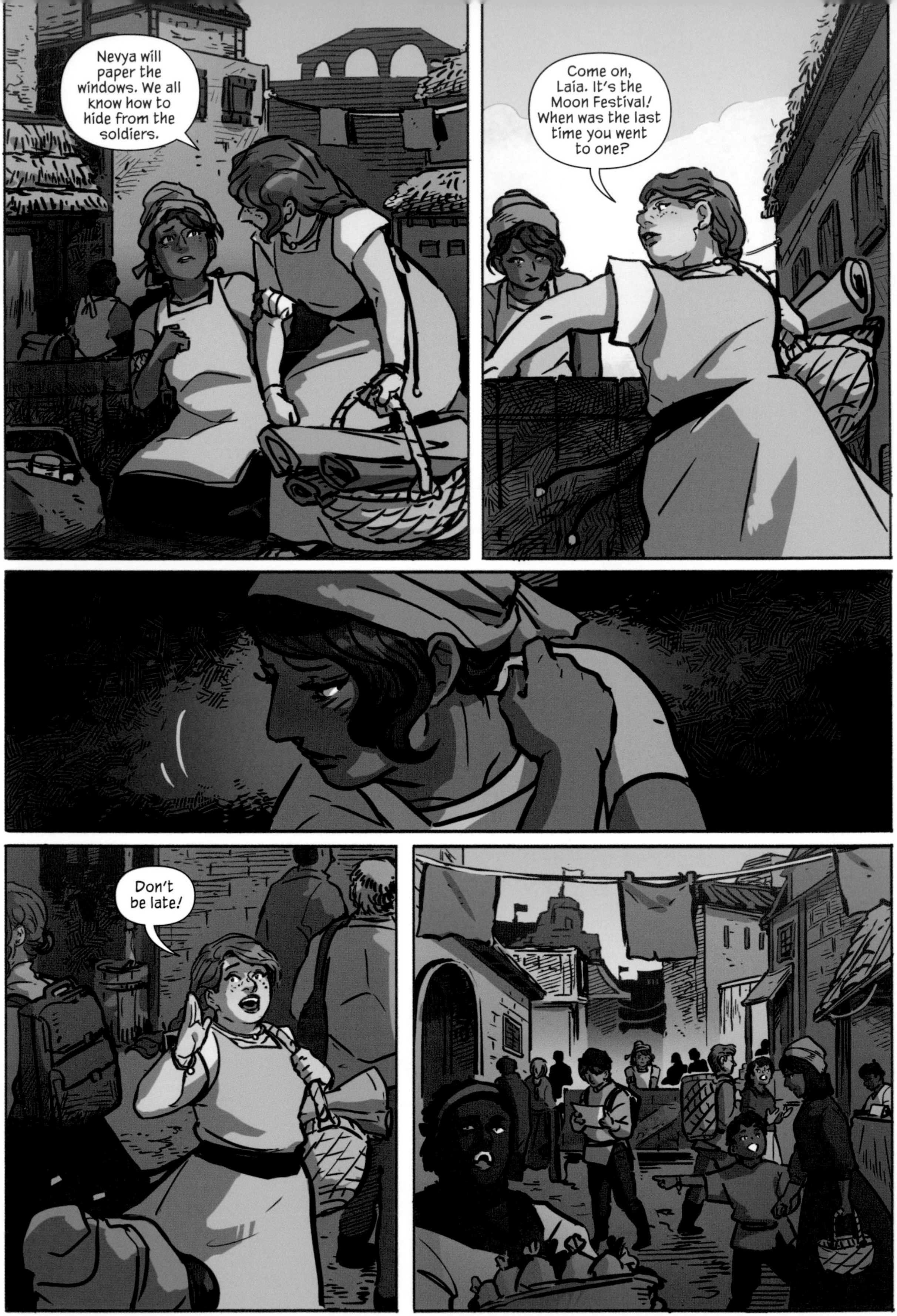
Nevya will paper the windows. We all know how to hide from the soldiers.
Come on, Laia. It's the Moon Festival! When was the last time you went to one?
Don't be late!

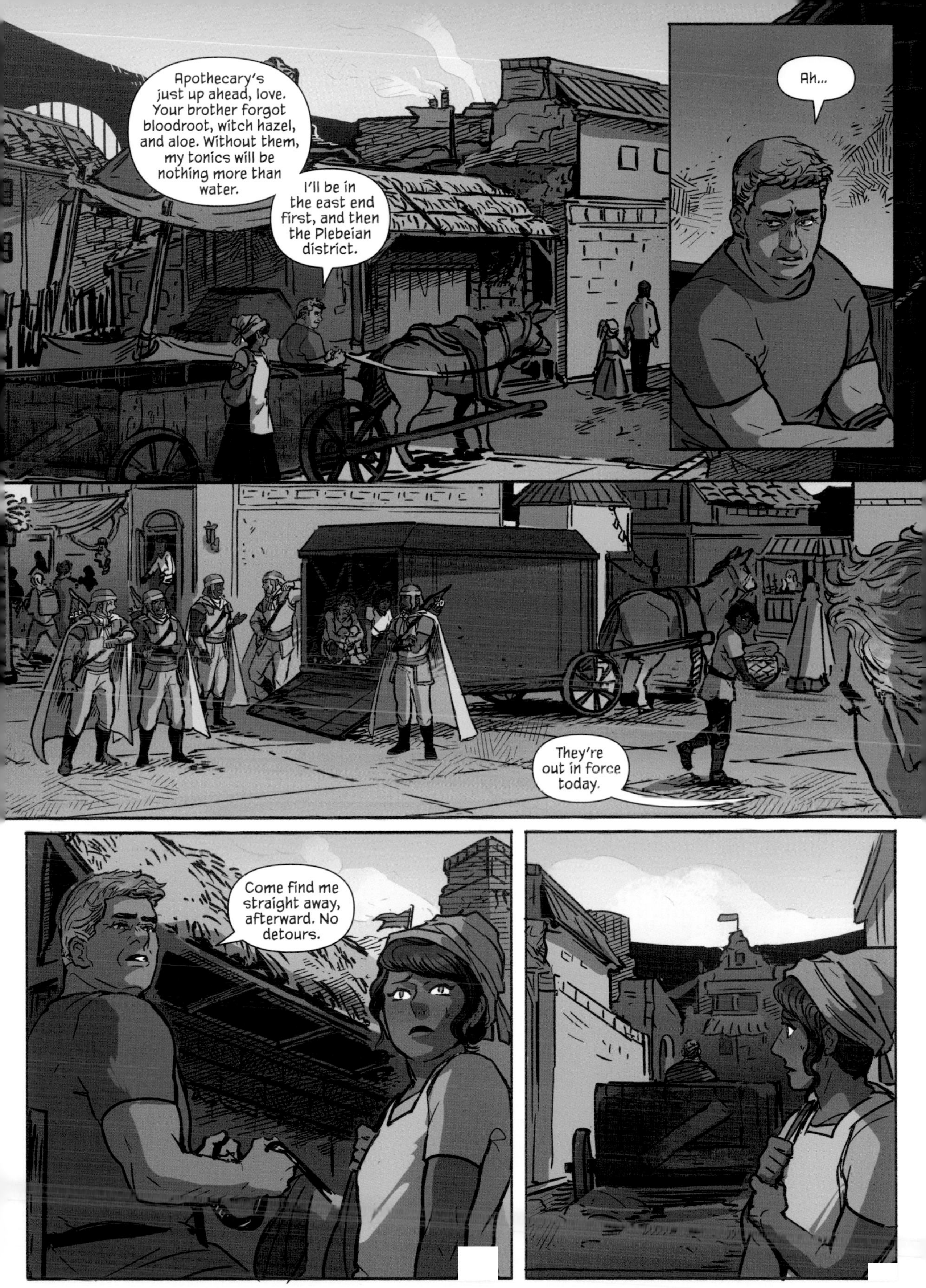
Apothecary's just up ahead, love. Your brother forgot bloodroot, witch hazel, and aloe. Without them, my tonics will be nothing more than water.
I'll be in the east end first, and then the Plebeian district.
Ah...
They're out in force today.
Come find me straight away, afterward. No detours.

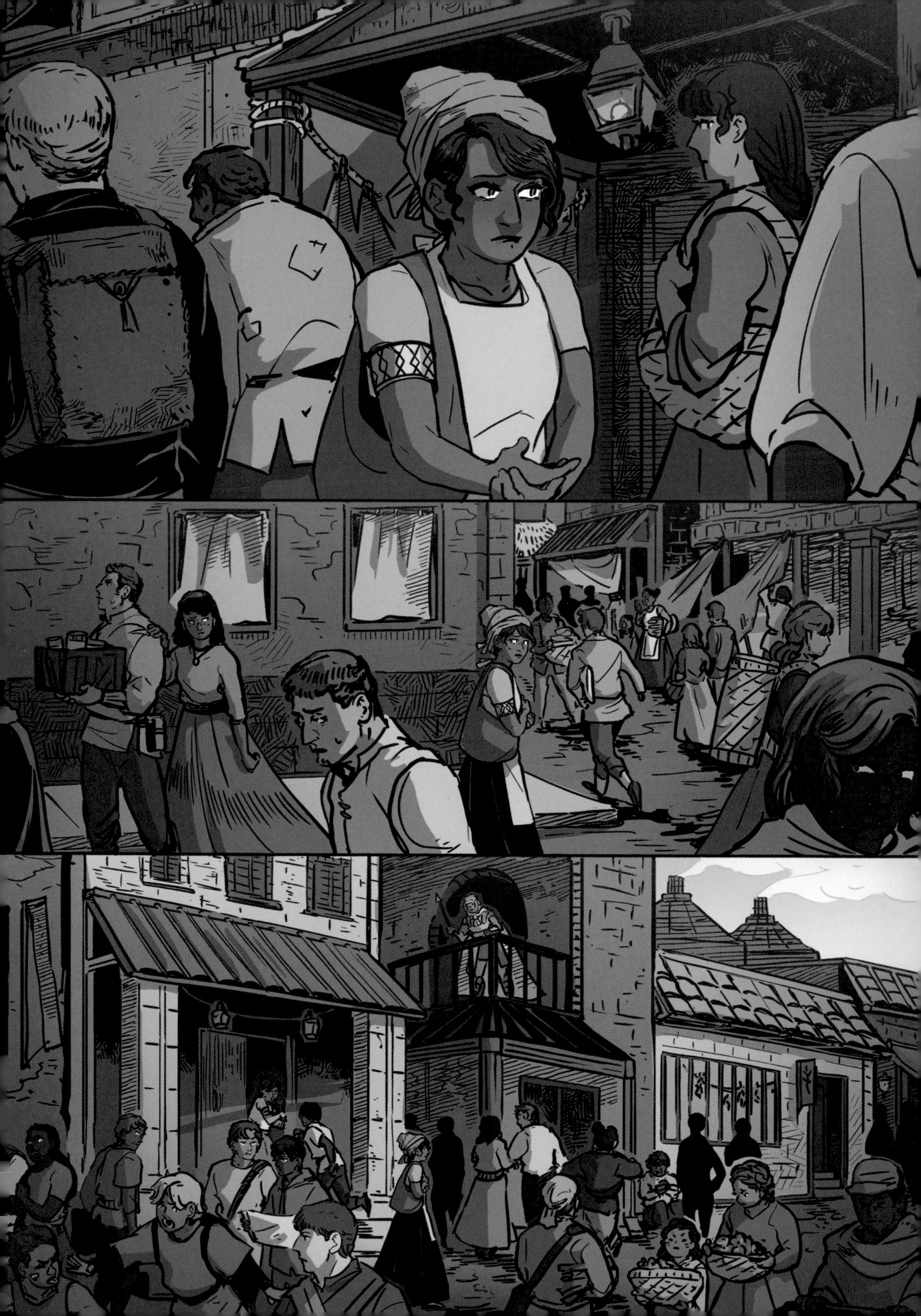

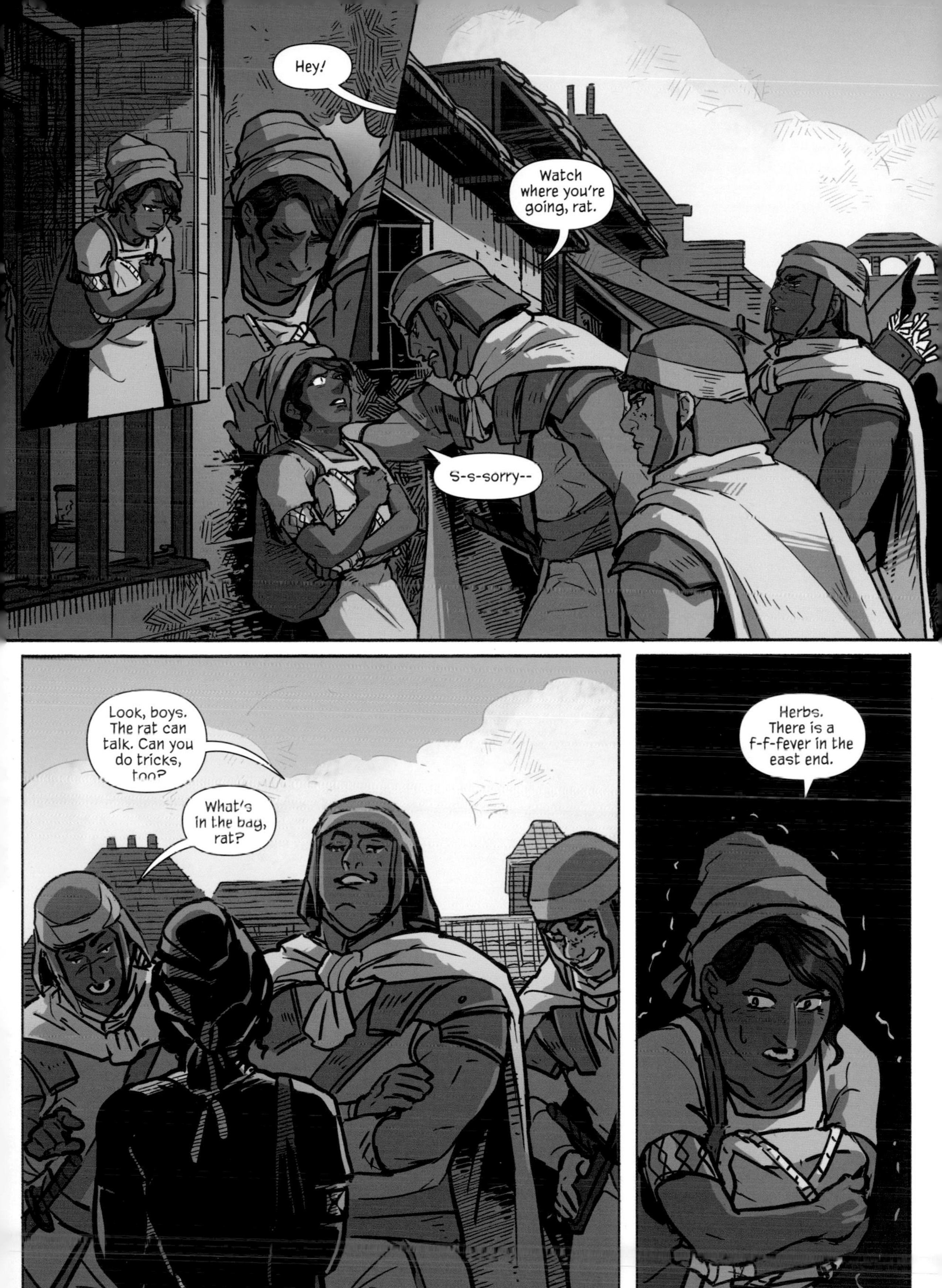
Hey!
Watch where you're going, rat.
S-s-sorry--
Look, boys. The rat can talk. Can you do tricks, too?
What's in the bag, rat?
Herbs. There is a f-f-fever in the east end.

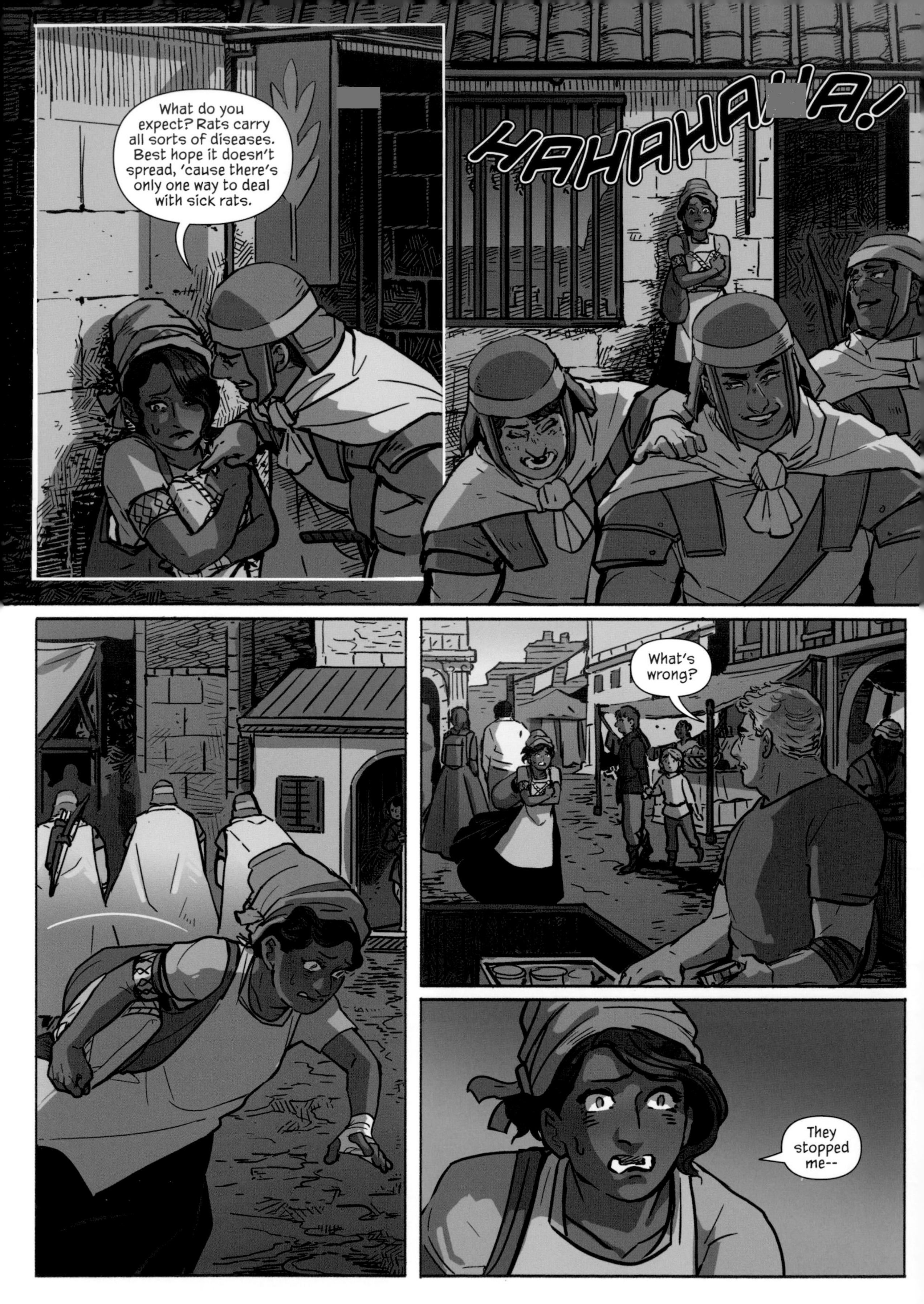
What do you expect? Rats carry all sorts of diseases. Best hope it doesn't spread, 'cause there's only one way to deal with sick rats.
What's wrong?
They stopped me--

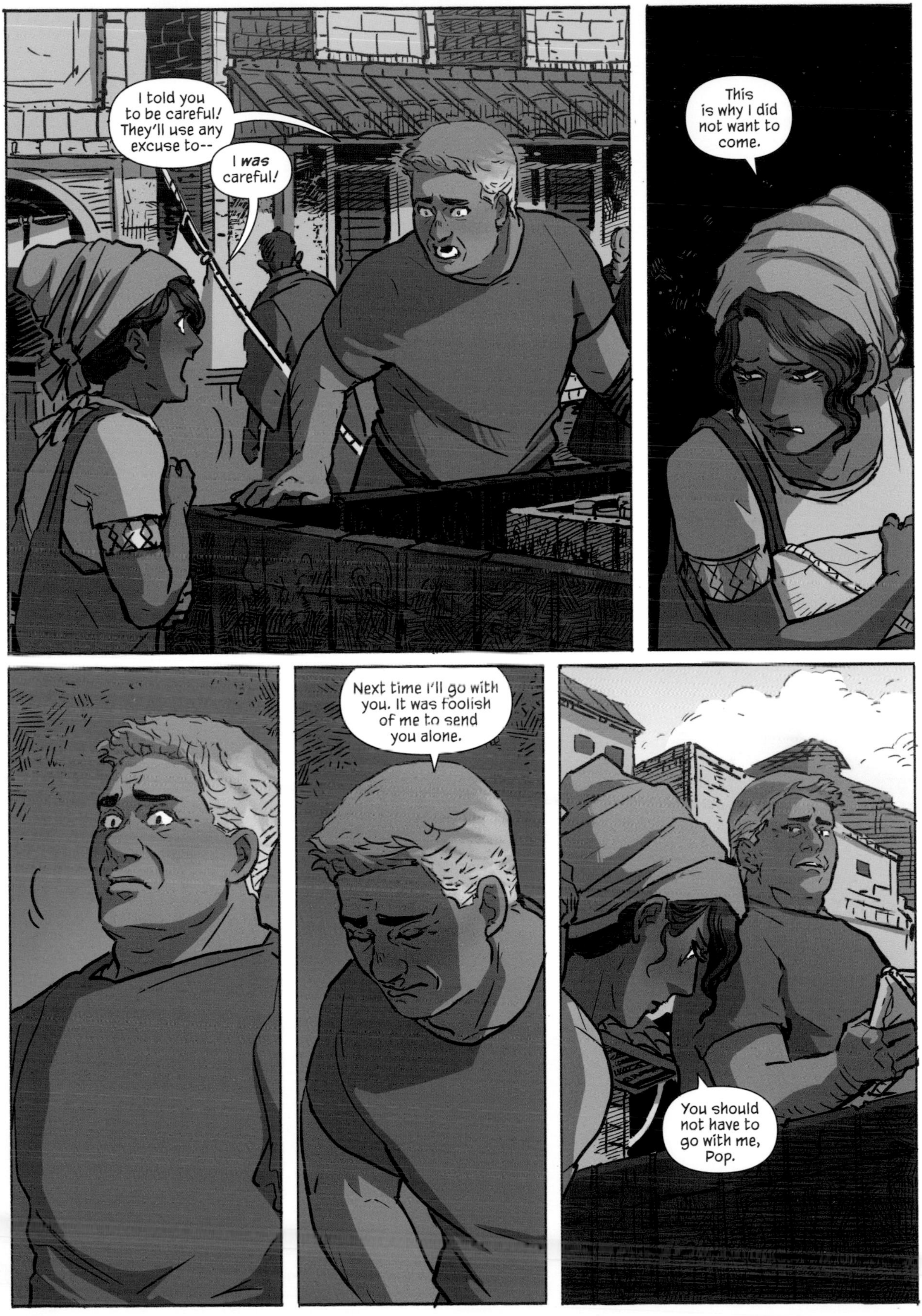
I told you to be careful! They'll use any excuse to--
I *was* careful!
This is why I did not want to come.
Next time I'll go with you. It was foolish of me to send you alone.
You should not have to go with me, Pop.

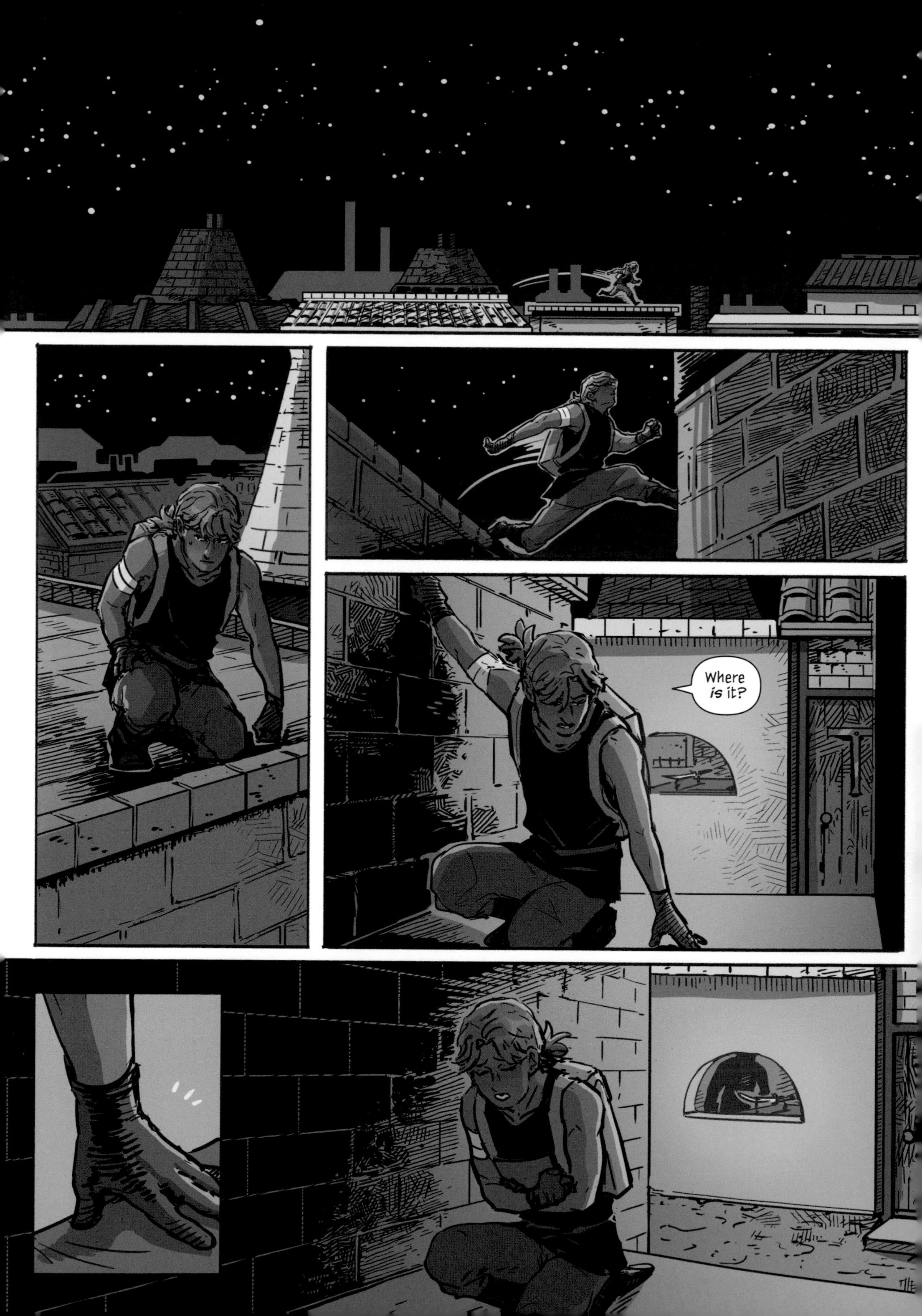
Where is it?

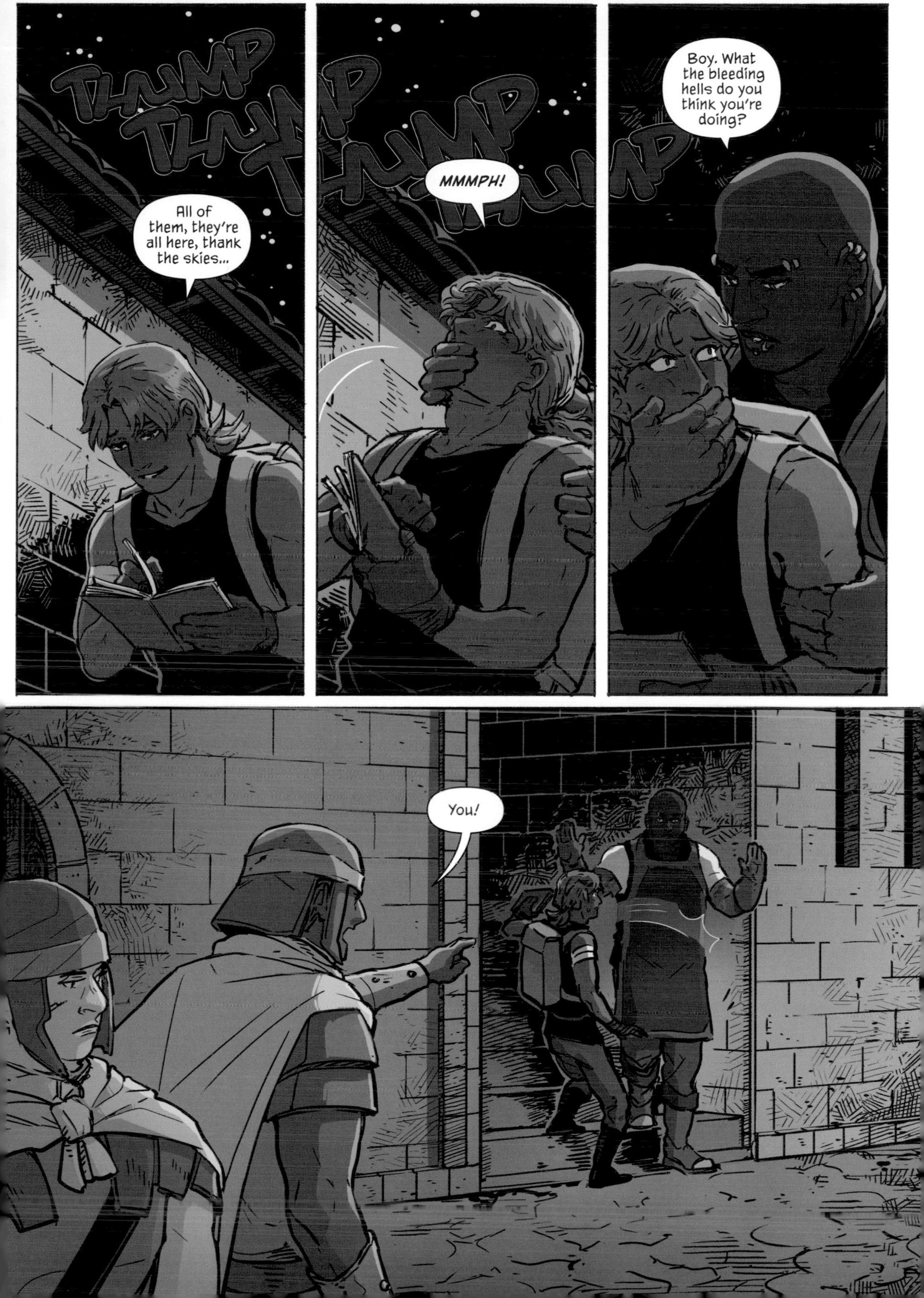

THUMP THUMP THUMP THUMP
All of them, they're all here, thank the skies...
MMMPH!
Boy. What the bleeding hells do you think you're doing?
You!

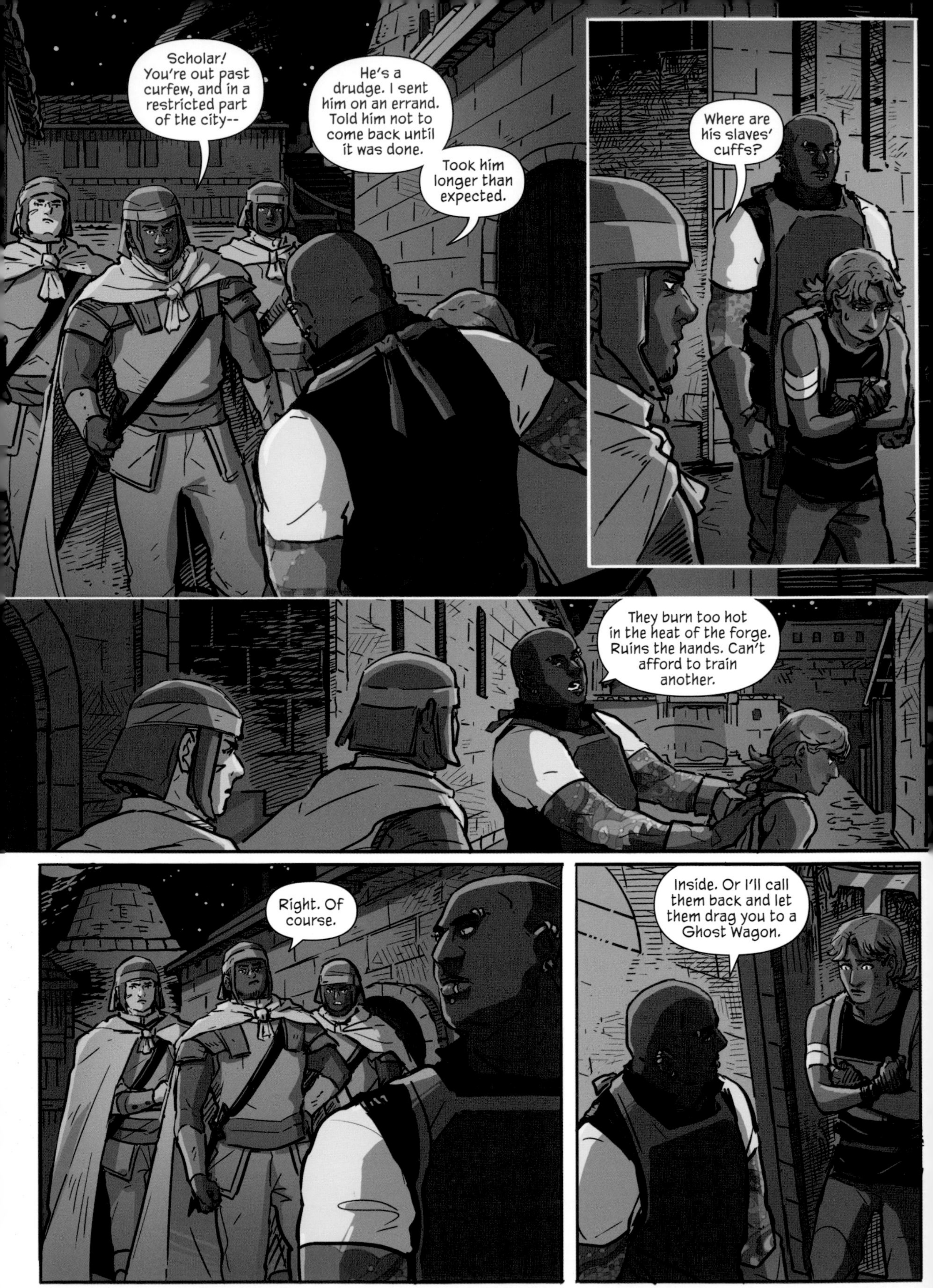
Scholar! You're out past curfew, and in a restricted part of the city--
He's a drudge. I sent him on an errand. Told him not to come back until it was done.
Took him longer than expected.
Where are his slaves' cuffs?
They burn too hot in the heat of the forge. Ruins the hands. Can't afford to train another.
Right. Of course.
Inside. Or I'll call them back and let them drag you to a Ghost Wagon.

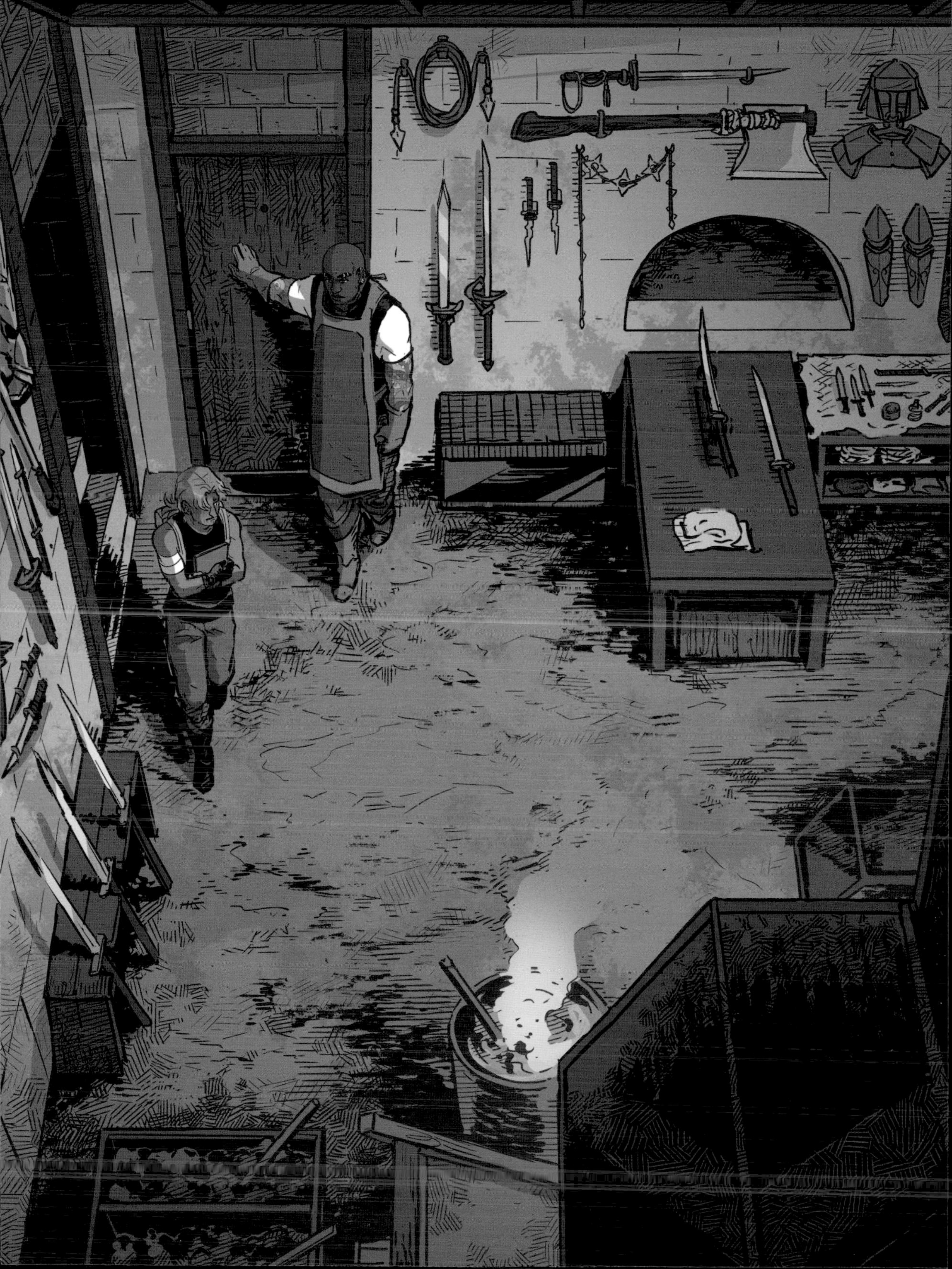

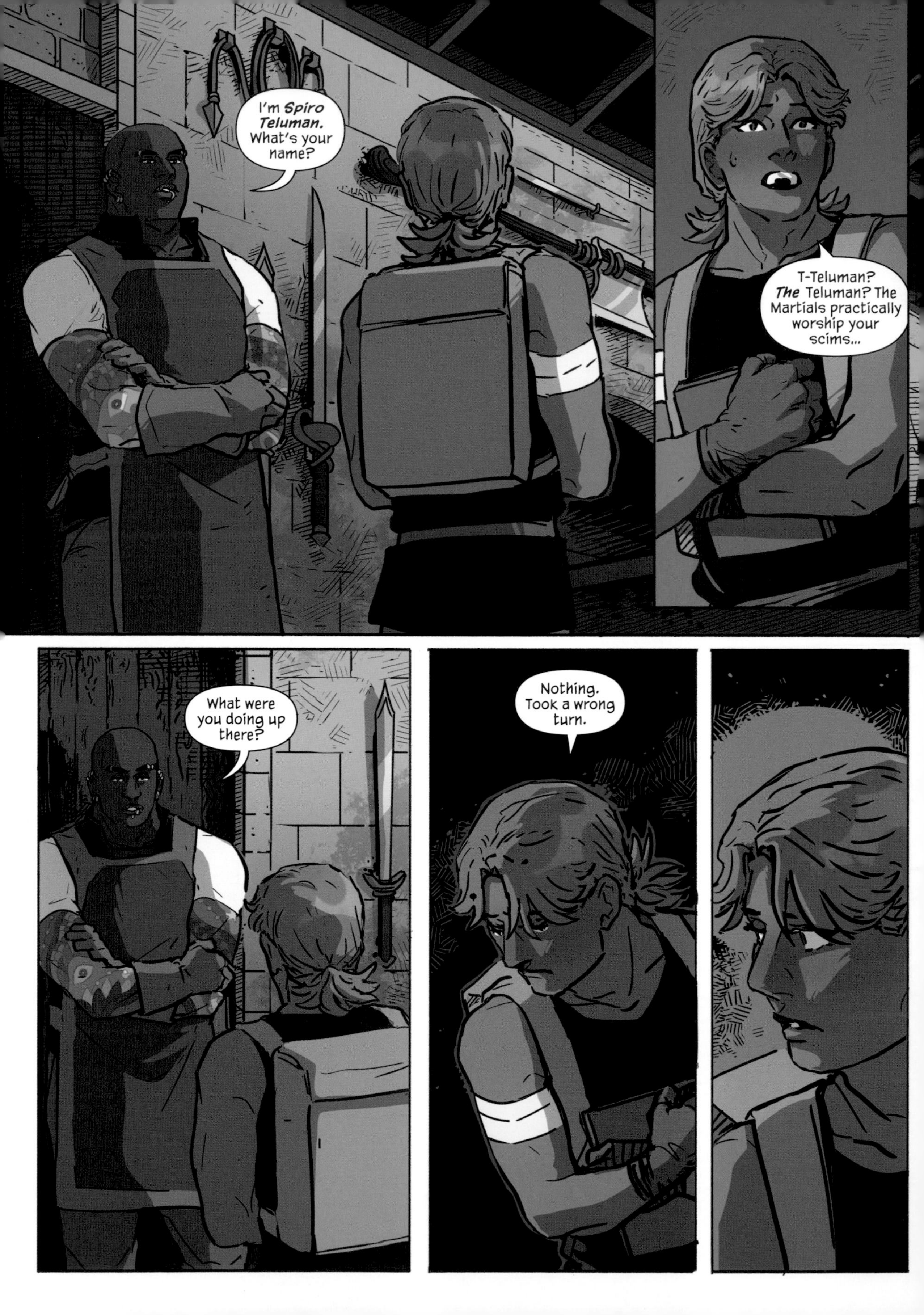
I'm Spiro Teluman. What's your name?
T-Teluman? The Teluman? The Martials practically worship your scims...
What were you doing up there?
Nothing. Took a wrong turn.

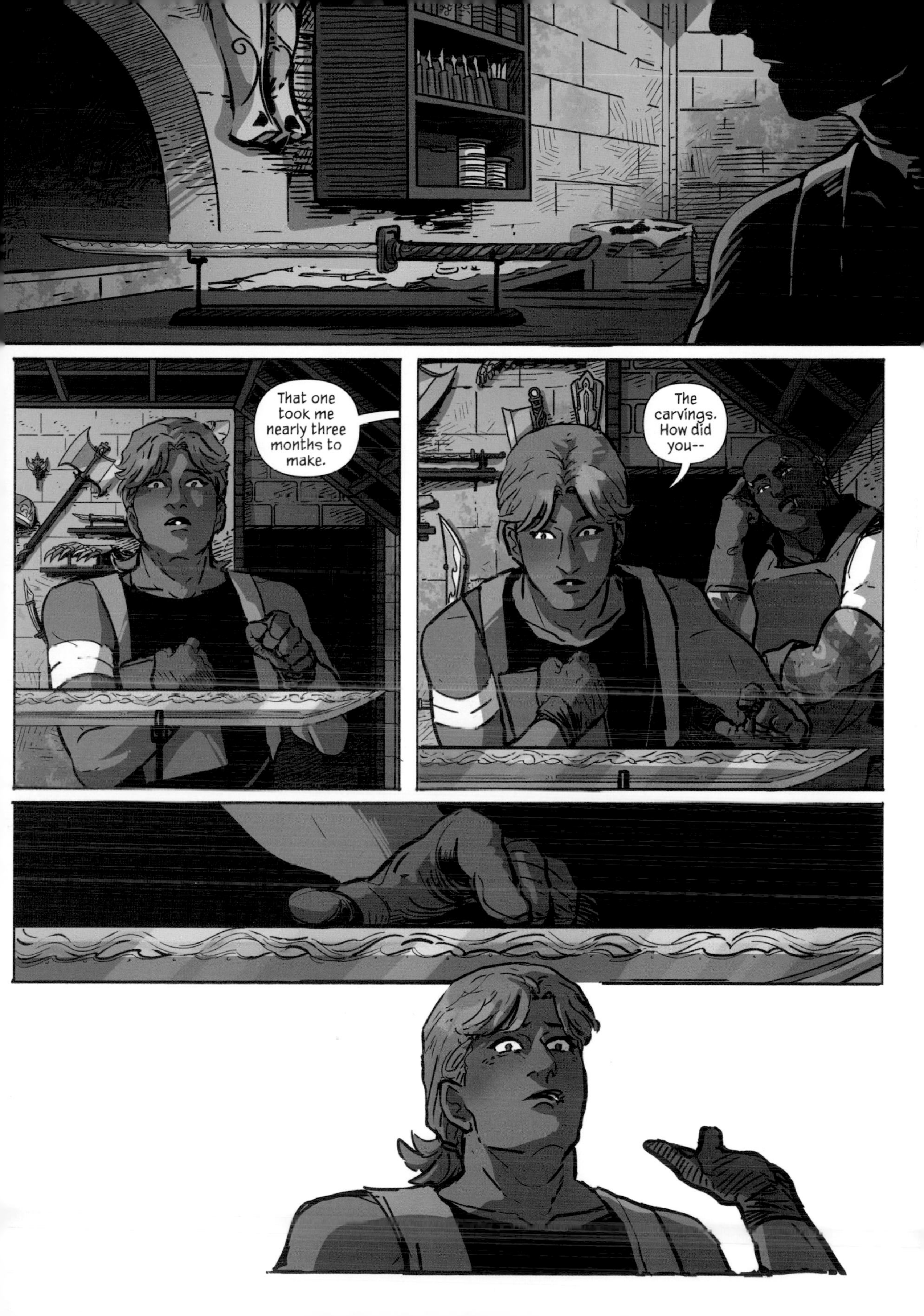
That one took me nearly three months to make.
The carvings. How did you--

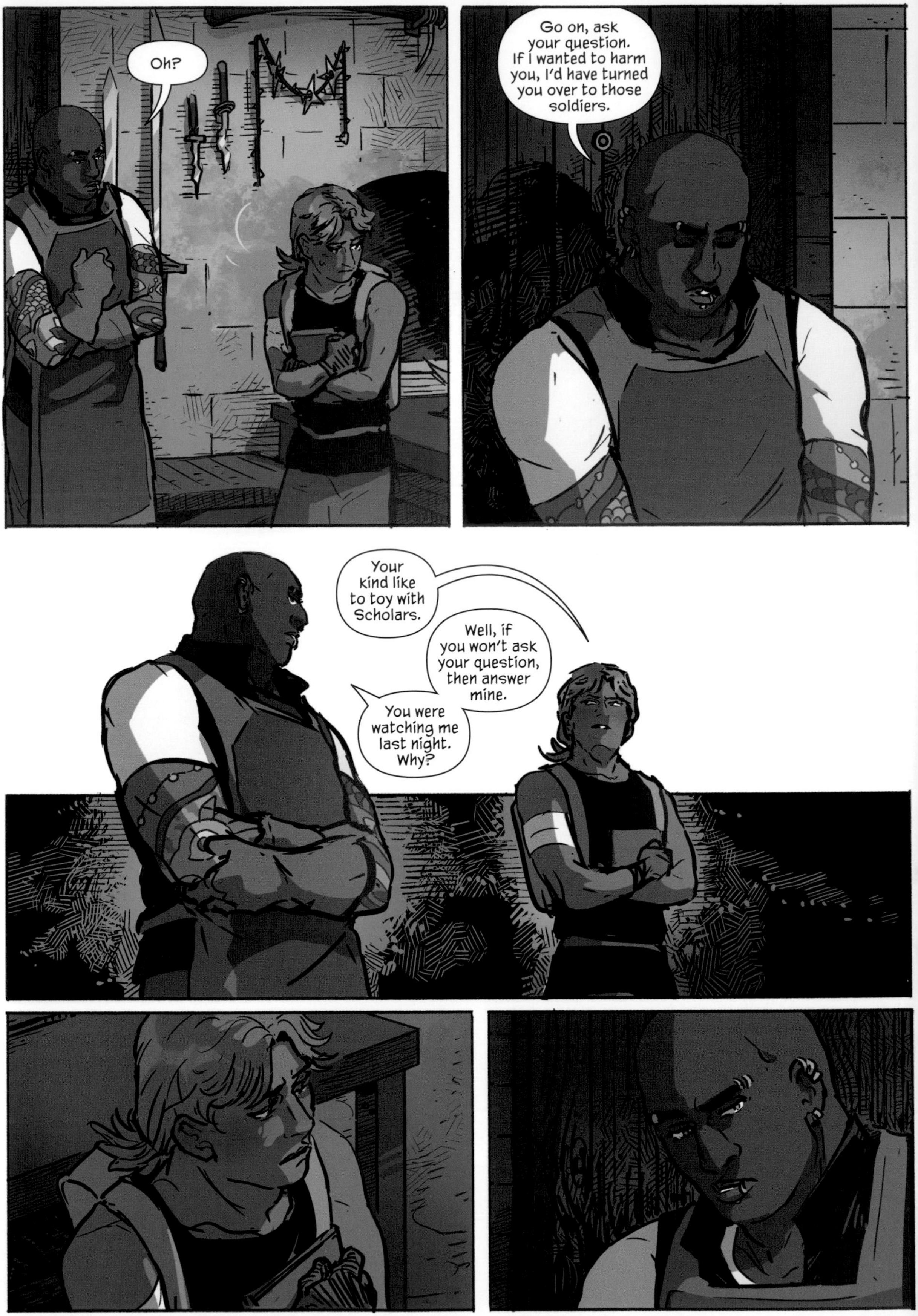
Oh?
Go on, ask your question. If I wanted to harm you, I'd have turned you over to those soldiers.
Your kind like to toy with Scholars.
Well, if you won't ask your question, then answer mine.
You were watching me last night. Why?

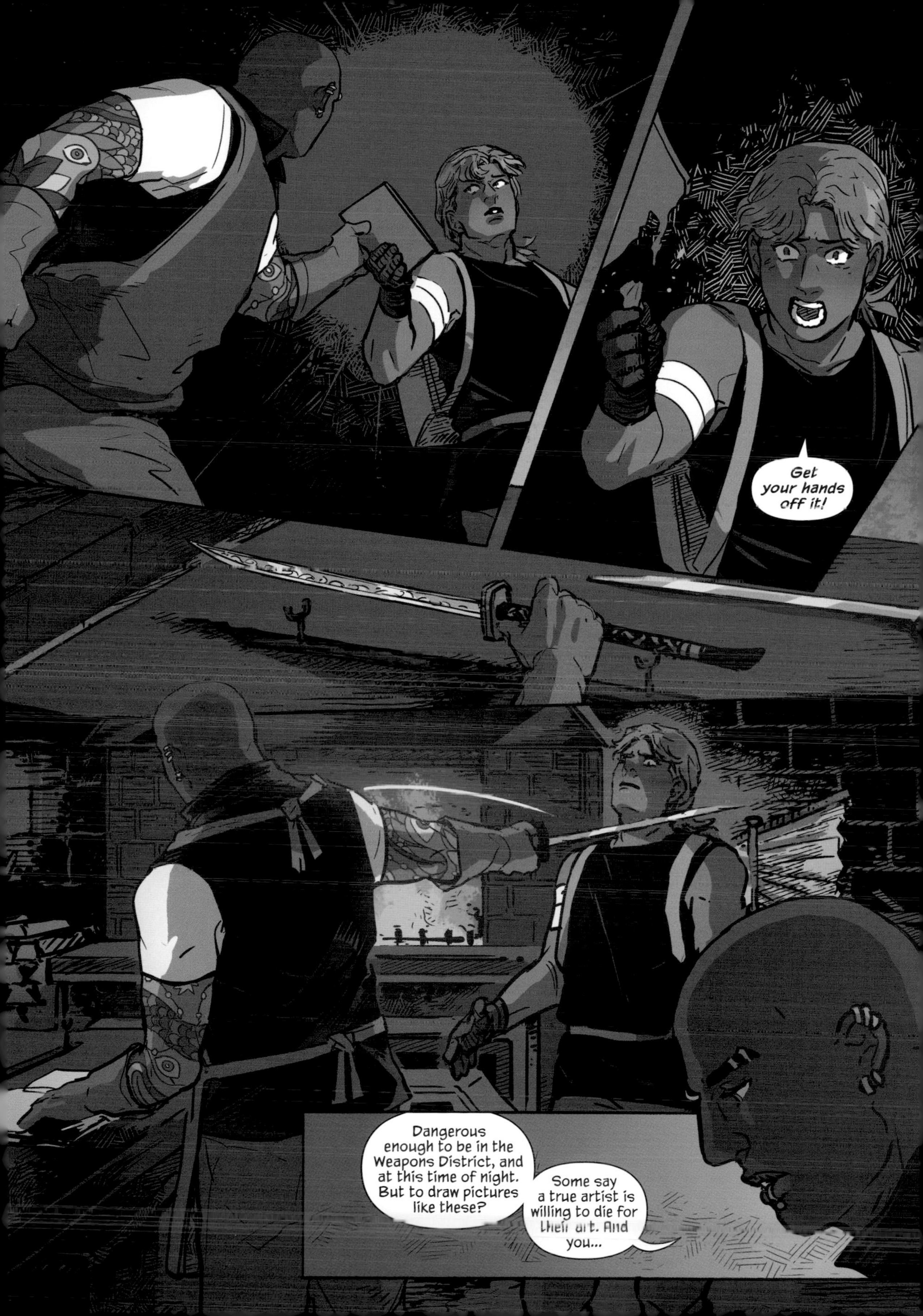
Get your hands off it!
Dangerous enough to be in the Weapons District, and at this time of night. But to draw pictures like these?
Some say a true artist is willing to die for their art. And you...

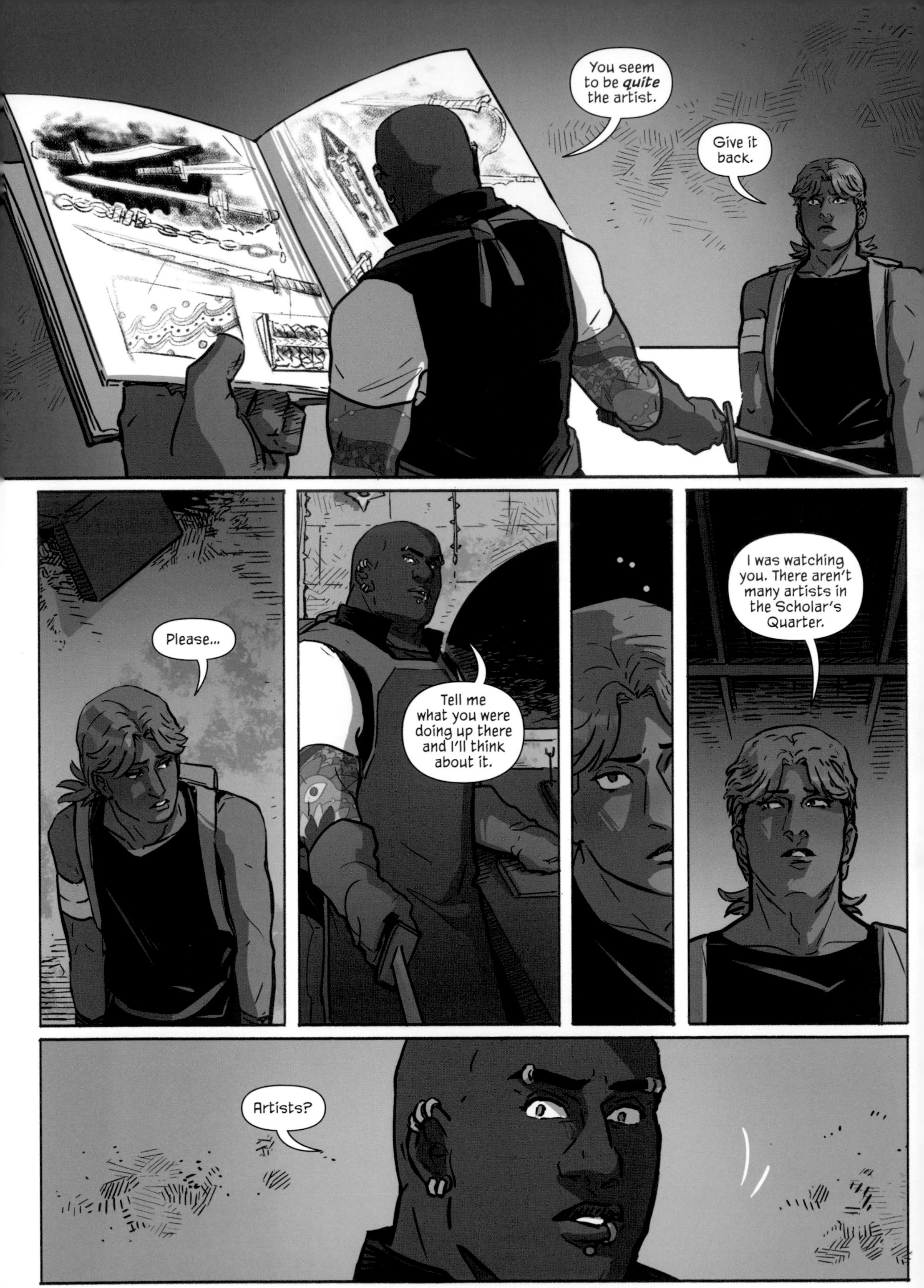
You seem to be *quite* the artist.
Give it back.
Please...
Tell me what you were doing up there and I'll think about it.
I was watching you. There aren't many artists in the Scholar's Quarter.
Artists?

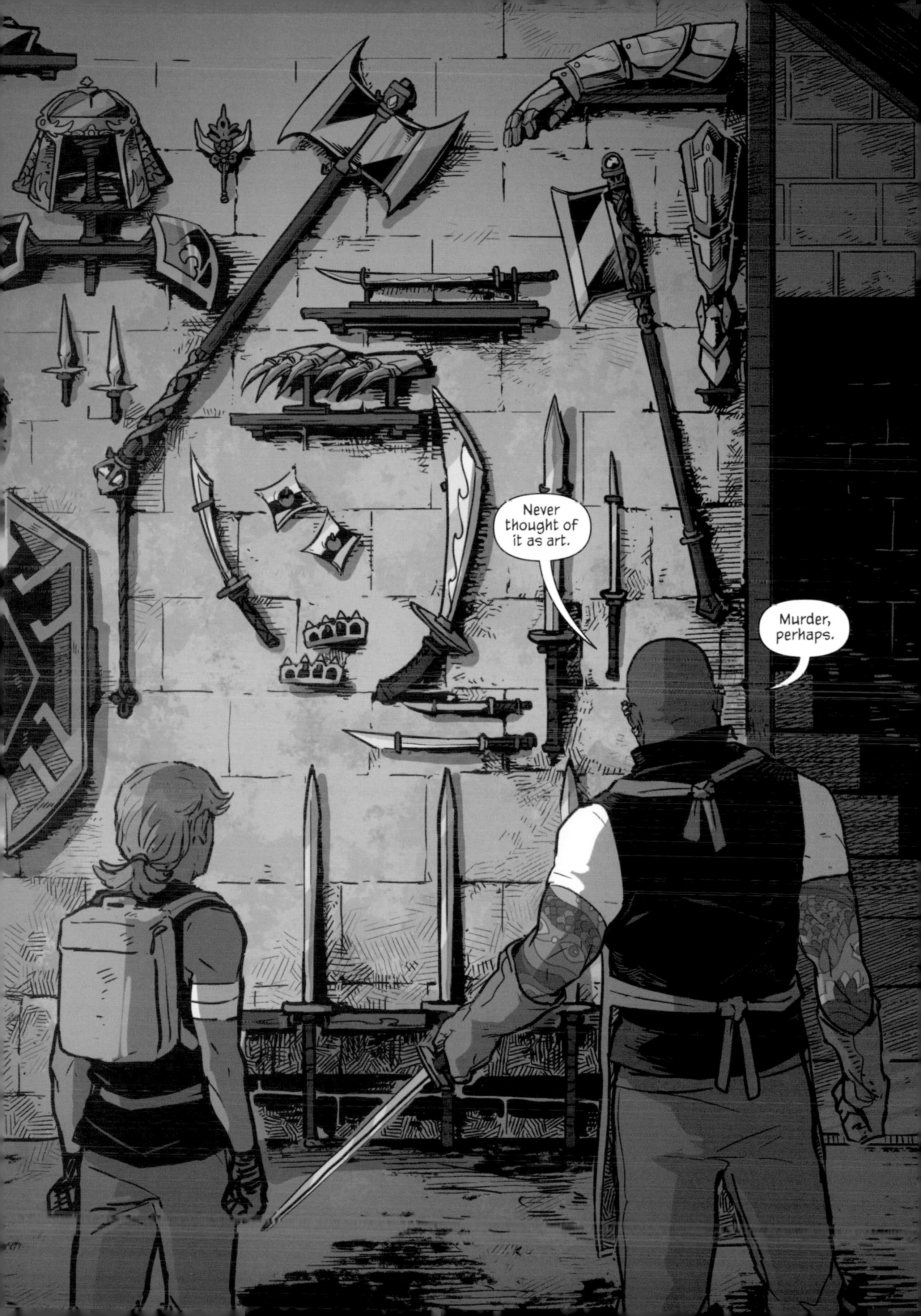
Never thought of it as art.
Murder, perhaps.

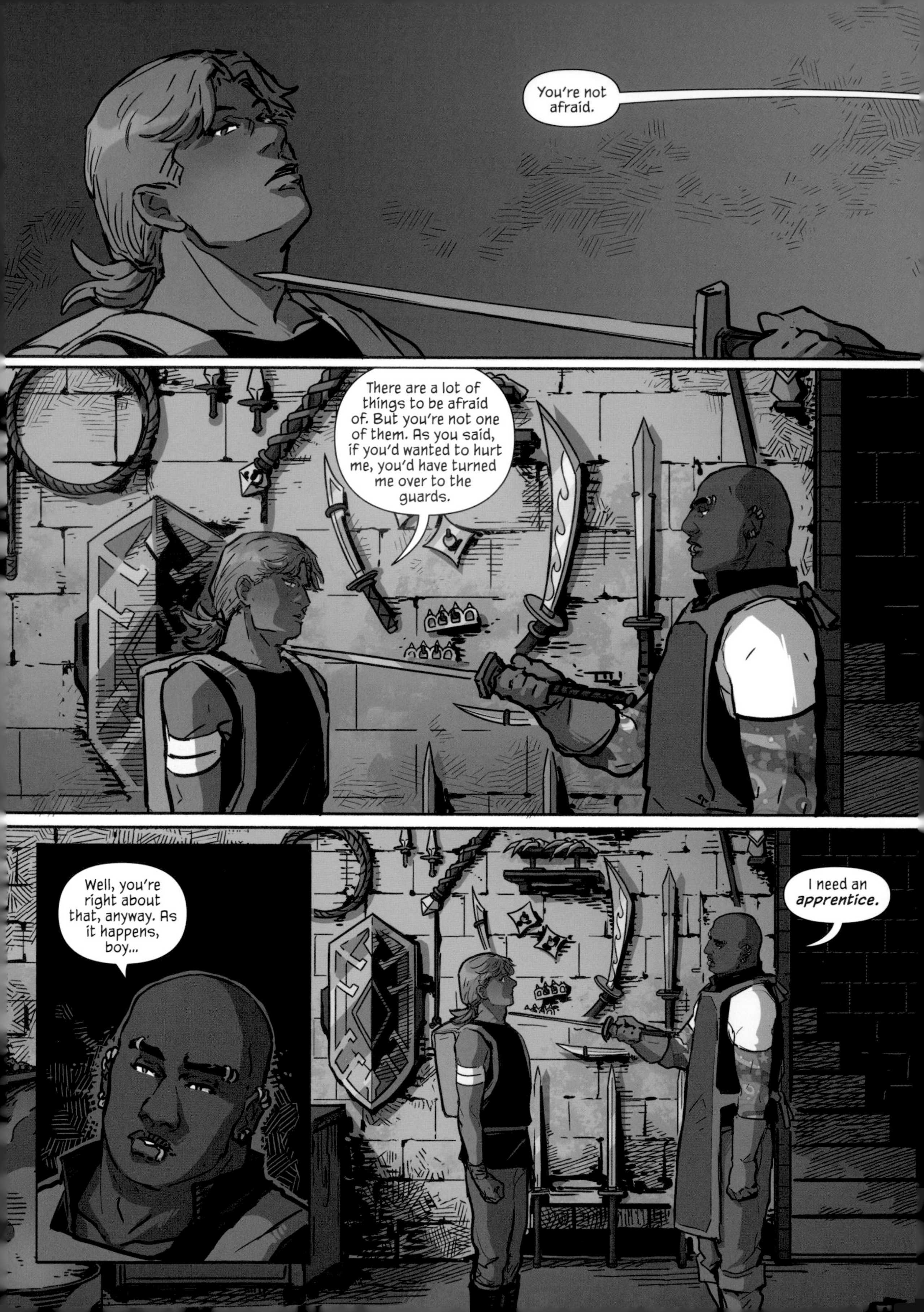
You're not afraid.
There are a lot of things to be afraid of. But you're not one of them. As you said, if you'd wanted to hurt me, you'd have turned me over to the guards.
Well, you're right about that, anyway. As it happens, boy...
I need an *apprentice.*

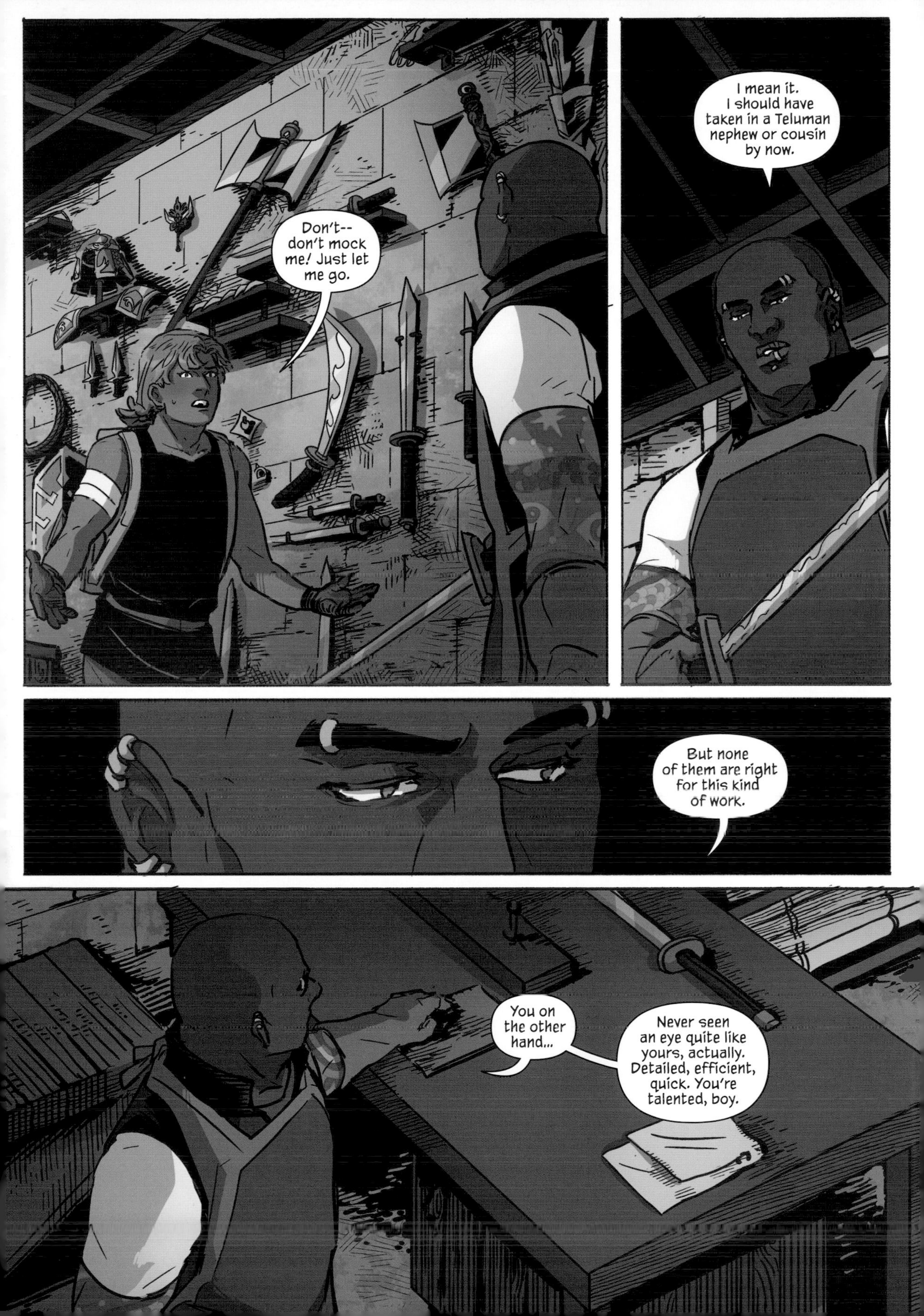
Don't-- don't mock me! Just let me go.
I mean it. I should have taken in a Teluman nephew or cousin by now.
But none of them are right for this kind of work.
You on the other hand...
Never seen an eye quite like yours, actually. Detailed, efficient, quick. You're talented, boy.

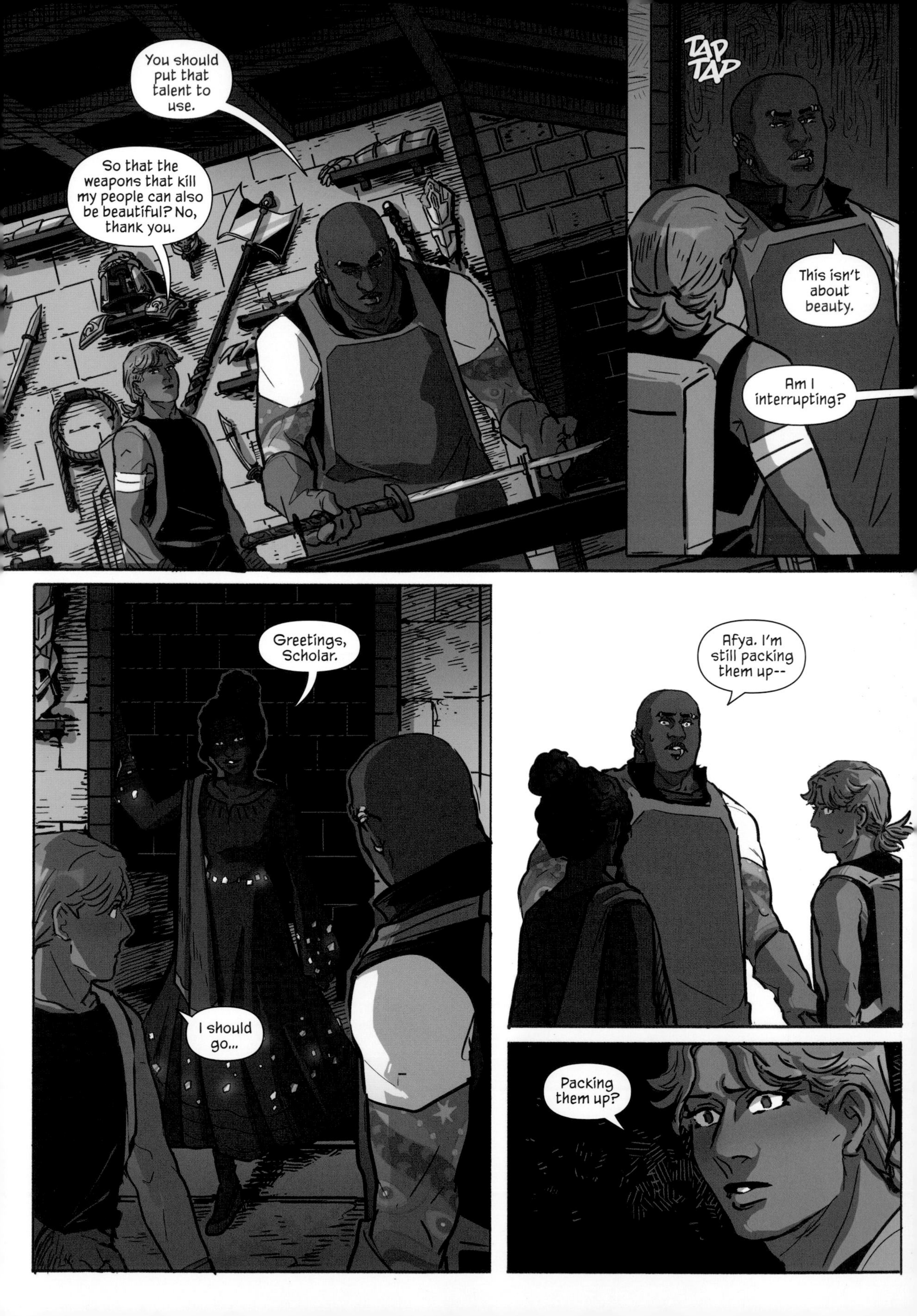
You should put that talent to use.
So that the weapons that kill my people can also be beautiful? No, thank you.
TAP TAP
This isn't about beauty.
Am I interrupting?
Greetings, Scholar.
I should go...
Afya. I'm still packing them up--
Packing them up?

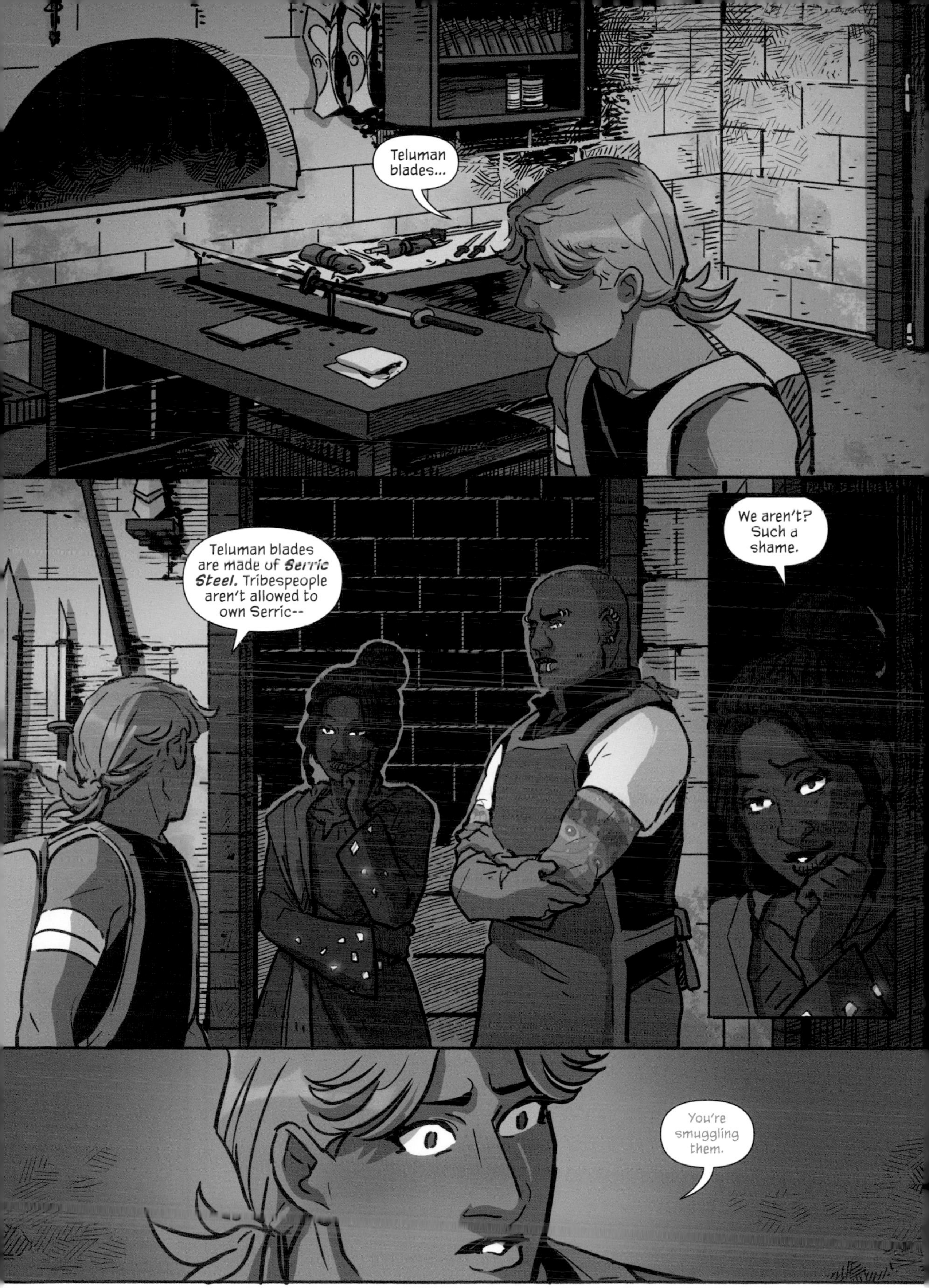
Teluman blades...
Teluman blades are made of *Serric Steel.* Tribespeople aren't allowed to own Serric--
We aren't? Such a shame.
You're smuggling them.

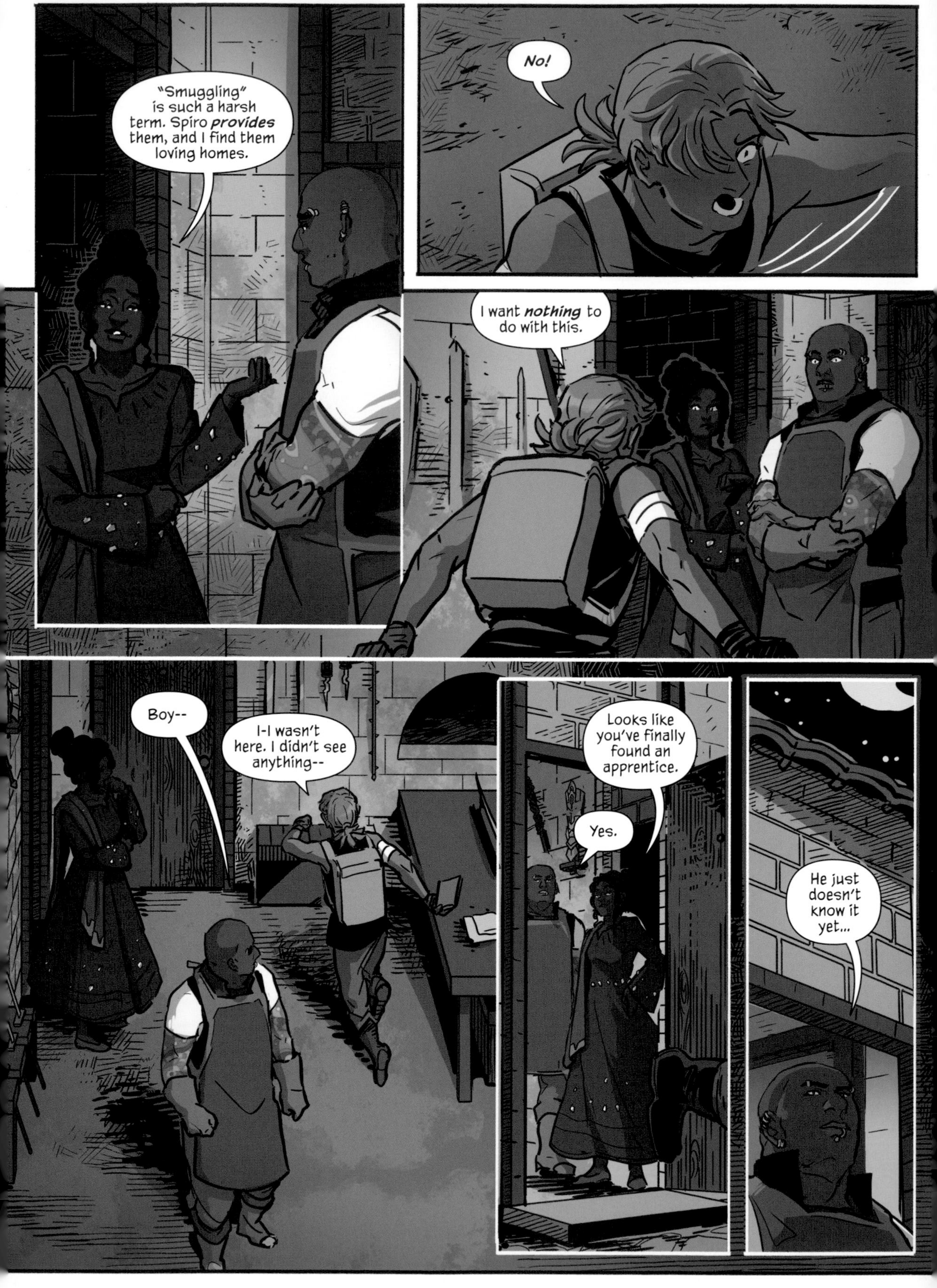
"Smuggling" is such a harsh term. Spiro *provides* them, and I find them loving homes.
No!
I want ***nothing*** to do with this.
Boy--
I-I wasn't here. I didn't see anything--
Looks like you've finally found an apprentice.
Yes.
He just doesn't know it yet...

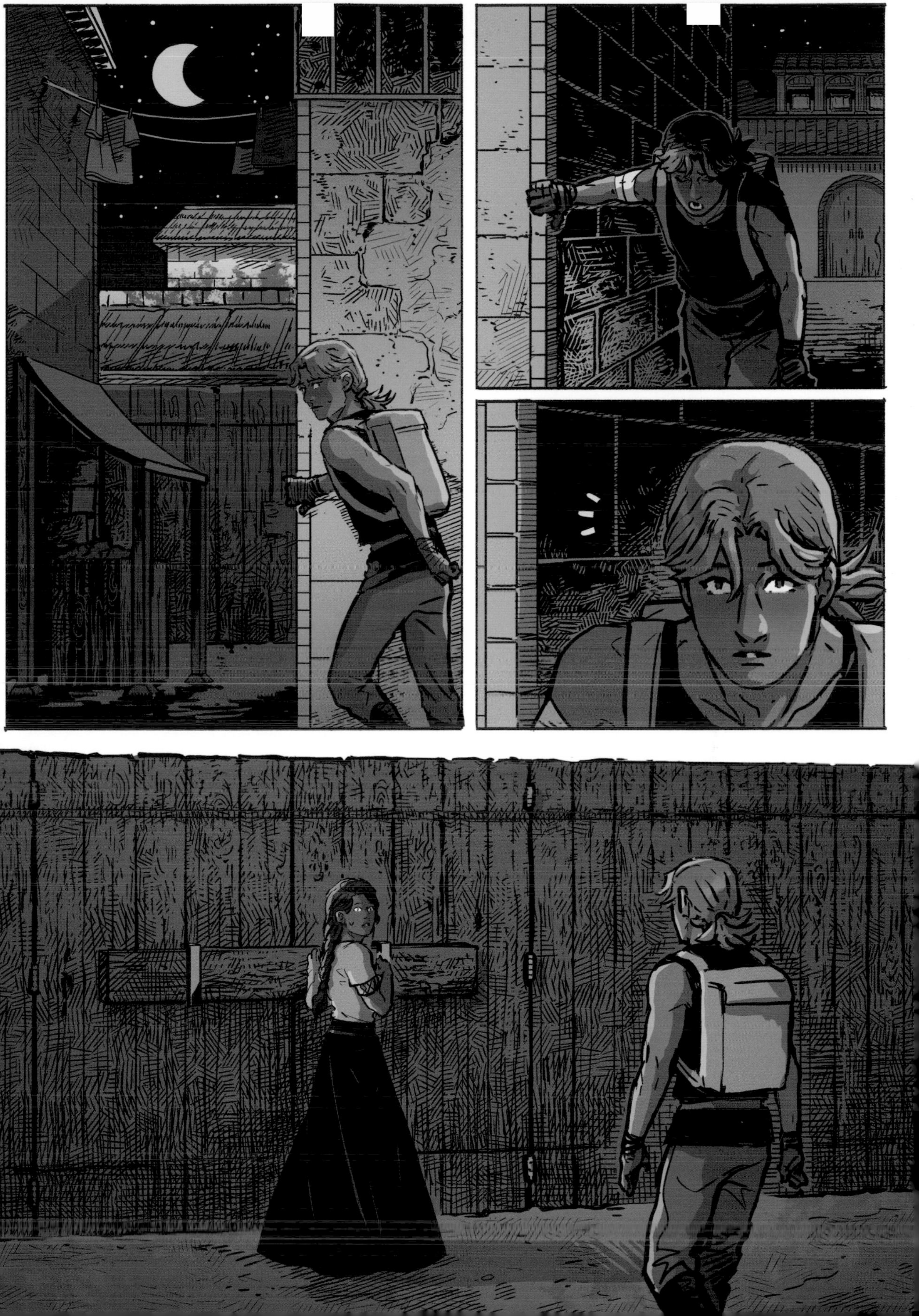

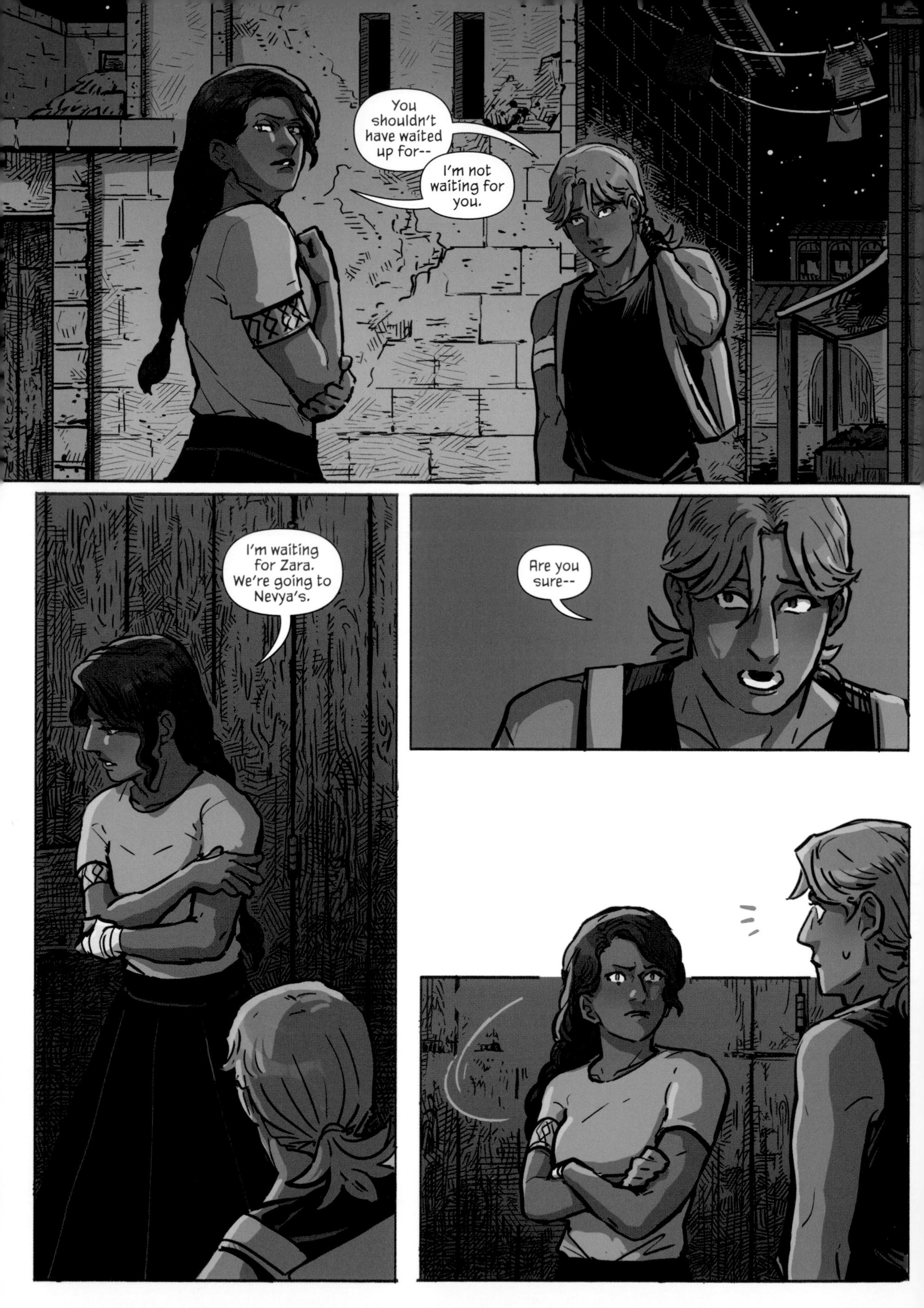
You shouldn't have waited up for--
I'm not waiting for you.
I'm waiting for Zara. We're going to Nevya's.
Are you sure--

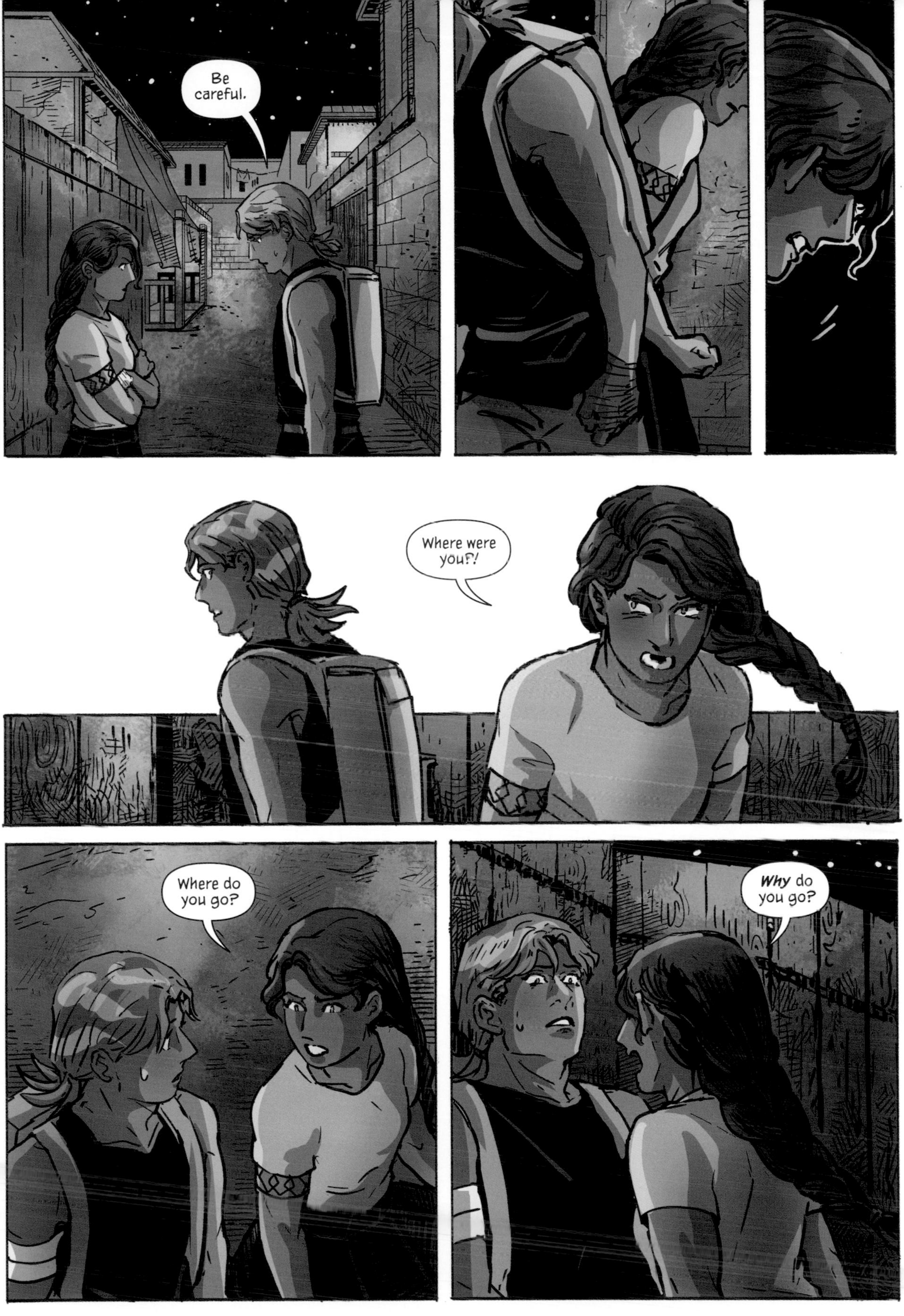
Be careful.
Where were you?!
Where do you go?
Why do you go?

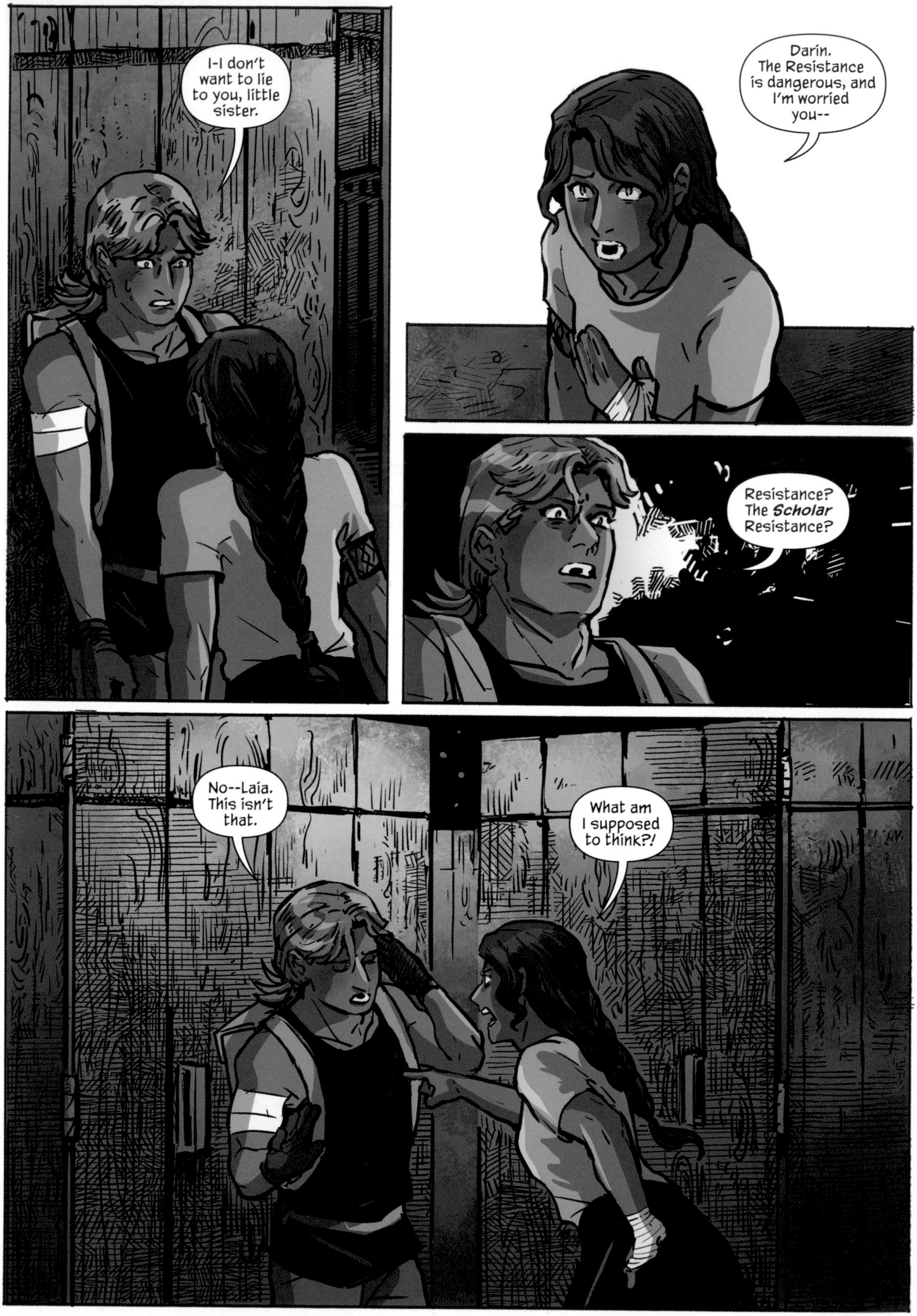
I-I don't want to lie to you, little sister.
Darin. The Resistance is dangerous, and I'm worried you--
Resistance? The *Scholar* Resistance?
No--Laia. This isn't that.
What am I supposed to think?!

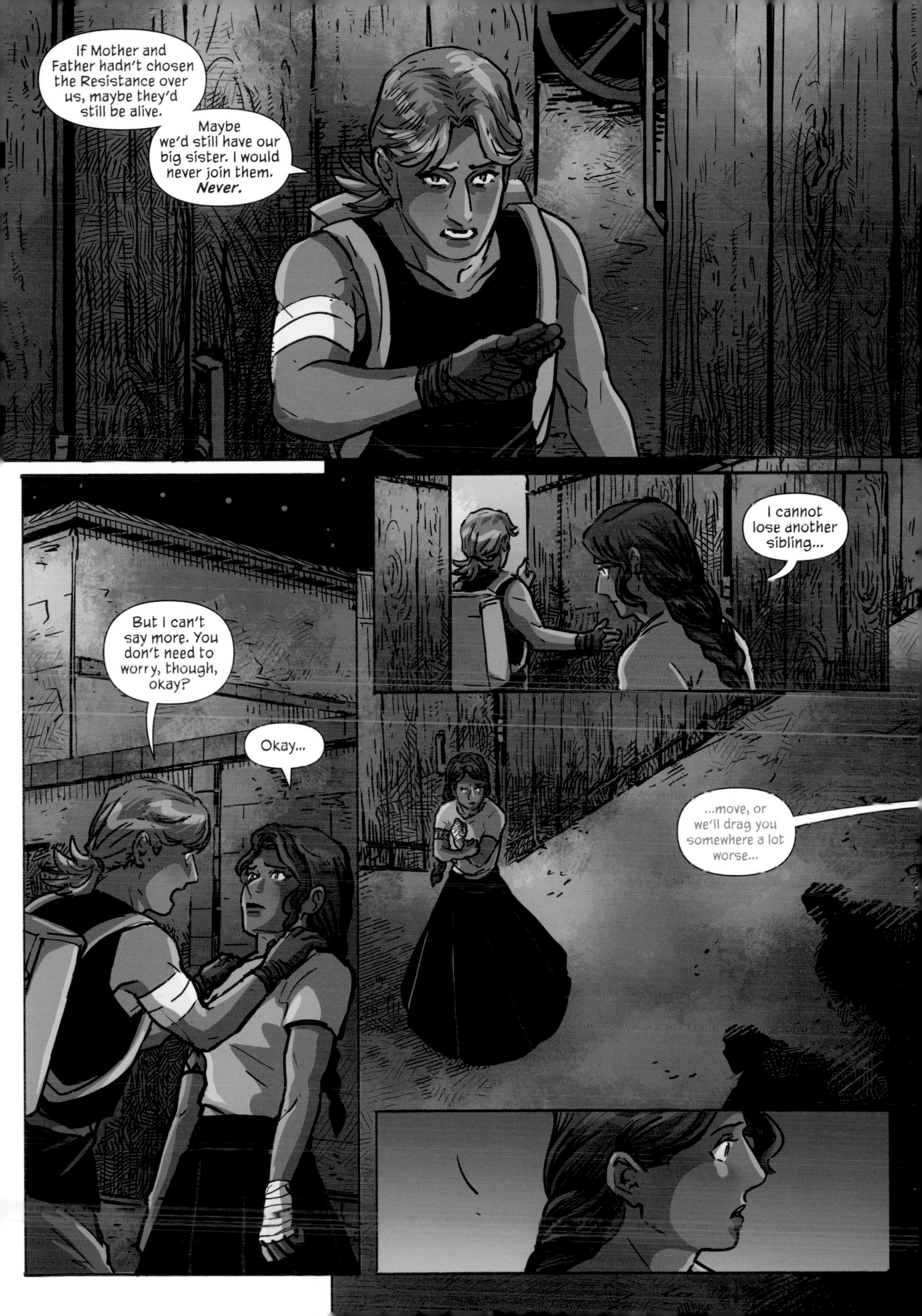
If Mother and Father hadn't chosen the Resistance over us, maybe they'd still be alive.
Maybe we'd still have our big sister. I would never join them. *Never.*
But I can't say more. You don't need to worry, though, okay?
Okay...
I cannot lose another sibling...
...move, or we'll drag you somewhere a lot worse...

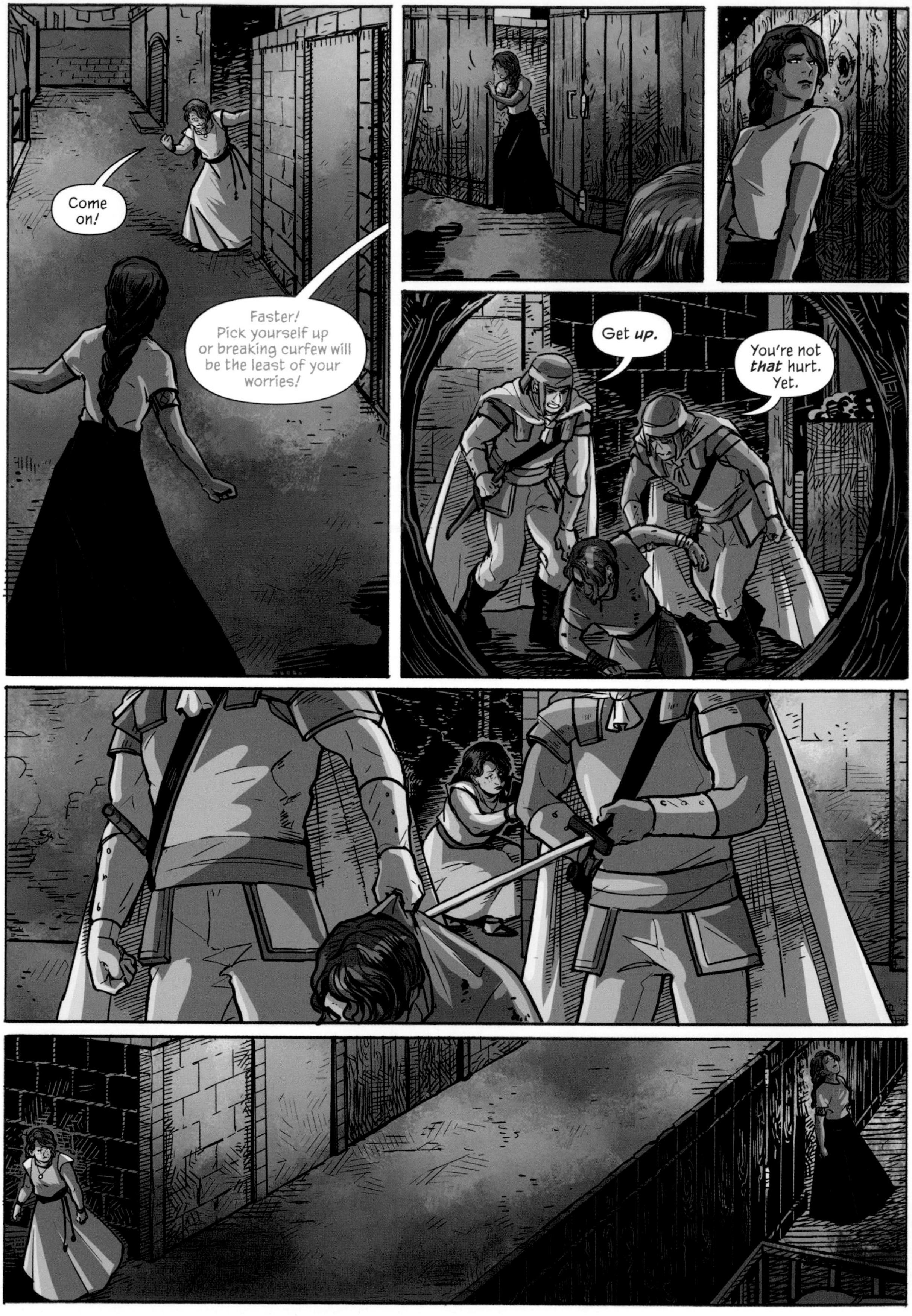
Come on!
Faster! Pick yourself up or breaking curfew will be the least of your worries!
Get *up.*
You're not ***that*** hurt. Yet.

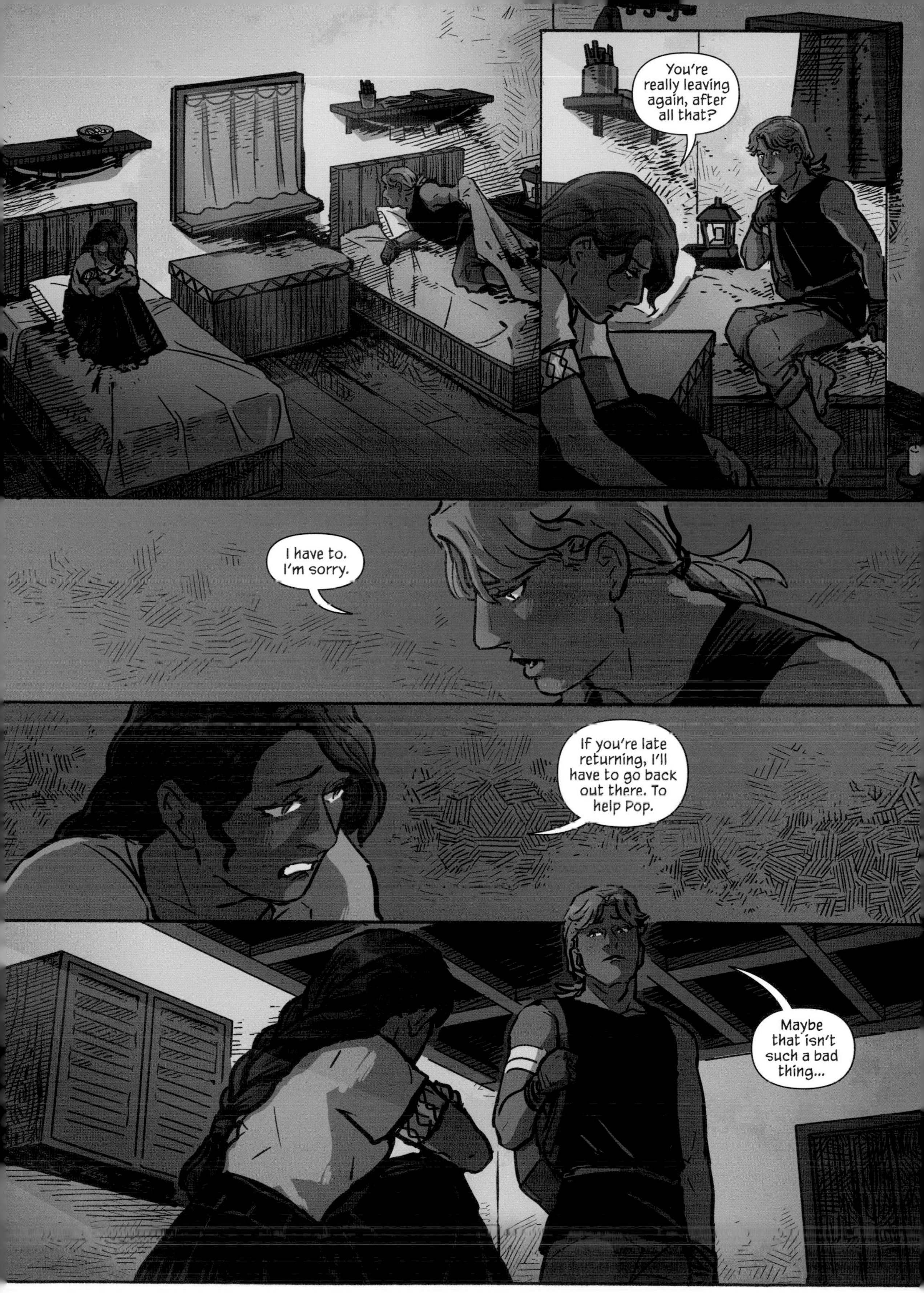
You're really leaving again, after all that?
I have to. I'm sorry.
If you're late returning, I'll have to go back out there. To help Pop.
Maybe that isn't such a bad thing...

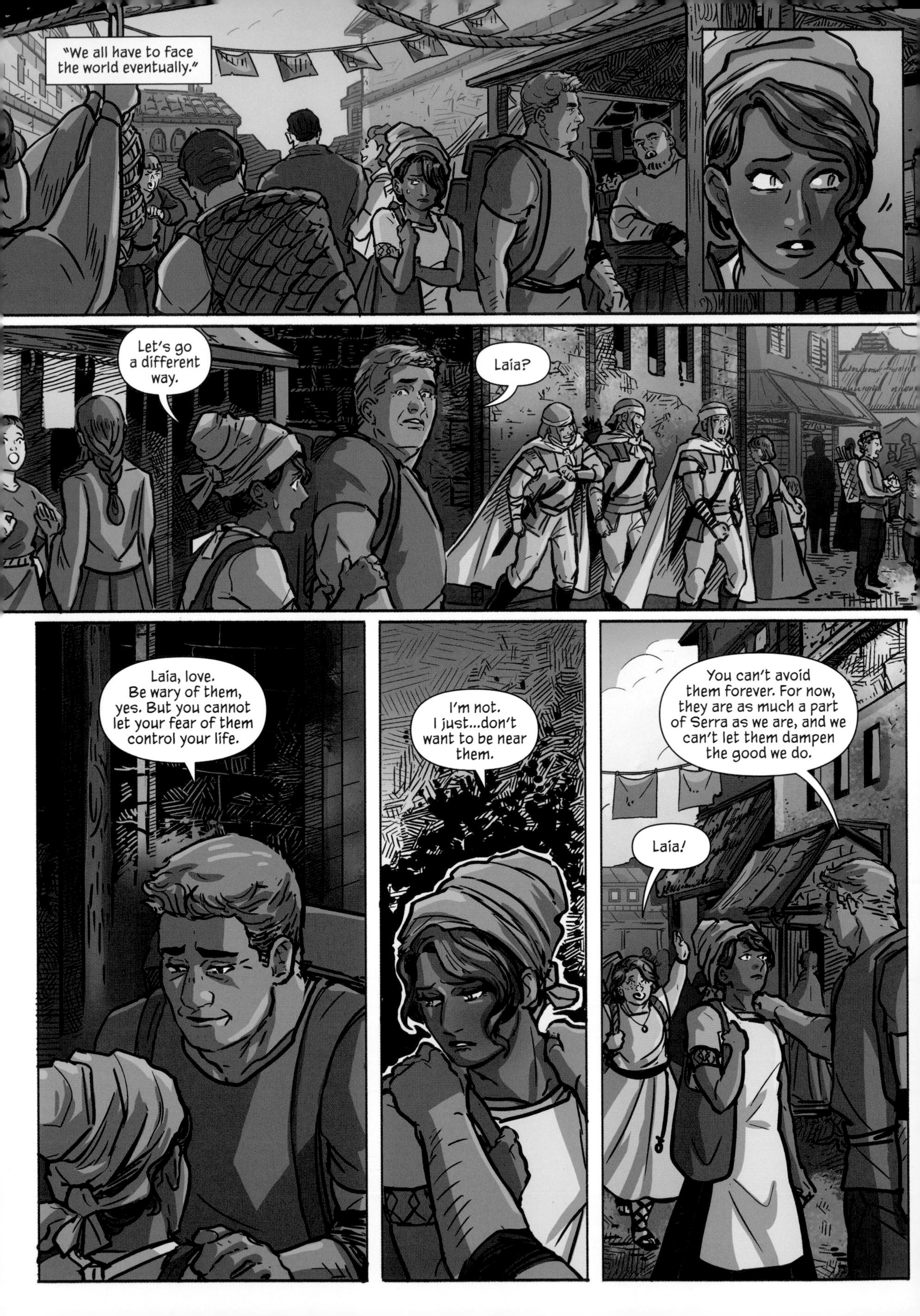
"We all have to face the world eventually."
Let's go a different way.
Laia?
Laia, love. Be wary of them, yes. But you cannot let your fear of them control your life.
I'm not. I just...don't want to be near them.
You can't avoid them forever. For now, they are as much a part of Serra as we are, and we can't let them dampen the good we do.
Laia!

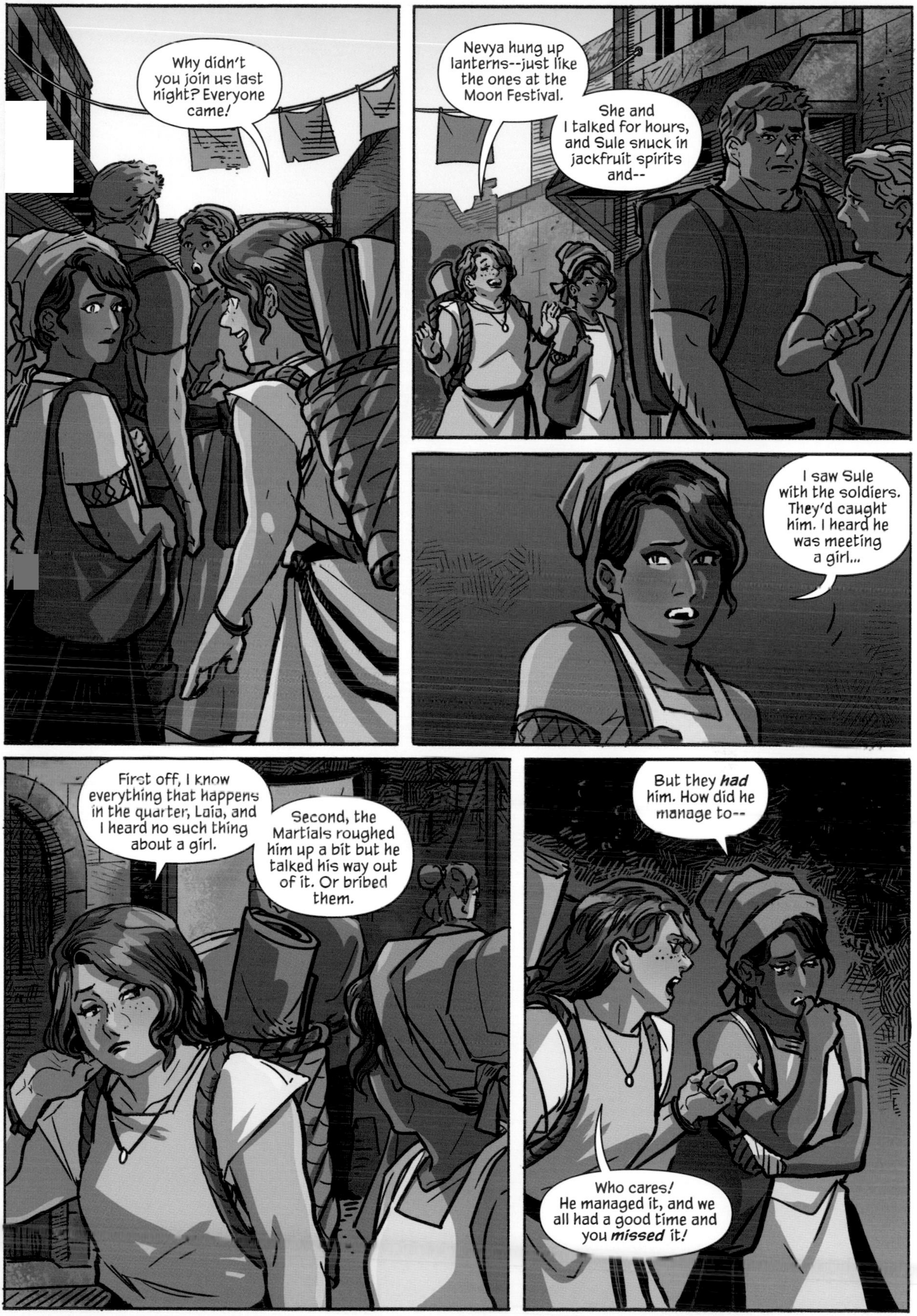
Why didn't you join us last night? Everyone came!
Nevya hung up lanterns--just like the ones at the Moon Festival.
She and I talked for hours, and Sule snuck in jackfruit spirits and--
I saw Sule with the soldiers. They'd caught him. I heard he was meeting a girl...
First off, I know everything that happens in the quarter, Laia, and I heard no such thing about a girl.
Second, the Martials roughed him up a bit but he talked his way out of it. Or bribed them.
But they *had* him. How did he manage to--
Who cares! He managed it, and we all had a good time and you *missed* it!

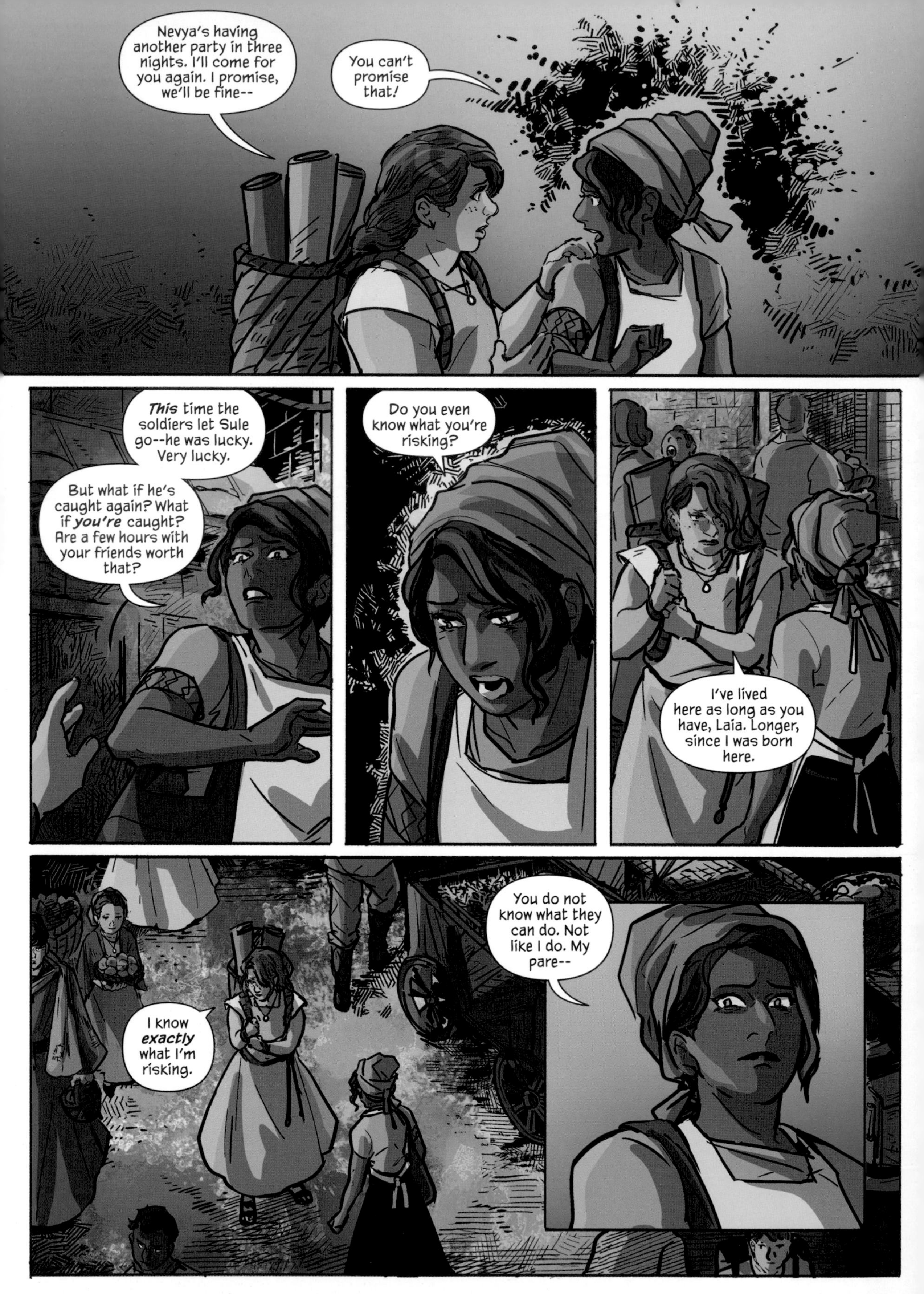
Nevya's having another party in three nights. I'll come for you again. I promise, we'll be fine--
You can't promise that!
This time the soldiers let Sule go--he was lucky. Very lucky.
But what if he's caught again? What if you're caught? Are a few hours with your friends worth that?
Do you even know what you're risking?
I've lived here as long as you have, Laia. Longer, since I was born here.
I know exactly what I'm risking.
You do not know what they can do. Not like I do. My pare--

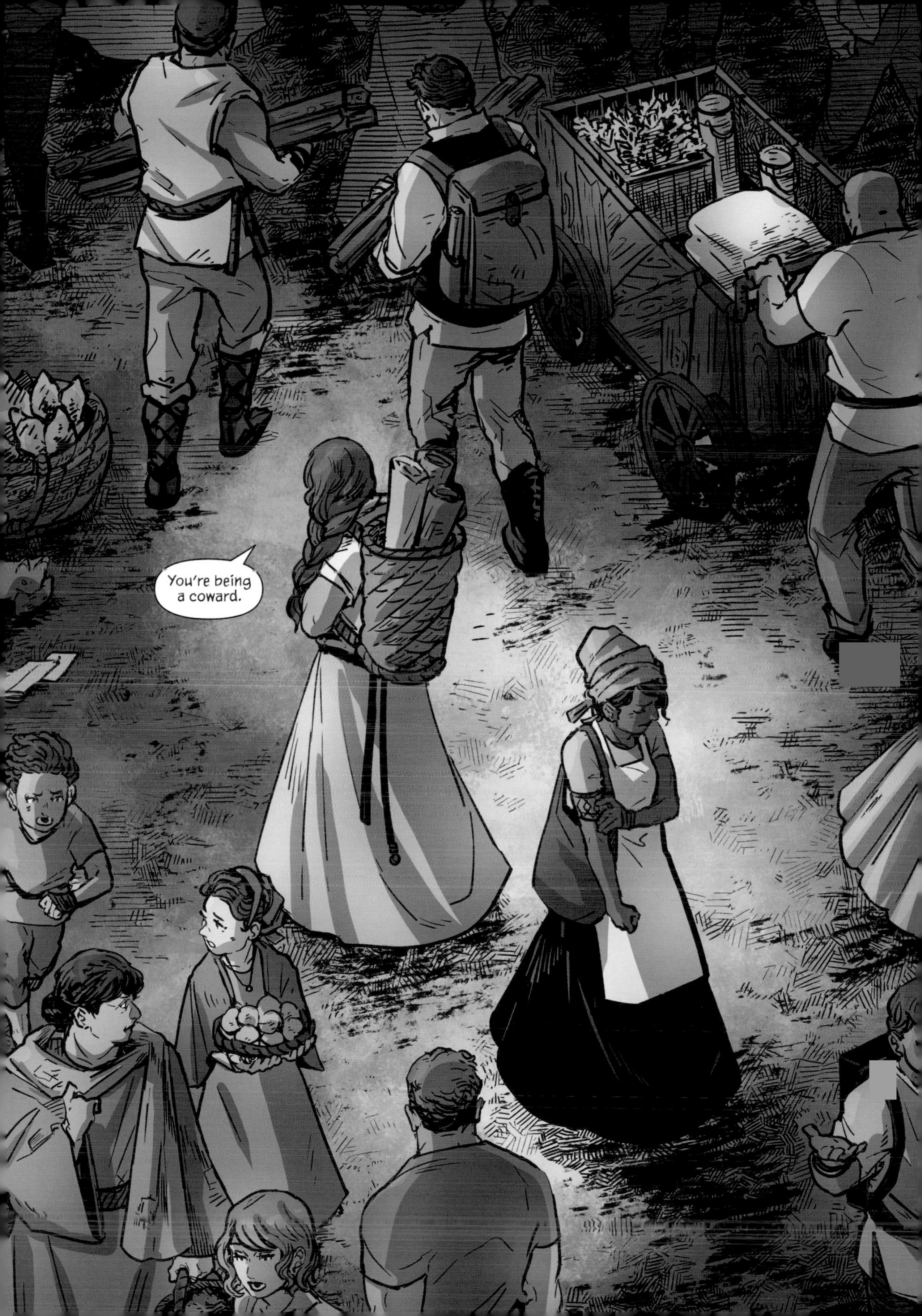
You're being a coward.

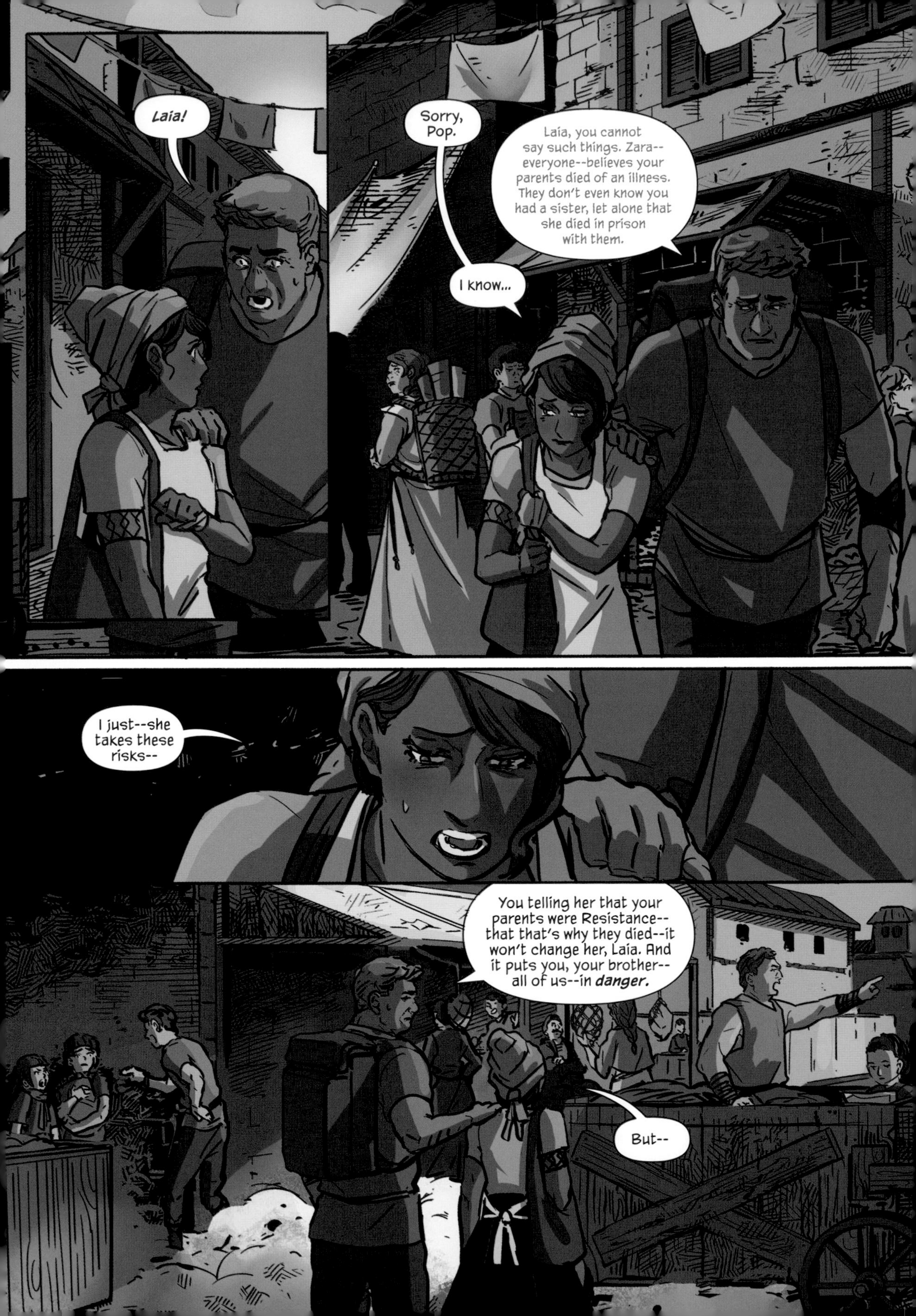
Laia!
Sorry, Pop.
I know...
Laia, you cannot say such things. Zara--everyone--believes your parents died of an illness. They don't even know you had a sister, let alone that she died in prison with them.
I just--she takes these risks--
You telling her that your parents were Resistance--that that's why they died--it won't change her, Laia. And it puts you, your brother--all of us--in ***danger.***
But--

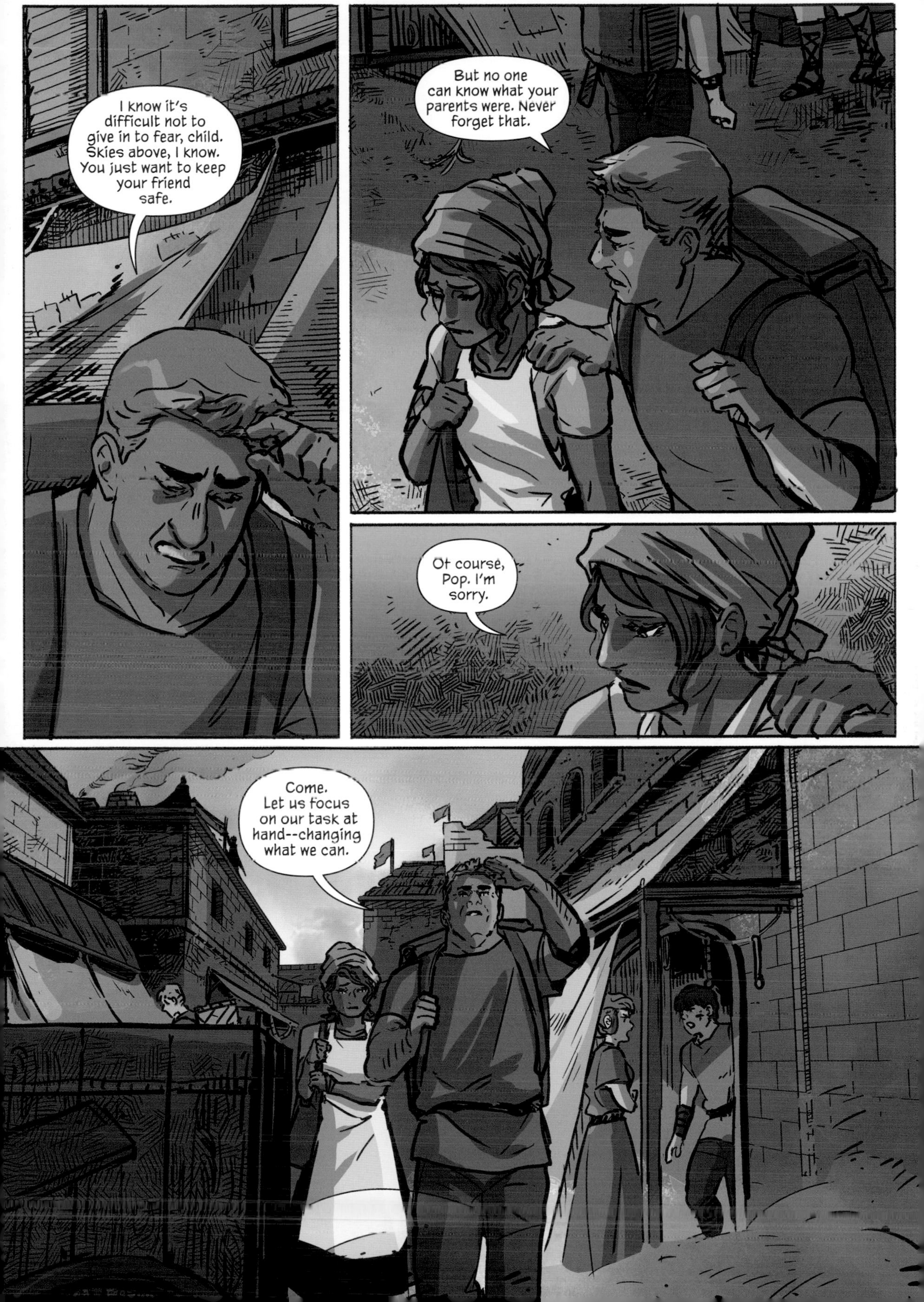
I know it's difficult not to give in to fear, child. Skies above, I know. You just want to keep your friend safe.
But no one can know what your parents were. Never forget that.
Of course, Pop. I'm sorry.
Come. Let us focus on our task at hand--changing what we can.

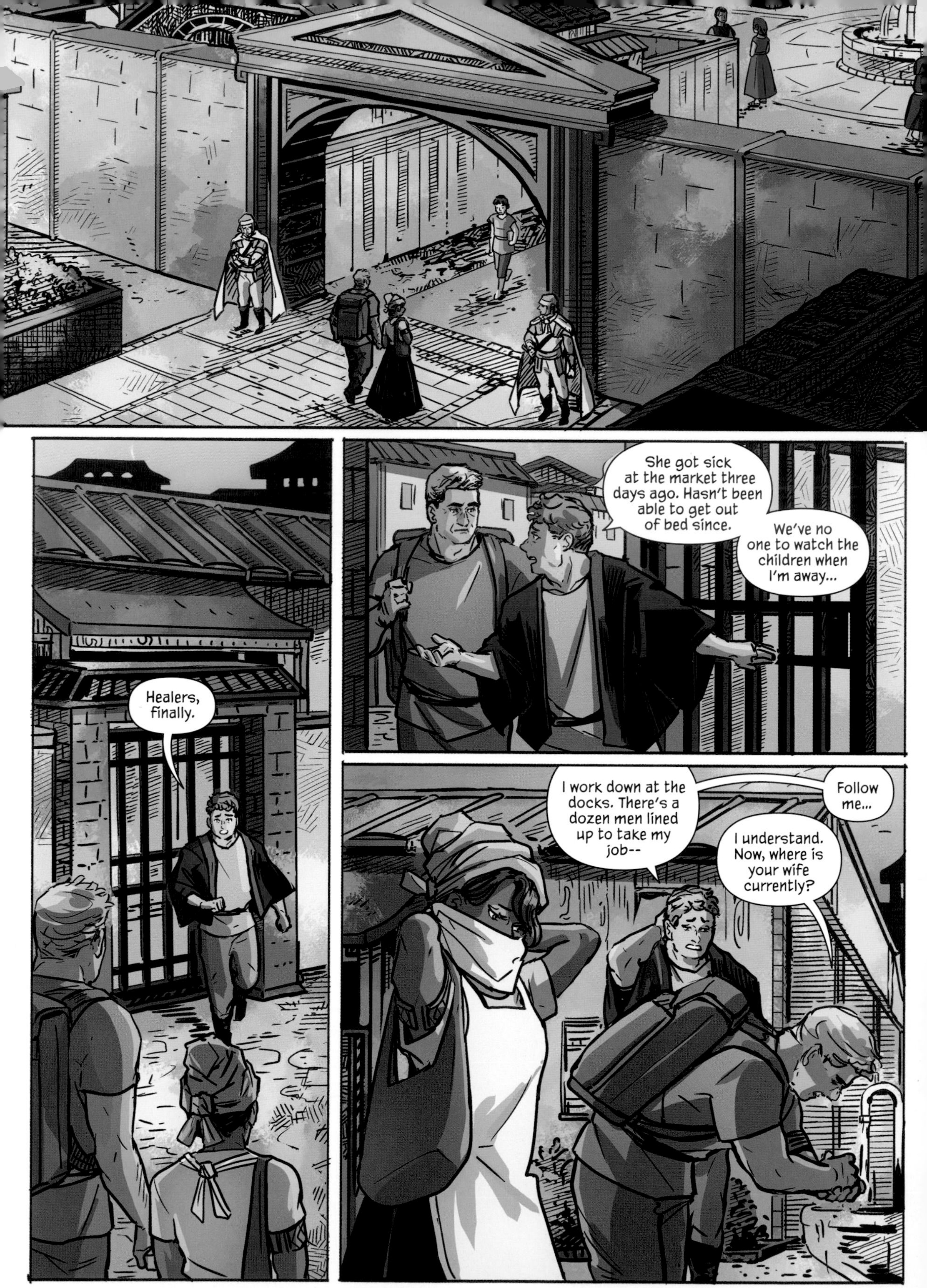
Healers, finally.
She got sick at the market three days ago. Hasn't been able to get out of bed since.
We've no one to watch the children when I'm away...
I work down at the docks. There's a dozen men lined up to take my job--
Follow me...
I understand. Now, where is your wife currently?

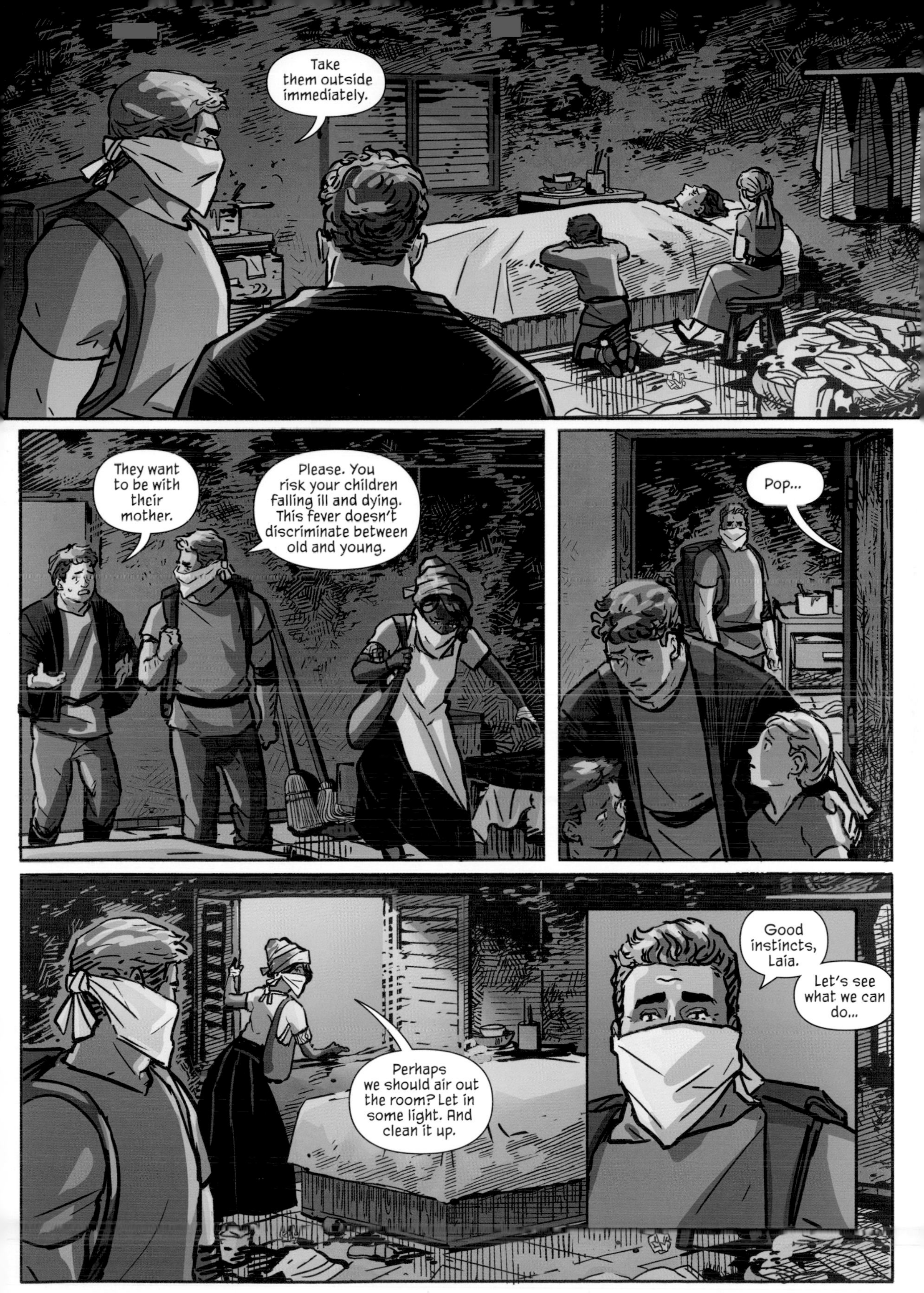

Take them outside immediately.
They want to be with their mother.
Please. You risk your children falling ill and dying. This fever doesn't discriminate between old and young.
Pop...
Perhaps we should air out the room? Let in some light. And clean it up.
Good instincts, Laia.
Let's see what we can do...

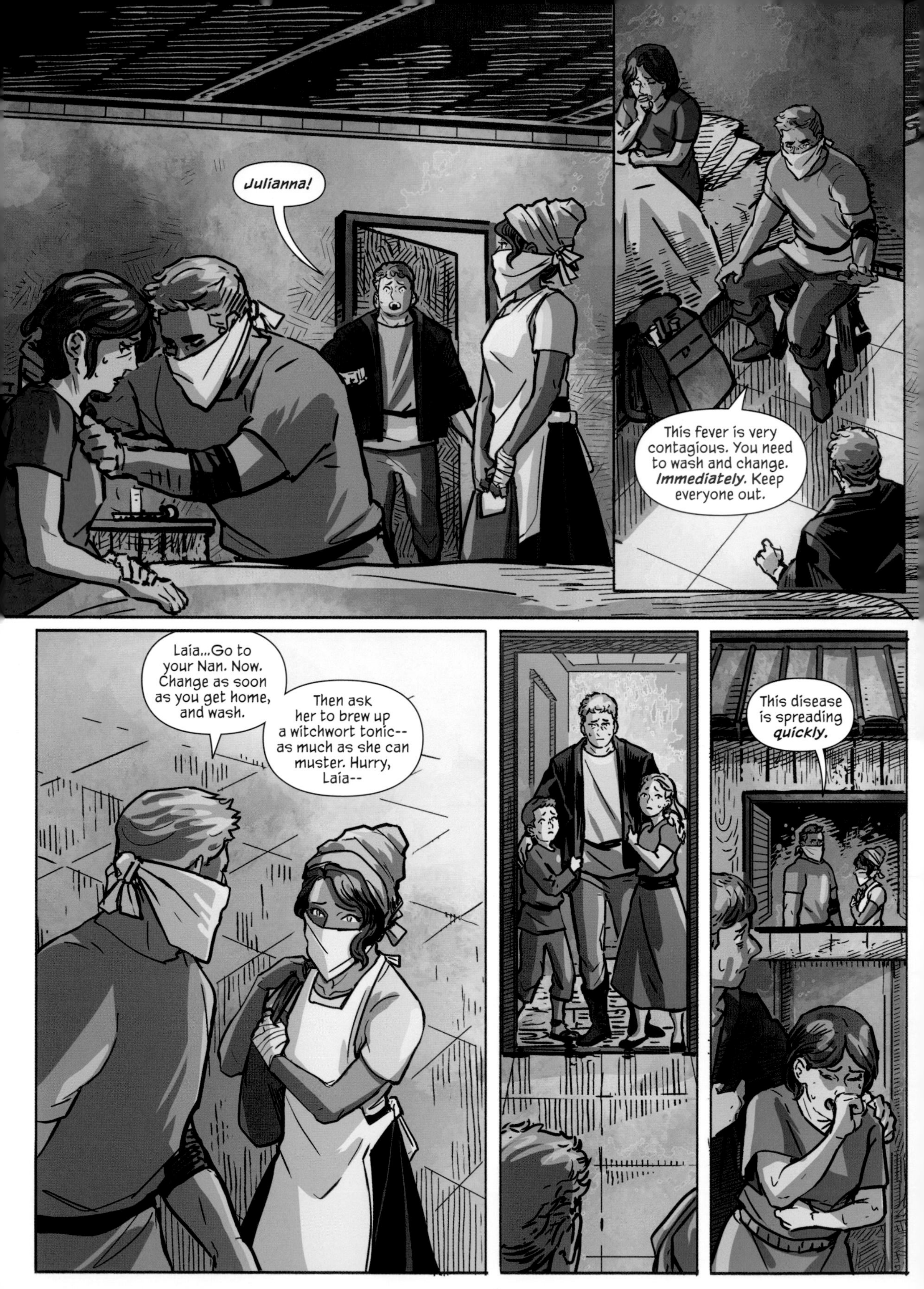
Julianna!
This fever is very contagious. You need to wash and change. *Immediately*. Keep everyone out.
Laia...Go to your Nan. Now. Change as soon as you get home, and wash.
Then ask her to brew up a witchwort tonic-- as much as she can muster. Hurry, Laia--
This disease is spreading *quickly.*

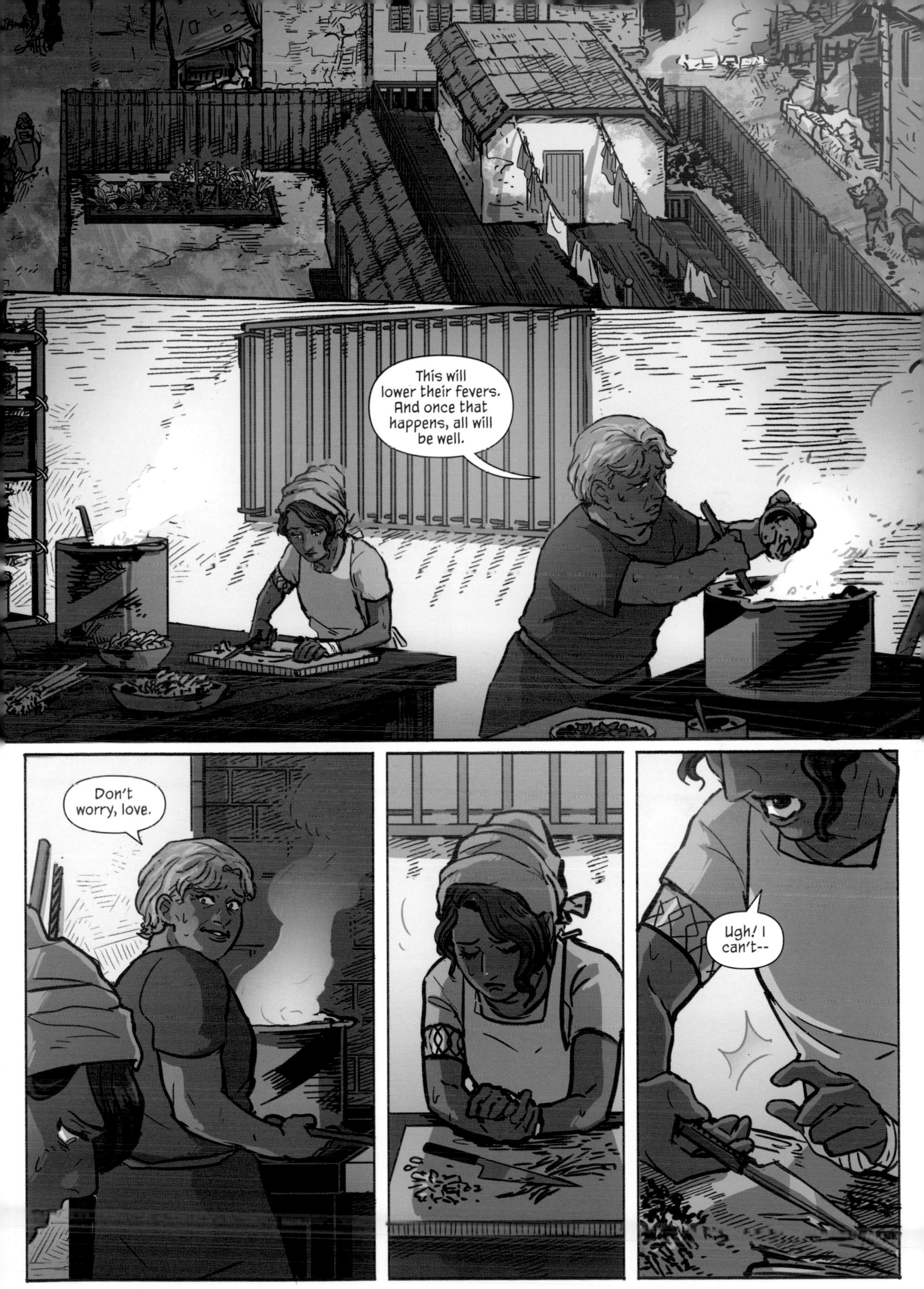
This will lower their fevers. And once that happens, all will be well.
Don't worry, love.
Ugh! I can't--

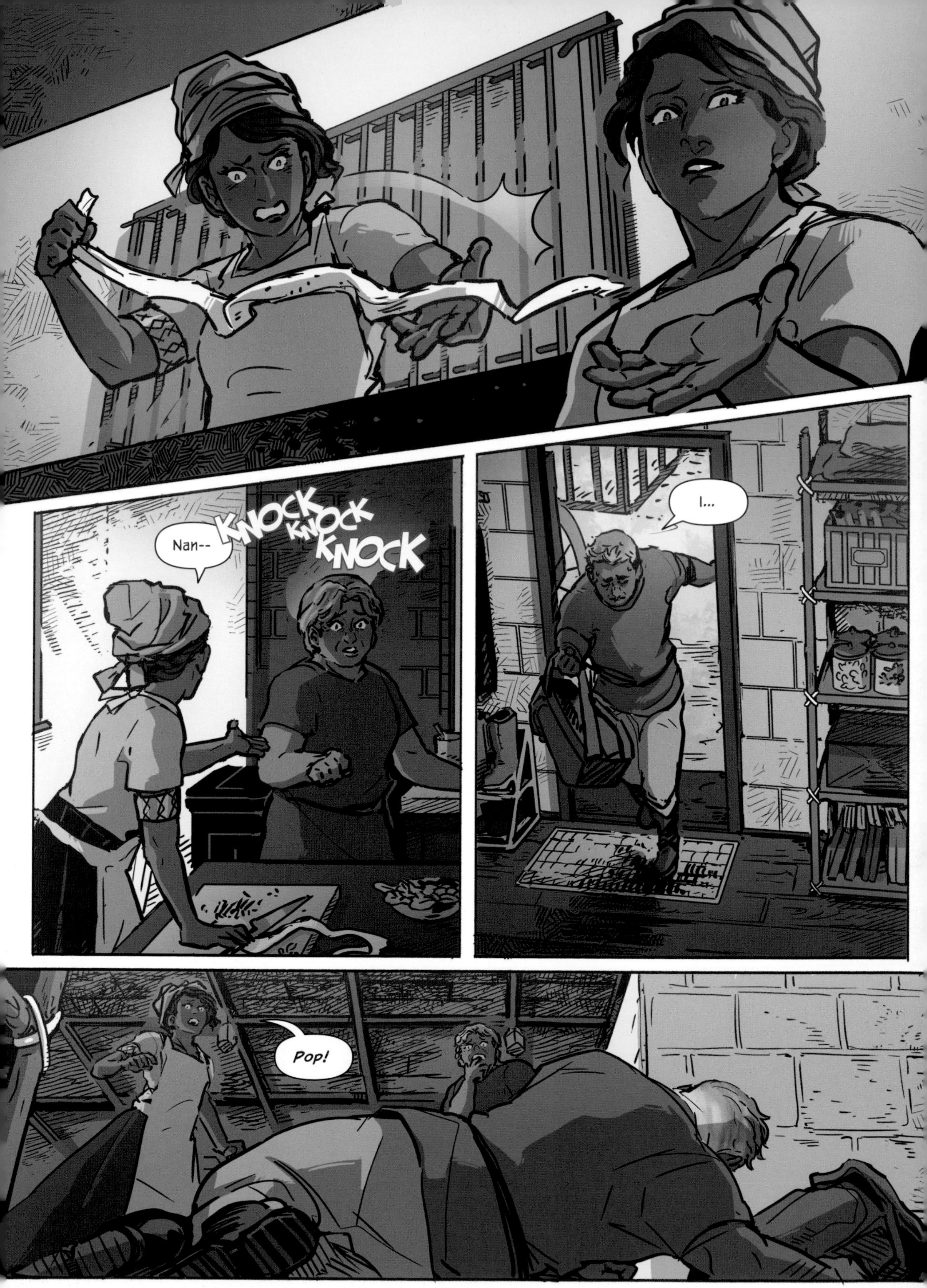
Nan--
KNOCK KNOCK KNOCK
I...
Pop!

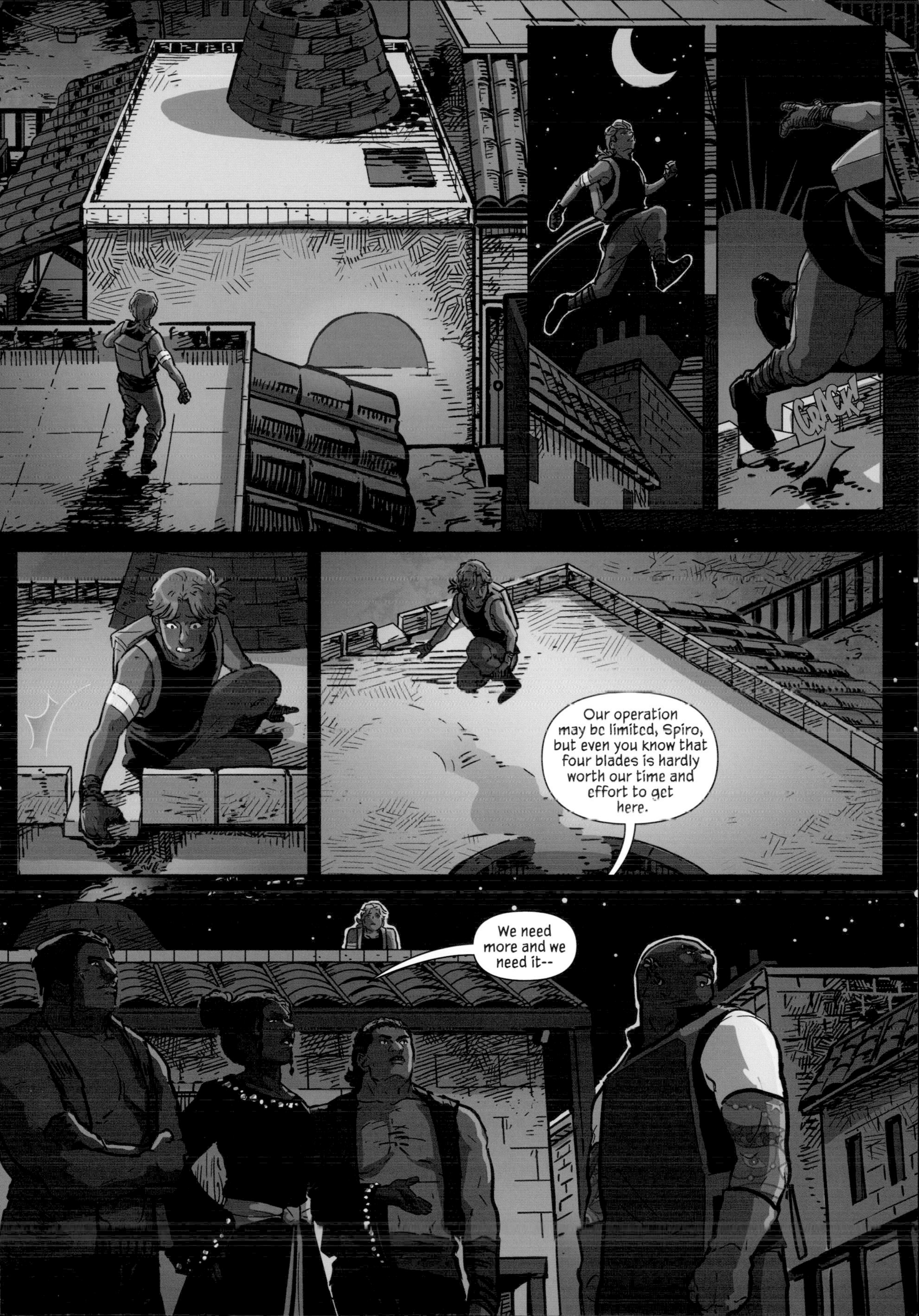
CRACK!
Our operation may be limited, Spiro, but even you know that four blades is hardly worth our time and effort to get here.
We need more and we need it--

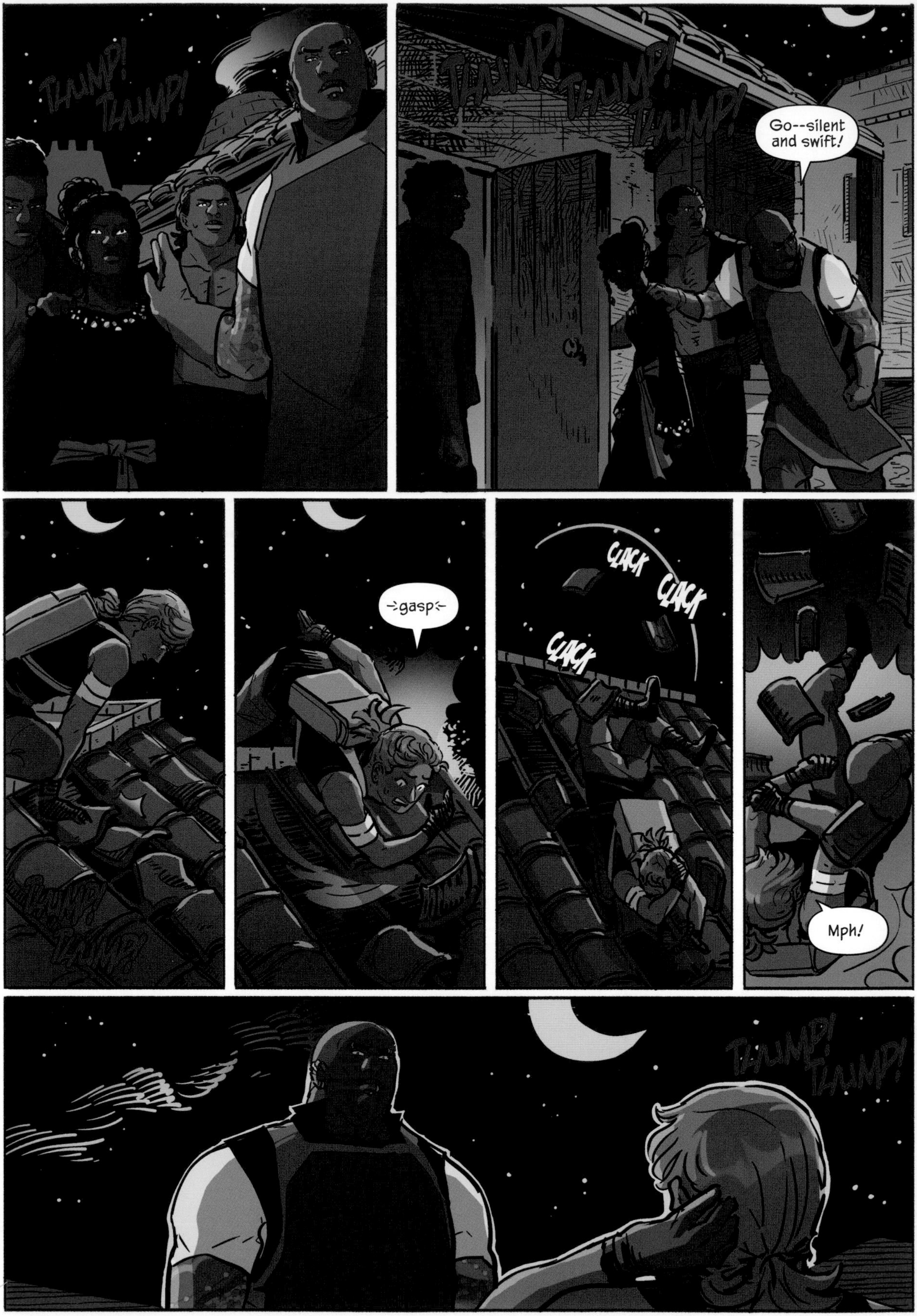
THUMP! THUMP!
THUMP! THUMP! THUMP!
Go--silent and swift!
THUMP! THUMP!
-gasp-
CLACK CLACK CLACK
Mph!
THUMP! THUMP!

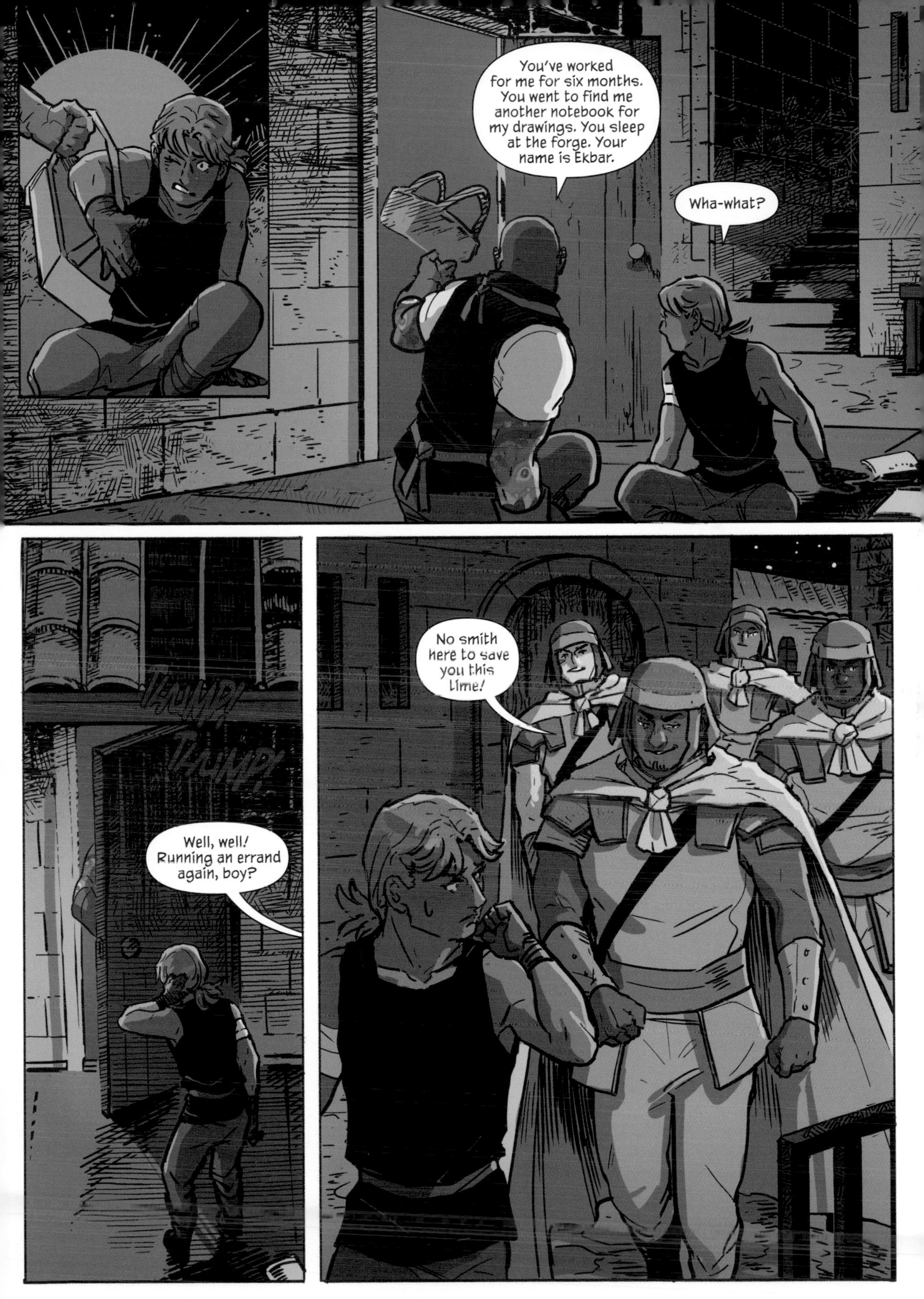
You've worked for me for six months. You went to find me another notebook for my drawings. You sleep at the forge. Your name is Ekbar.
Wha-what?
Well, well! Running an errand again, boy?
No smith here to save you this time!

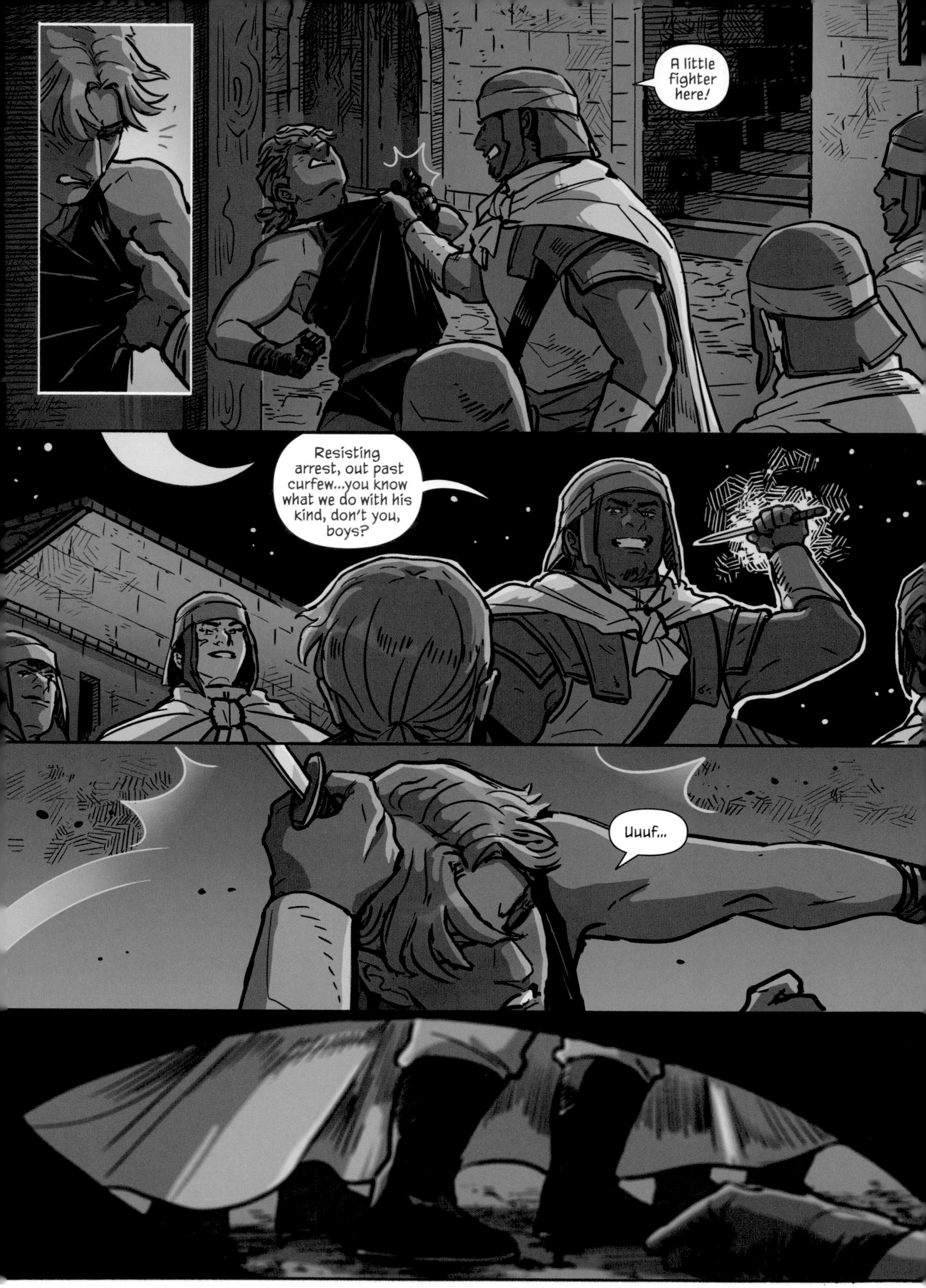
A little fighter here!
Resisting arrest, out past curfew...you know what we do with his kind, don't you, boys?
Uuuf...

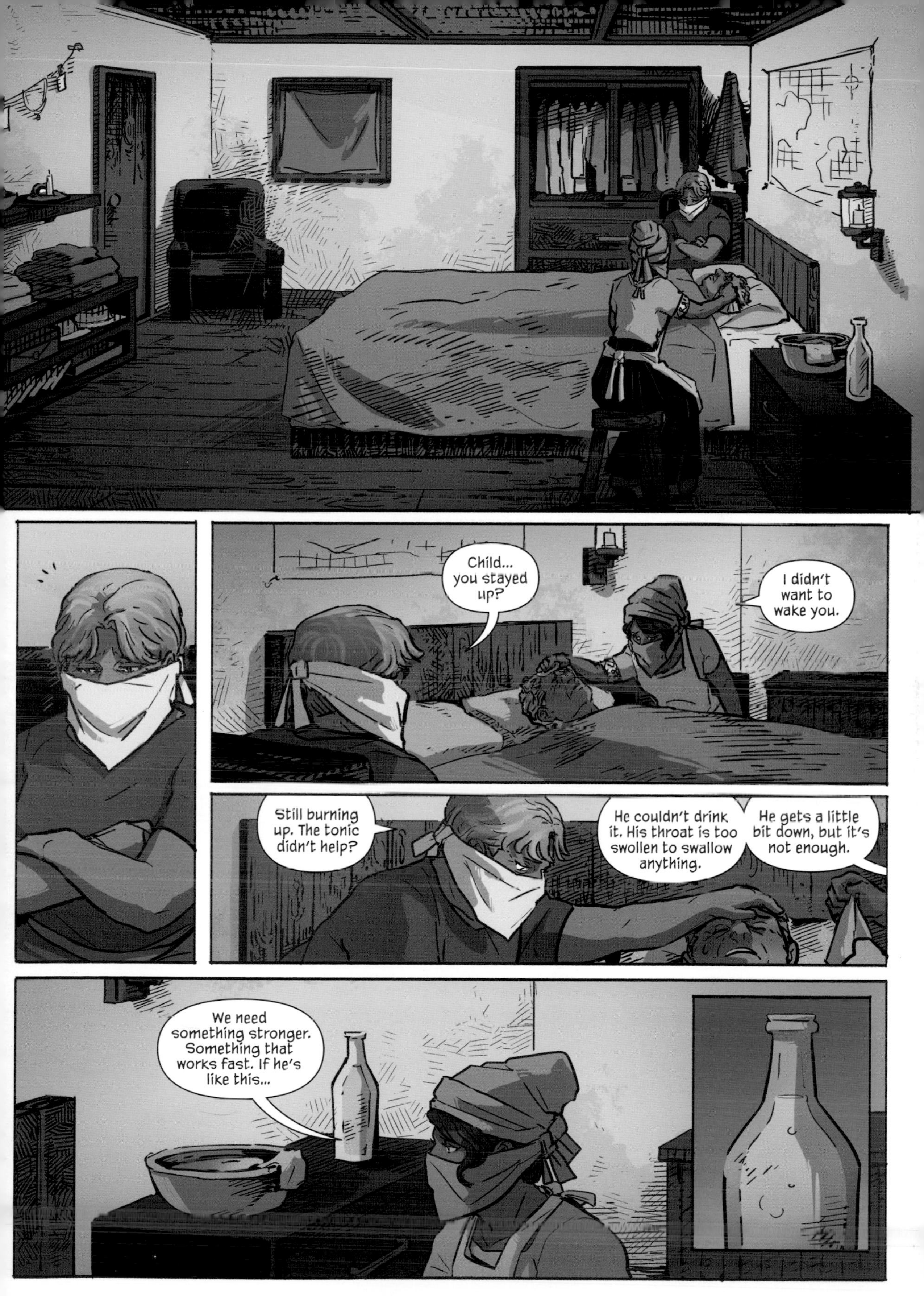

Child... you stayed up?
I didn't want to wake you.
Still burning up. The tonic didn't help?
He couldn't drink it. His throat is too swollen to swallow anything.
He gets a little bit down, but it's not enough.
We need something stronger. Something that works fast. If he's like this...

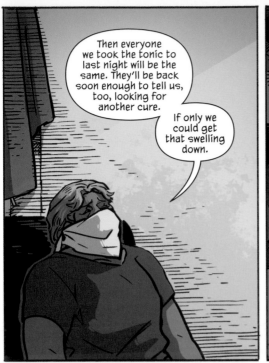
Then everyone we took the tonic to last night will be the same. They'll be back soon enough to tell us, too, looking for another cure.

If only we could get that swelling down.

Go wake your brother, love.

Yes, Nan.

Darin...

Darin?

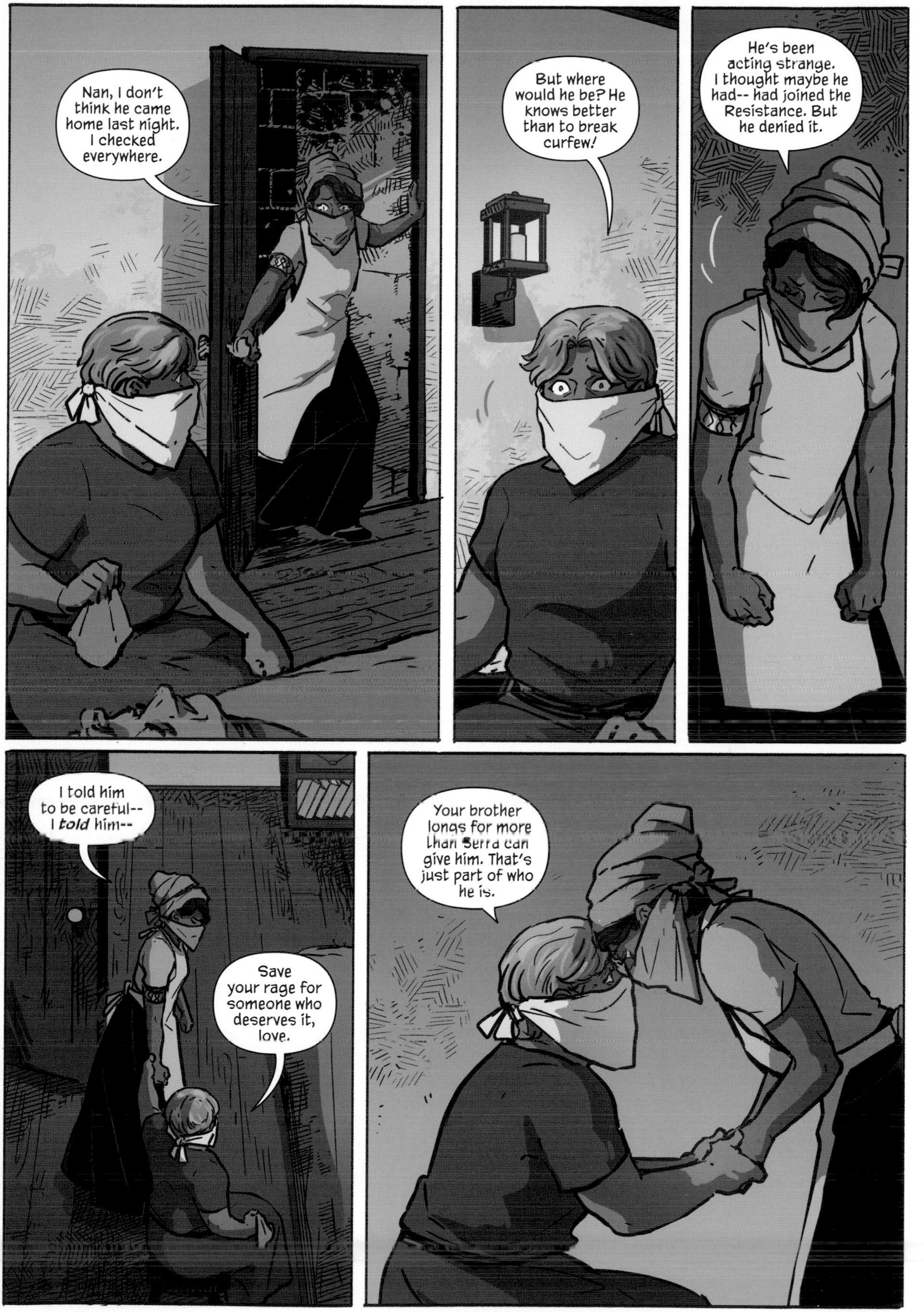
Nan, I don't think he came home last night. I checked everywhere.
But where would he be? He knows better than to break curfew!
He's been acting strange. I thought maybe he had-- had joined the Resistance. But he denied it.
I told him to be careful-- I *told* him--
Save your rage for someone who deserves it, love.
Your brother longs for more than Serra can give him. That's just part of who he is.

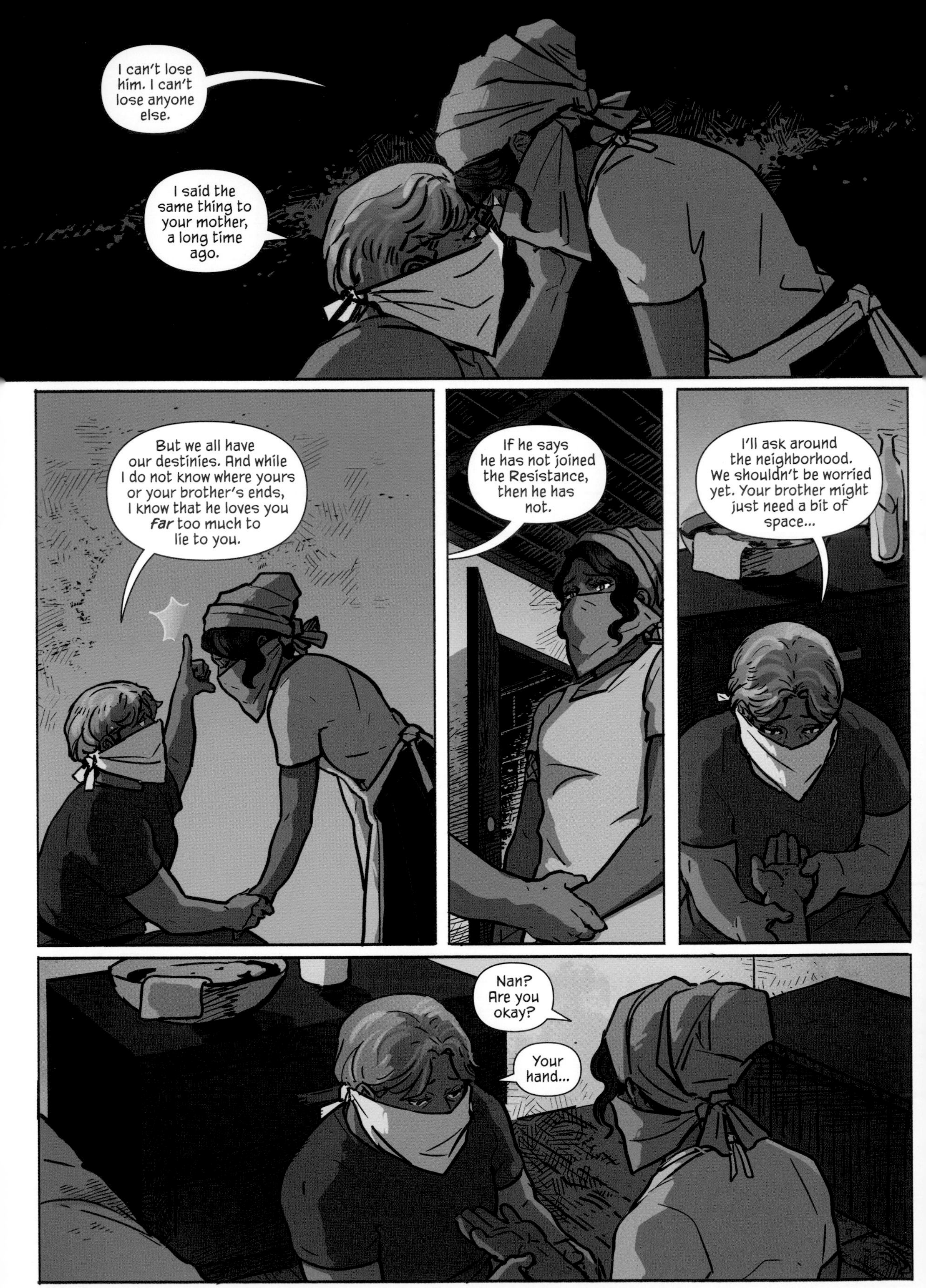
I can't lose him. I can't lose anyone else.
I said the same thing to your mother, a long time ago.
But we all have our destinies. And while I do not know where yours or your brother's ends, I know that he loves you *far* too much to lie to you.
If he says he has not joined the Resistance, then he has not.
I'll ask around the neighborhood. We shouldn't be worried yet. Your brother might just need a bit of space...
Nan? Are you okay?
Your hand...

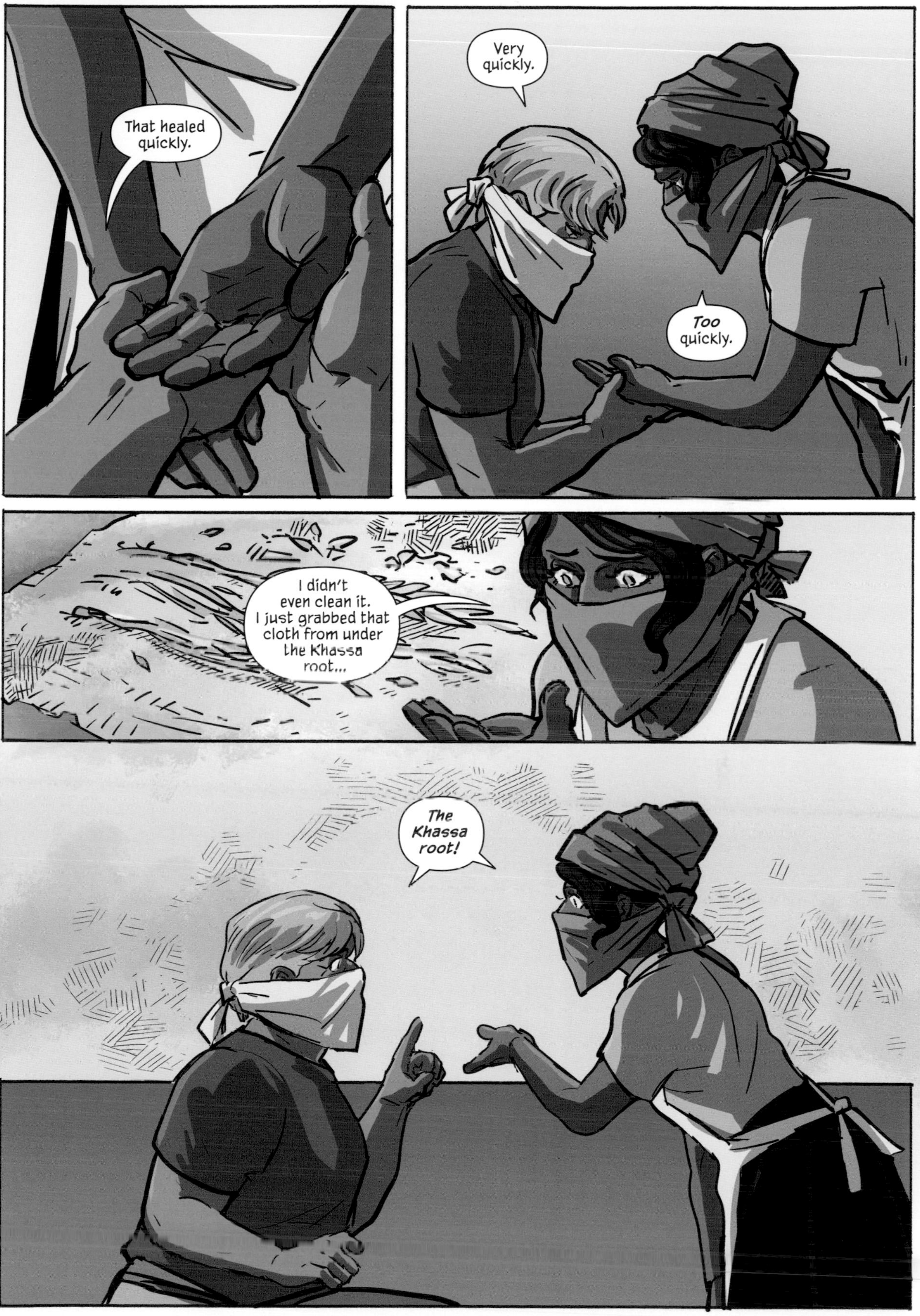
That healed quickly.
Very quickly.
Too quickly.
I didn't even clean it. I just grabbed that cloth from under the Khassa root...
The Khassa root!

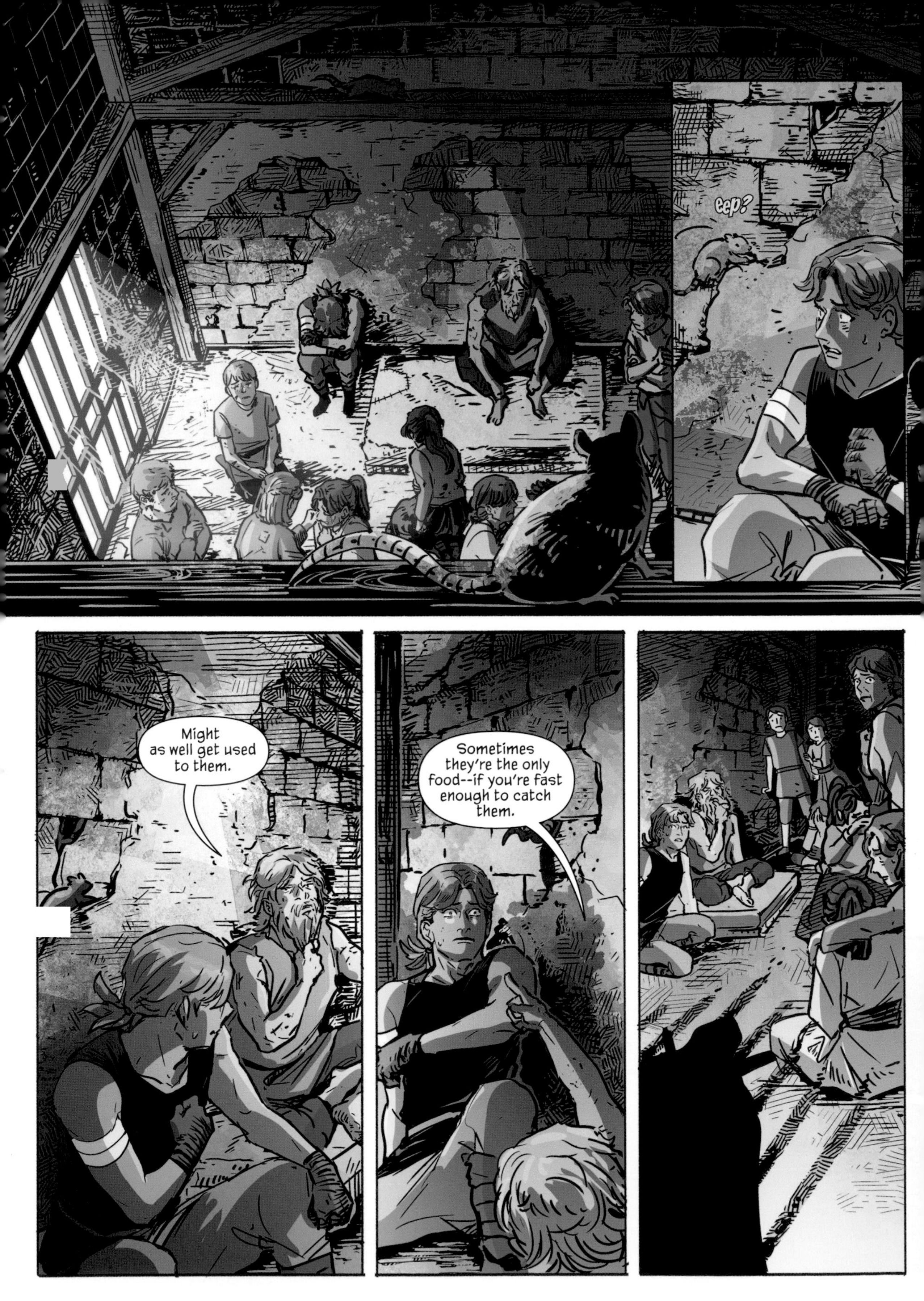
eep?
Might as well get used to them.
Sometimes they're the only food--if you're fast enough to catch them.

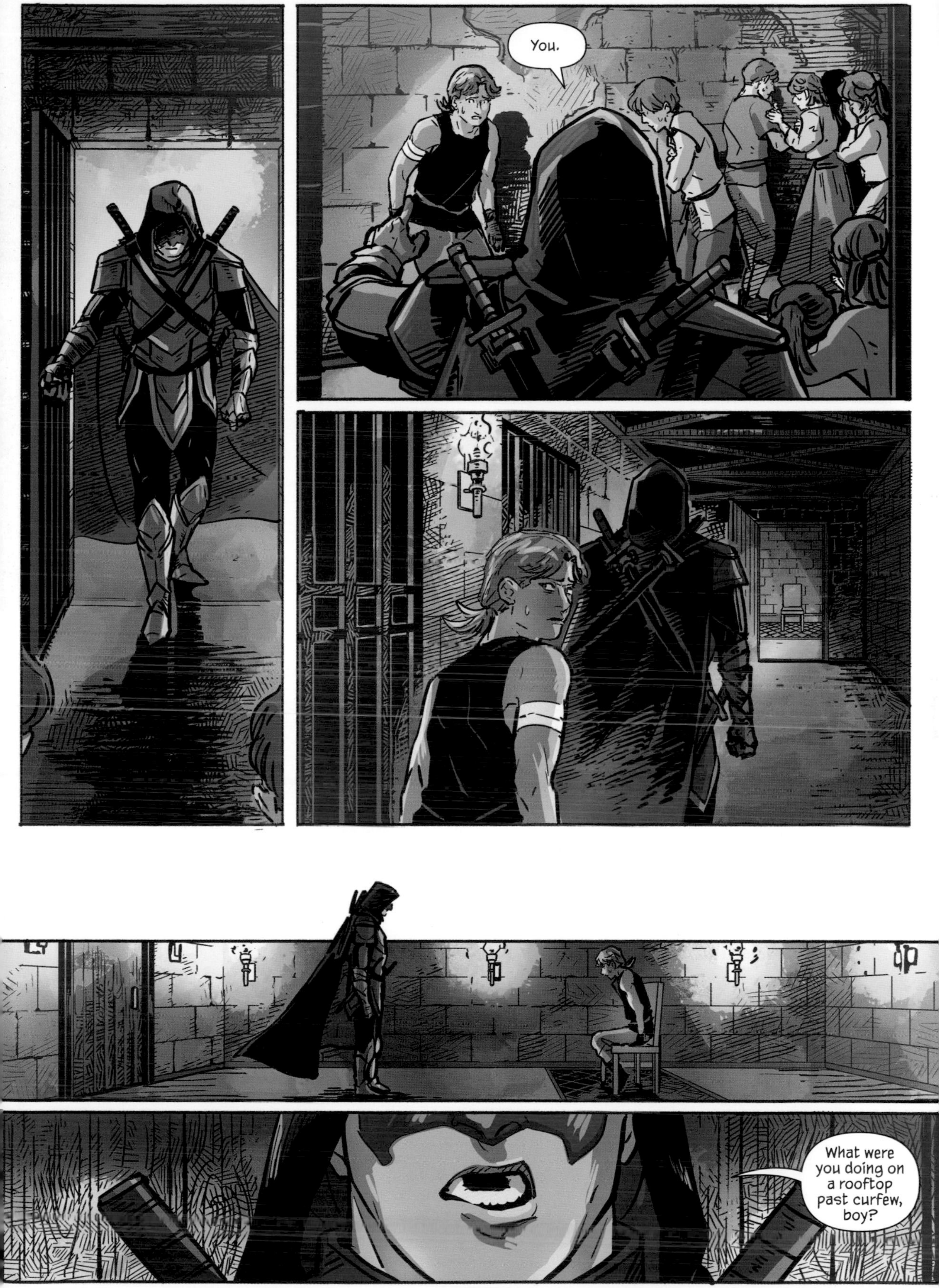
You.
What were you doing on a rooftop past curfew, boy?

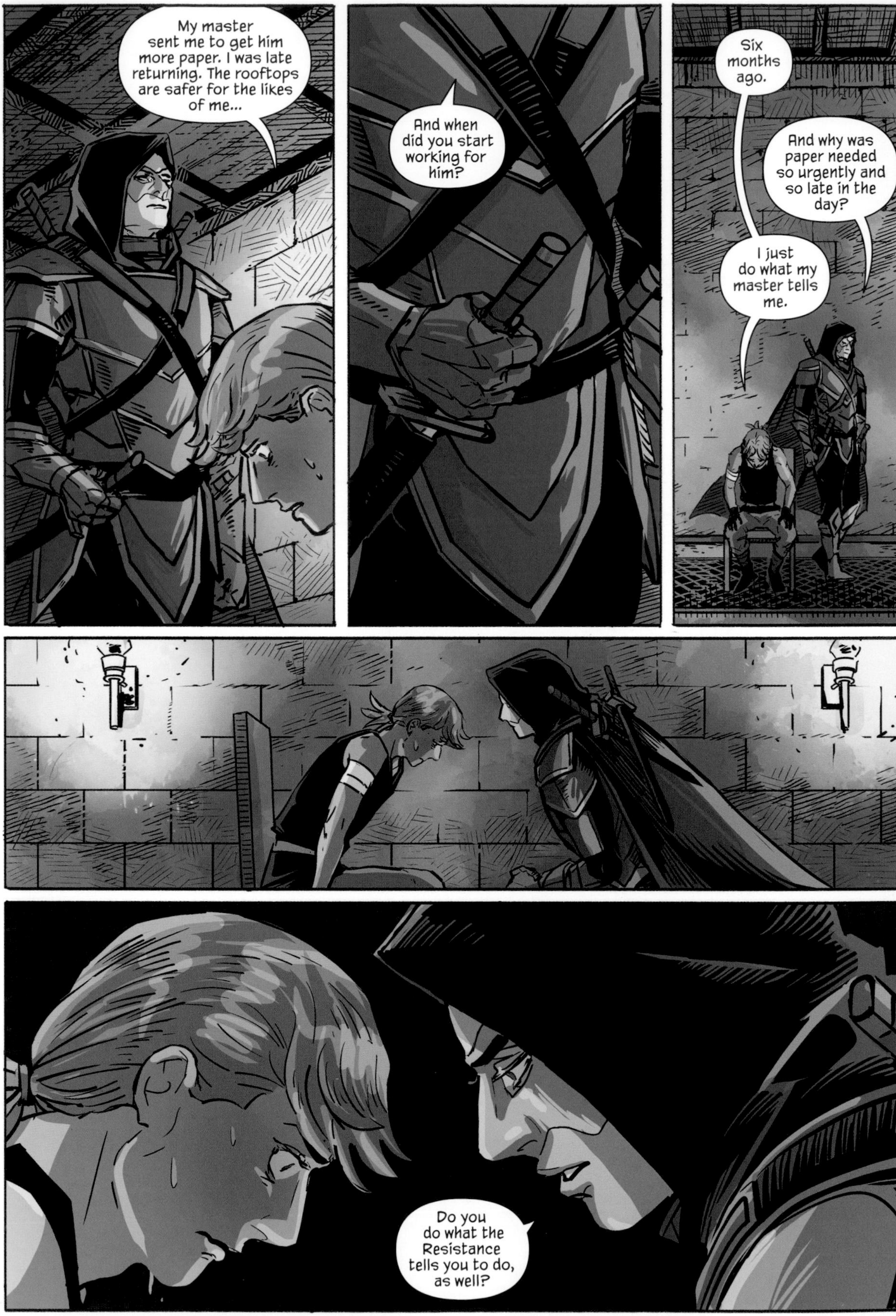
My master sent me to get him more paper. I was late returning. The rooftops are safer for the likes of me...
And when did you start working for him?
Six months ago.
And why was paper needed so urgently and so late in the day?
I just do what my master tells me.
Do you do what the Resistance tells you to do, as well?

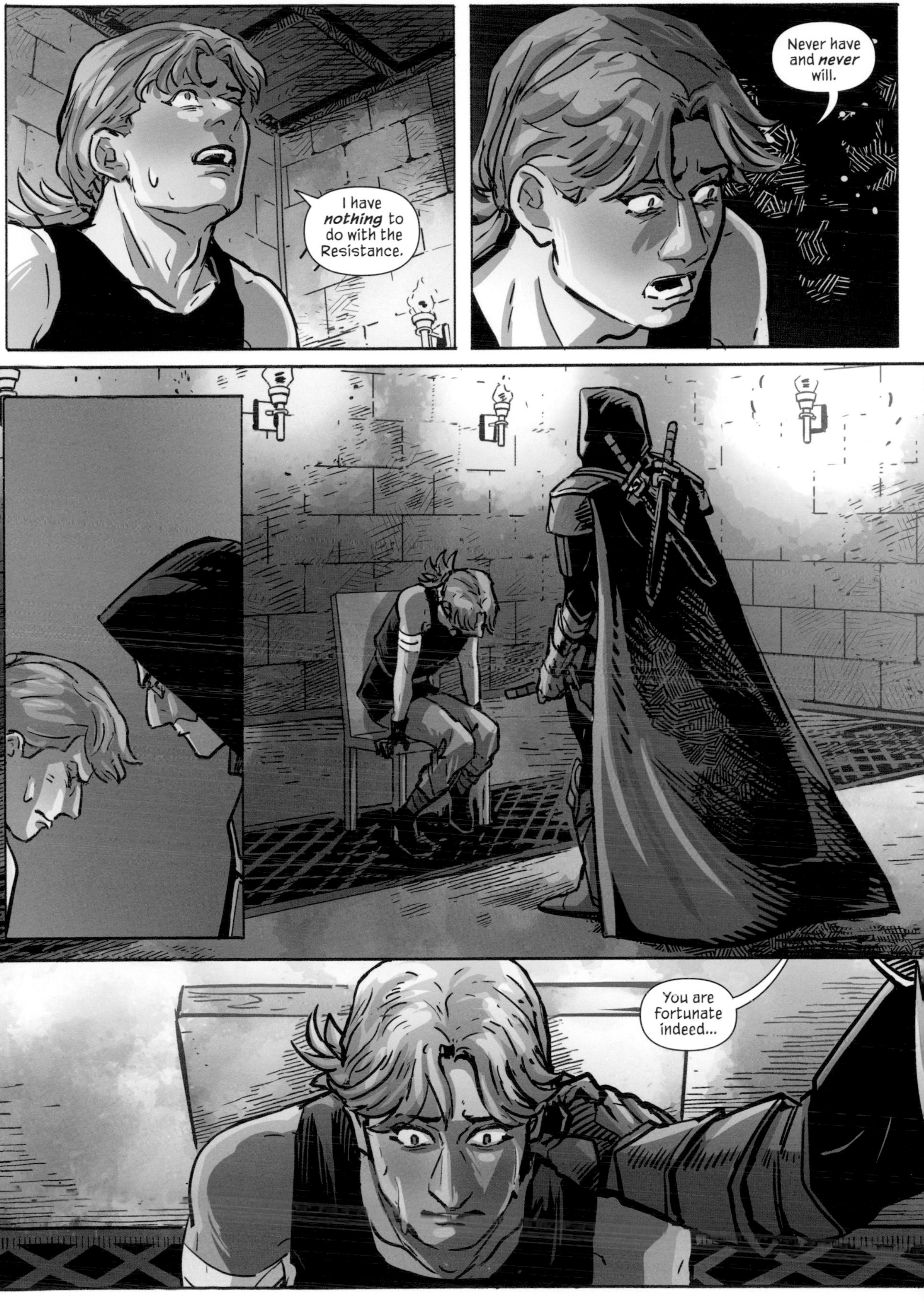
I have *nothing* to do with the Resistance.
Never have and *never* will.
You are fortunate indeed...

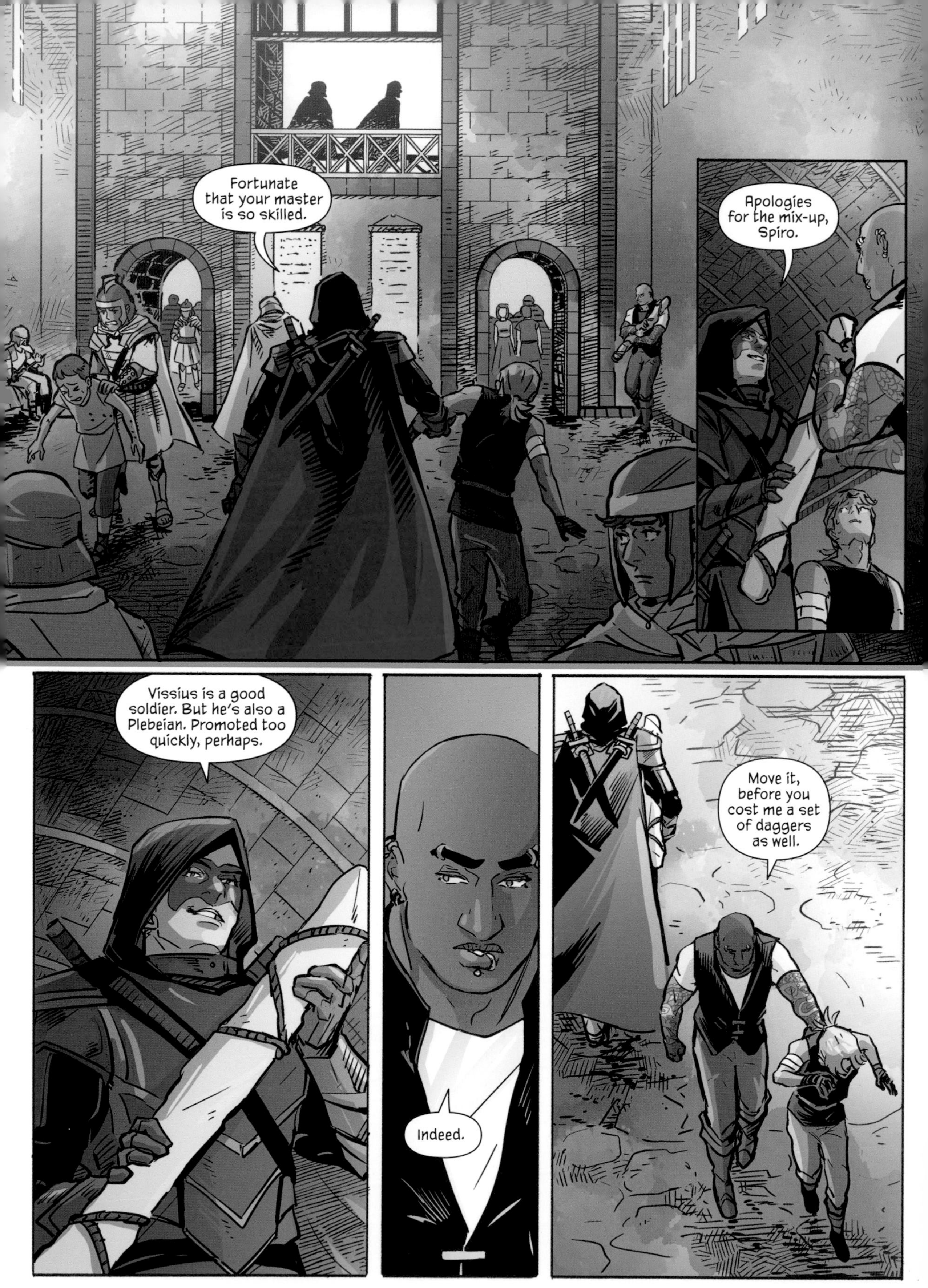
Fortunate that your master is so skilled.
Apologies for the mix-up, Spiro.
Vissius is a good soldier. But he's also a Plebeian. Promoted too quickly, perhaps.
Indeed.
Move it, before you cost me a set of daggers as well.

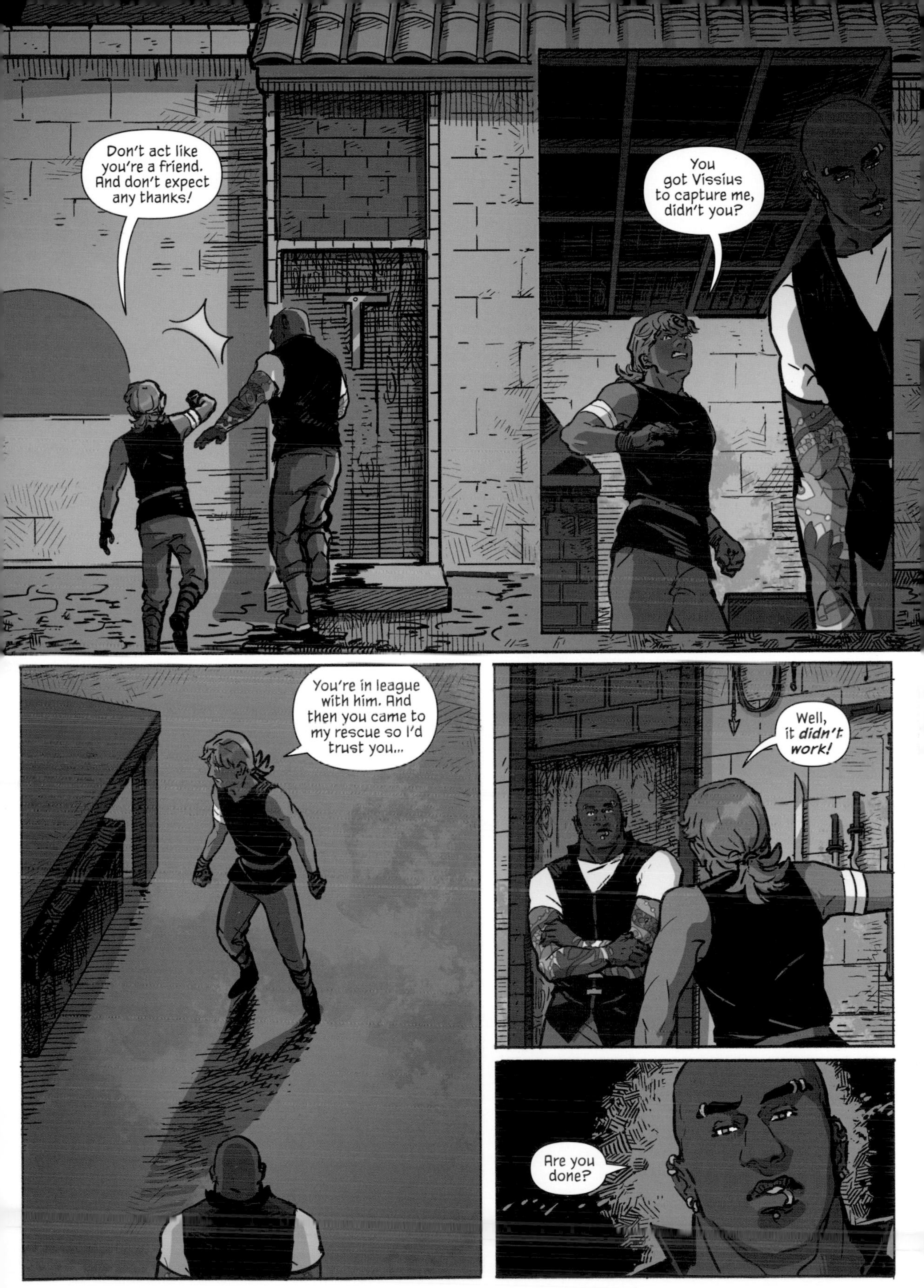
Don't act like you're a friend. And don't expect any thanks!
You got Vissius to capture me, didn't you?
You're in league with him. And then you came to my rescue so I'd trust you...
Well, it *didn't work!*
Are you done?

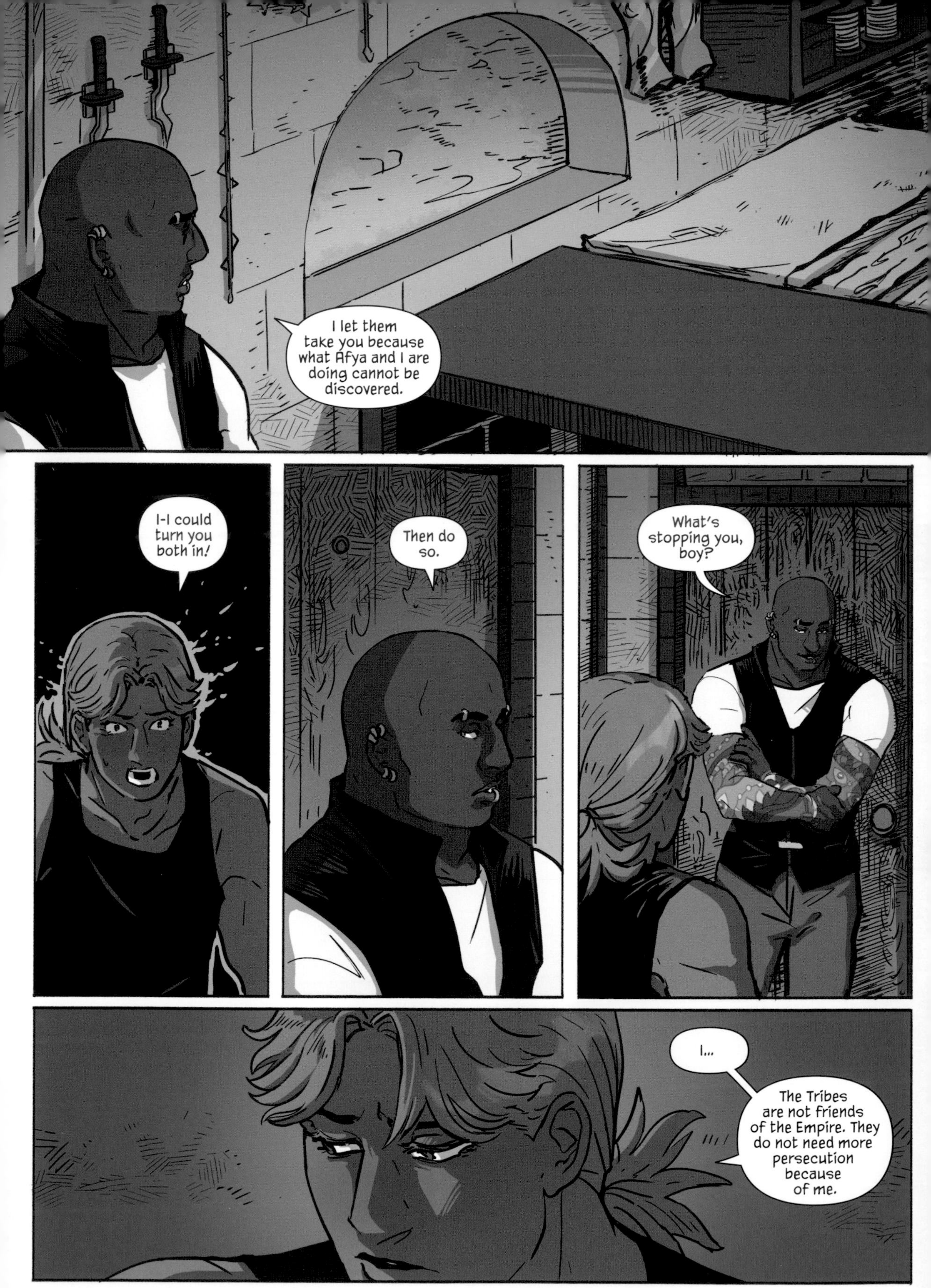
I let them take you because what Afya and I are doing cannot be discovered.
I-I could turn you both in!
Then do so.
What's stopping you, boy?
I...
The Tribes are not friends of the Empire. They do not need more persecution because of me.

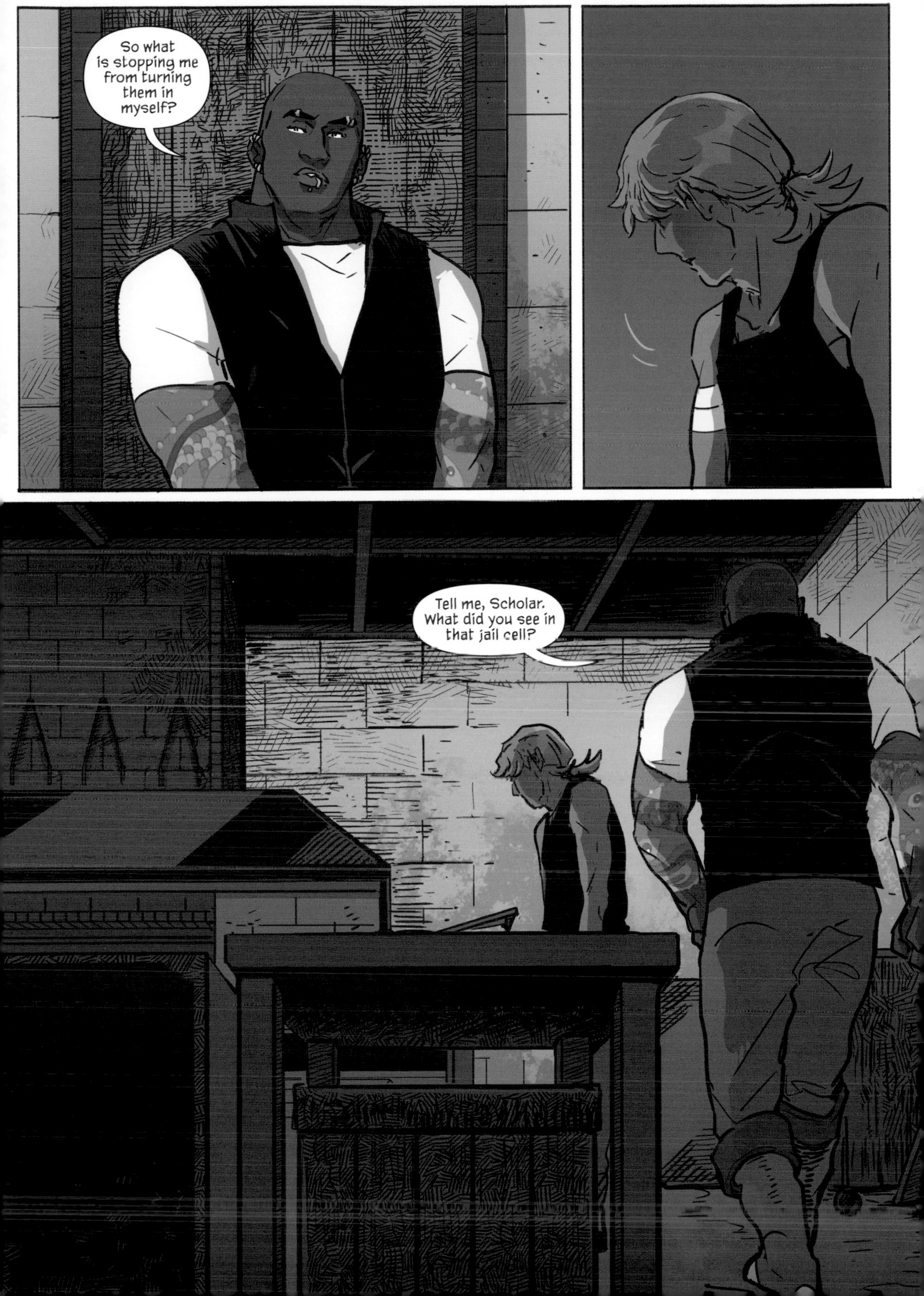
So what is stopping me from turning them in myself?
Tell me, Scholar. What did you see in that jail cell?

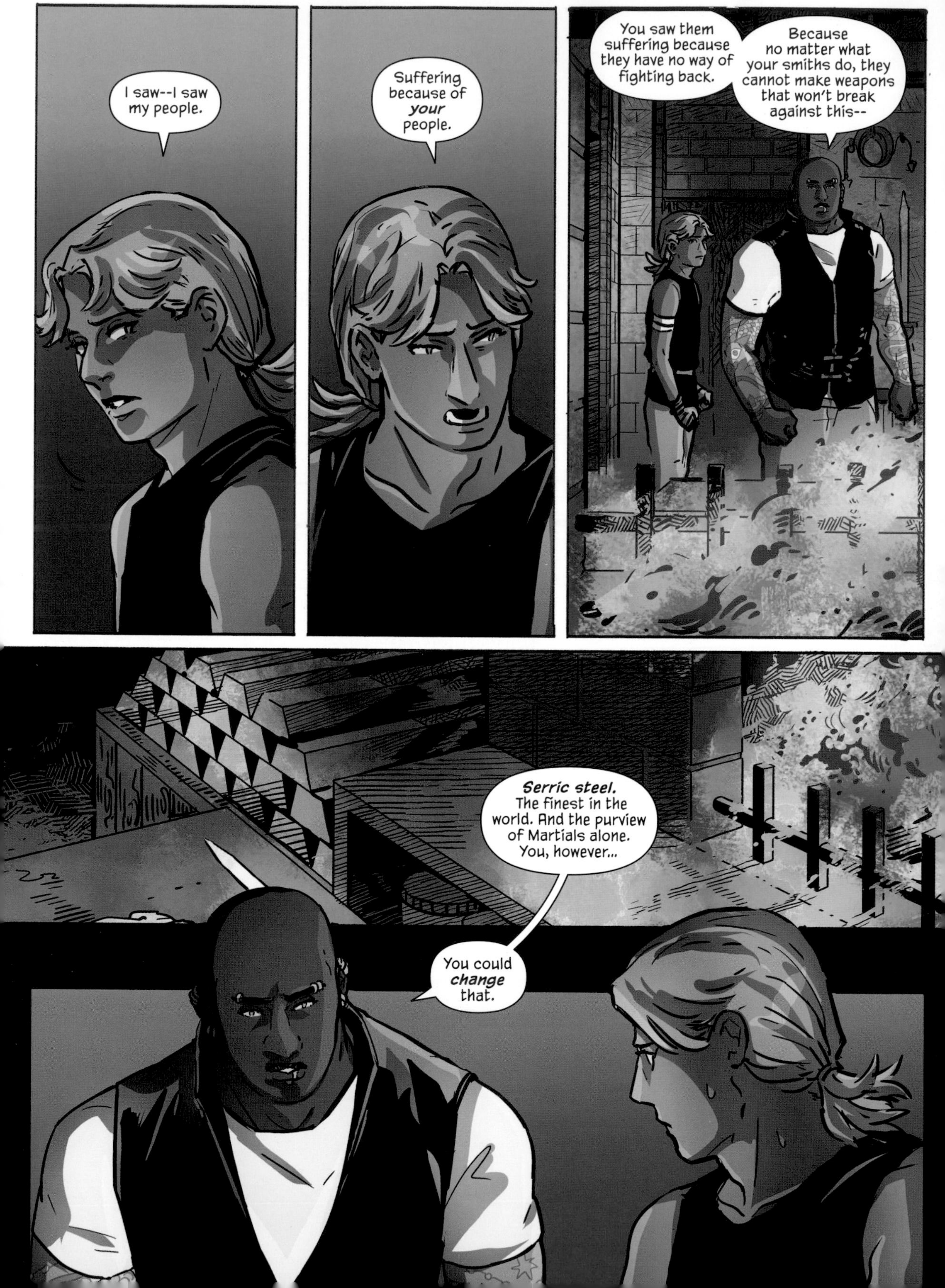
I saw--I saw my people.
Suffering because of *your* people.
You saw them suffering because they have no way of fighting back.
Because no matter what your smiths do, they cannot make weapons that won't break against this--
Serric steel. The finest in the world. And the purview of Martials alone. You, however...
You could ***change*** that.

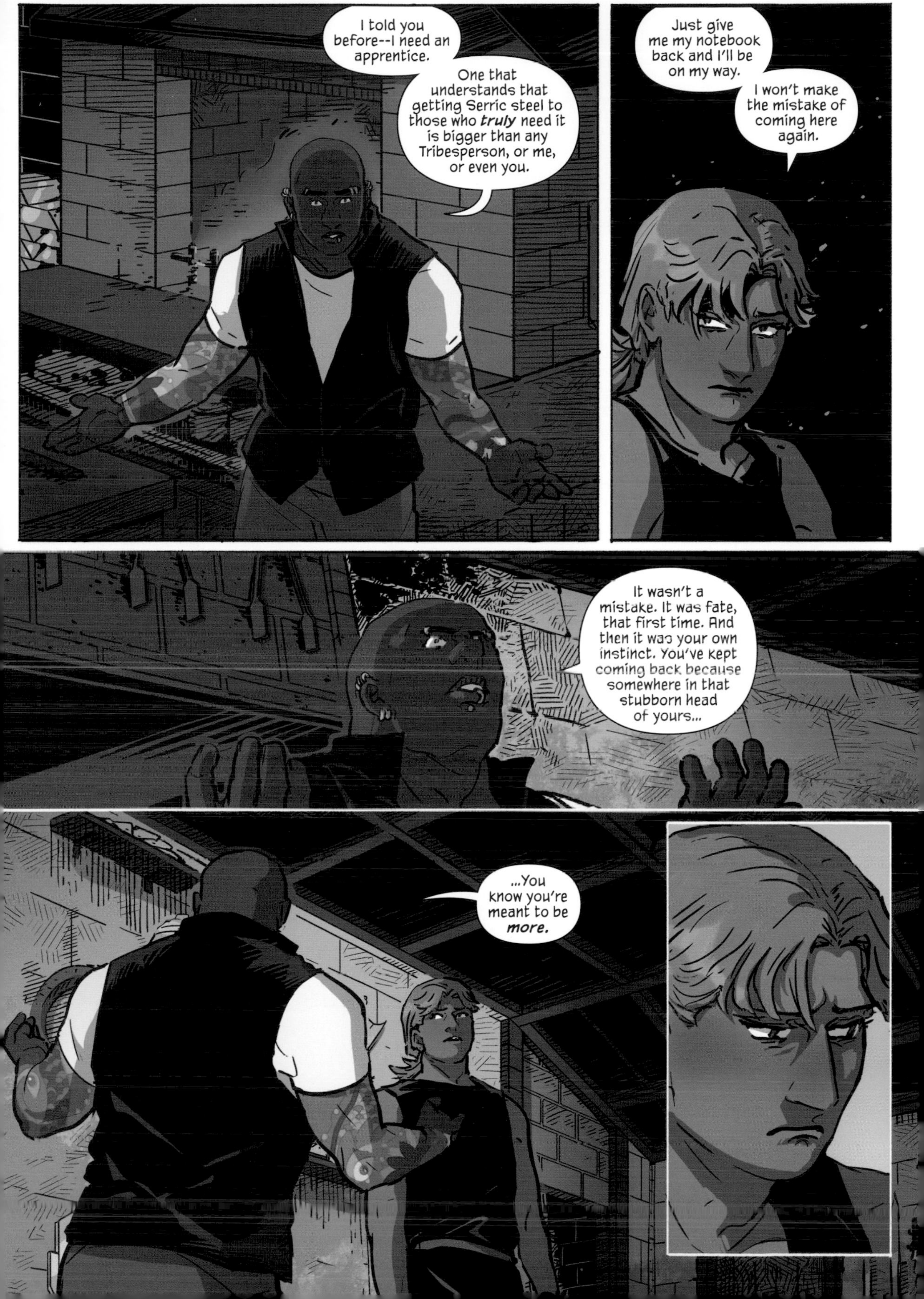

I told you before--I need an apprentice.
One that understands that getting Serric steel to those who *truly* need it is bigger than any Tribesperson, or me, or even you.
Just give me my notebook back and I'll be on my way.
I won't make the mistake of coming here again.
It wasn't a mistake. It was fate, that first time. And then it was your own instinct. You've kept coming back because somewhere in that stubborn head of yours...
...You know you're meant to be *more.*

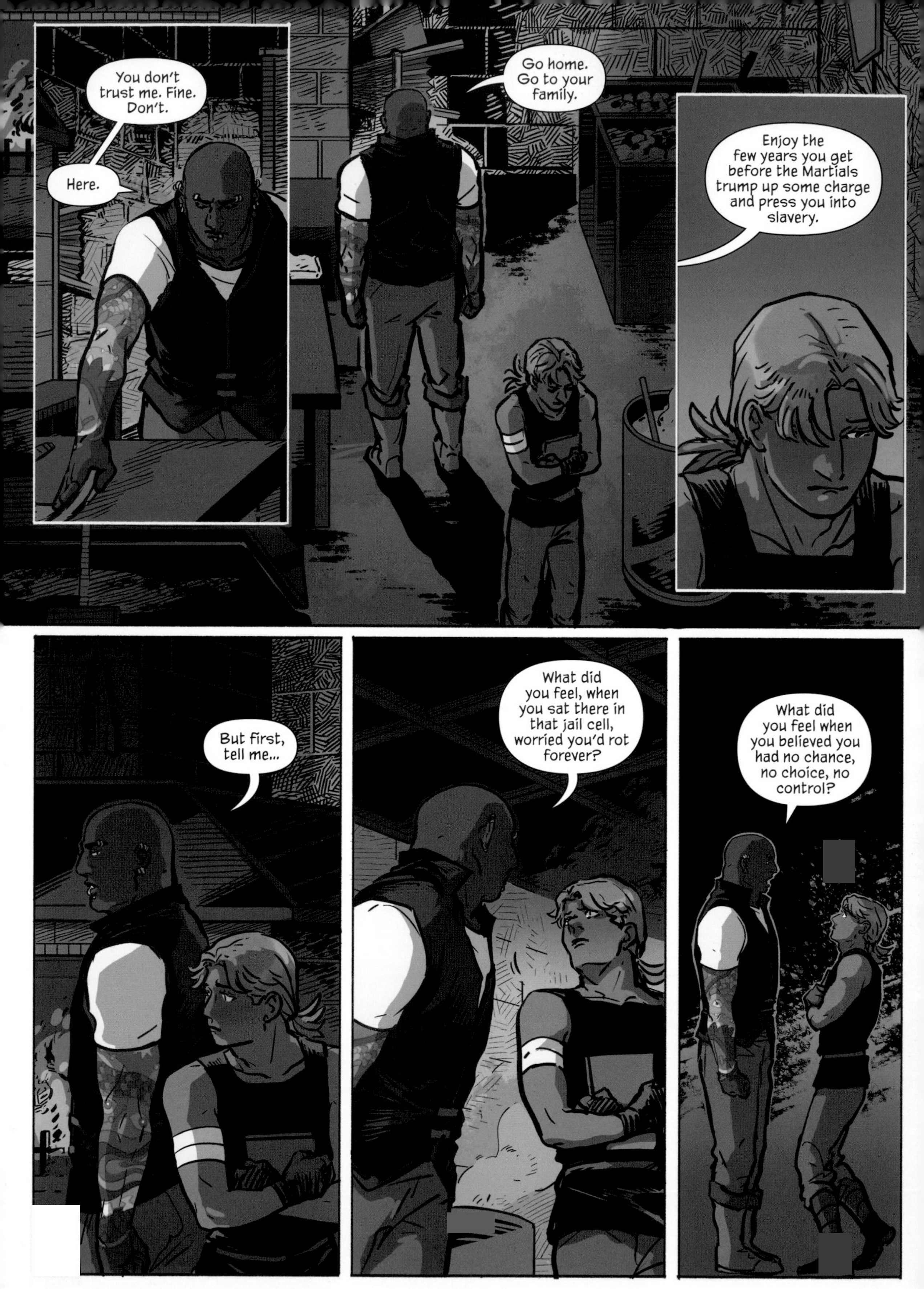
You don't trust me. Fine. Don't.
Here.
Go home. Go to your family.
Enjoy the few years you get before the Martials trump up some charge and press you into slavery.
But first, tell me...
What did you feel, when you sat there in that jail cell, worried you'd rot forever?
What did you feel when you believed you had no chance, no choice, no control?

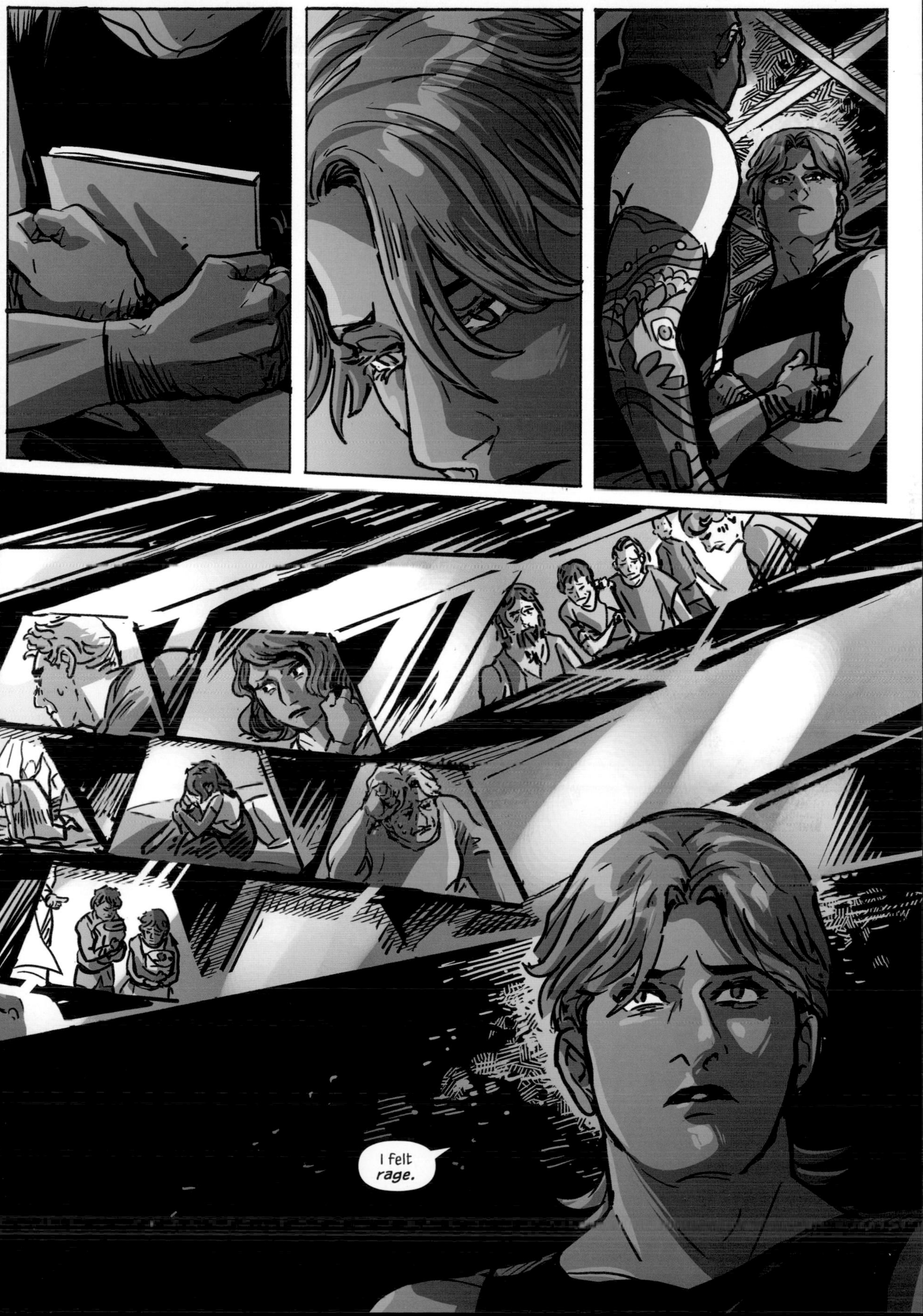
I felt rage.

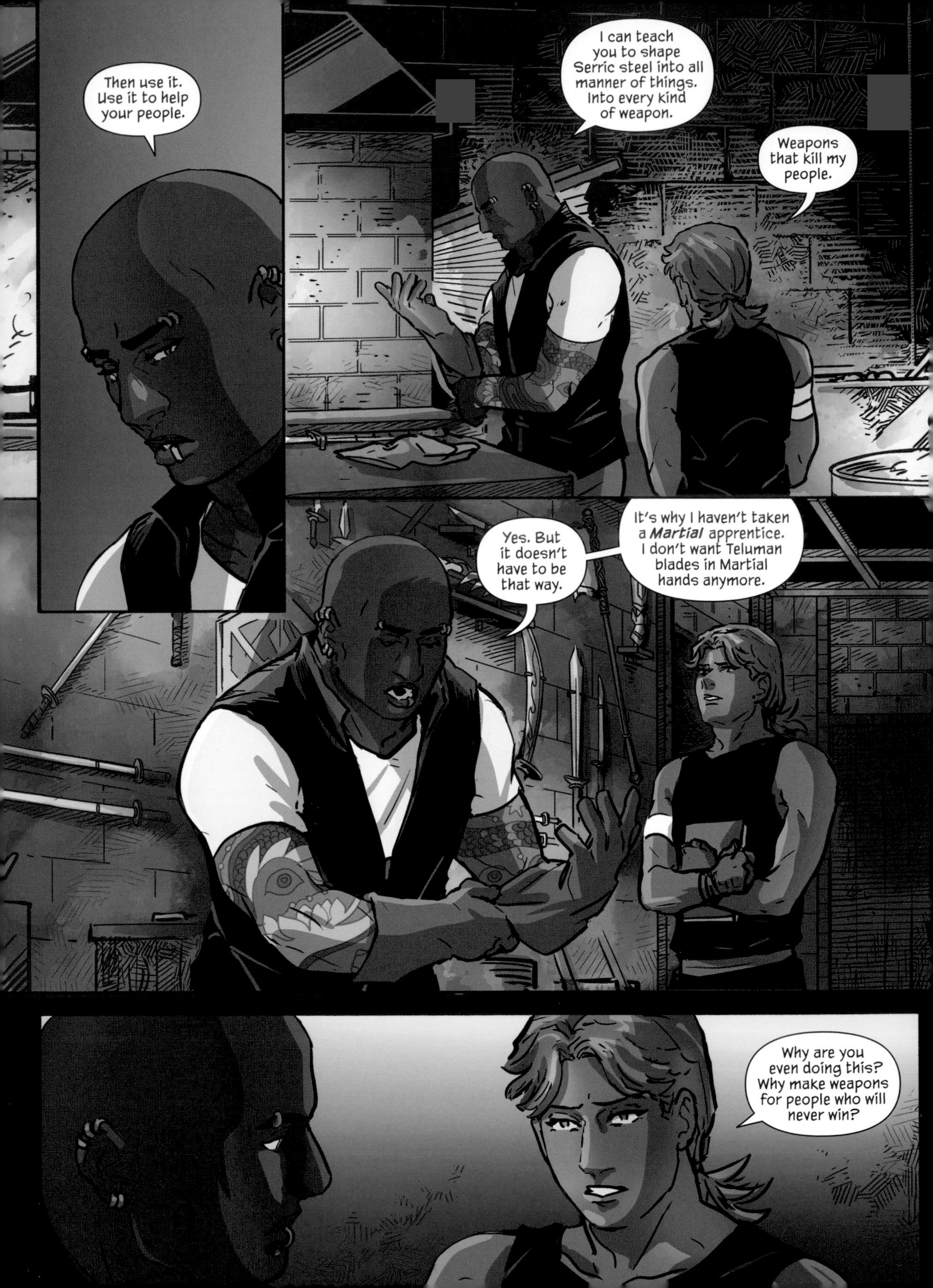
Then use it. Use it to help your people.
I can teach you to shape Serric steel into all manner of things. Into every kind of weapon.
Weapons that kill my people.
Yes. But it doesn't have to be that way.
It's why I haven't taken a *Martial* apprentice. I don't want Teluman blades in Martial hands anymore.
Why are you even doing this? Why make weapons for people who will never win?

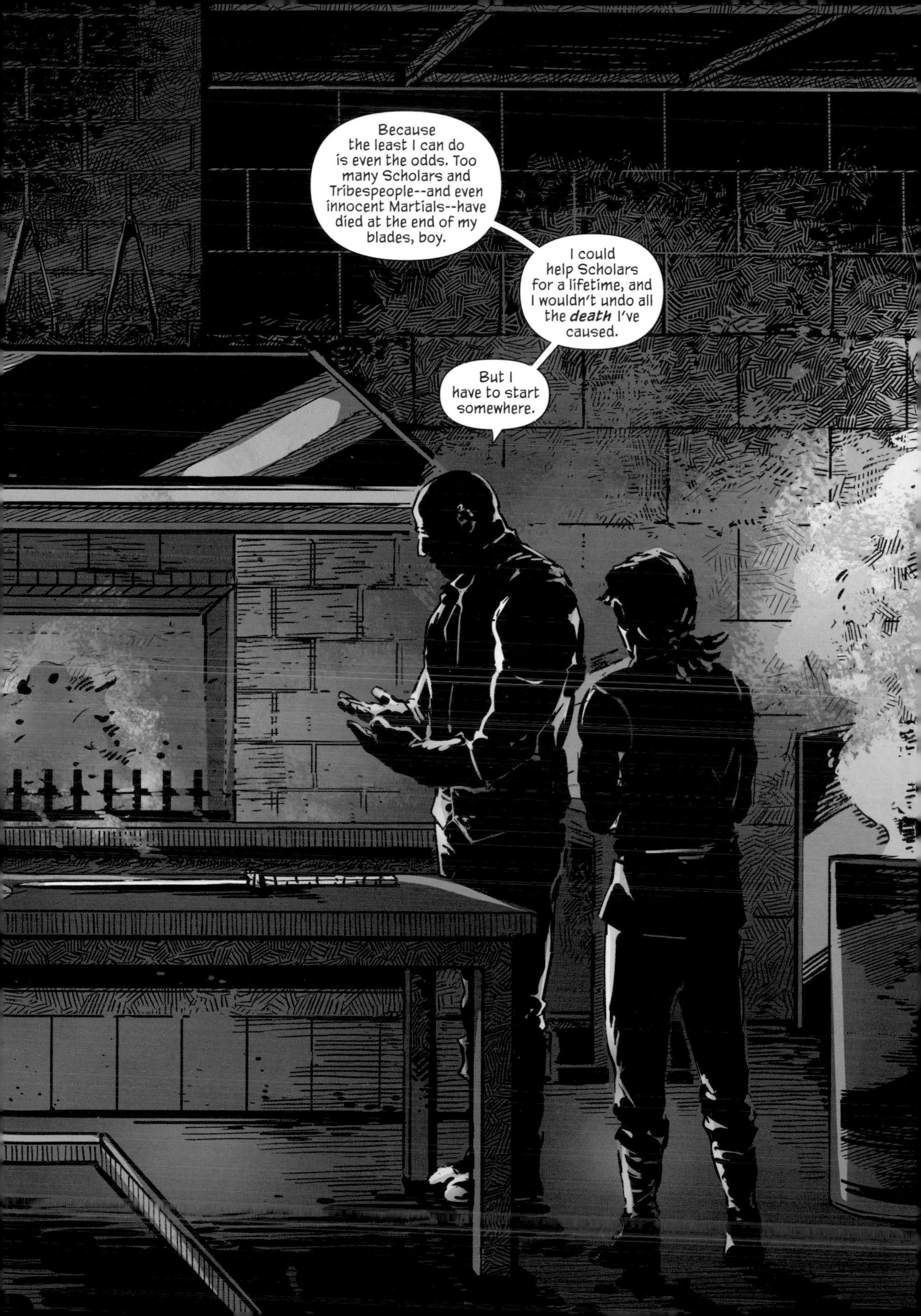
Because the least I can do is even the odds. Too many Scholars and Tribespeople--and even innocent Martials--have died at the end of my blades, boy.
I could help Scholars for a lifetime, and I wouldn't undo all the *death* I've caused.
But I have to start somewhere.

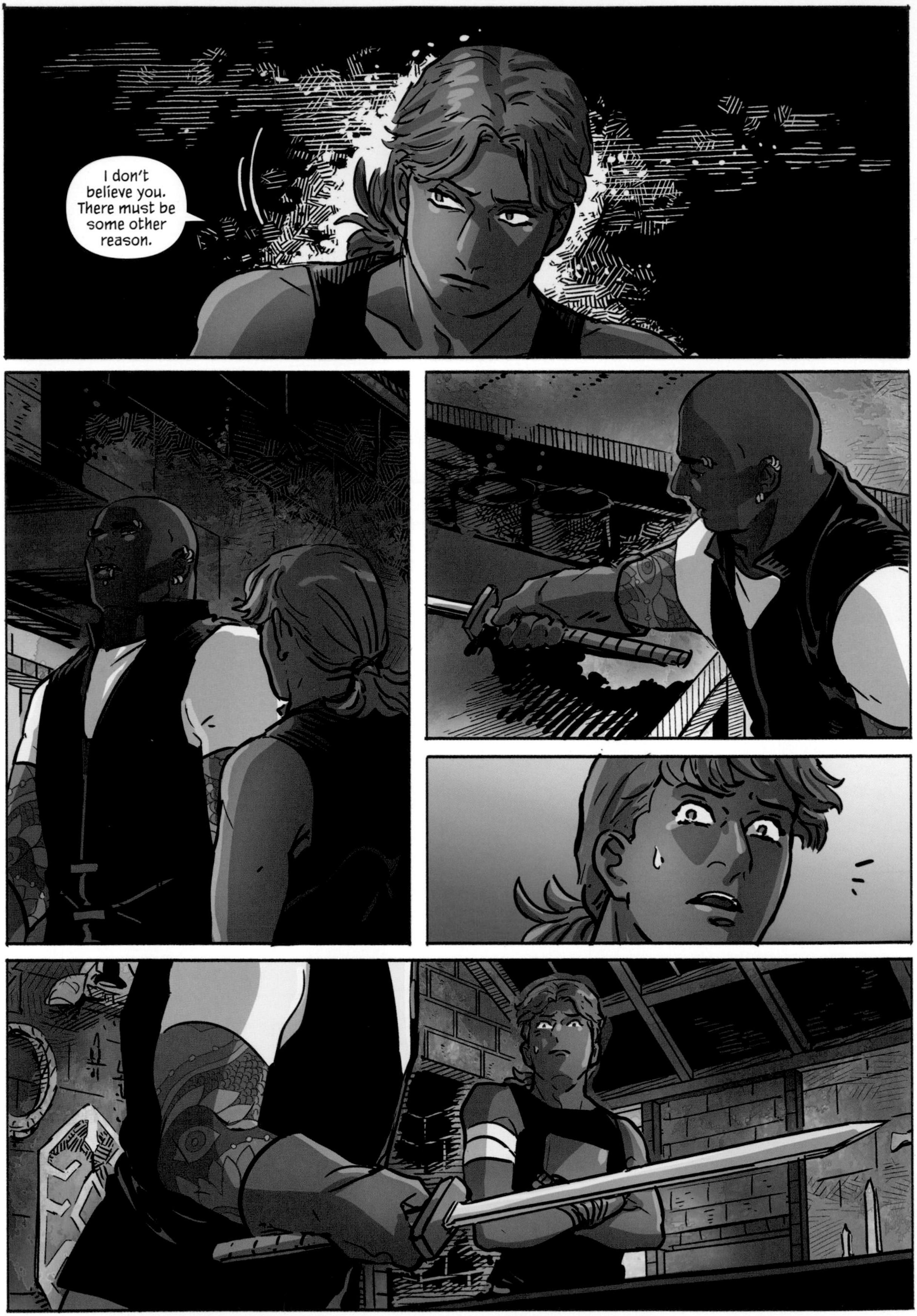
I don't believe you. There must be some other reason.

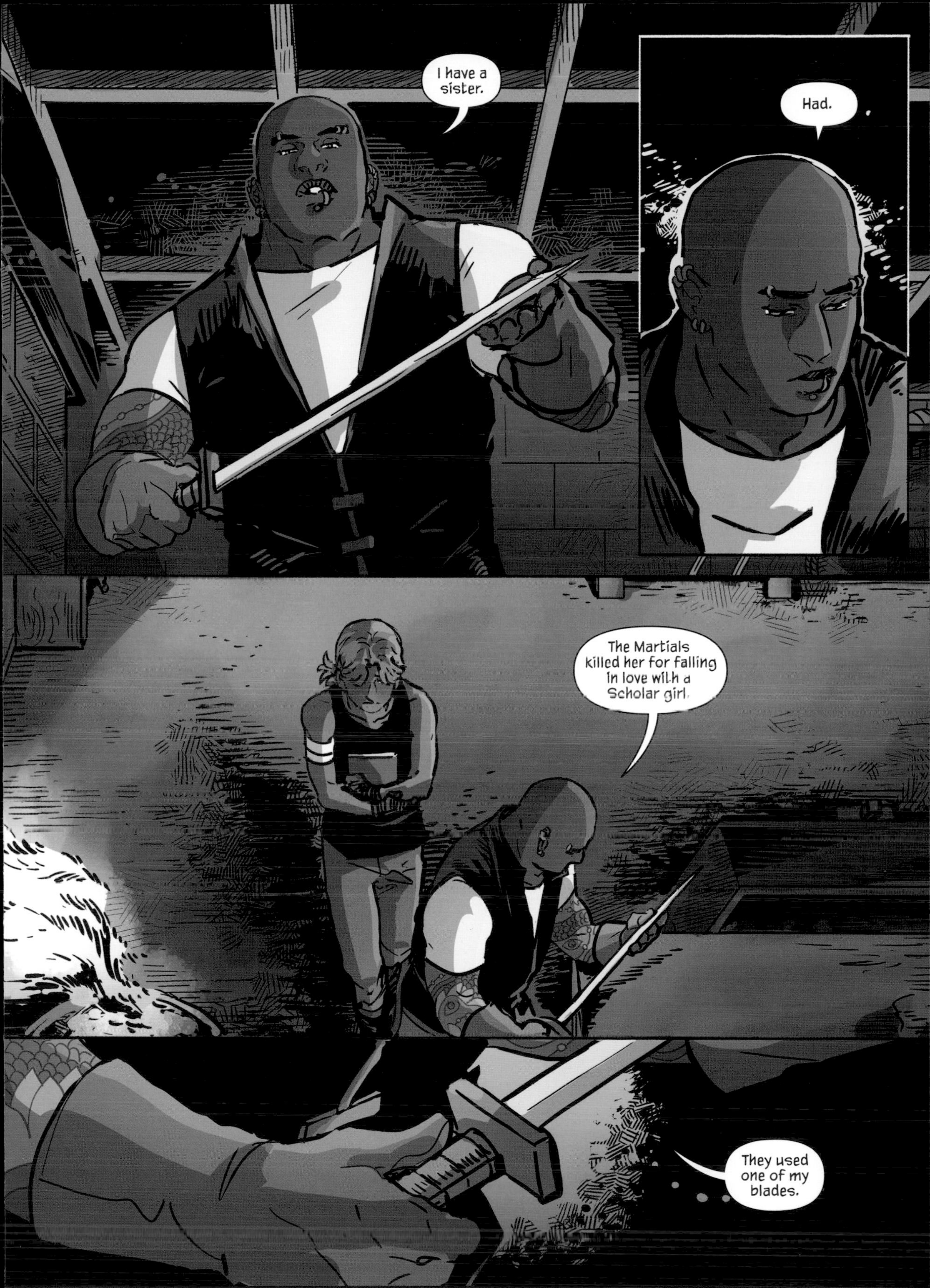
I have a sister.
Had.
The Martials killed her for falling in love with a Scholar girl.
They used one of my blades.

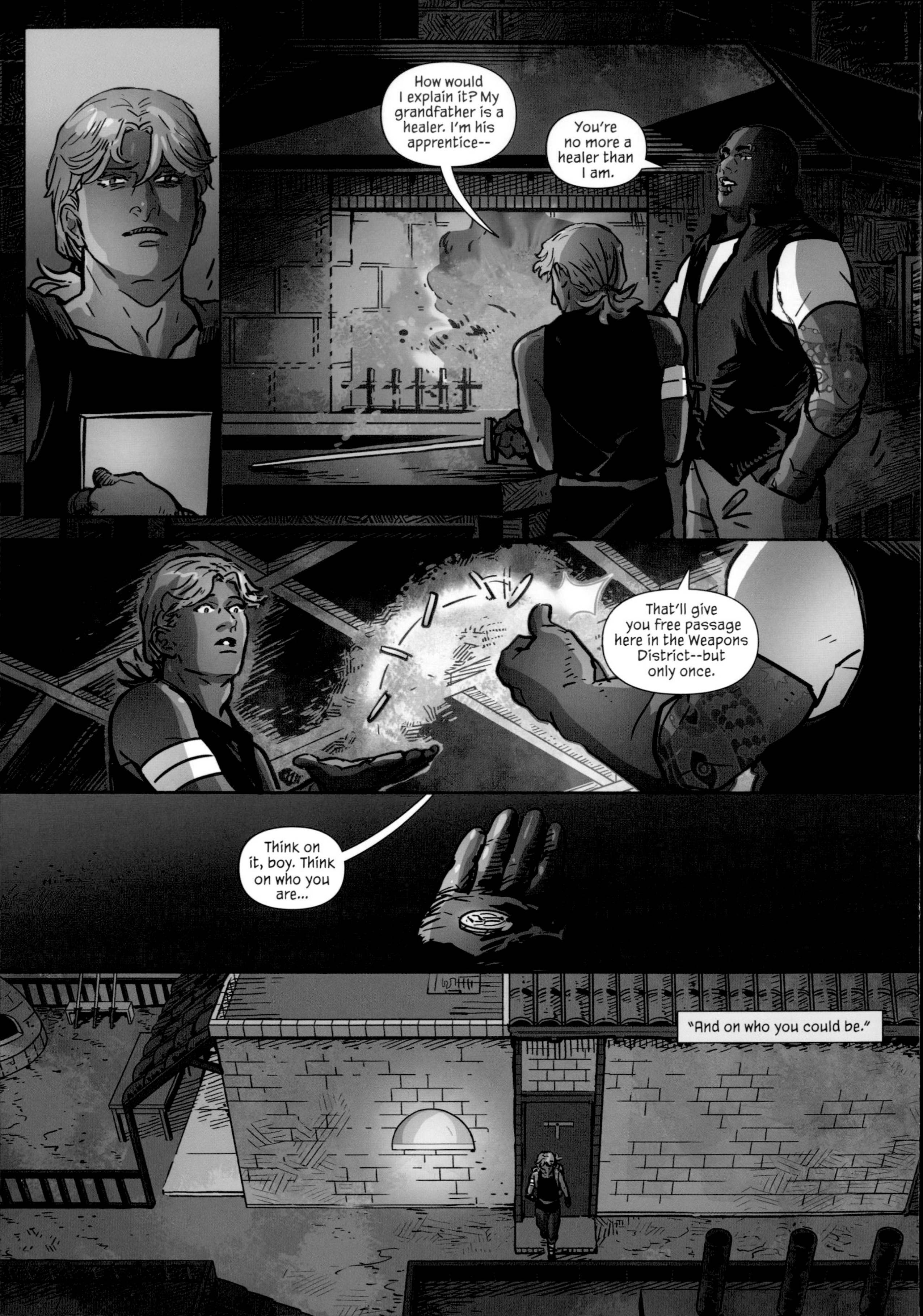
How would I explain it? My grandfather is a healer. I'm his apprentice--
You're no more a healer than I am.
That'll give you free passage here in the Weapons District--but only once.
Think on it, boy. Think on who you are...
"And on who you could be."

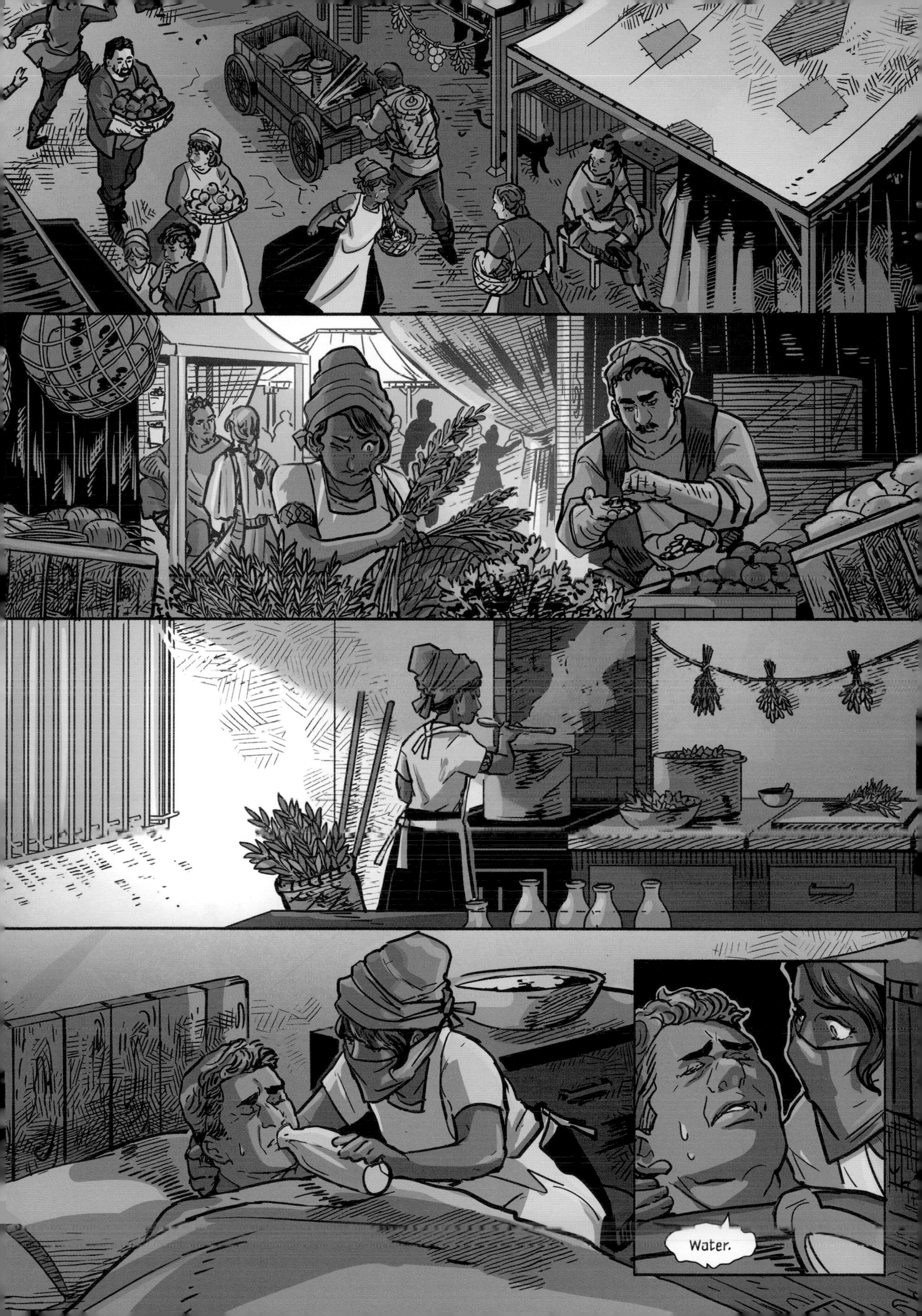
Water.

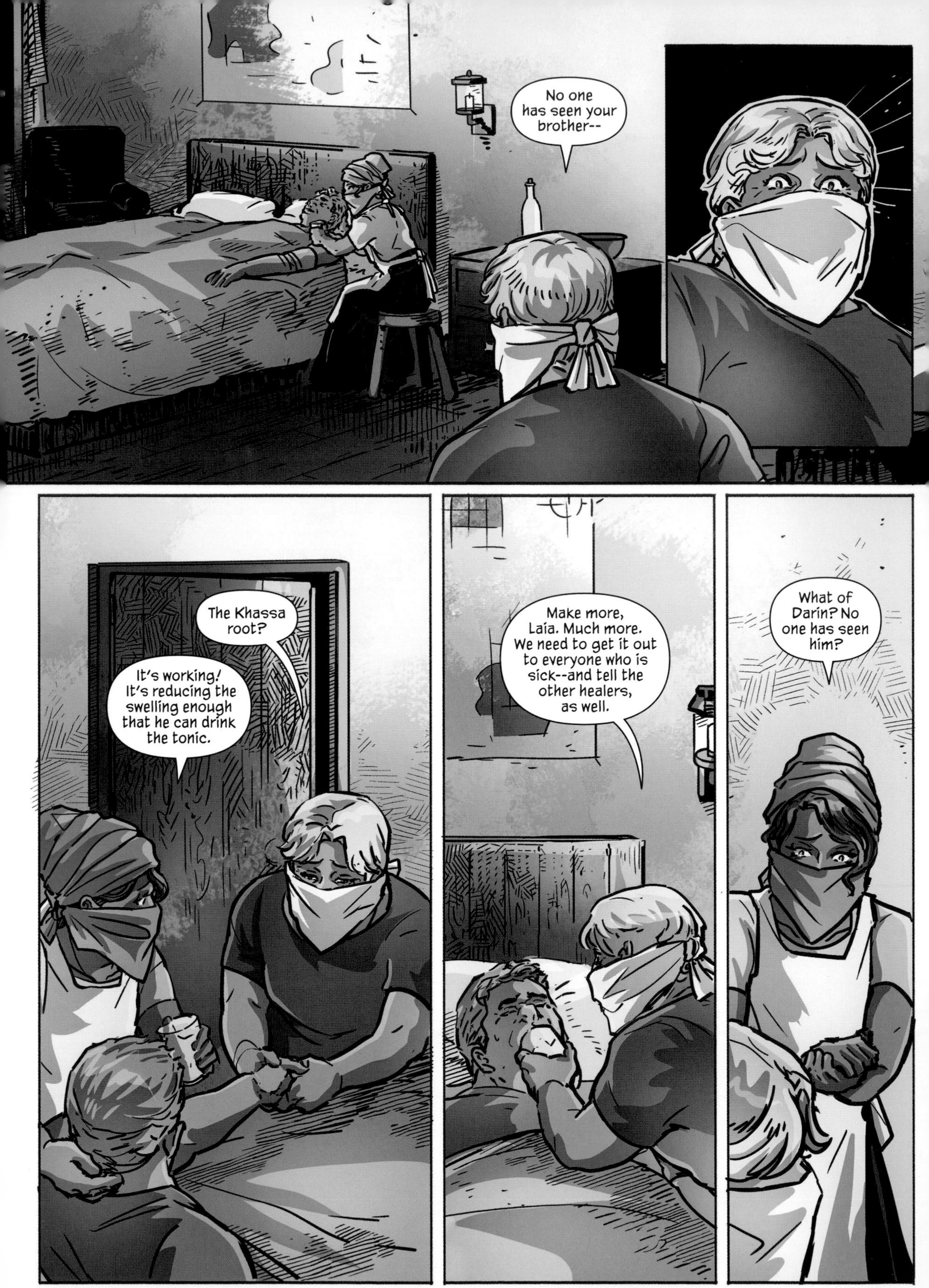
No one has seen your brother--
The Khassa root?
It's working! It's reducing the swelling enough that he can drink the tonic.
Make more, Laia. Much more. We need to get it out to everyone who is sick--and tell the other healers, as well.
What of Darin? No one has seen him?

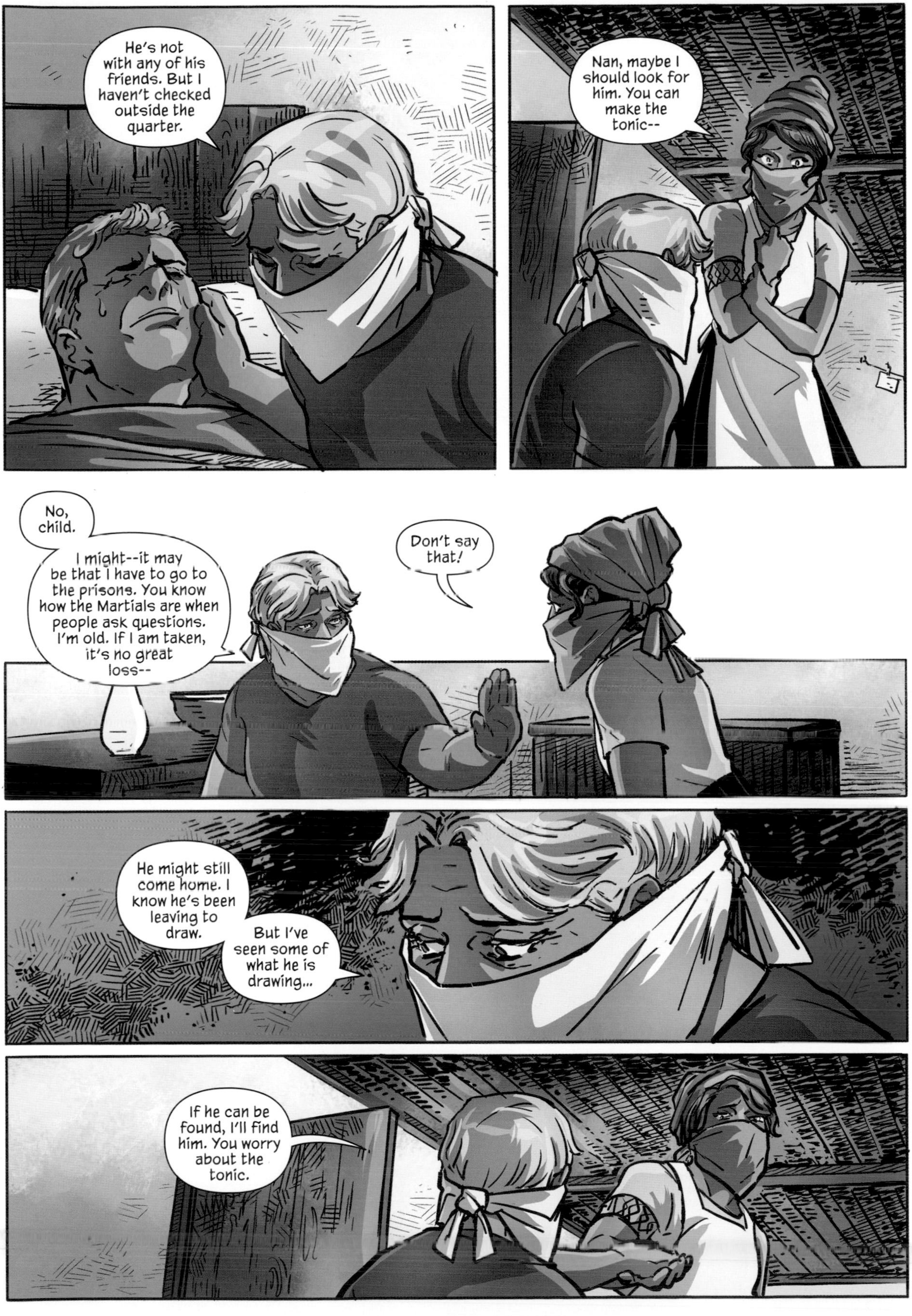
He's not with any of his friends. But I haven't checked outside the quarter.
Nan, maybe I should look for him. You can make the tonic--
No, child.
I might--it may be that I have to go to the prisons. You know how the Martials are when people ask questions. I'm old. If I am taken, it's no great loss--
Don't say that!
He might still come home. I know he's been leaving to draw.
But I've seen some of what he is drawing...
If he can be found, I'll find him. You worry about the tonic.

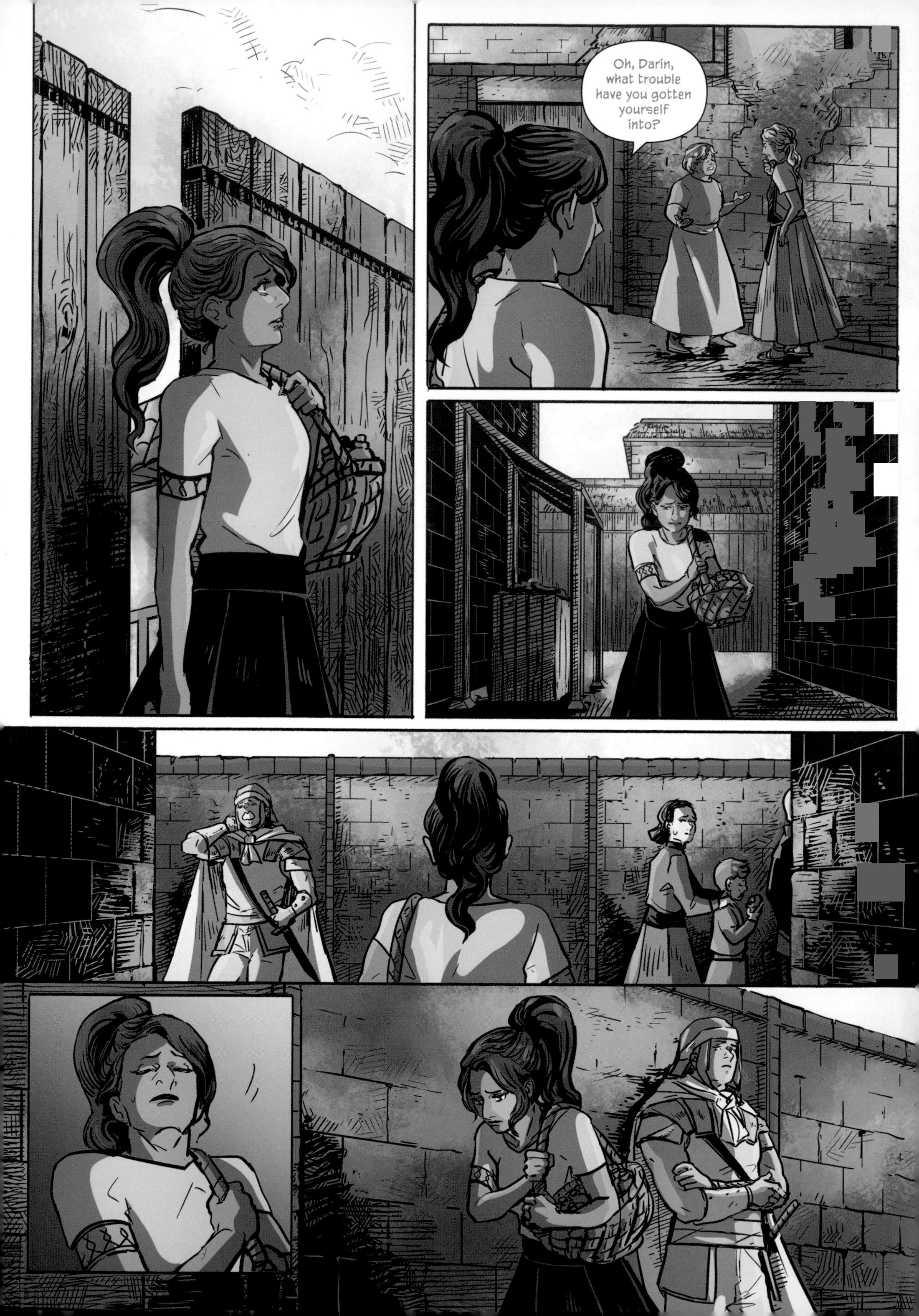
Oh, Darin, what trouble have you gotten yourself into?

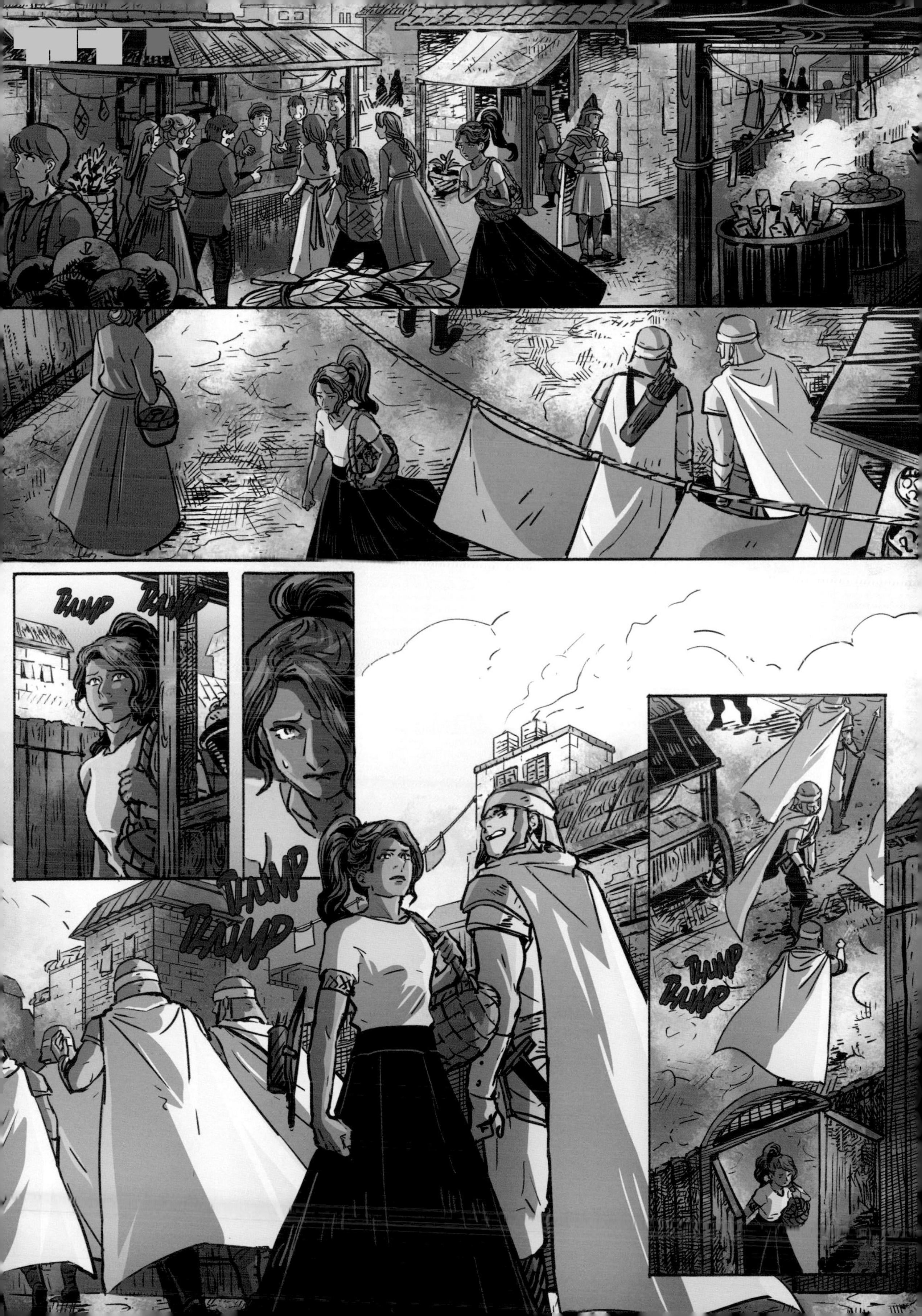
THUMP
THUMP
THUMP
THUMP
THUMP
THUMP

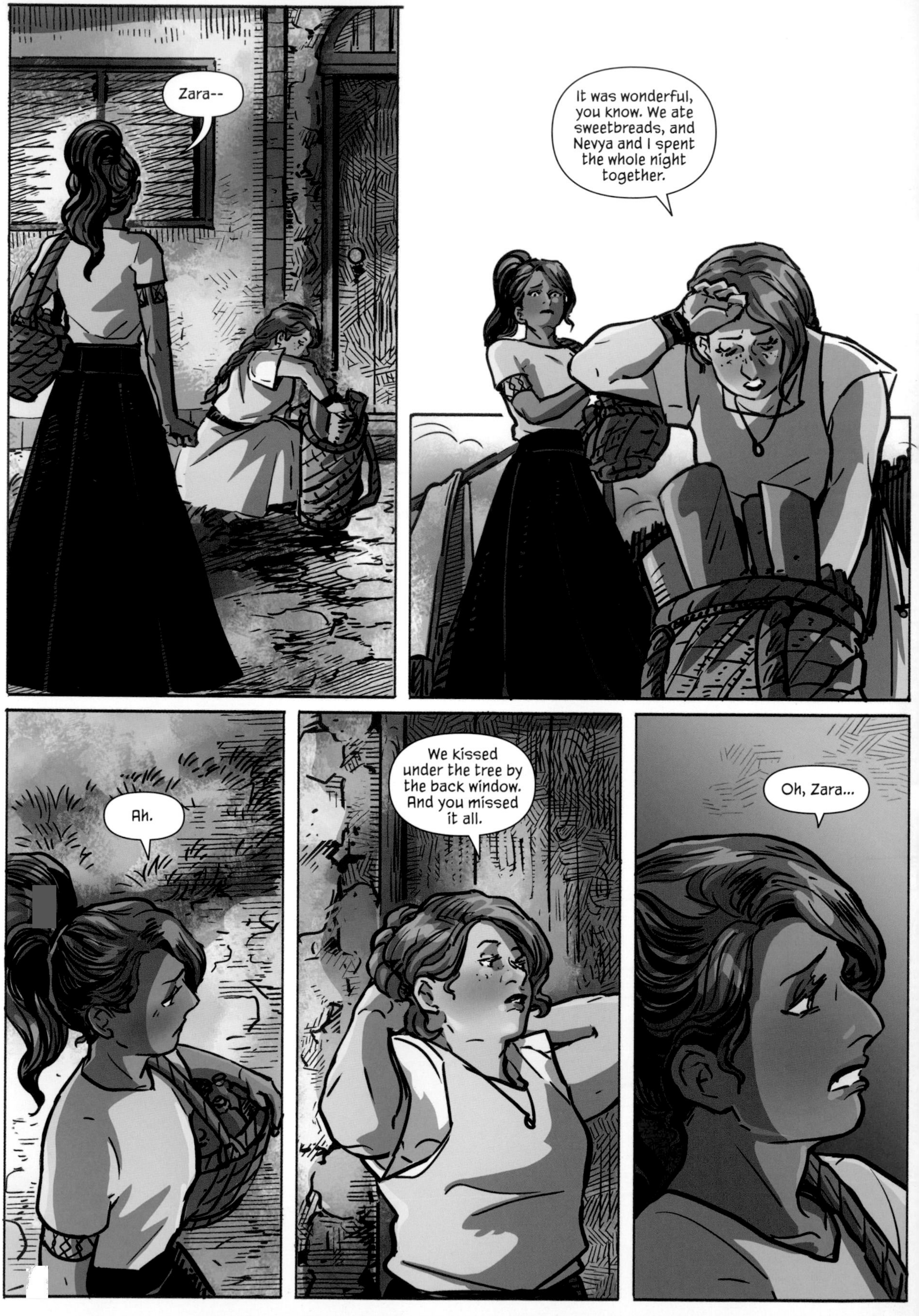
Zara--
It was wonderful, you know. We ate sweetbreads, and Nevya and I spent the whole night together.
Ah.
We kissed under the tree by the back window. And you missed it all.
Oh, Zara...

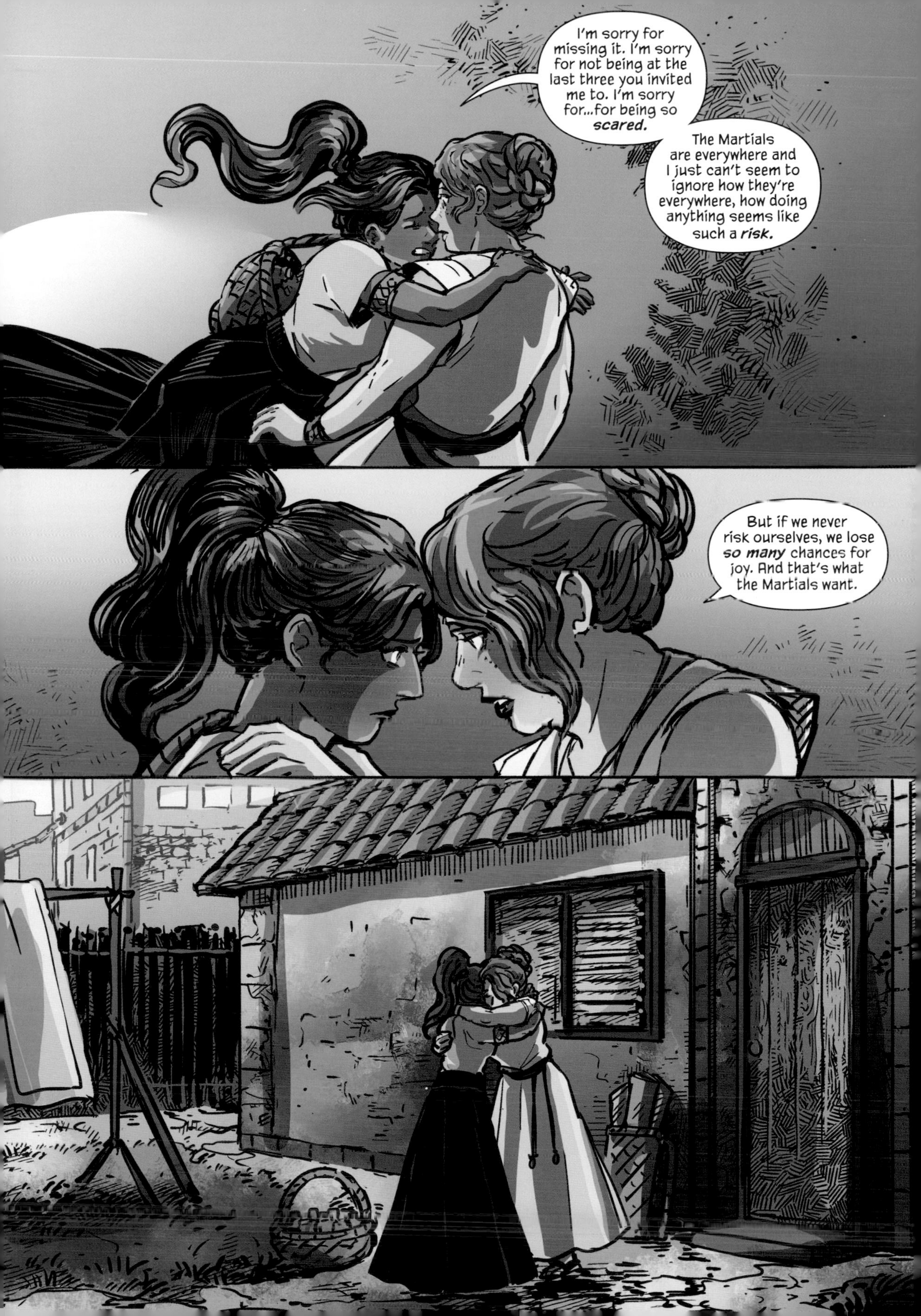
I'm sorry for missing it. I'm sorry for not being at the last three you invited me to. I'm sorry for...for being so *scared.*
The Martials are everywhere and I just can't seem to ignore how they're everywhere, how doing anything seems like such a *risk.*
But if we never risk ourselves, we lose *so many* chances for joy. And that's what the Martials want.

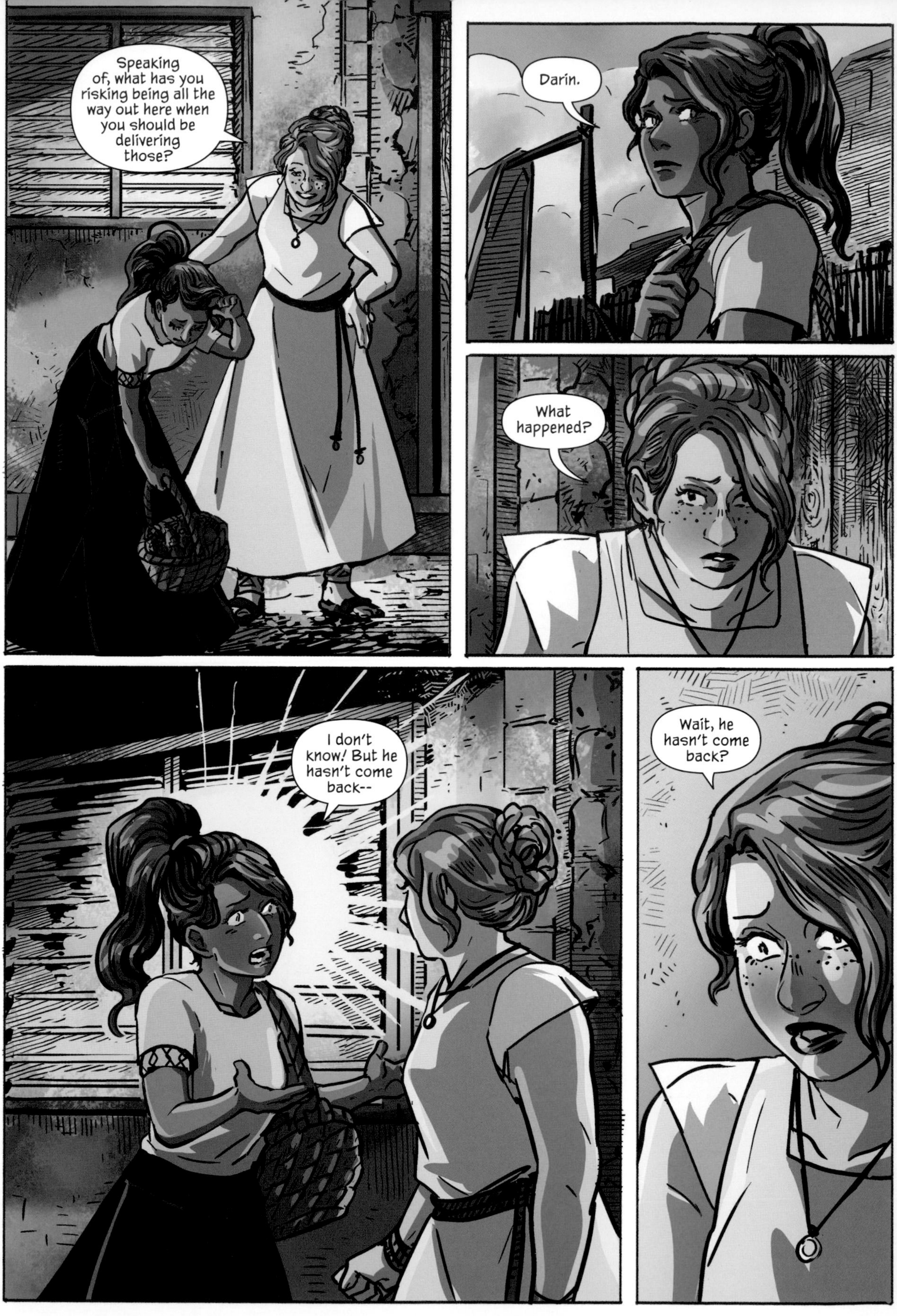
Speaking of, what has you risking being all the way out here when you should be delivering those?
Darin.
What happened?
I don't know! But he hasn't come back--
Wait, he hasn't come back?

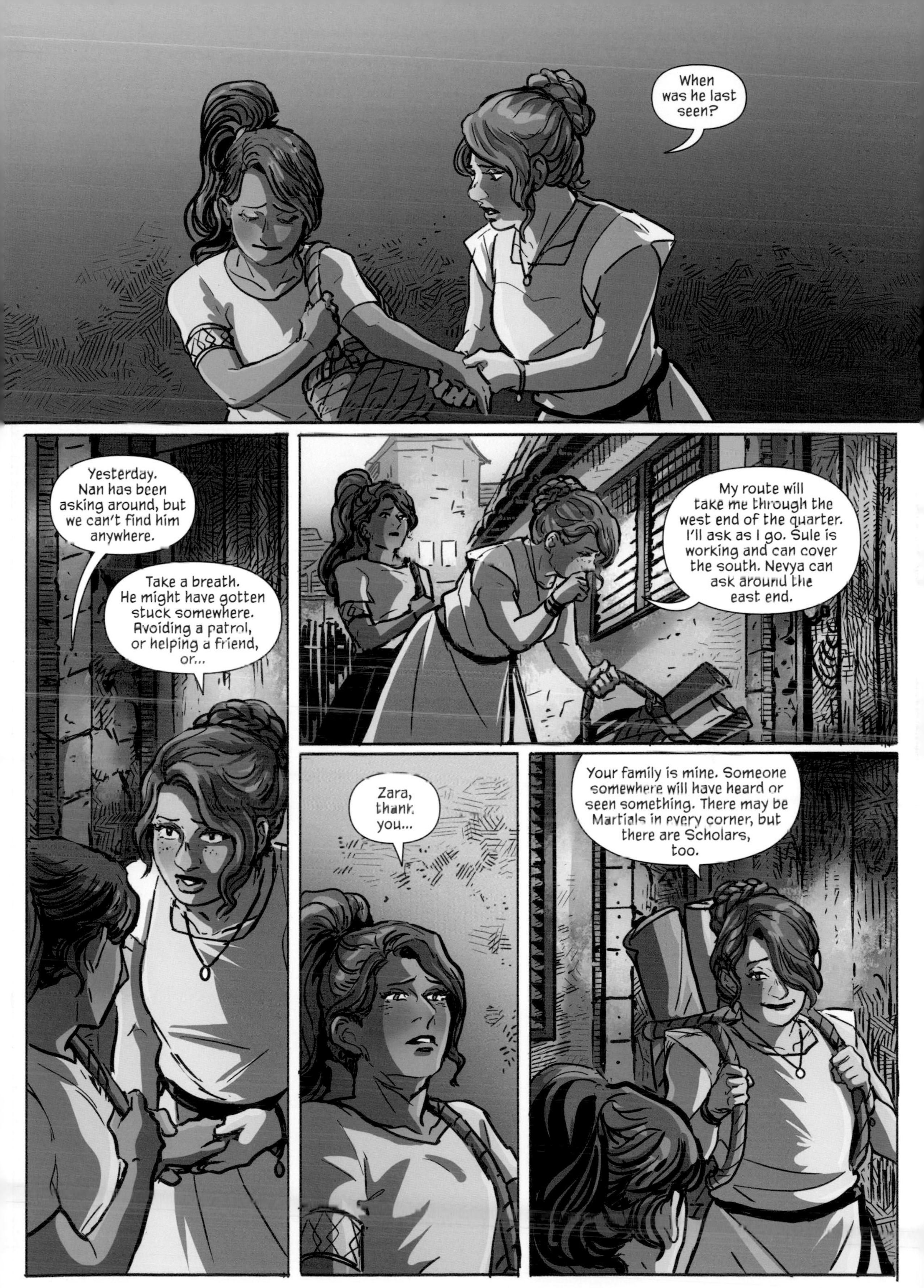
When was he last seen?
Yesterday. Nan has been asking around, but we can't find him anywhere.
Take a breath. He might have gotten stuck somewhere. Avoiding a patrol, or helping a friend, or...
My route will take me through the west end of the quarter. I'll ask as I go. Sule is working and can cover the south. Nevya can ask around the east end.
Zara, thank you...
Your family is mine. Someone somewhere will have heard or seen something. There may be Martials in every corner, but there are Scholars, too.

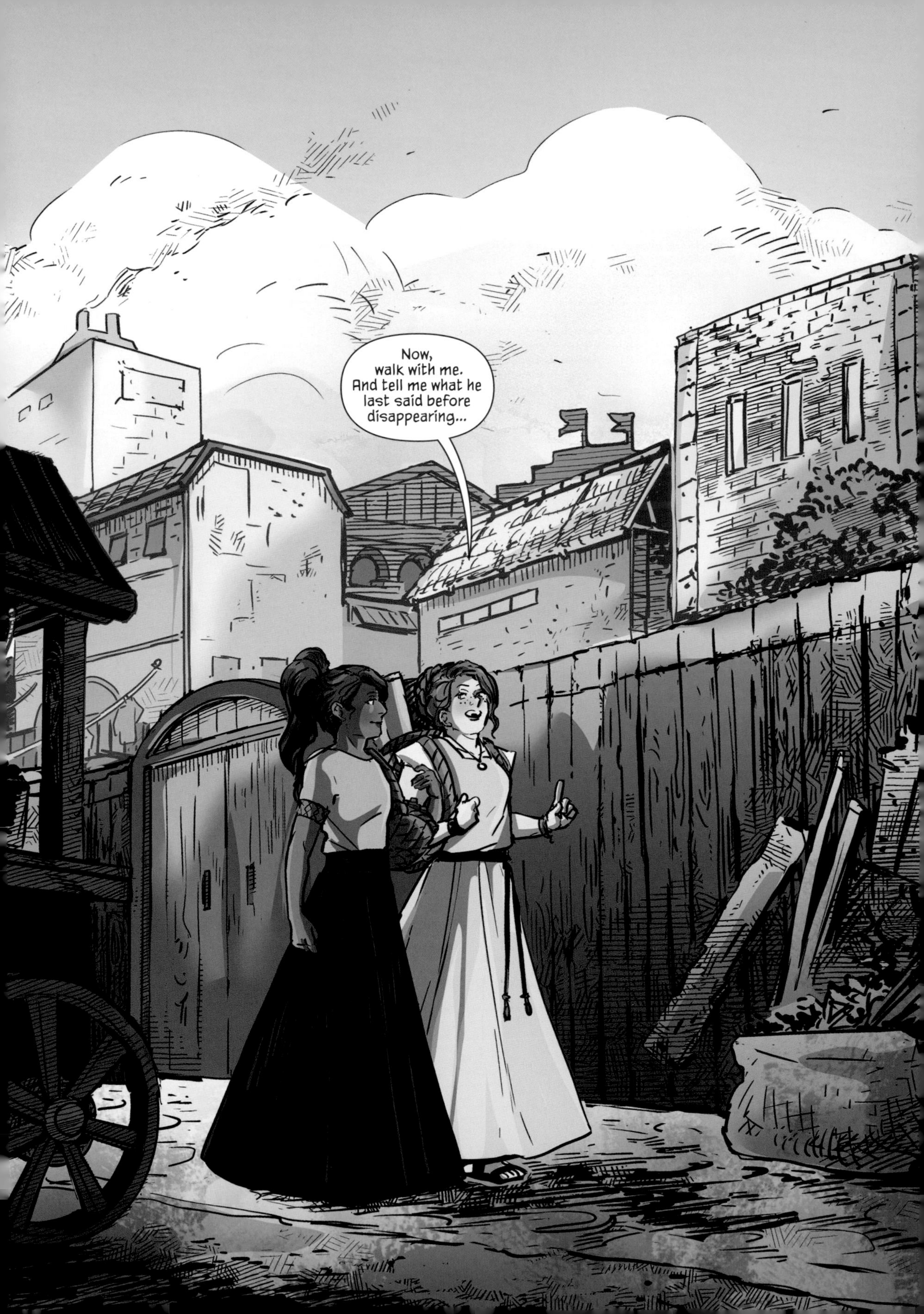
Now, walk with me. And tell me what he last said before disappearing...

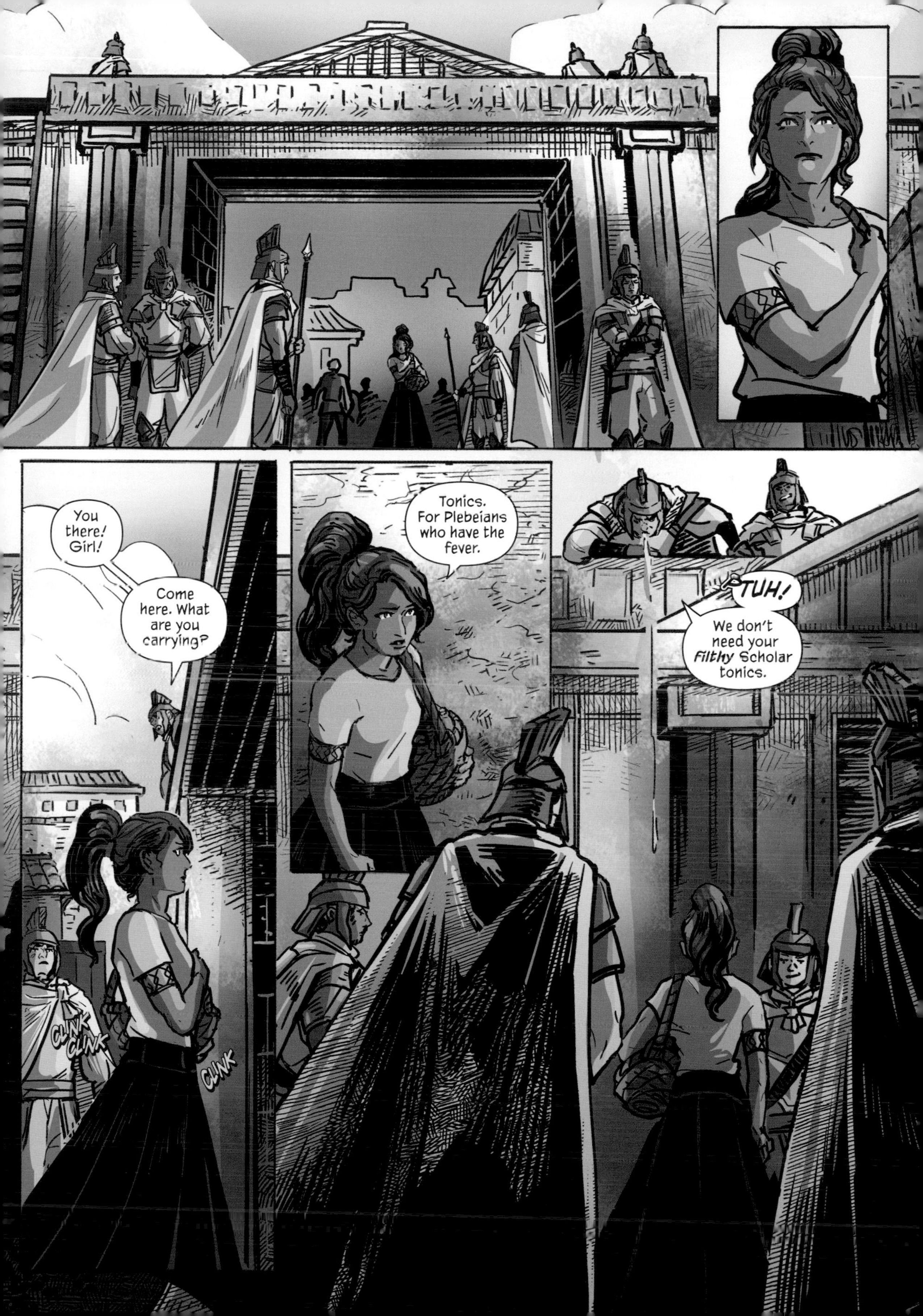
You there! Girl!
Come here. What are you carrying?
Tonics. For Plebeians who have the fever.
TUH!
We don't need your *Filthy* Scholar tonics.
CLINK CLINK
CLINK

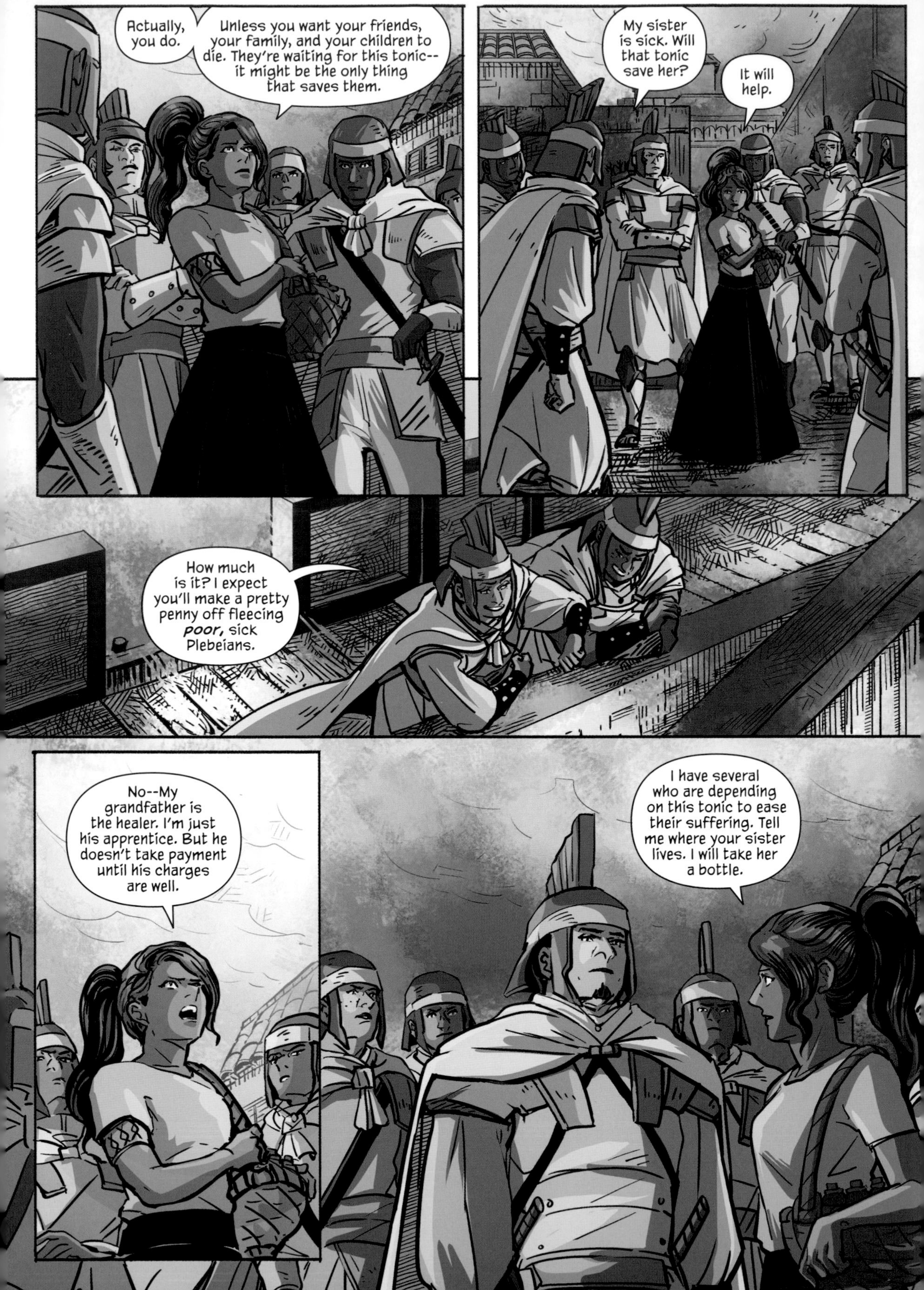
Actually, you do.
Unless you want your friends, your family, and your children to die. They're waiting for this tonic-- it might be the only thing that saves them.
My sister is sick. Will that tonic save her?
It will help.
How much is it? I expect you'll make a pretty penny off fleecing *poor,* sick Plebeians.
No--My grandfather is the healer. I'm just his apprentice. But he doesn't take payment until his charges are well.
I have several who are depending on this tonic to ease their suffering. Tell me where your sister lives. I will take her a bottle.

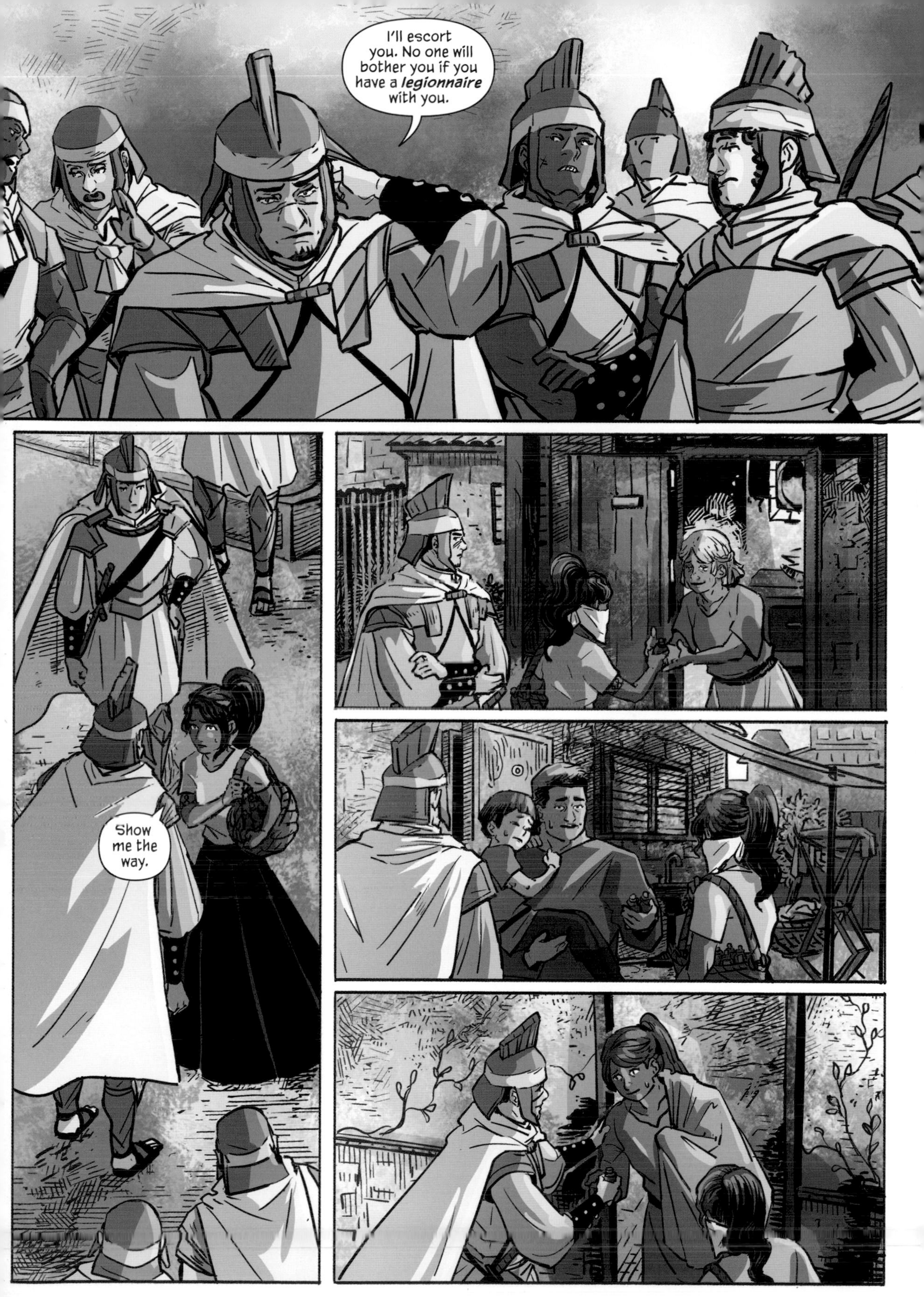
I'll escort you. No one will bother you if you have a *legionnaire* with you.
Show me the way.

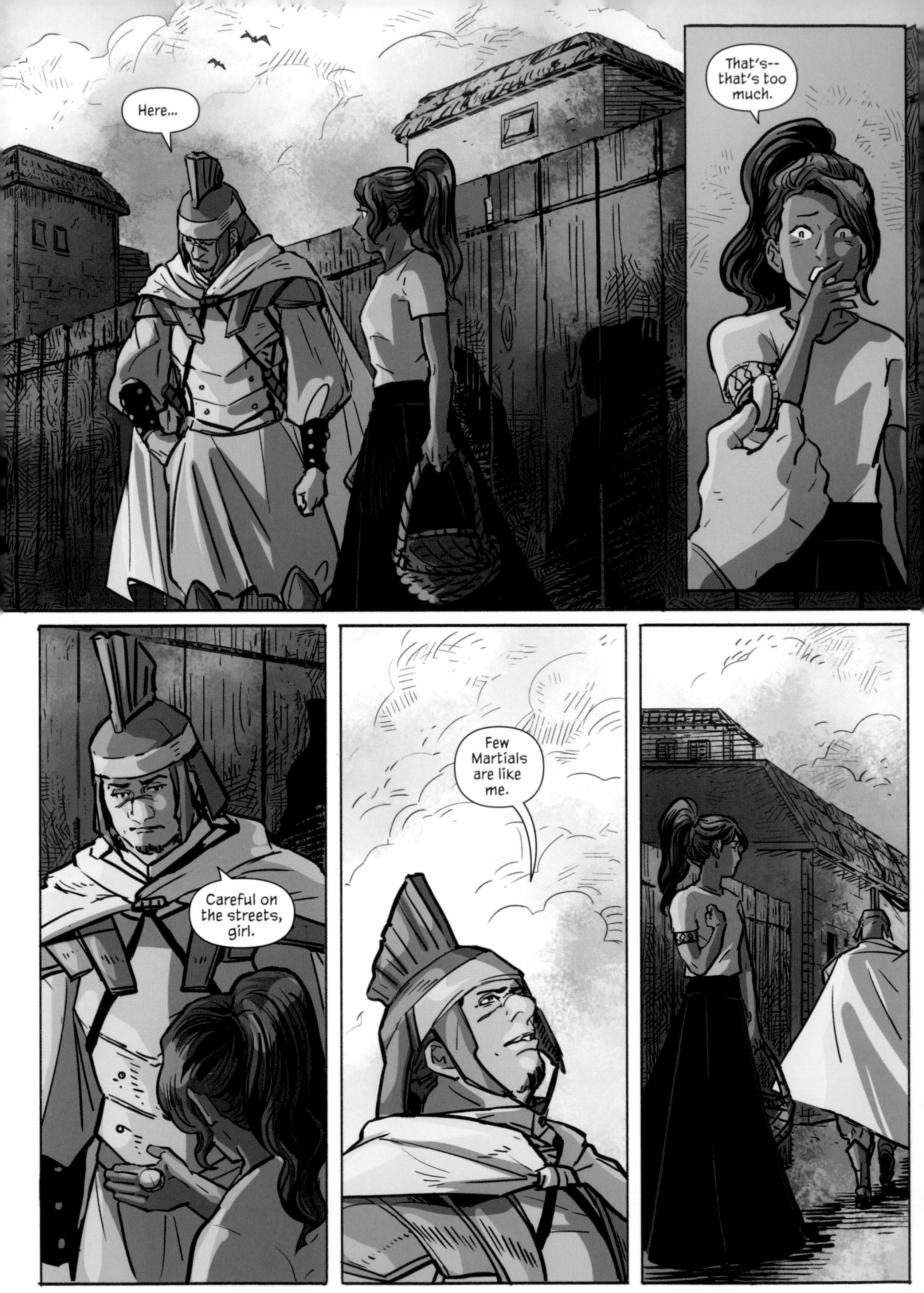
Here...
That's--
that's too
much.
Careful on
the streets,
girl.
Few
Martials
are like
me.

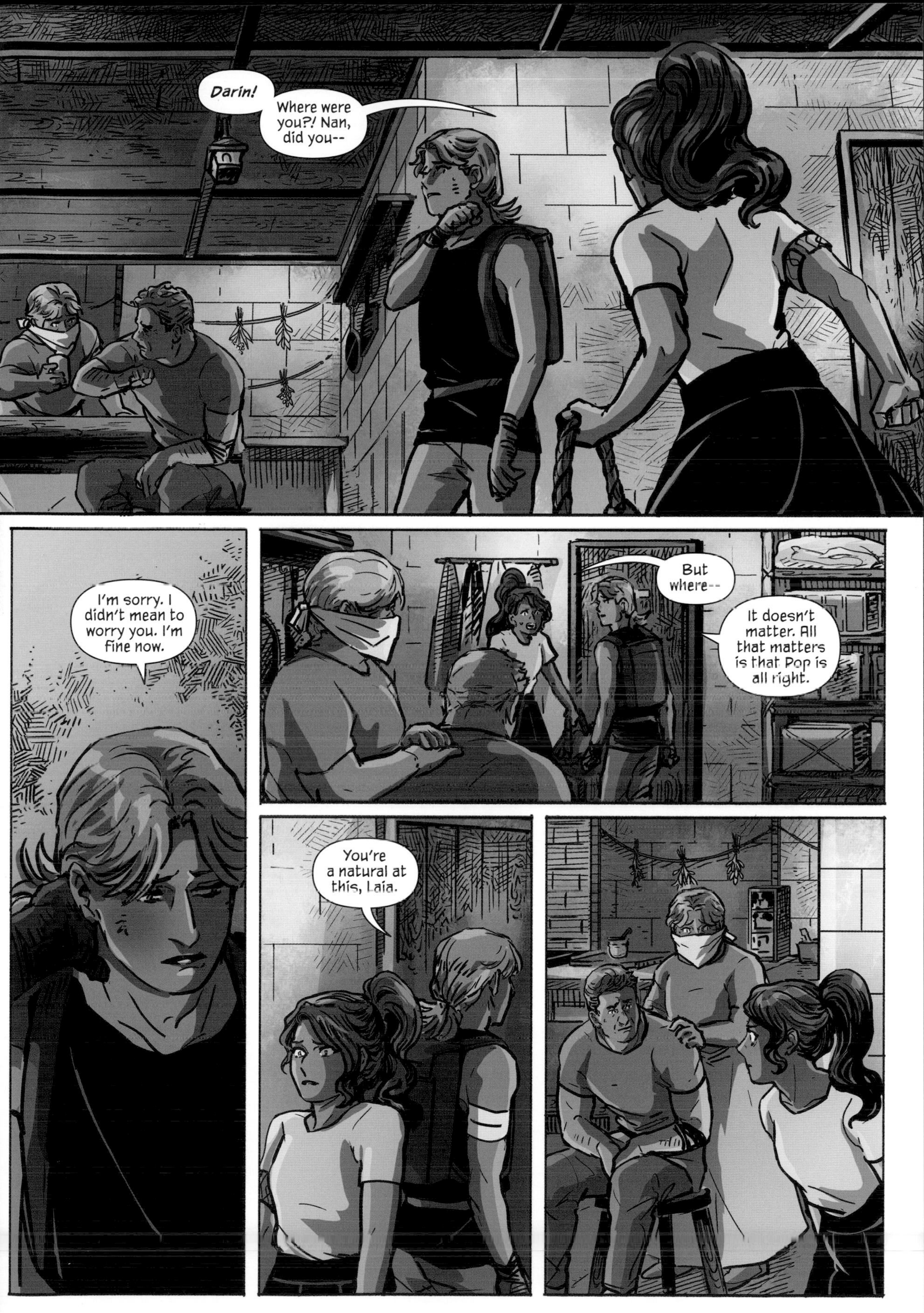
Darin!
Where were you?! Nan, did you--
I'm sorry. I didn't mean to worry you. I'm fine now.
But where--
It doesn't matter. All that matters is that Pop is all right.
You're a natural at this, Laia.

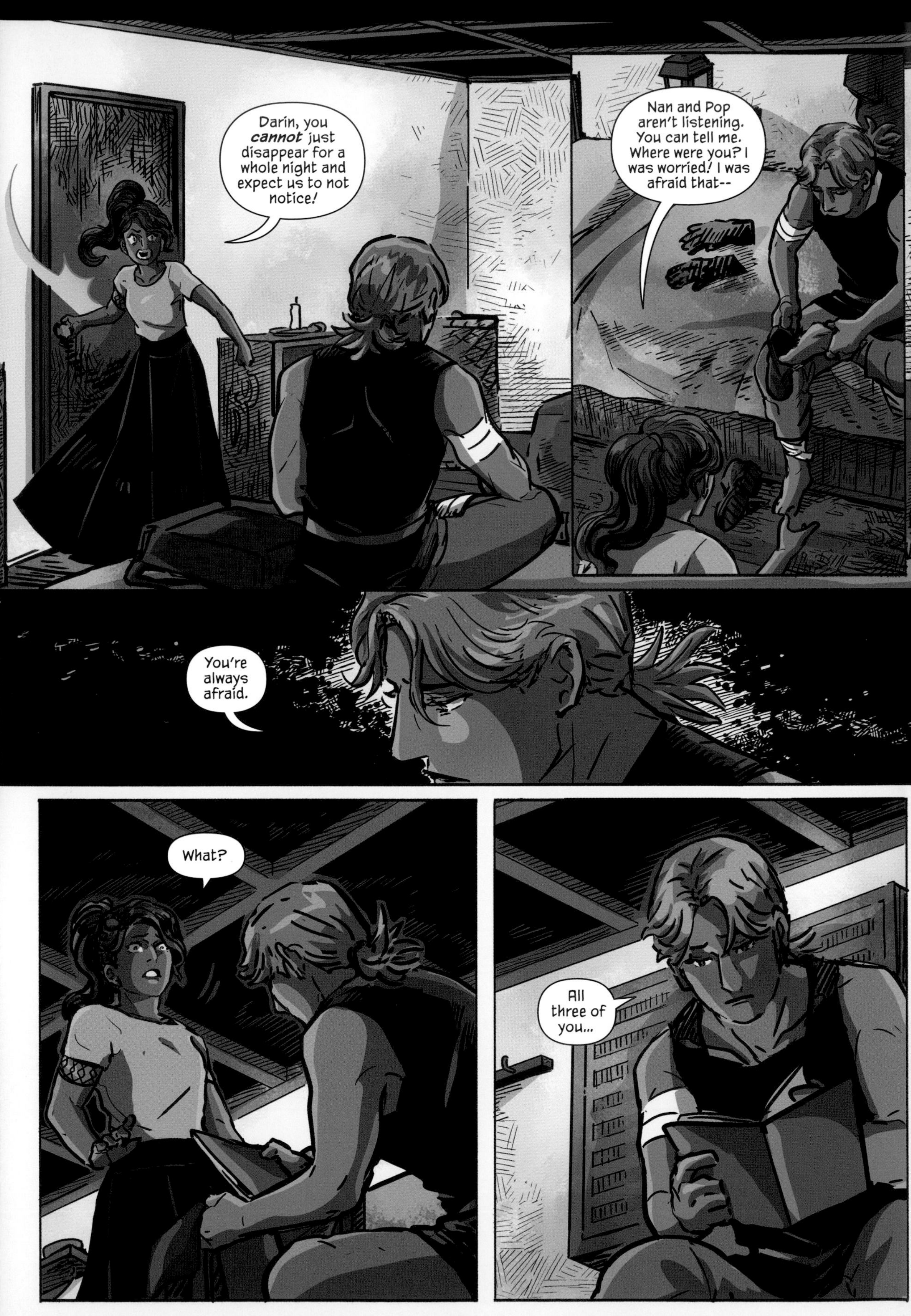
Darin, you **cannot** just disappear for a whole night and expect us to not notice!
Nan and Pop aren't listening. You can tell me. Where were you? I was worried! I was afraid that--
You're always afraid.
What?
All three of you...

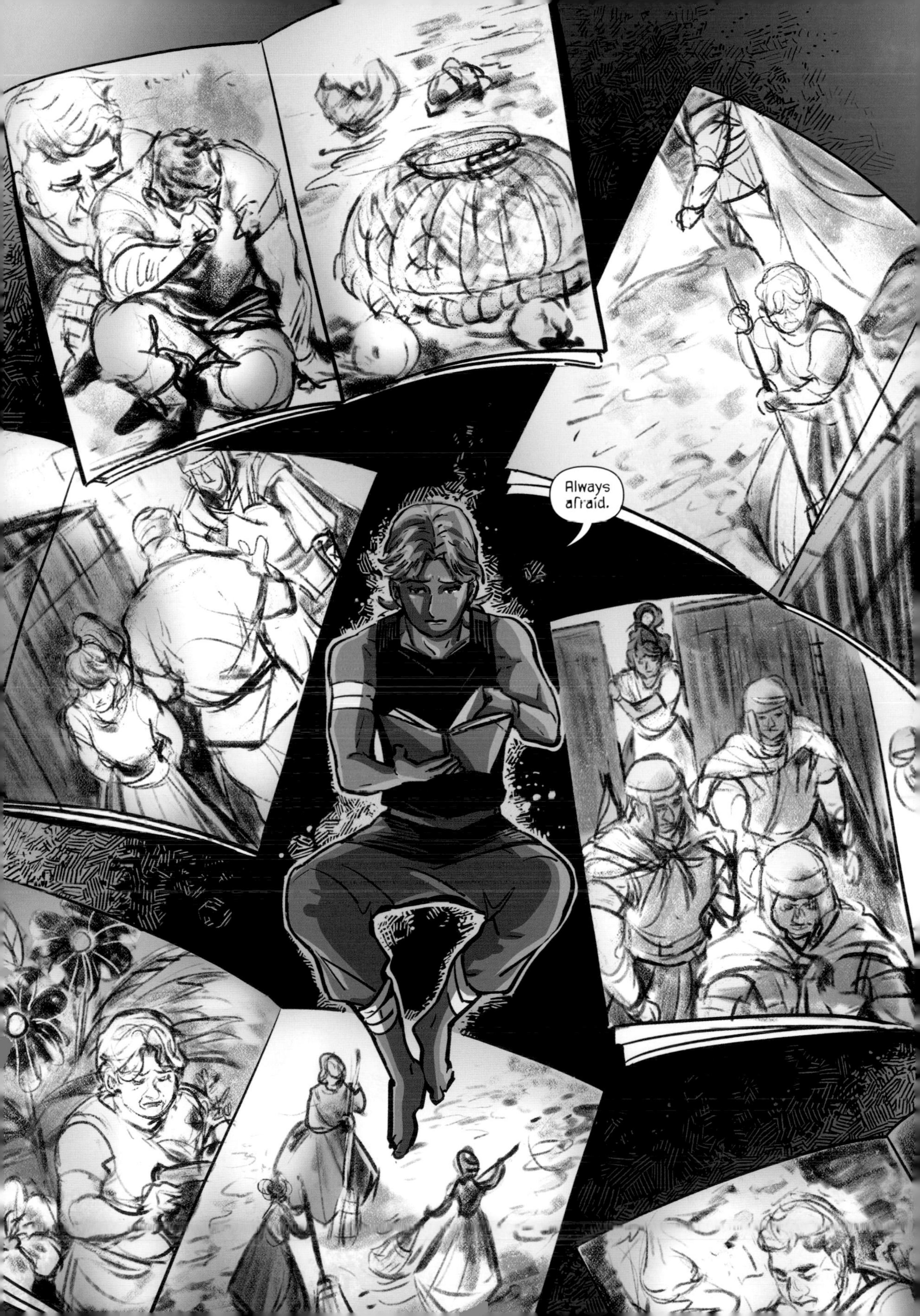
Always afraid.

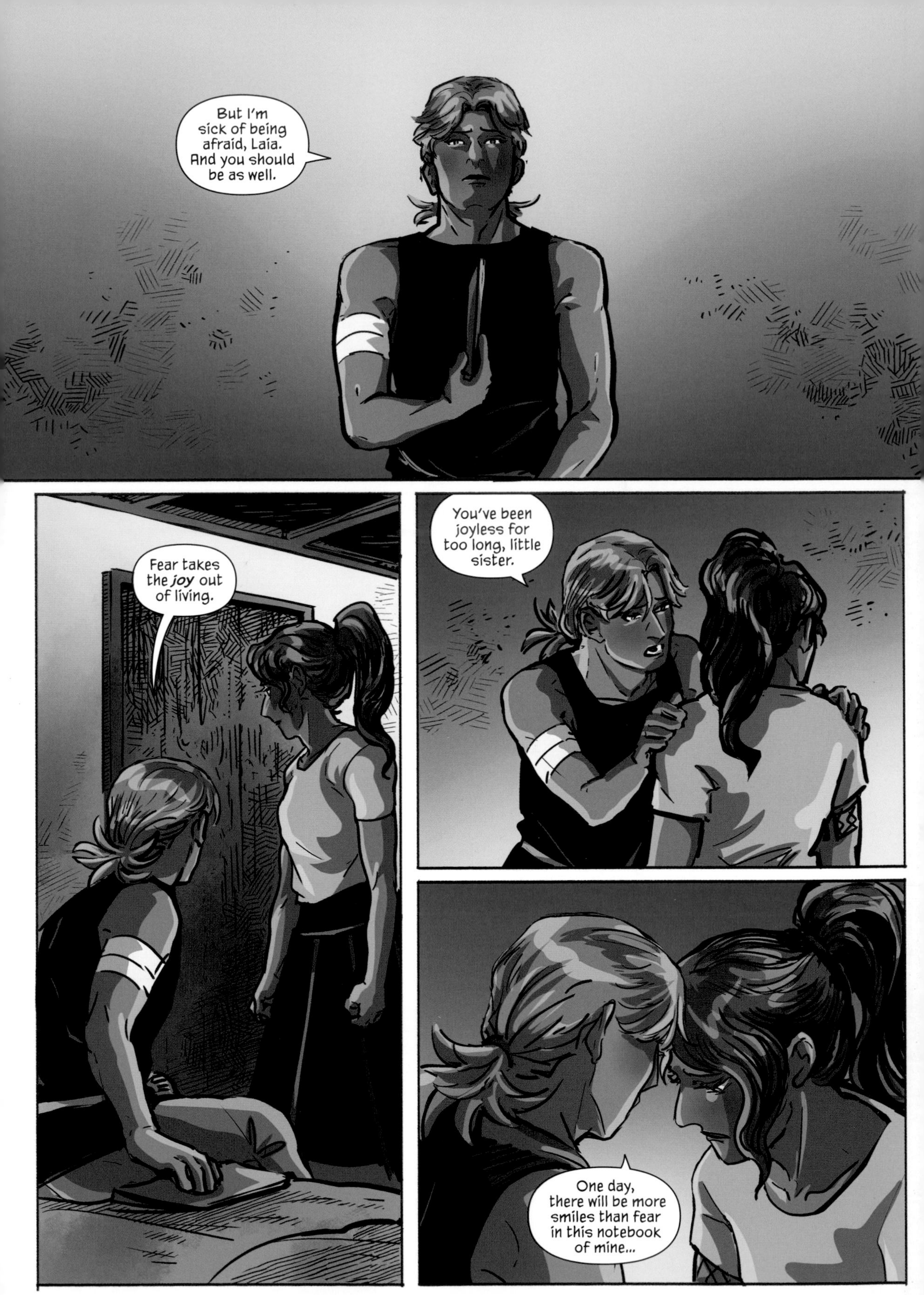
But I'm sick of being afraid, Laia. And you should be as well.
Fear takes the *joy* out of living.
You've been joyless for too long, little sister.
One day, there will be more smiles than fear in this notebook of mine...

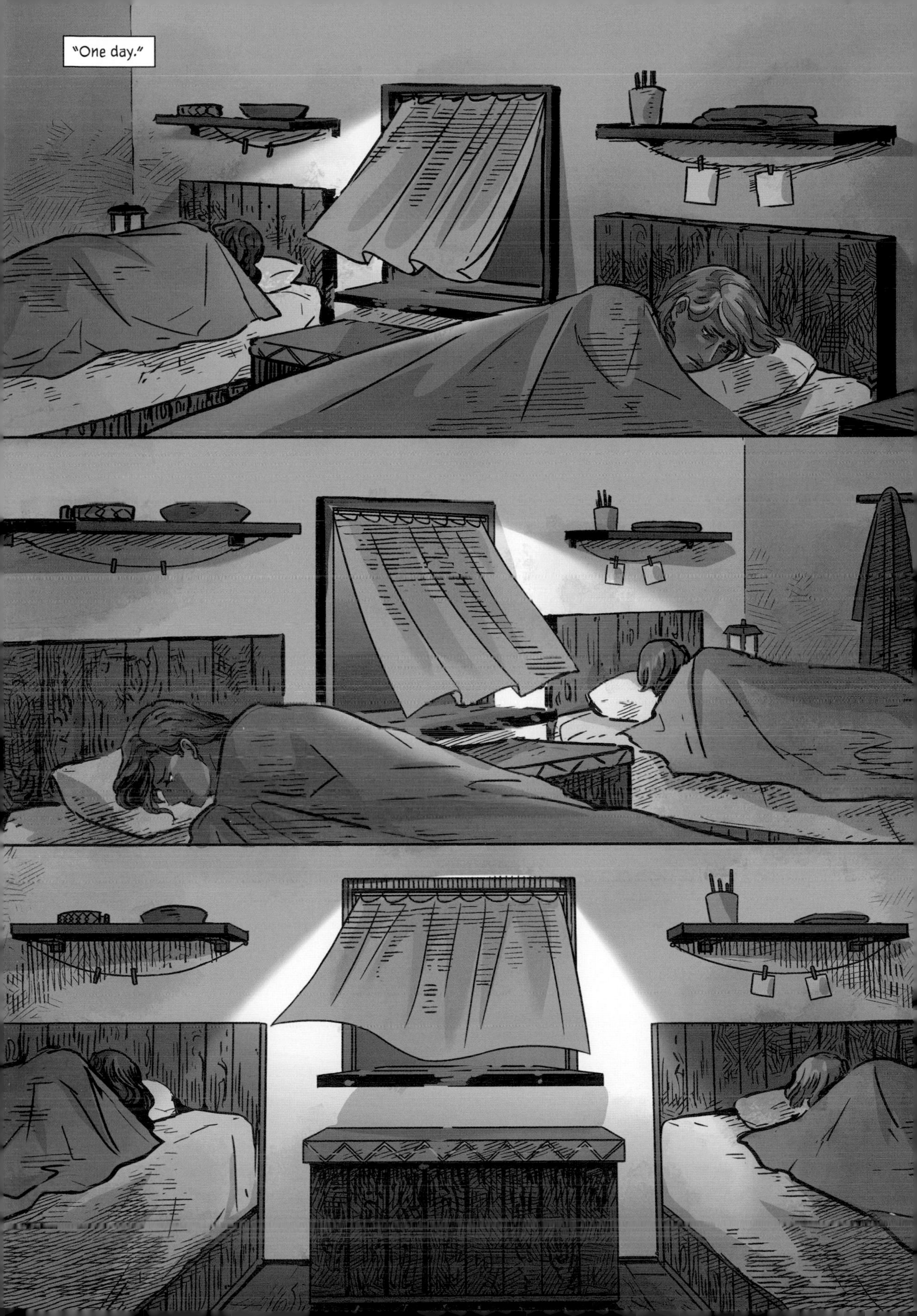
"One day."

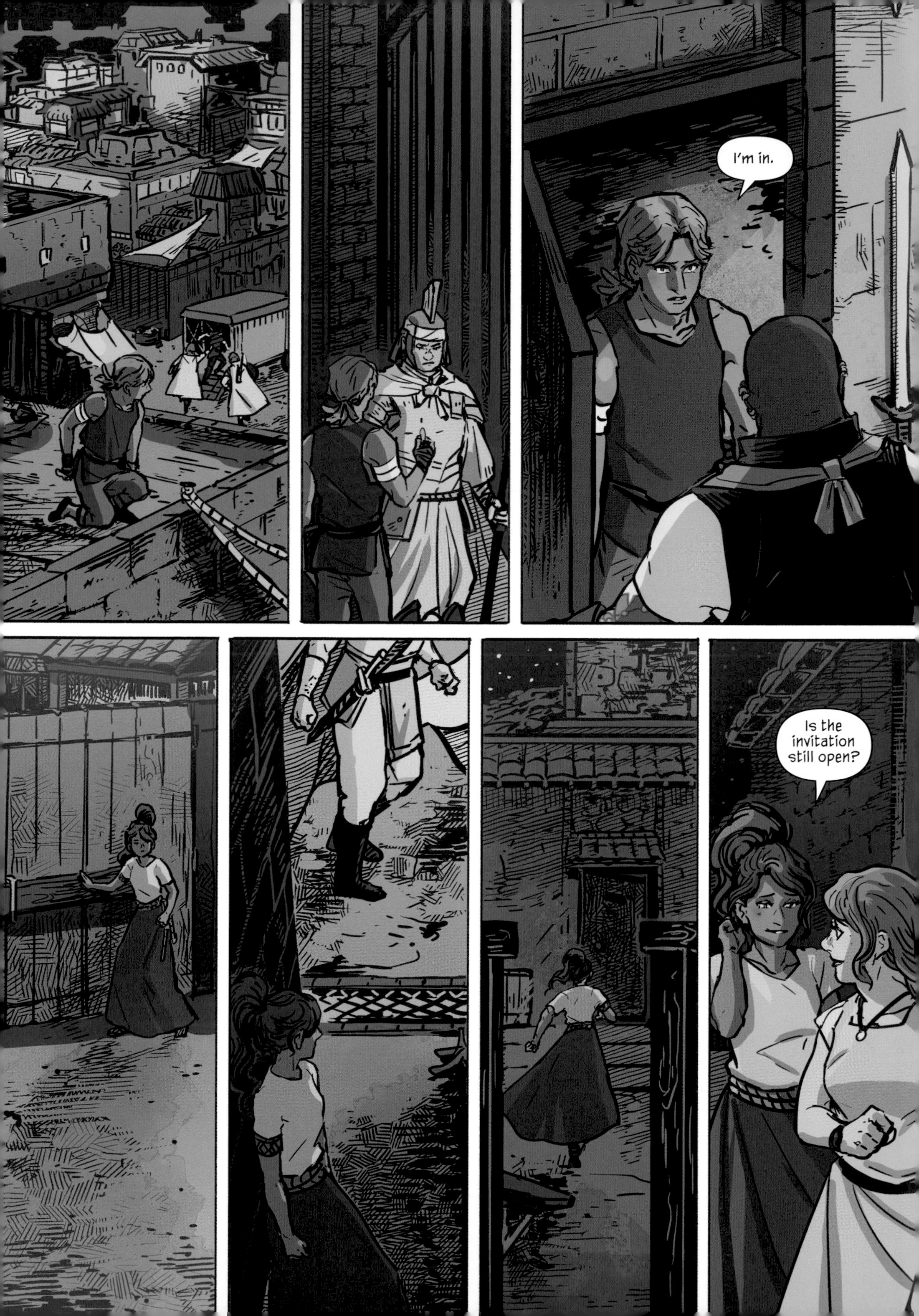
I'm in.
Is the invitation still open?

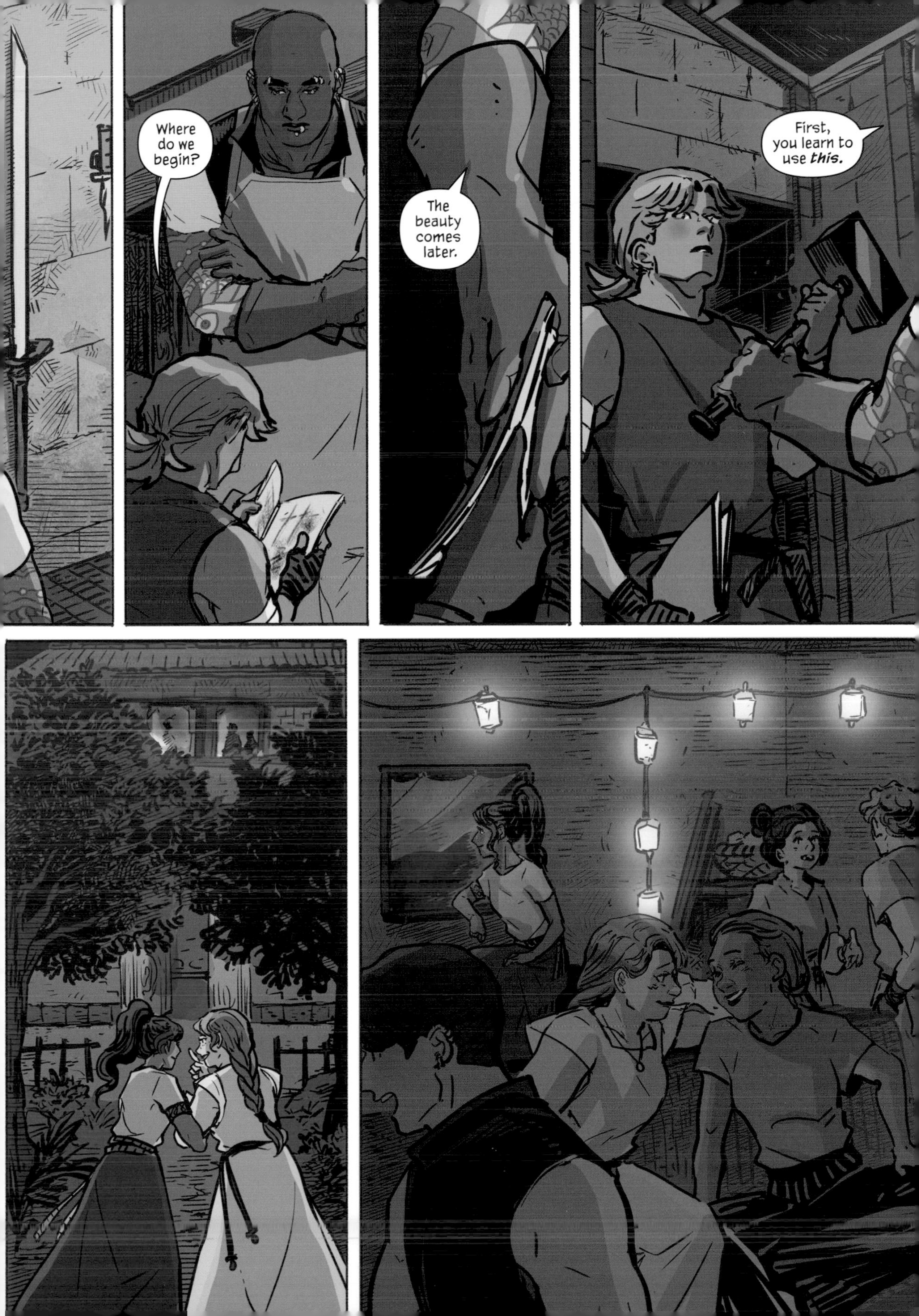
Where do we begin?
The beauty comes later.
First, you learn to use *this.*

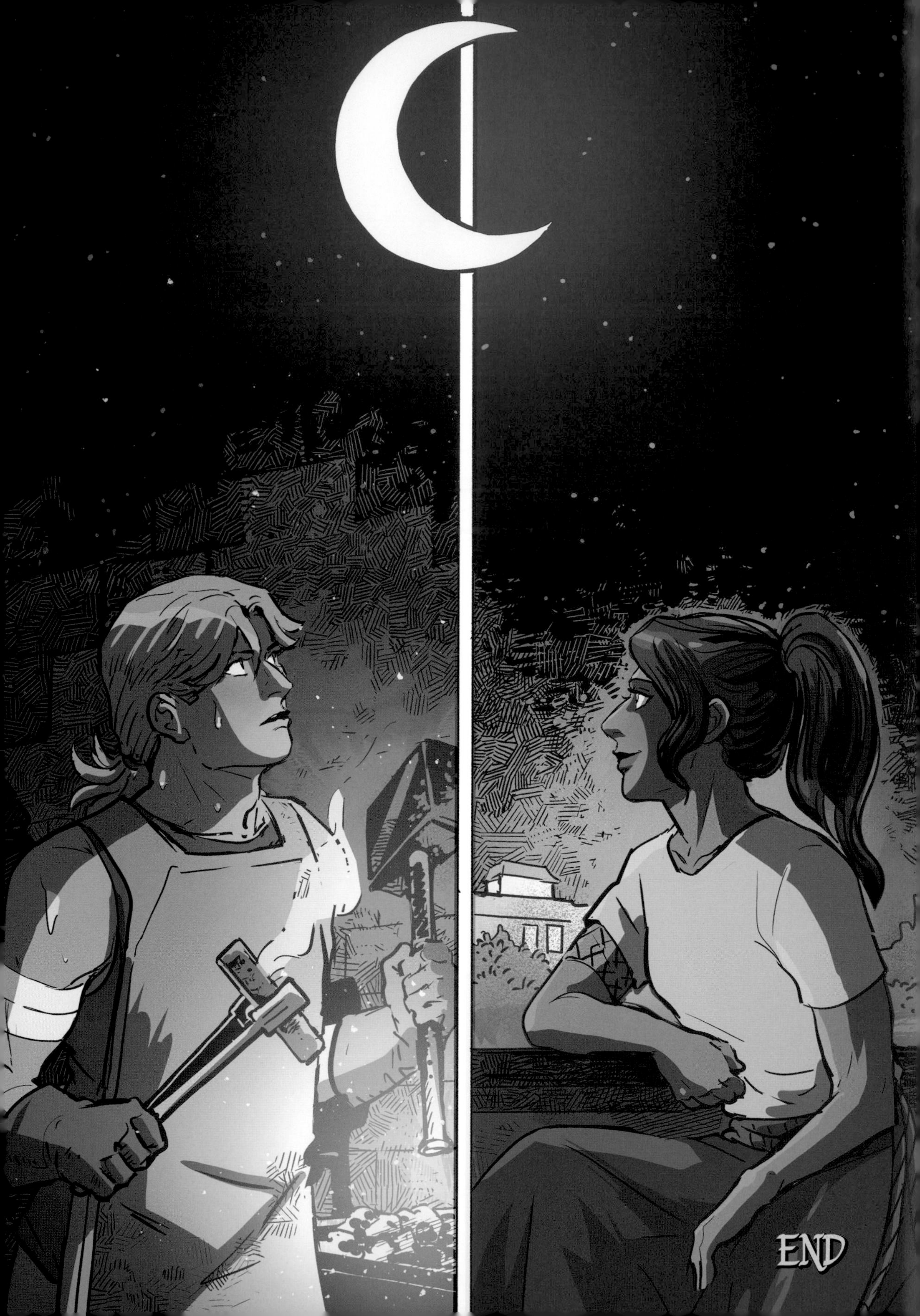
END

ABOUT THE CREATORS

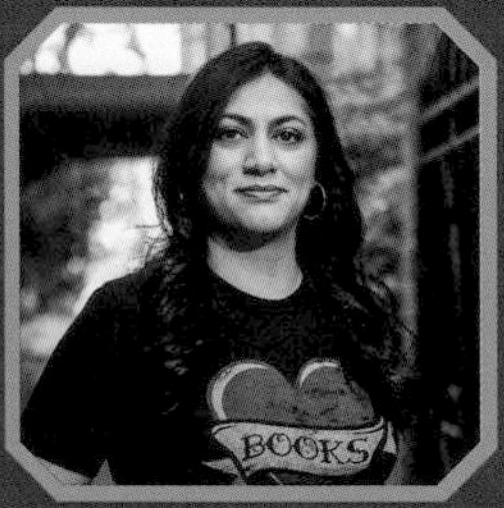
BOOKS

Sabaa Tahir is the author of the *New York Times* best-selling *An Ember in the Ashes* series. She grew up in California's Mojave Desert at her family's eighteen-room motel. There, she spent her time devouring fantasy novels, raiding her brother's comic book stash, and playing guitar badly. She began writing while working nights as a newspaper editor. She likes thunderous indie rock, garish socks and all things nerd.

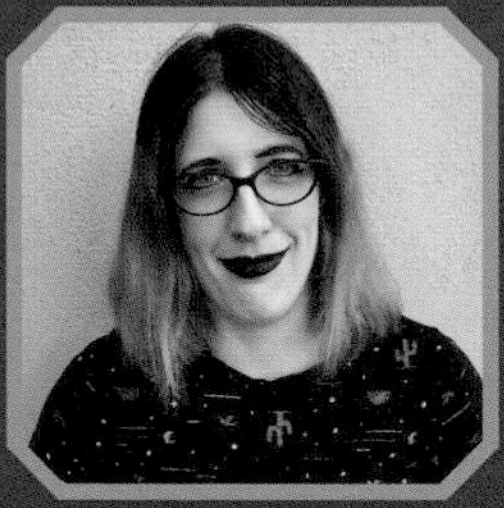

Nicole Andelfinger was crafting stories back when jelly shoes were cool. Since then, she's only continued to dwell in the realms of magic, monsters, and myth. When not changing her hair color or writing comics for some of her favorite franchises — such as *Jim Henson's The Dark Crystal: Age of Resistance, Regular Show, Rugrats, Steven Universe* and more — she works a day job best described as "emails." She lives with her absolutely, most decidedly perfect cat in Los Angeles.

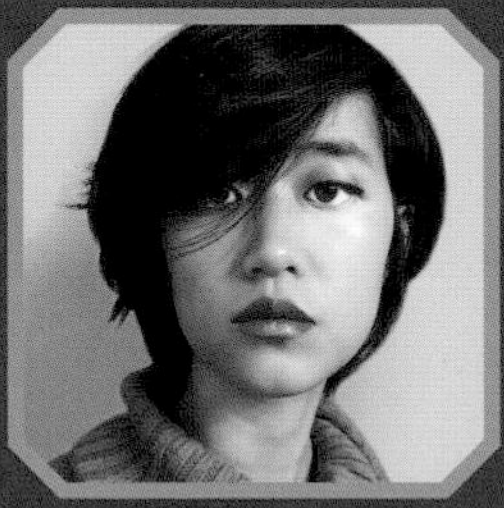

Sonia Liao is a comic artist based in Westford, Massachusetts. After graduating from MICA with her BFA in Illustration, she completed an internship at Fablevision and began life as a freelance artist. She was the main artist for the Curie Society graphic novel published by MIT Press in early 2021. She has also contributed art for projects by Sourcebook Fire, Red 5 Comics and Global Tinker.

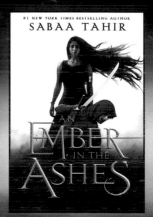

DISCOVER
GROUNDBREAKING TITLES

FRANK "BIG BLACK" SMITH
BIG BLACK
STAND AT ATTICA
JARED REINMUTH
AMÉZIANE
Four days in 1971 changed the course of American history.

FROM NEW YORK TIMES BESTSELLING AUTHOR
LEV GROSSMAN
WITH LILAH STURGES AND PIUS BAK
THE MAGICIANS
NEW CLASS

FROM THE NEW YORK TIMES BESTSELLING AUTHOR OF BAD FEMINIST
ROXANE GAY
TRACY LYNNE OLIVER
THE SACRIFICE OF DARKNESS
WITH REBECCA KIRBY & JAMES FENNER

KURT VONNEGUT
with RYAN NORTH & ALBERT MONTEYS
SLAUGHTER
or the children's crusade
HOUSE-FIVE
a graphic novel adaptation

SABAA TAHIR
WITH NICOLE ANDELFINGER & SONIA LIAO
A THIEF AMONG THE TREES
AN EMBER IN THE ASHES GRAPHIC NOVEL

EMEI BURELL
WE SERVED THE PEOPLE
MY MOTHER'S STORIES

Big Black: Stand at Attica
Frank "Big Black" Smith, Jared Reinmuth, Améziane
ISBN: 978-1-68415-479-1 | $19.99 US

The Magicians: New Class
Lev Grossman, Lilah Sturges, Pius Bak
ISBN: 978-1-68415-565-1 | $19.99 US

The Sacrifice of Darkness
Roxane Gay, Tracy Lynne Oliver, Rebecca Kirby
ISBN: 978-1-68415-624-5 | $24.99 US

Slaughterhouse-Five
Kurt Vonnegut, Ryan North, Albert Monteys
ISBN: 978-1-68415-625-2 | $24.99 US

A Thief Among the Trees: An Ember in the Ashes Graphic Novel
Sabaa Tahir, Nicole Andelfinger, Sonia Liao
ISBN: 978-1-68415-524-8 | $19.99 US

We Served the People: My Mother's Stories
Emei Burell
ISBN: 978-1-68415-504-0 | $24.99 US

Bear
Ben Queen, Joe Todd-Stanton
ISBN: 978-1-68415-531-6 | $24.99 US

Girl on Film
Cecil Castellucci, Vicky Leta, Melissa Duffy, V. Gagnon, Jon Berg
ISBN: 978-1-68415-453-1 | $19.99 US

Happiness Will Follow
Mike Hawthorne
ISBN: 978-1-68415-545-3 | $24.99 US

The Man Who Came Down the Attic Stairs
Celine Loup
ISBN: 978-1-68415-352-7 | $14.99 US

Waves
Ingrid Chabbert, Carole Maurel
ISBN: 978-1-68415-346-6 | $14.99 US

ARCHAIA

AVAILABLE AT YOUR LOCAL COMICS SHOP AND BOOKSTORE
To find a comics shop in your area, visit www.comicshoplocator.com
WWW.**BOOM-STUDIOS**.COM

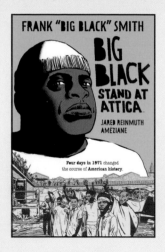

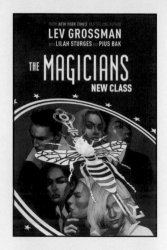

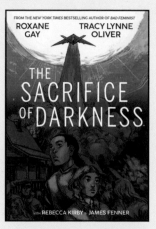

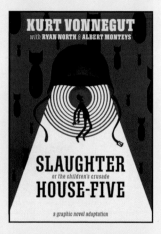

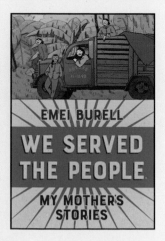